PRAISE FOR

The Sister Queens

"In her debut novel, *The Sister Queens*, Sophie Perinot breathes life into two of history's most fascinating siblings. What Philippa Gregory did for Anne and Mary Boleyn, Perinot has done for Marguerite and Eleanor of Provence. This is without a doubt one of the best novels I've read all year!" —Michelle Moran, author of *Madame Tussaud*

"Ms. Perinot, who seems like a very seasoned author, not someone presenting a debut work, has quite clearly put in the sort of exquisite attention to detail that resonates so deeply with true historical fiction lovers. I know it did that for me, swiftly drawing me back in time and placing me right there with her characters amid all of their conflicts and passions. Every page of *The Sister Queens* for me was like a morsel to savor. *The Sister Queens* is one of the most beautifully written books I have read in a very long time. Absolutely superb! I will certainly be adding it to my 'keeper' shelf." —Diane Haeger, author of *The Queen's Rival*

"*The Sister Queens* is a rich and stately medieval tapestry of a novel, with two royal couples weaving intertwined patterns of history and private life. Marguerite and Eleanor are the queens of France and England, yes, but Sophie Perinot reveals the living women behind the glittering pageantry—two young Provençal sisters, fiercely competitive and just as fiercely devoted. Through coronations and childbirth, wars and sieges, triumphs and betrayals, Marguerite's and Eleanor's lives are stitched against the colorful and meticulously researched background of thirteenth-century Europe—golden queens and steadfast sisters." —Elizabeth Loupas, author of *The Second Duchess*

continued . . .

"Sophie Perinot's debut tour de force, *The Sister Queens*, gives the reader a detailed and racy look into the very public and most intimate lives of English and French royalty. The sister queens have two very different personalities, yet Perinot's skills allow a modern woman to see herself in them and root for them both. This sweeping, compelling novel is a medieval, double-decker lifestyles of the rich, famous, and fascinating."

—Karen Harper, author of *The Queen's Governess*

"Sibling rivalry with the highest possible stakes! Sophie Perinot awards two of the luminaries of medieval royalty their due in a colorful and densely woven tapestry."

—Leslie Carroll, author of *Notorious Royal Marriages* and *Royal Pains*

"In her wonderful debut, *The Sister Queens*, Sophie Perinot breathes life into the world of the High Middle Ages, bringing us into the age of knights and chivalry, of courtly love and crusades. Caught in a web of politics, the young sisters Marguerite and Eleanor find themselves queens in foreign courts, where both women must learn to call on all their strength to become the queens they are destined to be. With lyrical prose, *The Sister Queens* tells a riveting story of sisterly rivalry and love, of war and betrayal. Marguerite and Eleanor remain united by bonds of love that cannot tarnish and that cannot break. A beautiful novel."

—Christy English, author of *To Be Queen*

"Here is a glimpse into the private and public lives of two sisters, Eleanor and Marguerite of Provence, who were destined to become queens of England and France. I found it irresistible. In an engaging style that draws the reader in, Sophie Perinot allows us to enjoy the rivalry and compassion that exist between two young women of very different character. At the same time, she gives us insight into the political intrigues in England and France that governed their lives. If you enjoy a tale of passion, intrigue, and sisterly devotion that will keep you turning the pages, then *The Sister Queens* is a must for your reading list."

—Anne O'Brien, author of *The Virgin Widow* and *Queen Defiant*

The SISTER QUEENS

SOPHIE PERINOT

NEW AMERICAN LIBRARY

New American Library
Published by New American Library, a division of
Penguin Group (USA) Inc., 375 Hudson Street,
New York, New York 10014, USA
Penguin Group (Canada), 90 Eglinton Avenue East, Suite 700, Toronto,
Ontario M4P 2Y3, Canada (a division of Pearson Penguin Canada Inc.)
Penguin Books Ltd., 80 Strand, London WC2R 0RL, England
Penguin Ireland, 25 St. Stephen's Green, Dublin 2,
Ireland (a division of Penguin Books Ltd.)
Penguin Group (Australia), 250 Camberwell Road, Camberwell, Victoria 3124,
Australia (a division of Pearson Australia Group Pty. Ltd.)
Penguin Books India Pvt. Ltd., 11 Community Centre, Panchsheel Park,
New Delhi - 110 017, India
Penguin Group (NZ), 67 Apollo Drive, Rosedale, Auckland 0632,
New Zealand (a division of Pearson New Zealand Ltd.)
Penguin Books (South Africa) (Pty.) Ltd., 24 Sturdee Avenue,
Rosebank, Johannesburg 2196, South Africa

Penguin Books Ltd., Registered Offices:
80 Strand, London WC2R 0RL, England

First published by New American Library,
a division of Penguin Group (USA) Inc.

First Printing, March 2012
10 9 8 7 6 5 4 3 2 1

 REGISTERED TRADEMARK—MARCA REGISTRADA

LIBRARY OF CONGRESS CATALOGING-IN-PUBLICATION DATA:
Perinot, Sophie.
   The sister queens/Sophie Perinot.
      p. cm.
   ISBN 978-0-451-23570-1
   1. Marguerite, Queen, consort of Louis IX, King of France, 1221–1295—Fiction.
2. Eleanor, of Provence, Queen, consort of Henry III, King of England, 1223 or -4–1291—
Fiction. 3. Sisters—Fiction. I. Title.
   PS3616.E7446S57 2012
   813'.6—dc23   2011044576

Set in Bembo
Designed by Ginger Legato

Printed in the United States of America

For my sister, Laura.
You were my first memory; you remain my best friend.

For my daughters, Erin and Katie.
Remember that sometimes you see yourself most clearly
through your sister's eyes.

For Frances,
my sister-in-writing if not by blood.

And for Colin.
You are my golden prince. May you grow up to be a good man
and a great leader.

PREFACE

The map of thirteenth-century Western Europe was a mosaic of regional kingdoms. Some—including France and England—still exist many centuries later; others—such as the Holy Roman Empire and the Kingdom of Castile—were eventually subsumed into different political configurations. Each piece of this patchwork was made up of both lands held directly by the kingdoms' rulers and lands held by vassals owing fealty to those rulers. As the High Middle Ages drew to a close, few of these realms resembled their images on maps today.

Early in the century, two young boys inherited the crowns of their fathers, ascending to the thrones of England and France. The boy who came to the English throne as Henry III was a Norman through his paternal great-grandmother, a descendant of Vikings who carved out a position of power on the peninsula of Normandy long before William the Conqueror set his eyes and ambitions on England. Henry was also a Plantagenet, and his grandfather, by his marriage to Eleanor of Aquitaine, claimed lands in the kingdom of France, including Poitou and various provinces from the Loire River to the Pyrenees mountains. Clearly then, though Henry's relations had ruled in England for 150 years, the new king and his kin remained thoroughly tied to continental Europe.

When nine-year-old Henry III inherited in 1216, his territories were both fewer and less secure than when his father, King John, inherited. John had managed to lose all of England's continental holdings with the exception of Gascony. He also depleted the powers of the English kingship by signing the Magna Carta under duress, and managed to lose part of his own island. At the time of his coronation, young Henry did not hold the eastern portion of England proper, not even the great city of London. Those territories were in the hands of a Frenchman, Crown Prince Louis VIII, who seemed poised to become King of England. As a child, Henry III had every reason to both dislike and fear the French. Years later, with the French driven from his shores and the initial challenge to his authority suppressed, Henry the man sought to regain English dignity and English lands lost before he was crowned.

A decade after Henry inherited, the second boy, the son of the Frenchman who had threatened to steal England, became the King of France. The ancestors of the boy-king Louis IX were no invaders. Rather, the first Capetian king was a man selected by his fellow barons to take up the kingship of France. Encompassing a realm expanded over the two previous centuries, Louis's territories included lands seized from the English, such as Normandy, Brittany, Maine, Anjou, and Poitou. Most of the former English holdings were fiefs of the King of France, but that never stopped the English from asserting otherwise, either while they were in possession of the territories or after they lost them. As ambitious as his predecessors, Louis IX worked to further consolidate Capetian power and expand the French realm. But in looking forward, Louis did not forget to keep one eye always on the English, wary of losing what his ancestors had gained.

As the first third of the century drew to a close, the boy-kings became men—men needing brides. Louis, guided by his mother, sought a connection that would give him more influence in the Midi, near the territory of Languedoc, which he already held. And what did Henry III want in a bride? On the surface, Henry sought a marriage that would strengthen his bid to regain English continental possessions. In the end, however, like most men who feel they are playing catch-up, Henry wanted whatever his rival had, so one family provided brides for both men. The queens of France and England were sisters, Marguerite and Eleanor, the two eldest daughters of Raymond Berenger, Count of Provence, and Beatrice of Savoy. And, while the Count of Provence was certainly neither a man nor a connection to be slighted, the girls' appeal as "brides worthy of kings" stemmed in largest part from their relation through their mother to the House of Savoy.

While we tend to think of "celebrity" as a modern concept, the idea of a person or a family so successful, talented, and glamorous that everyone else wants to be them or at least to be near them is as old as history itself. The Savoyards were celebrities in the High Middle Ages. A family of considerable martial and political power, with members renowned for their personal attractiveness, much of what was said and thought about individuals of the House of Savoy stretched to hyperbole. One of the girls' uncles was called "the second Alexander" by his contemporaries, while another was labeled "the second Charlemagne," and their mother's beauty was sounded in terms straight out of a troubadour's poem. People wanted to be like the Savoyards, and people, even kings and popes, wanted to be seen with them.

Louis and Henry, along with the ambassadors they sent south, were quickly beguiled by the Savoyard myth as displayed in all its shining, lavish glory at the court of Provence. Oh yes, there was glamour to be had in proximity, but would there also be love?

THE SISTER QUEENS

CHAPTER I

M,

    The sun is out and so should we be. Pray ask Mother to release us from our studies. She is sure to agree if you ask. You will be her "little queen," so she indulges your every whim. I wish you yourself were a little less satisfied with the title that will soon be yours. When I wanted to write you this note, I had a difficult time finding a scrap of parchment in our room not covered with "Marguerite, by the grace of God illustrious Queen of the French" in your handwriting.

                                        E

MARGUERITE
APRIL 1234
AVIGNON, PROVENCE

The sun is on my face and I can smell the spring squill as its blue blossoms, too numerous for the counting, brush against my gown as I walk. I do not stoop to pick them. My left hand already holds a bouquet of elder-flowered orchids, their orange throats glowing from within purple petals, their brown and orange speckles a happy reminder that spring has come to Provence.

We wintered here at Avignon this year. Not my favorite of my father's castles, nor my sister Eleanor's. We would have preferred to pass the colder months snug at Aix. But Avignon was more convenient for Giles de Flagy, representative of Louis IX of France, who was tasked with paying a "surprise" visit to my father's court for the express purpose of inspecting *me*.

Of course, we all knew he was coming. My father's great friend and adviser, the Catalonian Romeo de Villeneuve, has been negotiating with de Flagy for some time to see if I might not become Queen of France. So my father, a better host even than he is a diplomat, made certain that our lively court, always full of feast and fest, took on an even greater grandeur. Such dresses I wore! Such extravagant gifts were presented to the Frenchman! Such lavish banquets, each comprised of more than a dozen courses, were given in his honor!

And always the eyes of the French envoy were upon me. I was not the least shy at having such attention. Have I not been trained for this? Tutored in posture and dancing to improve my natural grace; instructed in chess, my native language of Lenga d'òc, and even Latin, so that I might be erudite in my discourse? Placed in the saddle hundreds of times to ride to the chase and given a falcon for my seventh birthday so that I might master that most noble of all sports? Have I not been given hour upon hour of religious instruction at Mother's knee?

Yes, I feel well prepared to be a great lady like my mother, Beatrice of Savoy, whose beauty, piety, tenderness, and wit are known far outside the borders of my father's territory. I am thirteen and well content to be looked at for a bride. But my darling sister Eleanor is less content. She has not my patience and could sorely use it, for she is second born, and, though she loves me dearly, Eleanor chafes to wait always behind me.

As if to confirm my thoughts, she bursts past me at a run—a blur of green and gold, skirts held nearly as high as her spirits.

"Ele-an-nor! Wait!"

The whining call is as inevitable as it is irritating. Mother insists that we take Beatrice with us on our rambles. But Beatrice is so very young—only three—that she is more of an annoyance than a companion.

Eleanor stops hard, turns with hands on hips, and regards Beatrice, who passes me with tears streaming down her face, with a saucy and somewhat malevolent air. "You had best stop your crying, Beatrice, before the Count of Toulouse hears you and comes to eat you."

"Eleanor!" My exasperation is evident in my tone. For now not only is Beatrice sobbing in earnest, but Sanchia, so quiet that I had momentarily forgotten she walked beside me, has silent tears rolling down her face despite being nearly nine years old.

"Elle me rend folle!" Eleanor responds defiantly, throwing up her hands.

It takes me a moment to realize what she is saying. We are not native French speakers, and both of us have just begun to learn. Or, rather, I have begun to learn so that I may converse easily in the court of my future husband, and Eleanor, quicker at languages than I, is helping me. Always a talkative bedfellow, she now exhausts me once the candles are out by initiating conversations solely in French.

"I do not care," I reply in Lenga d'òc, unwilling to struggle with my French even as I struggle with my sisters. I have reached Beatrice where she sits disconsolate on the ground. Squatting, I pull her into my arms and stroke her golden hair. "Bea," I say softly, "the Count of Toulouse is many leagues away. He and Father are not at war presently and even if they were, as dreadful as the Count of Toulouse may be, he does not eat little girls." I look up imperiously. "Eleanor."

Eleanor moves forward, reaching her hand to take Beatrice's.

"I am sorry, Sister," she says. But she is far from contrite and, it seems, also far from finished. "But I do wish you would keep up. You are worse than a pebble in my shoe."

Little pebble. Beatrice hates this moniker, which has lately begun to stick, but she smiles in a self-satisfied manner nonetheless. I know she will tell my father what has happened. Surely Eleanor must know it as well. Eleanor hands Beatrice off to Sanchia, who comes forward to hoist the toddler to her slender hip and bear her home again. As Sanchia struggles off uncomplaining under her burden, I lower my voice and say to Eleanor, "She will have your new samite mantle for this."

"It is far too big for her." Eleanor's confidence does not match her comment. She loves that cloak, all deep blue and gold, and knows better than any of us, as Beatrice's most frequent tormentor, that the youngest of us all is my father's openly avowed favorite.

"You must be nicer to her when I am married and gone," I coax Eleanor, "more fair in your treatment. She cannot help being little. Nor can she help being spoiled."

Eleanor looks as if she would take issue but instead changes the subject. "Are you frightened, Marguerite?" She reaches out to take my empty right hand and we begin to walk toward home.

"Why should I be frightened? All girls must marry unless they become nuns. And there is no question of that in my case. Father has dowry enough." I feel my face grow warm the moment the words are out of my mouth. Eleanor and I both know that while the word of my betrothal to Louis of France was greeted with great joy by all of Provence, the ten thousand silver marks that the White Queen, Blanche of Castile, demanded in recognition of our unequal ranks were not easy for my father to come by. He had not a thousand marks of ready money. The mighty castle of Tarascon had to be pledged to the French king as surety. And if de

Villeneuve had not managed by many clever means to raise one-fifth of the sum in plate and coin, this marriage, so provident for my family, might well have fallen by the wayside.

"Yes," Eleanor agrees, squeezing my hand, "but you will be so far away. And it is cold in France—both the weather and the people."

"Not Louis and my new mother, surely," I say with cheerful conviction. "Mother showed me one of Queen Blanche's letters. She seems a cordial lady and a charmingly attentive mother. As for King Louis, you know what Uncle Guillaume says of him."

"'The handsomest man and finest king in Christendom,'" Eleanor recites in a singsong voice.

Perhaps my Savoyard uncle *has* gone on a bit in praise of my betrothed's accomplishments and attributes, but I think Eleanor's constant impatience to do as I do and go where I go contributes materially to her mocking tone. A moment later I am sure.

"Will you not be lonely?" Eleanor asks. Her eyes show every evidence that she will be the next of my sisters to cry.

"I am not going alone. Uncle Guillaume and Uncle Thomas will accompany me," I remind her, "and at least one is sure to stay at the French court to provide me with good counsel in my role as queen." I wonder for a moment if my mother's powerful brothers, concerned as they will be with protecting the family's interests in my marriage, will have time to keep me company. Then, brightly, I plunge onward. "My nurse, Lisette, goes as well, along with a number of ladies-in-waiting. And surely you heard Father's fair promise to me last evening as we dined that I might take my favorite of the minstrels?"

Then, allowing myself to think for a moment of the greater separations lying at the heart of Eleanor's concern, I stop walking and throw my arms around my sister's neck. "I will miss you, my dearest Eleanor. If only you could come with me to France! How I wish King Louis could have two wives."

Standing back from her again, I clap my right hand over my mouth, horribly conscious of the blasphemous nature of my utterance. Men do not have two wives at once; this I know for sure. But as I look at my sister doubled over in mirth where only moments before she was on the verge of tears, I realize with a sudden ache that there are many things I do not know about husbands and their wives.

I glance into the distance and see that Sanchia has placed Beatrice on the ground and taken a seat beside her. I am conscious that I have shirked my duty as the eldest and allowed Sanchia, the frailest among us, to overtire herself. "Come, Eleanor. We had best go. There is still a long walk back, and you must carry Beatrice as your penance." I brace myself for the complaint that I know is coming. How many times in the last weeks have I heard her say, hands on hips, "You are not Queen of France yet, Marguerite, and even when you are, *I* do not live in France." To distract her from repeating this retort, I add, "Surely Father will pay less heed to her tale when he sees how gently you bear his little angel home."

Eleanor smiles slyly. The mantle is not lost yet. "You will be a good queen, Marguerite. You have the skills of a diplomat already."

MY UNCLE GUILLAUME ARRIVES FIRST. He is thirty-three and has been the bishop-elect of Valence for most of my life. I think he looks more like my mother than any of her other brothers. Besides being handsome, he knows everyone—His Holiness the Pope, the Holy Roman Emperor, and my soon-to-be husband, King Louis of France. He sweeps into my mother's apartments, where we ladies have gathered to pass the afternoon.

"Beatrice," he says, embracing Mother warmly before his eyes turn naturally to me. "And here is the little bride. Come, Marguerite, see what I have brought you." Drawing a small velvet bag from the pouch at his waist, he upends it into my eager hand.

"Uncle!" I hold a ring-brooch more beautiful than any I have ever seen, even among my mother's ornaments. Gold with rubies, it is certainly of great value.

My mother must be thinking the same thing, because even as I throw my arms around my uncle's neck in thanks, she chides him, "Guillaume, it is too generous a gift."

"Shall I tell King Louis to take it back then?" he teases. "For 'twas he who sent it and he who selected the inscription."

I look more closely at the treasure in my hand and find the words *Ave Maria G*, a Latin abbreviation for "Hail Mary, full of grace." I wonder, does my betrothed call down the Virgin's blessing upon me, or does he compare me to Our Blessed Lady?

"This will be a great match," my uncle continues, rubbing his hands together; then, noticing Eleanor's poorly guarded jealous look in my direction, he puts a hand under her chin, draws her face up ever so slightly, and adds, "for all the members of the houses of Provence and Savoy. Make no mistake, Niece, you may perchance make a better marriage because your sister marries well before you. Now, help Marguerite to pin that on."

I hand the brooch to my sister, who does as she is bid. And if she pricks me in the process, there is no point in my mentioning it. No one will believe the gesture intentional because no one else saw the flash in her dark brown eyes as she did it.

Before the sun sets, Uncle Thomas arrives. He is older than Guillaume, but neither so handsome nor so prominent in the church. Mother always says she would not be surprised to see Uncle Thomas leave the church entirely and marry should a good opportunity present itself. Eleanor is Uncle Thomas's favorite, and, although she is nearly eleven years old, he swings her up in the air when he thinks no one is looking. He has a mind for detail. "I will see the clothing before retiring," he tells my mother as we settle down to dine. He is speaking of what I will wear on the long progress from Avignon to Lyon and then onward to Sens where I am to be wed. "And the list of those courtiers and clergy who will accompany Lady Marguerite's train."

My father, far from being put out by these demands, laughs aloud. "My Lord of Piedmont, I have it on good authority that when the archbishop of Aix heard you were to be one of our party, he summoned his tailor at once. I hope you come prepared to compete."

"Always, Raymond, and in every venue."

"Well, I will lay odds on you every time." My father slaps Thomas on the back and then summons a nearby servant for more wine. "Perhaps alone you can be bested, but you are never alone, not with six brothers for support."

"Do you hear this, Beatrice?" Uncle Guillaume speaks over my father, appealing to my mother who sits on Father's other side. "Your husband slights you."

"By no means!" Father takes Mother's hand on top of the table and regards her with the frank admiration that I am used to seeing and she is used to receiving. "To the contrary, my lady wife has political and diplomatic skills equal to either of yours in every respect. Why do you think I married her?"

"Because I was beautiful," my mother suggests playfully.

"That too," Father replies, "and you still are." He raises Mother's hand to his lips, then calls for the evening's entertainment to begin.

Sitting between Eleanor and Sanchia with the latter's drowsy head in my lap, listening to my father's best minstrel play his harp and sing, I cannot imagine a life better than my own or a place warmer than the bosom of my family. Why am I leaving? I touch Louis's brooch to ward off tears.

TWO WEEKS LATER I PONDER the same question. The party from Sens arrived at Avignon three days ago.

We went in great splendor to the gates of the city to meet them. I rode the most beautiful palfrey imaginable, a white of great price selected by my uncle Guillaume as a symbol of my purity. The smooth, ambling gait of the beast did little to slow the agitated beating of my heart. I could not wait for someone to spot the French.

Like the animal beneath me, I was bedecked in every splendor. Each detail of my attire had been carefully selected and approved by Uncle Thomas, who sought to present me as the queen I will shortly become. My tunic was made of the rich blue *perse* for which my father's county is so rightly famous. Elaborate bands of golden embroidered orphrey decorated its bottom as well as the ends of my tightly fitting sleeves. My *surcote*, of heavy samite the color of fresh cream, was so luxurious that I had to remind myself not to keep fingering it as we sat waiting. Finally, my mantle, held fast by Louis's ruby brooch, was the *orchil* of a spring violet and lined in softest gray and white vair, with a rolled trim of that same luxurious fur.

I sat between my mother and father, each also magnificently mounted. Beatrice, too young to be thought any competition to me, sat before Mother on her saddle. But Eleanor, nearly marriageable herself, and Sanchia, so beautiful that from the youngest age she stopped the breath of men, were kept well back with their nurses. It would not do, my uncle Thomas told my father solemnly, for there to be any confusion as to the identity of the bride or any opportunity for comparison that might render me less superior in the minds of the Frenchmen. So, arranged on either side of my mother and father, instead of their remaining children, were my Savoyard uncles—not just Guillaume and Thomas, but the Count of Savoy, Amadeus IV, who made the journey with his family and a portion of his court and men-at-arms for the occasion, and Mother's younger brothers, Peter and Boniface. It is a firm tenant of the Savoyards that in family lies the root of all power and glory.

We were so many and so lively a party that I was certain we would dazzle the archbishop of Sens and the senior ambassadors of my betrothed. Nor was my confidence much shaken when the French at last arrived, for while the days they passed among us showed them to be elegant and well educated, my father's court did not suffer by comparison.

But now, on the evening before I must leave my home forever, with all the preparations for my departure complete, I feel neither dazzling nor confident. My mother orders me early to bed. I must be well rested; a journey of more than one hundred thirty-five leagues lies before me. I take leave of my parents with only muted sadness. They will ride with me as far as Lyon, so separation from them is still distant enough to forestall the melancholy that must accompany it. But my eyes linger long on the great hall itself, and on every feature of my walk to my bedchamber.

Eleanor is with me, uncharacteristically solemn and silent. Her nurse and mine trail behind. Tonight every moment of our ordinary readying for bed seems to take on the sanctity of ritual: the stirring of the embers into a cheery fire by Lisette; the undressing; our sitting side by side on matching stools while our nurses comb through our waist-length hair thrice with different combs—each finer toothed than the one before it—as a remedy against lice; the warming of our cups of spiced wine. But it is *not* the same as most nights. Not a word passes between me and Eleanor. The only conversation is between Lisette and Agnes who natter in the background, their words no more distinct to me than the humming of bees.

Then, as Eleanor and I sit beside the fire to take our evening libation, she speaks at last. Turning partway round, she regards the nurses where they are carefully laying out my garments for the morrow and covering them with chainsil cloths.

"Leave us!"

For a moment I hear not my Eleanor, but the commanding and sometimes imperious voice of my father. Such hauteur from a girl only now approaching the age of marriage! I am astounded. I do not know whether to admire it or fear where it may lead my sister. Upon the nurses, who are accustomed to doing without complaint the bidding of others, the effect is immediate. They slip from the room, gone too quickly to see that Eleanor's firm self-possession is illusory.

As the door shuts behind them, my sister begins to weep. But she does not surrender quietly, even to sobs. Rounding on me with near-wild eyes, she demands, "How can you leave me? Who will I have to gossip with when I surprise one of the serving girls in a corner of the garden with a stable boy? Who will sing me to sleep when the air is so full of summer flowers that my head aches and I have difficulty drawing breath?"

Now I am crying too.

Eleanor throws herself into my arms, equally heedless of the cup she casts aside and the wine that spills from it.

"Oh Eleanor, if only you could come with me! How cruel that Jeanne de Toulouse is betrothed to one of the king's brothers rather than you! The lady is no doubt vile like her father, and even were she not, even were she all accomplishment and good humor, no one can bear me such company as you do. You hold all my secrets and I yours."

My chest is heaving. I am crying so hard that I cannot continue. Even if I could, what would I say? No words of mine uttered in either protest or prayer can change my destiny. I will be Queen of France and must therefore be parted from the sister whom I love more than any other person.

Her continued distress allows me to rein in my own. I must make an effort to support her spirits. "Eleanor, do you remember the time, at Mother's castle, at Brignoles, when we planned to run away and become trobairitz?"

Eleanor sniffs, and, wiping both eyes, manages to look ever so slightly saucy. "Are we going now?"

"That would be ill-advised," I reply. "For, if you remember, we gave the scheme a miss, upon discovering that neither of us has a facility for rhyme, though I sing as beautifully as a lark."

"You? I have the sweeter voice." Eleanor is smug, and that is better than seeing her miserable.

"And I the sweeter temperament." I feel my own spirits rise as the evening suddenly becomes very much like thousands of others we have passed in similar banter. A friendly competition, like a joust or a contest among troubadours, is what we have. Eleanor may win one day and I another, but the pleasure lies in contesting the other, not in vanquishing her.

"You must write to me often," I demand.

"What shall I tell? Nothing will change here."

"And that is precisely what I will wish most to hear; that all I love remains as I left it."

"Then I promise to write to you nearly as often as I will think of you."

"Nearly?"

"I cannot be at my escritoire every minute. And you must write to me in return. As queen, you will be better able to command messengers into the saddle than I will."

"I will write," I reply, suddenly feeling solemn again. "And let us exchange tokens of our promise." I rise and go to the foot of our bed, expecting to find my trunk, but it is not there. I stop dead, feeling panic rising within me. All my things are packed away for my journey north. I have nothing left in the rooms of my childhood but the clothing I took off this evening and the clothing I will don at sunrise.

Lifting the protective coverings from my new garments, I wonder what I can give to Eleanor without being caught by my mother or my eagle-eyed uncle Thomas. My glance alights on my new slippers with the wonderfully pointed toes and a strap that closes them at the ankle above an open instep. Made of soft, light-colored doeskin, they are embroidered with a myriad of small gold stars. Such shoes are meant to be seen protruding from the bottom of my skirts once I am astride my horse rather than to be walked in. However, if I am careful with my skirts, I may easily wear the plain black slippers that I took off this evening with no one being the wiser. So I catch the pretty slippers up and hold them out to Eleanor. "Here. Only pray don't lift your skirts when you wear them, or Mother will know."

Eleanor laughs. "And what do you expect her to do? You will be many leagues away, a married woman."

"But not, I suspect, safe from maternal scolding. Mother can write to me as easily as you can."

Eleanor appears genuinely puzzled by my reply. When she is convinced she is right, words have never been enough to persuade her otherwise. She doubtless cannot imagine being chastened by a letter. Going to her own things, she returns with the fine woolen broadcloth *aumônière* she has been laboriously embroidering for months. Eleanor does not like to embroider; she has not the patience for it, while I excel at it. But, having been struck by the idea of decorating the bag with the poppies that are everywhere about Aix by the beginning of the summer, she has lavished much attention on this particular work. Always drawn to displays of finery, she planned to wear the *aumônière* suspended from her favorite scarlet girdle.

"You must take this, Marguerite, and make sure when you wear it that one of my letters is always inside with your coins and other things."

"Are you certain?"

"Entirely, for I love no one so much as you."

But I notice as I take the bag from her hands that she holds on to the strings until the last possible moment.

CHAPTER 2

Eleanor, my dear sister,

    I do not know when I shall have the opportunity of sending this. I am carried onward, like one of my trunks, without any effort on my part. This is just as well as my will to go forward falters since Lyon where I bid a tearful good-bye to Mother and Father. How can a crown take the place of seeing you and our dear parents every day as I am used to? Uncle Guillaume assures me that this aching for home will pass once I see my handsome husband. I pray he is right, for at the moment I think myself as likely to cry as curtsy when we are introduced.

            Yours,

            M

MARGUERITE

MAY 1234

OUTSIDE SENS, FRANCE

I cannot breathe. My nurse, squatting beside me where I sit, squeezes my hand. She has spotted him too. The little party is very close now. A handful of young gallants and their attendants riding toward our larger party, magnificently dressed like the knights in the poems and songs of my great-grandfather Alfonso of Aragon, a "troubadour among Kings" (though he would always have it a "King among troubadours").

Most beautiful of all those riding toward us is Louis. *My* Louis. I know who he is by his armor. It is gold—all gold. The chain mail, even his spurs. But I must confess, though his magnificent attire draws my eyes, it is his more personal attributes that hold them. At twenty years old, he is *so* tall and *so* well favored. He has tawny golden hair blunt cut at his shoulders, a long straight nose, and lips that while unsmiling presently are appealingly full. And his eyes are blue. Not the crisp, sometimes harsh blue of a summer sky over Aix, nor the gray, weeping blue of a woad-dyed dress, but an altogether softer, warmer blue than I have ever seen.

Those clustered about me, where I take my rest underneath the shade of my tent, part like the biblical seas as my soon-to-be husband dismounts and moves forward to greet me. He is followed by two other richly dressed gentlemen and half a dozen attendants bearing a variety of objects. I rise from my seat and fall again immediately into the deepest curtsy I have ever made, keeping my eyes modestly downward. When I rise again, Uncle Guillaume, who has also finished making his reverence, provides the introductions.

"Your Majesty, may I present my niece, the Lady Marguerite of Provence, by God's grace your affianced wife."

"Marguerite, may I present His Majesty, Louis, by God's grace King of France; His Highness, Robert, Count of Artois; and His Highness, Alphonse, Count of Poitiers." I know these are Louis's brothers, and I notice that neither has his poise or good looks. Alphonse seems very near to my own age, and I struggle to remember just how old he is, as I am sure I have been told.

"My lady." Louis's voice is warm. He reaches out to take my hand, bowing over it solemnly. "All of France welcomes you. We convey particular greetings from our dear mother, Blanche, by the grace of God Queen of France, our sister Isabelle, and our brother Charles, each of whom is overjoyed at your safe arrival. We bring also some little tribute as testament to your beauty and value to us." With this, Louis beckons forward his attendants, ticking off the gifts they carry: "Two ceremonial saddles and a bridle of gold for a lady we know by report to be a most excellent horsewoman; a collection of jewels, the greatest of which is made to seem insignificant in comparison with your beauty; a cloak of sable as soft as your eyes; and, most important, a golden chalice for our nuptial Mass that we may share the blood of Our Lord and be made one with fitting dignity."

Acknowledging the gifts with another curtsy, I find that my training is happily sufficient to overcome even my awe. "Your Majesty, we thank you humbly for these gifts. They are of great value in themselves but even more so in our eyes as tokens of your love and respect for us." Then, remembering my uncle Guillaume's constant admonition that Louis prizes piety above all, I add, "We give thanks daily to God and to his Blessed Mother for sending us such a husband."

Uncle Guillaume smiles at me. The king smiles at me. Those gathered on every side smile at the sight of the king and me standing together. I have done well. And like that, the formality in Louis's manner drops away.

"My lady, shall I ride beside you on the way into Sens?" he asks, holding out his arm.

"Your Majesty," I reply, laying my hand upon it and feeling a sudden thrill as I do so, "I would be beside you from this moment on whenever you will have me there."

When we reach the palace of the archbishop of Sens, my uncles and I discover we are to be parted. I must take my leave of them as attendants carry in my chests and Louis disperses his men. Lisette and several of my ladies are shepherded inside by an imposing-looking woman of advanced age. The archbishop himself stands prepared to lead me in once my good-byes are completed.

"I apologize, Thomas," he remarks, "but thanks to the events of the morrow, the city strains at the seams and so too my palace." The archbishop's contrition appears genuine; no doubt he was hoping to impress my uncles with the lavish nature of his dwelling and is sorry to be deprived of the opportunity. "We thought it most fitting to install the Lady Marguerite here with the rest of the royal family, as tomorrow she will join it. It seemed also pressing to find room for some of her attendants so that they might prepare the bride, a task where gentlemen will not be wanted."

I nearly laugh out loud. How little His Grace knows my uncles! They might not dress me themselves, but no two persons, once my parents were left behind at Lyons, have been more instrumental in preparing this bride!

"I have secured lodgings for you at the chapter house," the archbishop continues, oblivious both to my suppressed mirth and to the displeasure of my uncles, which I can read clearly in their pinched lips and flared nostrils.

"Are we not to be received by Her Majesty Queen Blanche?" Uncle Guillaume's tone is more insistent than inquiring.

"Certainly." Louis has returned to my side. "Our mother is eager to show you every gratitude for your good offices in delivering the Lady Marguerite, but would allow you time to retire and refresh yourselves. We shall all dine together this evening, and she will greet you then."

There is no answer for this, and clearly there will be no moment of privacy offered to me and my Savoyard kin. I want to embrace both my uncles, but such a show of open affection with so many eyes upon us seems sadly out of place.

"Until tonight then," I say, trying to project cool confidence. Then on Louis's arm and preceded by the archbishop, I am whisked through the stone entrance. I assume I will find my women just inside, but apparently *I* am not to be given any time to rest or recover before facing my new family.

"Here she is, Mother." Louis's words are directed to a trim figure at the bottom of a great staircase. The woman is surprisingly imperious for a lady of such small stature, and surprisingly dour for a woman still of an age to be beautiful. She remains silent and expressionless for a moment, content to look me up and down as if appraising a horse for purchase. Then one side of her mouth rises slightly, giving not so much the impression of a smile as of a wry smirk.

"Pretty. We have not been misled in that. Come here, child." I glide forward and, stopping directly before the Dowager Queen— for who else would dare speak to me so boldly?—slowly sink in reverence. I stay down. "You may rise." Her voice holds a note of grudging, cautious approval. "How was your journey?"

"I make no complaint of it, Your Majesty, for it brings me to you."

"And are you prepared to be a good wife and obedient daughter?"

"I have been an obedient daughter to my own mother lo these thirteen years, and I offer Your Majesty all the same respect and duty. The role of wife is new to me, but I am prepared, with the grace of Our Lord, to subject myself always to my husband's will and to be attentive to his every need."

Blanche smiles, but the gesture is brittle, and I cannot shake the feeling that a certain superior air, a subtle irony, underpins her look of approbation. "Beatrice of Savoy has my compliments. She clearly knows how to raise daughters."

And suddenly I know that I am being dismissed, even before the archbishop steps forward to lead me away. The king looks as if he will say something; take some leave of me, but his mother's voice interrupts the impulse.

"Louis," the Queen Mother asks sweetly, "do you not greet your mother?" And like that I am forgotten as the king moves past me to kiss his mother. The lady's actions seem deliberate, but surely I am only overtired from the road and overexcited by my arrival and the prospect of my wedding tomorrow, for why in the world would Blanche, who arranged this match, be deliberately unpleasant to me?

BEFORE MY MOTHER TOOK HER leave of me at Lyon, she gave me the most rudimentary idea of what would happen on my wedding night. "There will be pain," she said earnestly, holding my two hands in hers as we sat side by side, turned slightly together so that our knees just touched, "just as there will be when you bring forth the heirs of your husband's body. This is the price for the sinful pride of Eve. But in it also lies a lesson: almost everything that you will take joy from in this life starts first with sacrifice. Happiness must be paid for."

I am a married woman. Our vows were exchanged this morning on the steps of the Cathédrale Saint-Étienne while the carved figures of the ten virgins watched from above the central door. And now I stand, virgin myself, trembling at the center of a bedchamber in the archbishop's palace. It is richly hung with silks and strewn with flowers, just as the whole city is bedecked for the occasion of my marriage; yet I barely noticed. Word has come from the king that I am not to be undressed. My ladies think this strange.

"Perhaps," I hear Alix de Lorgues murmur to the others as they open the door to depart, "he wants the pleasure of unwrapping her himself." The thick oak door falling shut behind them barely muffles the laughter this comment evokes.

I have nothing to do but wait in terror, and that will not do. "The women of Savoy are prized for their serenity." I can hear my mother's voice in my head admonishing Eleanor on the subject—a frequent occurrence. Would that my mother were here now, to hold me in her arms and soothe me. I have missed her daily since we said our good-byes, but never more than at this moment. Taking a seat on the edge of the bed, I am determined to busy my mind with a closer examination of the room. It is in most respects ordinary, lavishly furnished to be sure, but ordinary. It does, however, contain the most elaborate prie-dieu I have ever seen. The prayer stool seems to be made for two as it is very long. It is heavily carved with extraordinary tracery and biblical scenes. The carvings on the left side portray scenes from the life of the Virgin. In the largest, a gilded Holy Spirit dips low over a swooning Mary. Her hands are clasped and her eyes are closed, whether in joy or fear I cannot say. At the moment the two emotions seem perilously close. The right side has carvings of an altogether different nature. They offer scenes of the apocalypse and, as they provide no help for my nerves, I quickly turn my eyes elsewhere. The cushion on the portion meant for kneeling is precisely the same blue that I have seen in Louis's standard, but it covers only half the length of oak supporting it. It is patterned with Louis's fleur-de-lis. At either end of the rail where one might rest one's arms, magnificent candleholders rise, each with a half-dozen wax tapers in place. The prie-dieu faces a miniature altar, above which, on the wall, a large crucifix has been hung.

The door creaks. My heart is in my throat. Yet even so, I am aware of a strange sensation in a more private region, as if my blood is rushing there as well. Louis smiles at me from the doorway. He is so handsome. I feel as if I know a secret or as if I have drunk too much of Father's good wine, as Eleanor and I did once hiding beneath a table in the great hall at Aix.

Rising quickly from my seat, I drop low to a curtsy. The effect of these rapid movements in combination with the wine I took at my nuptial dinner is enough to make me dizzy. My unsteadiness must be noticeable, for Louis comes forward quickly with gentle concern in his eyes and takes both my hands. He touches the gold band that he placed on my third finger this morning. "My lady wife, you are unwell?"

"No, Your Majesty, only tired. There has been so much excitement." Then, worrying that I might be mistook, and my comment taken as complaint, I quickly add, "In all my life, I have never beheld such wondrous things as in the last hours."

"Your life, Marguerite, has not been very long yet," replies Louis with an indulgent smile. "I trust that today will be but the beginning of many 'wondrous' occasions."

"With God's grace, Your Majesty, I pray that I shall indeed have many years to prove myself a faithful wife to you and a worthy queen to your kingdom."

The earnestness of my tone is not lost upon Louis and serves to light up his face in a manner I have never yet seen. He literally glows. Pulling me to him, he whispers in my ear, "You must call me Louis when we are alone." Then his mouth finds mine. Fear is driven back by the pressure of his lips. As his tongue suddenly enters my mouth, I find that I want him to touch me, even if there will be pain. But as I press myself closer to him, his mouth leaves mine and a groan like that of a man in agony issues from him. What have I done?

Louis pushes me to arm's length with great effort. Gone is the radiant look. Instead, his eyes have a hungry and beseeching quality. "Will you pray with me?"

"Of course, Louis, if you wish."

Turning from me, my husband lights one of the tapers from the prie-dieu at a wall sconce, then uses it to ignite the others. Taking my hand again, this time touching only the tips of my fingers, Louis leads me to the kneeler. I realize at a glance that only one of us will fit on the portion covered by the cushion.

Perhaps seeing my look of confusion, Louis says, "I had the pillow made for you. I myself prefer to eschew such comfort, but surely Our Lord will not expect you as a woman to subject yourself to such rigors."

Together we kneel down, and my husband leads me in prayer.

Hours later, I hear the bells of the cathedral where we were married chime thrice. Louis, who, like myself has been praying in silence for some time, crosses himself and says aloud, "O God, you are my God, I seek you, my soul thirsts for you; my flesh faints for you. . . ."

It is the prayer for Matins; we are halfway to dawn. When he is finished, he rises stiffly. "I would be in my rooms for Lauds," he says by way of leave-taking. It is not clear whether he offers this information as explanation or excuse.

When he is gone, I get off my knees with great difficulty. Despite my cushion, my legs are stiff and my feet nearly without feeling. I stagger rather than walk to the great bed and fall upon it face-first, fully clothed. I am asleep before I can call for someone to undress me. Asleep before I can even roll over.

———

TWO MORE NIGHTS ARE SPENT in hours of solitary prayer in accordance with my husband's wishes. Louis assures me that he is likewise praying in his own chamber.

It is a strange way for a bride to pass her time, and I am exhausted each morning when Lisette comes to wake me with worry in her eyes. But my pains are rewarded by Louis's smile as he greets me with obvious delight at High Mass, and also in the sweet hours we spend watching jousters and jongleurs, dancing, and feasting side by side. Sometimes, under the table, Louis places his hand on my leg. I can feel the warmth of his flesh, even through my *surcote*, tunic, and chemise. Or perhaps I only imagine the sensation, but it is, nonetheless, both delightful and confusing.

Then, on the evening of the third day following my marriage ceremony, the sumptuous festivities are at an end. Tomorrow we begin our journey to Paris.

I do not even think of Louis as my ladies undress me for bed. I am comfortable now in the archbishop's rooms and eager for sleep, a whole night's worth as Louis gave no orders for prayer before we parted. Tucked between the feather bed and a coverlet of silk lined luxuriously in softest miniver, I am naked. This is how I slept in Provence. I am already drifting off, thinking of the gorgeous crimson *surcote* trimmed in ermine that I will wear tomorrow, when I hear the door open.

I sit bolt upright, clutching the covers, and see Louis in his shirt standing with a candle at the foot of the bed. Rounding the bed and setting his light down on the table without putting it out, he wordlessly draws the covers off me. Self-conscious but mindful of what my mother told me, I fight the urge to pull the blanket back again and instead force myself to lie down stiffly, perfectly still, averting my eyes from my husband. I feel the bed beside me sink beneath his weight, and I cannot resist glancing. He is lying next to me. I begin to shake, just slightly, but visibly. My modesty and trepidation seem to please Louis.

Rolling toward me, he puts his lips to my ear and whispers, "'Marriage *is* honorable among all, and the bed undefiled.'" It is strange to hear the Bible quoted in such a situation.

He kisses me, and the Holy Book is forgotten. There is no pulling back this time, no call to prayer. Then he is on me, and I am a maid no longer.

THE NEXT MORNING EARLY I am awakened by someone I do not know. "Where is Lisette?" I ask. "And Alix de Lorgues and the others?"

"I do not know, Your Majesty, but I am Marie de Vertus, and I will be Your Majesty's *chambrière*. I have been sent to help you rise and dress."

This seems strange and makes me obstinate. Especially on a morning such as this, I want Lisette. "I am not inclined to rise yet. I will get up when Lisette is found."

"Your Majesty, Her Majesty Queen Blanche and the bishop-elect of Valence wait just outside to inspect your linens. Surely you will not greet them in the nude?"

It costs me much dignity to hear this. But mine are not the only cheeks that burn, and Marie's pleading tone and obvious embarrassment make me like her more and not less. I spring out of bed and find that it is painful to walk. The insides of my thighs are tender as is that place that before last night man had never touched. Holy Mary, if it hurts to walk, how will I sit in the saddle all day?

A handful of other ladies I do not recognize join us, and my toilet is quickly complete. Marie opens the door to admit Blanche, an elderly gentleman of officious mien whom I do not recognize, my uncle Guillaume, and one of his attendants. The unknown gentleman walks to my bed and with a single swift motion turns back the cover. There on the sheet below is a darkened splotch—my maidenhead. I am mortified. I do not know where to look, but the others seem singularly unmoved by my embarrassment.

"That is that, then," Queen Blanche remarks dryly. She nods to the gentleman who pulls the sheet from the bed, folds it, and hands it to Uncle Guillaume. I cannot imagine why, but my uncle does not appear the least surprised. He merely hands the cause of my shame to his attendant, who places it in a bag apparently brought specially for the purpose.

The queen turns to my uncle. "Your Excellency, I again wish you the safest of returns south. You will want a moment of private leave-taking with Her Majesty."

Blanche stops before me just long enough for us to exchange curtsies and then, with her official in her wake, swiftly passes from the room. Uncle Guillaume sends his man out. I nod at Marie with a curtness I did not know I possessed, and she goes likewise, leading the other ladies.

"Niece," my uncle says, and I am relieved to hear him address me as he always has, for so many other things seem altered, "we have not much time. Already the train that will bear you north, no doubt to glory, gathers in the courtyard. The Count of Piedmont and all who accompanied you here are *not* with it."

"What?" I am both confused and discomforted. "Surely I mistake you! You told me that you and Uncle Thomas would go with me to Paris and would remain there to be my counsel in all things."

"And so I intended. So had the whole family intended. But His Majesty the King of France, or more precisely His Majesty's mother, has other plans. Last evening after you retired, the Queen Mother called Thomas and me to her. The most elaborate compliments were paid us and also you. Generous gifts were bestowed. I alone received a draft for two hundred thirty-six livres, and even Lisette was not forgotten. Then we were dismissed."

"Dismissed?"

"All of us. From myself to your minstrel."

I begin to weep. "Lisette? My ladies?"

"Must go back to Provence." Uncle Guillaume takes me by the shoulders and looks me squarely in the eye. "Marguerite, you are your mother's daughter—clever, beautiful, patient. You are surprised, but you are *not* undone. You have a duty to yourself and to your family to make of this marriage what you can. We will not abandon you. While you may be alone at Paris for now, your family will support your position in every possible manner."

I dry my eyes on my sleeve. Uncle Guillaume is right. I am Queen of France, and that is nothing to weep over. And I am not alone; I am astonished that my uncle even used the term. I have Louis—handsome, gallant Louis. What is the loss of a childhood nurse or even separation from my uncles in comparison to this?

WE ARRIVE IN THE GREAT city of Paris on the ninth of June. I do not exaggerate when I use that appellation. Never could I have imagined such a place! It teems with people. Louis tells me quite offhandedly that he believes there are more than one hundred fifty thousand souls living within the walls. And the streets are paved! At least those we travel. Louis assures me the rest will follow as he is continuing the work of his grandfather in that vein. Throngs of people line the streets. So many flowers are thrown at me or offered me that the arms of my ladies—no, they are not *my* ladies I remind myself—the arms of the ladies given me are filled with blooms. We ride directly to the Palais du Roi, which sits on an island in the middle of the Seine. It is so large, I wonder how long it will take me to learn my way about.

"Come," Louis says, handing me down from my horse. "I will show you your apartment." We enter the palace and, moving along the ground floor, come to a goodly sized hall with views of an enclosed garden. I notice that the roses are beginning to bloom. "This shall be yours. And through here"—my husband opens a door as he speaks—"are your withdrawing chamber and your bed-chamber." Yolande of Dreux, wife of the Duke of Burgundy and now a member of my household, moves forward to throw open the shutters, revealing a beautifully furnished withdrawing chamber of charming proportion.

"And what of your bedchamber, Louis?" My husband seems uncomfortable, and I realize with embarrassment that I have addressed him by his Christian name in front of Lady Yolande. The lady, perhaps conscious of it as well, retreats to my hall, draw-ing the door shut behind her to keep the other members of my household from intruding.

I have never seen Louis blush. "My rooms are in the north wing of the palace where they have always been." Then seeing my con-fusion, he continues. "The rooms en suite to mine would have afforded you no view and no access to the gardens. Besides, I have much business of state to attend to, and my mother fears you will distract me."

"Do I? Do I distract you, Louis?" I do not mean the words to be provocative, but at less than two weeks married, Louis is easily excited, as I learned along our journey home.

"Indeed, Marguerite, but most pleasantly." He moves forward

and takes me into his arms, kissing the side of my neck. "Do not be angry with me, little queen," he pleads.

"Never, Louis." I can feel his member swollen beneath his tunic, and my hand moves confidently down to touch the bulge. I am no longer the little girl I was a fortnight ago. My husband moans with desire and then, grabbing my hand, pulls me through the door to my new bedchamber. Without turning back the covers, he pushes me onto the bed and, grasping the hem of my skirts, lifts them above my hips to reveal my nakedness. Still half sitting, I eagerly help him lift his own tunic and draw down his hose and braies. Unlike the night he took my virginity, I no longer look away but watch with fascination as he disappears inside me. My body, though still tight, offers no resistance but rather flows warm and wet around him. There is no longer any pain involved, only pleasure as my mother promised. I kiss my husband's face, his ears, his neck.

The urgency of Louis's need for me makes our coupling brief. After a few-dozen swift hard strokes, penetrations that pin me to the bed with their force and leave me gasping for air, Louis closes his eyes and pulls his head up and back in that peculiar way I now recognize. A moment later he makes a strangled cry and, jerking as a rabbit caught in a snare, spills his seed into me. We lie quietly for a few moments, both content, and then a knock sounds on the withdrawing chamber door.

"Yes," Louis calls out in obvious displeasure, withdrawing his now-shrunken member from me.

The voice of some unidentifiable attendant comes back across the length of the two rooms separating us from the door. "Your Majesty, the Dowager Queen would see you in her chambers if you are finished settling the Queen Consort into her apartments."

Louis looks exasperated, but immediately straightens his tunic and calls out, "Tell Her Majesty we will come at once." Then, looking down at me, my knees still lifted and naked from the waist down, he offers a rakish smile and says, "Consider yourself settled."

A MONTH LATER I DO indeed feel settled in. I know which of my French ladies I can trust and which I cannot. I know that I am the best dancer at my husband's court and that my manners are far above what passes for proper behavior here. I know I must write to the Vezian family of Montpellier if I want any really good rose water, for the stuff that can be secured in Paris is not worth wearing. This last is particularly important as Louis likes the smell of roses, in the royal gardens and on my person.

I am going to the gardens to meet him now with a Latin grammar book in my hands, for the king likes to amuse himself with improving my Latin. Entering the walled space from the archway nearest my rooms, I see him sitting beneath a pear tree, contemplating a book of his own, a religious work by a Cistercian monk. He is very taken with the Cistercians just now. Six years ago he founded an abbey for them at Royaumont. He goes there quite often to wait upon the monks as an act of charity and contrition, and he has promised to take me before the summer is out so I may see the refectory of which he is particularly proud.

As soon as Louis hears my footfall, he puts down his book. "Little queen," he says, his delight evident. "How is my Latin scholar this morning?"

"Very well, Your Majesty," I reply demurely, and then, opening my eyes as wide as I can, I add in feigned innocence, "But then I slept so very well last night."

Louis chuckles. He knows that he kept me awake to all hours—so late, in fact, that he feared discovery as he crept back to his rooms. Blanche, our mother, has given him a lecture on his "marital duties," admonishing him that while the relations of the marriage bed are no sin, they are meant for procreation and as a remedy against fornication. Therefore, in her august opinion, engaging in them more than once nightly is lascivious self-indulgence. I wonder what she would think if she knew we engaged in them during daylight.

"Come, sit beside me and we will get to work." He pats a spot on the carpet that he has spread beneath the tree. This is his favorite way to sit, and I find no fault with it though that officious, self-righteous Marie de Montmirall says it is unseemly and more appropriate for a shepherd than a king. Honestly I loathe that woman. In which opinion I am heartily joined by her daughter-in-law, Lady Elisabeth of Coucy, who is as favored a member of my household as her mother-in-law is disliked.

I drop down willingly at Louis's side, and we set to studying. After some time, Agnes d'Harcourt, Princess Isabelle's *chambrière*, passes on the path nearby.

"Spy," I grumble to Louis.

"Never mind, little queen, we are quite blamelessly occupied."

"How can you be so sanguine about it?" I ask, hands on my hips. For a moment I am more my sister Eleanor than myself. I lose my patience. "The spying I mean. This is *your* palace. You are *king* and I your queen; yet we must sneak about to see each other."

Louis looks pained. I am myself again and bitterly wish the words unsaid. Only a few nights ago we had a dreadful argument on a similar topic. For the first time I took aim directly at Blanche of Castile and learned an important lesson. I may outsmart the lady, but I dare not complain of her. She is *perfect*. She is, according to *mon mari*, the reason he has a throne to sit upon. Good God! But she is old, and I am pretty. I will outplay her, or outlast her.

"Never mind," I say, gently touching Louis's hand where it holds my book. "It is an adventure. We are like the lovers in the epic poems, defeating all to be together."

We resume my Latin, but I know Louis is not yet at his ease. His posture tells me as much. Agnes d'Harcourt shuffles past again, and I make certain she can hear my conjugations, reciting in a particularly crisp, clear voice.

When she disappears into the palace I say, "I believe my hard work and scholarship deserve a reward."

"Hm." Louis pretends to consider me very severely, but I make a face and he laughs at once. "And what do you demand, little queen?"

"Might we walk in the rose garden?"

"Bien sûr." He rises with a grace born of natural athleticism and extends a hand to draw me upward. Together we move in the direction of the roses, which are in their full glory. The smell is intoxicating. Behind a particularly full bush Louis steals a kiss.

Yes, I think, *I will give Louis what Blanche cannot, and love will conquer all.*

HOW I LOVE PONTOISE. IN a single day's ride, my position in the battle between my "dear" mother and me, or as Yolande and I now refer to her privately, "the dragon from Castile," improves markedly. I wheedle Louis to bring me here quite often and, given that he likes it as well as I do, I am generally successful unless the dragon can think of some manner of business that must be handled from the Ile de la Cité. This trip was particularly easy to arrange as the Foire Saint-Martin will be held in a week on Saint Martin's feast day. As I told Louis, such a venerable fair, more than sixty years old, is not to be missed.

So the November-afternoon sun finds us in the king's rooms, reclining near a set of windows with a view of the Oise River below while we play chess. We have already played at other things. And perhaps because Louis was satiated in that game, he is letting me win this one.

"Be careful," he chides. "You are in danger."

"Never, Husband, with you here to protect me." I smile and rub my foot against his bare leg. In dressing after our encounter he did not bother to put on his hose.

"No, I mean your queen. Look to your queen."

I see what he means and move accordingly, striking with that same queen to remove the threat. "Perhaps the queen can take care of herself." I shake my head, putting my hair, uncovered and hanging to my waist, in motion.

"Can she?"

"Yes, but she *prefers* to take care of her king." I rise and, going to a nearby table, pour a goblet of wine and bring it to Louis. Taking it, he motions for me to sit on his lap, and I sink there willingly.

"You are a very devoted wife, lady." He offers me a sip, and then sets the glass of wine down on the floor beside him and takes my face in his hand, drawing it close to his. I know what is coming. Already my nipples stand at attention beneath my soft woolen tunic. And then there is a rap at the door.

"She comes," says a muffled voice from the other side, and I spring up like a doe surprised by a hunter.

Grabbing my hose and shoes from a nearby stool, I race to the spiral staircase connecting my husband's chamber to my own. Down the stairs I plunge. Slipping two steps from the bottom, I skin my calf badly and land in a heap. Elisabeth and Yolande are there to help me up. "Quick!" I whisper, but the admonition is needless. The scene in my chamber has already been carefully set, and I need only be tidied and placed into the tableau. Three stools sit in a circle by the fire with an embroidery frame before each. Needles threaded and at the ready are stuck into two. On the stool before the third, a harp sits, and, even as Yolande fastens my shoes and tightens a girdle around my waist, Elisabeth seats herself and begins to play. Yolande hands me an amber-colored crespine. I give my hair a vicious twist and force it into the net, over which she places my coif and the barbette needed to hold it in place. In another instant I am on my stool, needle in hand.

Yolande carefully closes the door at the bottom of the stairs before taking her seat.

I can well imagine what is going on upstairs. Blanche has entered Louis's chambers and is looking for evidence of me. She will not find any. When I go to Louis's room, I take nothing. I drink nothing unless it be from his glass. We even have a special cloth we place upon Louis's bed, when we use the bed, that is folded afterward and tucked away, so that Blanche may not spot or smell the product of our loins and discover us in that manner.

Generally, once she is satisfied that I am not with Louis, the dragon sits with him herself as long as she can—sentinel against him passing a pleasant hour with me. Occasionally she will appear at my door and be announced, searching for traces that escaped her *en haut*. Hence the very deliberate picture we have arranged and my choice of loyal company.

A moment later, the door at the bottom of the interior staircase bursts open. She has never done this! How bold she grows! Or perhaps, how desperate.

"Your Majesty," I say, rising to offer the obligatory curtsy, "how you startled us." I am not obliged to stand in her presence, so I return, as nonchalantly as possible, to my stool. I do not take up my needle for fear that my fingers might tremble noticeably. I may hate Blanche, but I also fear her. "Will you join us?"

"And how have you passed your afternoon?" Blanche makes no move to sit and little effort to soften her voice to an acceptable level of *politesse*.

"As a Christian woman should, doing her duty." I keep my eyes wide and innocent, enjoying the fact that I have made a statement that, while literally true, hints at the very activity she hoped to catch us in. "My ladies and I are working on pieces for the Eucharistic vestments His Majesty asked me to complete for the priest at Royaumont." I gesture toward my frame, but Blanche shows no inclination to examine the work, so the effort that my ladies made last evening to advance it appears to have been wasted. "Pray, Your Majesty, how was the king, my husband, when you left him?"

"Rather indolent, and behind in important matters." Blanche narrows her eyes and peers fiercely at me. "I fear for him. It is so easy for a young man to be led astray by temporal matters. He swore at his coronation to be *'rex et sacerdos,'* king *and* priest, and I would not have him break that oath. No, as I have told him since he was a boy, I would rather see him blameless dead than in commission of a mortal sin."

The strident nature of Blanche's pronouncement chills me to the bone. Piety is greatly to be admired. This I was taught and truly believe; and none can question my own family's religiosity. Every clergyman in my father's territory, nay the Holy Father himself, would confirm that the Count of Provence is a fast friend to the church. But this woman from Castile has a faith altogether different from my own. It possesses her; yet rather than bringing her comfort, it seems to leave her full of fear.

"Your Majesty, I pray daily that my husband may be a good

king and a worthy Christian, but surely there is little reason for concern on that score. Did he not, before we left Paris, order several hundred of the poor fed in the courtyard of his palace? Does he not, in your company, visit the city hospitals to pray with the sick? Does he not rise up at night to hear the hours?"

"Yes, but his immortal soul and his kingdom would be better served if he spent more time on his knees and less time between yours."

Next to me the music stops, and Elisabeth covers her mouth with her hand in shock at such a blunt and coarse reference to my marriage bed. I myself am undone by it. I blush crimson and begin to weep both in anger and in shame.

"Your Majesty, I am your son's wedded wife, and it was you who chose me for his bride. Surely a man may lie with his wife without accusations of depravity. Is it not my duty to provide him comfort thus and to furnish heirs of his body?"

"Are you with child then?"

"No." I am stung by the question although I have been a married woman only half a year.

"Then speak no more of 'duty' until you have done yours. Keep your mind on God that you may be a fitting vessel for His Majesty's sons. Only a woman who gives herself to her husband in fear of God shall find her womb quickened, whereas the woman who, like a strumpet, revels in the animal pleasure of the event is odious to the Lord and unworthy to be called mother. I will send you a hair shirt this afternoon that you may do penance for your carnal nature. And Louis likewise. And make no mistake, lady, I shall expect proof that you wear it when we dine this evening."

Then, without another word, the dragon turns on her heels and lets herself out of my apartments by the main door.

CHAPTER 3

My dearest Marguerite,

Everything was settled with the English king with surprisingly little difficulty, and soon I will be on my way to him. On my way to you. I do not dare confess to anyone save yourself that I look forward to my arrival at Paris most. Not that I mean to insult my newfound lord by this. He is a great man and a king, and I am suitably honored at the prospect of becoming his queenly wife. But I do not know him and do not love him, whereas you are as my own heart. How I have missed you these last eighteen months.

Yours faithfully,

Eleanor

I have grown since you saw me last, and I believe I am now as tall as you are.

ELEANOR
NOVEMBER 1235
CASTLE OF TARASCON, PROVENCE

"Marguerite had more gowns." My mother, looking about at the great number of trunks in the process of being packed by an equally large number of servants, draws her brows down sternly and sighs in disbelief.

But she will have to do better than that if she thinks to shame me into silence.

"And shoes. I distinctly remember my sister had two dozen pairs. I have only eighteen."

"Eleanor! *Pro es pro!* Your father spent a mighty sum to see you married in style. You will have more than three hundred in your train when you set out in the morning, and yet you complain. If the King of England could hear you, what would he think? Perhaps he would reconsider his choice of bride."

"It is too late for that—the *verba de presenti* were exchanged yesterday. Henry of England has committed himself, and so have I." I try to sound nonchalant even as I remember that my future husband went so far with Joan of Ponthieu, only to turn back.

Mother, no doubt thinking the same, shakes her head again. Then her eyes, without warning, drop to the hand I have half hidden behind me. "What do you have there?"

I know that I am caught, but I refuse to be embarrassed. "Only the shoes I plan to wear tomorrow." I open my eyes wide, trying to keep my tone guileless like that of my sister Sanchia.

Mother's suspicions are not assuaged. "Let me see."

I bring the slippers out from behind me and hold them forward. A look of bewilderment passes over Mother's face. Whatever she was expecting, it was not this. "Those are not yours." She pauses, her eyes momentarily glassy as if, rather than seeing what is before her, she is trying to glimpse the past and remember where she saw the shoes before. Then her head snaps up, and she looks me in the eye. "Those are Marguerite's shoes, made for her journey to France." Reaching out, she touches the pointed toe of one of the doeskin slippers—as if by touching the shoe she can better recall the daughter whom she has not seen in more than a year and a half.

"I did not take them," I insist defiantly. "She gave them to me."

"She would." Mother's smile is sweet yet touched by a certain sadness. Her voice catches as she continues. "Will you return them when you see her?"

I glance at the shoes, hard worn since I saw my sister last. How beautiful they were. How they have changed. Marguerite would not recognize them. Will I recognize her? "No," I reply, drawing them back against me until they are hidden in my skirt, "they are not grand enough for the Queen of France. But I will give her the gifts from Father and yourself." *Perhaps,* I think, *those will not be grand enough either.* For a moment my doubts get the better of me. Then I swallow them. Marguerite may be a mighty queen, but she is still my sister.

GRAY, COLD, AND WET; THAT is how the city of Paris appears, looming not far in the distance. That is also how I feel, riding beside Uncle Guillaume.

"This is English weather," he remarks offhandedly. It is a comment hardly calculated to make me feel better. I pull my cloak closer and grit my teeth. All the pleasant hours passed as a guest of Thibaut of Champagne, King of Navarre, seem ages rather than days ago.

"Then I no longer want to go to England."

My uncle barks a laugh before looking more closely at me and seeing I do not laugh as well. Considering me, he says, "London is not the frontier you think it."

"Is it Paris?" I challenge.

"No. But with God's grace and Savoyard help, perhaps it can be made so." It is my turn to laugh and my uncle's turn to be serious. "Listen, Eleanor. Henry of England waits to be pleased. He *wants* to be pleased. Your vigorous, fiery temperament can be captivating when you make it your business to be so. Capture the king's heart, and I will help you do the rest."

Peering at my uncle through the increasing drizzle, I feel my spirits lift slightly. He is a man capable of many things—of any-thing. Am I not blood of his blood? Am I not as ambitious as my Savoyard uncles? As beautiful as my Savoyard mother? As capable as my sister the French queen? "Never fear, Uncle. I will make Henry of England feel as young, handsome, and loved as Louis of France."

"One thing is sure, your need to equal your sister in everything will be an asset to us in this undertaking." Uncle Guillaume's com-ment catches me off my guard, like an unexpected slap. I said noth-ing of my burning desire to be thought Marguerite's peer, but he knows me well—too well. "Just remember, Eleanor, your sister is more than a stick to measure yourself against. She is an ally. She worked to secure your safe passage through her husband's territo-ries, and she pays a price for your marriage to the English king."

"A price?" I am intrigued. Though my father and uncle saw fit to tell me much about the negotiation of my marriage, admonish-ing me that such was a part of my political education, I cannot see how my becoming Queen of England directly affects my sister, except perhaps to make her feel more superior than usual.

"Blanche of Castile uses your alliance with her son's rival to challenge your sister's loyalty and question her trustworthiness. She thinks that Henry of England desires to regain Normandy, which was lost by his father, and that Provence and Savoy will help him get it."

I feel suddenly colder, and not because of the weather. No, this cold comes from within. It is the sort of icy feeling that strikes me when I am very angry. How dare that woman, that *masca*, cast aspersions on my sister! I may not think Marguerite perfect, but no one outside the family is entitled to suggest otherwise. Perhaps my Henry *should* take Normandy back just to teach Blanche of Castile better manners!

My Henry. I have never thought of him that way before. I scarcely allow myself to think of him at all, except abstractly as the King of England and the reason that I will wear a crown. Tucking my chin down against a gust of wind and raising a hand to pull my hood as far forward as I can, I wonder if it was so for Marguerite as she traveled to meet Louis for the first time. Did she worry that she would be repulsed at first sight of him? That they would have nothing to talk about either in company or alone? That she would color scarlet when faced for the first time with the sight of a naked man? About the physical act of being taken to wife?

No. I cannot imagine that she did. Louis of France is twenty-one years old and the subject of story and song, rumored to be so handsome that no woman can resist him, and so virtuous that they have no need of trying. My betrothed husband is twenty-eight. Is it any wonder then that I feel envious of my sister even as I am eager to see her?

When we reach it at last, the French royal palace is warm, thank God. Or maybe it is only the absence of rain that makes it feel warm. We pass through the doors with some difficulty as servants swarm in and out around us, managing our baggage and horses. I may be out of the rain, but I am still wet—wet through. I cannot believe that I must present myself to the King of France and my sister for the first time looking like a drowned rat.

As I raise a self-conscious hand to my hair, Uncle Guillaume says, "Do not make yourself uneasy. This is not your formal reception. That will happen later. There will be plenty of time to recover and bedeck yourself in something splendid before the eyes of the French court are upon you."

Before I can make any answer, I realize that my sister's eyes are on me *now*. Passing through a vaulted arch, I see her just ahead, and beside her the king. Holy Mary, he is handsome, and she is grand. She looks like Mother, not in her features perhaps, as she has always been a good mix of Savoyard and Provençal, but in her expression and in her bearing. She seems so much older than two years my senior. She is as serene and radiant as any queen I have ever seen in a manuscript illustration. Instead of just feeling damp and miserable, I suddenly feel childish and tongue-tied.

"Your Majesties." My uncle's voice brings me to my senses, and, along with him, I sink before my sister and her husband—the King and Queen of France.

"Your Excellency, Lady Eleanor, we are happy for your safe arrival." The king's voice is formal, his expression correct in every particular, but this was not what I imagined, though I can scarce say what I did expect, as I rode the many leagues from Provence. My eyes sting as I turn them to Marguerite.

When they meet hers, something remarkable happens. Heedless of her rank, her beautiful clothing, and the fact that I am dripping wet, Marguerite springs forward and throws her arms around me. There is no more Queen of France. There is only my sister.

MARGUERITE AND I ARE CURLED close before her fire, silent and content on the third evening after my arrival, when I finally have the courage to mention it. Something I have never said aloud to anyone—not to Mother, not to Uncle Guillaume during our travels. "I am marrying an old man."

My sister, who has been gazing at the flames, looks up, startled. "Eleanor, no. You are the English king's first bride. Surely he must be a man in his prime."

"He is not ten years younger than Father." My voice unexpectedly comes out in a whisper, as if all the air has been choked out of me by my fears.

Marguerite sucks in her breath audibly. This is not the reassurance I hoped for. "Still," she says, her voice with a note of forced cheerfulness, "he is not thirty, and did you not tell me by letter that Uncle Guillaume calls him a 'fine man'?"

"You have the handsomest man in Christendom!" I feel my cheeks grow warm as I say so. Over the past days I have been forced to admit to myself that the King of France is all my uncles and my sister said he was. He is so handsome that he appears to shine. He dances better than anyone I have ever seen. Everything he does, everything he says, conveys an easy, kingly authority. My stomach tightens into a knot. Perhaps I should have said nothing to my sister.

"This is not about what I have." The sympathy and superiority in my sister's eyes are maddening. "All our lives you have measured what was yours against what was mine—everything from your complexion to your newest cloak. It has to stop. It will only make you unhappy."

That does it. I find my voice and loose my anger. "So," I cry, springing from my chair to stand before Marguerite, "you believe that you have already won! That your husband, your palaces, your kingdom are all destined to be better and greater than mine!"

My sister, looking up at me, blushes.

I am glowering, but I don't care. My sister deserves to feel uncomfortable. "I may have been born second, Marguerite, but I will not remain behind—not in honor and not in dignity. England will not be second to France!"

"I do not want to outdo you," Marguerite protests somewhat feebly. "I only want you to be happy. If you are not, I will grieve. I could never take pleasure in the disappointments of others."

Her ludicrously misplaced piety breaks the back of my anger. I take a step away from her and laugh, or rather snort, something I am prone to do despite my mother's constant reminders that it is unbecoming. "Never? Oh no, Marguerite, I will not let you paint yourself the saint! I well remember the times you bested me at hawking and reveled in the fact. And all the times you *thought* that you bested me in lessons—"

"Thought?" Marguerite rolls her eyes. "*Did.* But though I *am* the better student, we will *both* be great queens."

"You sound like Uncle Guillaume." I return to my seat. "Before I left, I heard him talking with Father. 'Two queens,' he kept saying, 'four daughters, and two of them queens.'"

"Two of us queens *together.*" Marguerite reaches for my hand, and I give it to her willingly. "And if your Henry is not young, he must certainly be kind and more than a little enamored of you. After all, he made no fuss about your dowry."

"True. I just hope he is not very ugly"—I scrunch up my nose in a manner calculated to make my sister laugh, even though the fear that I feel, I feel in earnest—"or I might have to close my eyes every time he kisses me."

My time at Marguerite's court is so full of delightful activity and abundant opportunities for sisterly companionship that I find myself thinking less and less frequently of my husband-to-be. There are days when I do not think of Henry of England at all. Days when I do not worry about kissing him. Then, when I have been with Marguerite nearly a month, a letter arrives from my groom. It is addressed to my sister, not to me.

"Listen to this, Eleanor." Marguerite is in my rooms, having interrupted my evening's toilet to share the content's of my betrothed's missive. "'I hope you will not consider me bold, but since the illustrious bishop-elect of Valence has gone on a matter of business to the court of Emperor Frederick, Your Majesty seems best situated to send me news of my intended, your dear sister the Lady Eleanor. We pray she is well despite all this damp weather.'" Raising her eyes from the paper, Marguerite says, "He is very attentive."

I turn at the dressing table, frustrating Agnes, my childhood nurse, who is trying to plait my hair, beguiled in spite of myself by my soon-to-be husband's concern for me. "He is well-informed too," I answer, "for surely our uncle made no mention of his travels to His Majesty. Not after admonishing us to avoid the subject."

Marguerite nods in agreement, then lowers her eyes and reads silently for a moment. "Your groom grows impatient," she remarks, placing her finger upon a particular passage. "'We approach Your Majesty affectionately, asking that you speed our lovely affianced bride on her way to her new home in England. We have been eagerly awaiting her since our marriage contract was confirmed at Vienne.'"

Marguerite sets the letter down before me so that I can read the rest myself. But before I can complete a single sentence, she speaks again. "I think you must continue your journey as soon as our uncle can return to accompany you." Her voice is agitated, but I cannot imagine why. She paces away and then turns back to face me, wringing her hands slightly. "We cannot risk the English king's impatience growing into something more—into a search for another bride."

"Marguerite, calm yourself. Surely there is no need for exaggerated concern. I believe I will reach England before His Majesty tires of waiting." My response is meant to set Marguerite laughing, but instead her shoulders fall and she gives a deep sigh. Turning completely in my seat despite Agnes's clucking tongue, I ask, "Whatever is the matter?"

"I . . . I will miss you." My sister's face hangs like that of an old woman. "The last weeks have been like a return to Provence."

"Do you wish yourself back in Provence?" I ask. I cannot believe what I am hearing. Much as I was sad to leave home, and much as I have enjoyed my sojourn in France and the respite it has offered from my apprehensions over my upcoming marriage, being with my sister has awakened a burning desire in me for my own court. I am convinced our destinies lie in being queens. I would not go back to being only a count's daughter.

"No," she says, "but I wish I had a sister here."

I know what she means. Her new sister, Isabelle, is the strangest little thing. I asked her if she liked my gown at the banquet celebrating my arrival and complimented hers, and, unbelievably, she told me that such vanity is offensive to God. I hope that my own new sister, with whom, auspiciously, I share a name, will be more to my liking.

"You will always have me," I say. "Wherever I go, for as long as I live."

THE WINTER WINDS, IT SEEMED, wished me in England as urgently as His Majesty. As a result, my ship touched ground earlier than anyone expected. I was sincerely glad of it. This sea voyage was my first, and I did not enjoy it. From the moment we left Wissant, Agnes and I took turns being sick. I thought my stomach could not feel more agitated. I was wrong. As we pass through the gates of Canterbury, word comes that the king is already in the city.

"He must have left London before we landed, for he traveled more than three times our distance," Uncle Guillaume tells me. "He waits for you at the steps of the cathedral."

"At the cathedral?"

"It appears he intends to be married today."

In my surprise, my ice-cold hands drop my reins. Thankfully I am not the type to swoon, or I might well be lying on the cold January ground beside my palfrey this very minute.

Still, my countenance must be pale, for the king's proctor, Sir Robert de Mucegros, says bracingly, "I am sure His Majesty will be postponed until tomorrow in deference to his lady's fatigue. It is only His Majesty's naturally enthusiastic temperament running ahead of him."

I sit up straight, gathering both my reins and my wits. I am here to marry Henry of England whether the man or the thought be palatable or no. What must be done is best to be done quickly. "Sir Robert, I am at His Majesty's disposal. If he likes, he may wed me straight from the saddle, though I would beg an hour to warm myself and change my gown."

When we reach them, we find the cathedral's grounds enormous, though not large enough for my party, so only a score or so of the most important ride on with me. Even so, we spill off the frozen path and overhang the square beside the church where we pull up to dismount.

Another large party is already there. All of them are male. All are noblemen sumptuously dressed and wearing heavy fur-lined cloaks, though I doubt there is enough fur on this island to make the weather bearable. None are young. I do not allow myself to hope for much, and it is just as well. As my uncle helps me from my horse, a man outstrips his companions and clasps Robert Mucegros in an embrace. The gentleman is short and square. Dear Lord, I know that my husband is old, but must he be short as well? Sure enough, it is Henry of England. Releasing Sir Robert, he turns in my direction. He is not at all handsome. His face is ruddy from the cold and one eyelid droops alarmingly, giving him a sleepy look.

But his smile is merry, and his curly hair and beard give him a comfortable look. He is also beautifully and meticulously dressed. If he is a man of fashion, we shall at least have something in common.

"Lady Eleanor," he says in a voice as deep and as warm as his smile, "Our Lord and Saint Edward be praised for your safe arrival! We have gathered the first among our magnates to greet you and pay their respects. We have also brought gifts meant to honor you. But we see now that all our efforts pale to insignificance in the shadow of your beauty."

He executes a bow as easily as a younger man would. And I find myself, all in all, rather more satisfied than not. It could certainly be worse. And as Uncle Guillaume promised me, he appears to have good teeth. "Your Majesty does me great honor by his compliments and even greater distinction by giving me his hand." I curtsy and then, knowing already the king's inclination, I add, "When, sir, shall we wed?"

"Where is Edmund Rich?" the king asks of those surrounding him. The group parts slightly to make way for an ancient-looking cleric in a miter. This then must be the influential archbishop of Canterbury. "Your Grace, we would be married as soon as practicable."

"But the feast," says a man standing near to the king. I cannot know his name, but I am sure I soon will, for his manner of address suggests great familiarity with my future husband. "All the preparations."

"We will save the celebration for the Lady Eleanor's coronation. If she does not object, surely no one else can." Henry looks again, rather meaningfully I think, at the archbishop.

"If Your Majesty wishes, I can be ready in an hour," the prelate replies.

"His Majesty does wish."

MY NUPTIAL MASS DRAWS TO a close. Like the ceremony of betrothal at the cathedral door preceding it, I felt strangely absent from the service. Still, I do believe I smiled and spoke as the situation required, and everyone around me looks abundantly pleased with me.

As we leave the altar, the king turns to Edmund Rich and says, "You had best come at once and bless the marriage bed."

"At once?" The venerable archbishop forgets his manners in his amazement.

"I have waited many years for a wife," Henry replies, his eyes sparkling. "I will not wait an hour longer."

I am bustled without ceremony to an apartment in the castle where I made ready for my wedding. While Agnes and my ladies undress me, a host of servants stoke the enormous fire in the grate, bring in wine, and warm the sheets on a large, carved bed, which they garland with swags of costly fabrics in rich colors. I am redressed in a chemise of finest chainsil so delicate that I can see every curve of my own body as I sit before the mirror of polished steel to have my hair combed. Before Agnes can finish, a knock sounds at the door. She pulls me to my feet and covers me with a fur-lined pelisse even as the door swings open to reveal the archbishop of Canterbury, still magnificently clad in the vestments in which he celebrated my nuptial Mass. With him are several priests swinging censers of incense, and behind them a half-dozen noblemen whom I saw in church, escorting my husband. Like the others, he is still in his court finery.

My ladies lead me to the foot of the bed, and the archbishop makes the sign of the cross over me as his attendant priests circle me and nearly choke me with their incense. After praying over me,

the archbishop turns to the bed and, after his priests administer a
goodly dose of incense there as well, sprinkles it with holy water,
praying all the while. I am too nervous to pay much attention, but
I hear mentions of Sarah, Rachel, and Rebecca, matrons of the
House of David, and numerous allusions to the Blessed Virgin.

Then, quick as they came, they are all departing, Agnes with a
quick peck on my cheek as she goes. Henry of England and I are
alone.

Stepping forward, the king takes my hand and leads me not to
the bed but to stand before my mirror. Directing my attention to
my own image by gesture, he says, "You are beautiful."

And I am. My hair is a glorious mass of auburn touched with
gold; my cheeks are flushed pink with agitation.

As I watch in the mirror, Henry lifts the pelisse from my shoulders and drops it to the ground. I hear a sharp intake of breath. His
hands take my waist from behind, pulling me against him, and I
feel the heat of his body through my shift. He kisses my neck
where it meets my shoulder, his right hand wandering over my
body to cradle my breast, and it is my turn to gasp. Then turning
me, the king takes my face in his hands. At this distance his drooping eyelid gives him a sly rather than sleepy look. Pulling me to
him, he puts his mouth upon my own. He nips at my lower lip and
slides his tongue between my lips. So this is kissing. It is not
unpleasant, though I do close my eyes without thinking.

My husband takes his mouth away and lifts my shift up over my
face and head. Caught up in my new experiences, I had momentarily forgotten what comes next. My sudden nakedness has a
sobering effect. I shiver both with cold and trepidation.

The king scoops me up in his arms as if I were a child and
deposits me on the bed. Then, regarding my trembling form with
a kindly expression, he pulls the covers over me and says, "Some

wine, I think." Pouring me a glass he commands, "Drink it all." I do the best that I can with shaking hands and a throat suddenly closed with fear. When the glass is drained he is not satisfied. "And another."

I have had nothing to eat since I broke my fast this morning, so I can feel the second glass even as it goes down. His Majesty must see its effects, for he nods his head contentedly and takes the glass from my hand. Then he begins to undress rapidly.

My good nurse advised me to look away, as if I were about to have a splinter removed from my finger. But I cannot. It is in my nature to face what I fear. As the king's braies come off, I catch sight of it. I have never seen such a thing, not even when I stumbled upon a stable boy and kitchen maid engaged in the act of love behind a garden wall, for then all I could see was his back and her face as she panted and moaned. My husband's member is like the slightly gnarled limb of a flesh-colored tree. It stands straight out from his body. I cannot fathom how such a thing will fit inside me; yet this is what must happen, according to my mother's description.

Lifting the covers, the king slides into bed beside me and begins to kiss me once more. I hold my body back from his, as far as I can; yet I can feel the tip of it brushing my legs. I want to put my hand down and push it away, but I dare not. Moving his mouth to my ear, my husband says, "Eleanor, I will try to be gentle, but you must relax. Do you understand?"

"Y-yes, Your Majesty," I stammer.

"Henry."

"Yes, Henry." I cannot see what difference it makes what I call him at a moment like this!

Sitting up, the king rolls me onto my back. "Draw up your knees," he instructs. And when I lie helpless and uncomprehending, he arranges my legs himself as if I were an inanimate thing.

Between my legs and kneeling over me, Henry kisses me again. Pressing his mouth once more against my ear he says, "Promise you will tell me if I hurt you."

I can only shake my head by way of response. I have lost my tongue.

I feel his fingers spreading me, and for a moment something round and smooth, like the tip of a nose, hesitates at the entrance to my *cloistre virginal*. Then with slow steady pressure he begins to slide into me. My eyes tear, but he cannot see them, for his head is buried in my hair and he is kissing the side of my neck. And I refuse to cry out, no matter what I promised, even when a sudden shove causes me a sharp pain. I close my eyes and clench my hands into fists beside me against the pain of subsequent thrusts. Thankfully, after perhaps half a dozen more, Henry gives a great cry and slumps down upon me, pulling me to him in a tight embrace. Withdrawing from me, he pulls the blankets, which have come off during his efforts, up to cover me modestly, then lies beside me, stroking the hair back from my face.

"You were very brave," he says solemnly, "and have made me very happy."

"I am glad," I mumble. I suddenly feel very sleepy, even though it is only late afternoon.

"I promise next time will be better." His voice is soothing, as is his touch upon my face. I have a hard time focusing my eyes on him. "Sleep," he croons, "sleep, my beautiful bride. My treasure."

NEVER IN ALL MY LIFE have I met anyone more desirous of seeing me pleased than this man who has known me less than a week. On our travels from Canterbury to Westminster, where we are now ensconced, His Majesty spent nearly every minute trying either to keep me warm or to draw me out on the subject of my likes and dislikes. There was no use telling him how much I hate the English weather, with its constant rain and a cold beyond any I have ever known. So, I confined myself to more pleasant topics. Finding that tales of chivalry delight me, he promised to take me to Glastonbury to see the resting place of the noble and much celebrated King Arthur. I have been allowed to wait for nothing, to want for nothing.

Now, shortly before my coronation is to begin, he arrives, full of excitement, at my apartments. "Eleanor, come to the window!" Striding through the cluster of ladies who have been buzzing about me adjusting my attire, he catches my hand and draws me to the casement before I can say a word. A truly dazzling site meets my eyes—hundreds of riders, clad in silks of every color and mounted on horses of every description, are approaching the palace in orderly ranks. Each rider has something gold or silver before him on his saddle.

"Who are they?"

"The wealthiest men in London, my love, bearing goblets to serve our guests at your coronation banquet."

I feel suddenly giddy with delight. In a short time I will be a queen, and every moment of my coronation day, every detail of the event, promises to be as grandiose as the sight of these cup-bearing riders. I throw my arms around my husband's neck and kiss his cheek. He laughs with pleasure at my being pleased, then steps back to examine me.

"Madam, you are a vision."

I twirl so that he may see me from every side. Then stop and look squarely at my husband. "Your Majesty looks quite exceptionally fine as well." And in truth, he does. Magnificent clothes cannot make him younger, but they do seem to make him more dashing. He is undeniably regal.

"Henry," he corrects me. He cannot stand for me to call him anything but Henry, even in front of my ladies. "And thank you. A compliment from the most beautiful woman in England is well worth having."

The most beautiful woman in England? Certainly the most celebrated, I think an hour later as, following my husband, I make my way along a path of blue ray cloth from the palace to the Westminster abbey church. A thousand eyes must be upon me as I walk beneath a canopy of purple silk suspended between the silver lances borne by barons of la Cinque Ports, and I thank God again that for once the endless English rain is not falling. Small silver bells at the canopy corners above my head tinkle merrily with every step. I am flanked by a pair of bishops. One is my uncle; the name of the second I have already forgotten in my excitement.

Inside the church, I am greeted by hundreds of expectant faces. My husband's knights, barons, clergymen—all of the most important men in his kingdom—fill the church, turning it to a sea of brilliant hues, sparkling with a smattering of gold and silver. Prostrating myself before the high altar while Edmund Rich intones a prayer, I feel my own breath but also something more—a humming as if the church itself is breathing. The archbishop invokes the blessing of the Virgin upon me, that I may be fruitful and continue the line of English kings. I know my duty in this area and am prepared to do it, but hearing the subject raised in church embarrasses me. I am glad my face is down beyond the sight of the crowd for I am sure it colors. I am mortifyingly certain that every man standing among the pews is thinking of what my husband does to me in an attempt to seed my womb. And still the archbishop sounds the subject, naming all the great matriarchs of the tribe of David, the bearers of some of the world's most important sons.

At last there is silence. I draw myself to my knees. The

THE SISTER QUEENS 55

archbishop leans down and, removing the golden circlet sitting upon my hair, anoints my head with holy oil. I am keenly aware of the fragrance of the unction and also of incense. I pray, even as the archbishop blesses my ring and slides it onto my finger, that my shortness of breath, my wheezing sickness, will not be engendered by the scented heaviness of the air.

I watch with rapt attention as His Grace raises a crown, *my* crown, for all to see—a marvelous ring of golden lilies, shining in the light of numberless candles. It is surprisingly heavy as he places it upon my head. I hope that I can do it justice. That like Esther, whose compassionate example the archbishop extorts me to follow, I can intercede with my husband to the benefit of his kingdom, *our* kingdom. As I accept the virge and scepter, magnificent sound swells to fill the vaulted spaces surrounding me, voices singing, *"Christus vincit, Christus regnat, Christus imperat."* Christ rules indeed, and so do I. I defy any to think me less than my sister Marguerite now.

CHAPTER 4

My dearest Marguerite,

Thank you for the ring you sent for my natal day. Henry gave me one as well, along with many pretty presents, but I assure you that I like yours best. I have much to celebrate. To be fourteen, a queen, and well loved is no mean thing. Only one happiness is lacking, I would give my Henry a son. He insists that there is no hurry, although we are more than a year married, and that a daughter would do as well (for he is a man most desirous of a large and varied family), but I know my duty, and as he loves me so very well, would do it. We attend to the task of conceiving a child with much frequency and enthusiasm. I confess that, despite my prodigious love for fine gowns, shoes, and the like, I am not at all sorry to spend so much of my time without my clothing. Have I shocked you, my darling sister? Surely not, for you have a fair husband of your own.

Yours,

E

MARGUERITE
JUNE 1237
PALAIS DU ROI, PARIS

"I have heard from my sister the Queen of England."

"Hm." Louis does not look up from the letter he is read-ing beneath the pear tree—the tree that used to be ours. "I truly believe this fellow is being abused by one of my barons. He sought help with his grievance at the local Franciscan monastery, and the abbot writes to me." Unlike in former times, he no longer pats the spot on the carpet beside him and asks me to sit. And this fact makes me both sad and angry.

"Her husband the king surprised her by hiring an artist to paint her bedchamber at the Tower of London while she and all the court were at Westminster." I will not be distracted, certainly not by some barefoot mendicant from the countryside. I do not begrudge the time Louis spends sitting where once we studied my Latin, meting out justice to his subjects both high- and lowborn. But *surely* he should do me justice as well, and give me a modicum of his attention. "Louis, did you hear me?" I put my hands upon my hips. Have I become a shrew? My husband looks up, startled. He thinks of me, when his mind strays in my direction at all these days, as a mild woman, a woman of patience. And so I have been, but to what end?

"Your sister is at Westminster." He appears genuinely puzzled.

"No, my sister has just returned from Westminster to find her rooms painted with hundreds upon hundreds of delicate roses at the King of England's behest."

"How singular, and what a waste. Just think how many of the poor he might have fed with the same monies."

"That would indeed have been a noble enterprise, but surely

giving pleasure to his wife is also worthy? The two are not in opposition to each other. Henry of England may give to the poor and also to my sister Eleanor."

"So it seems." Louis looks down again and turns another page. Then, as if struck by something, looks up at me again. "If you want your rooms painted and your incomes and allowance do not permit it, I shall be happy to advance you the money. I sincerely hope, however, you will select a more exalted theme. Perhaps the parables."

I feel as though Louis has slapped me. Mild-mannered Louis, who shows the most exquisite kindness to the sick in our city's hospitals; who cleans their filth and changes their dressings. Can he not see that I do not envy Eleanor her freshly painted rooms, but the solicitude of her husband—a man who, from what my sister's letters tell, rises each morning intent on finding some novel manner of delighting or pampering his wife? My eyes sting. But even if a loss of composure might recall my husband's attention, I cannot bear to expose my feelings to someone so clearly indifferent to them. Turning on my heels, I retreat as quickly as I can without appearing to run. I lose control of my temper for only a single moment before reaching my rooms. Rushing past Agnes d'Harcourt, who never seems to be absent when Louis and I are in the gardens together, I do not allow her sufficient time to make way, and the clumsy little spy tumbles off the path and headlong into a bed of butterbur.

Bursting past a collection of ladies in my hall, I gain my bedchamber before the tears come. My women know well who is welcome to follow me uninvited into the private parts of my apartment and who is not, so only Marie, Elisabeth, and Yolande trail behind. I crumple to the floor on my knees, sobbing. Taking up a handful of my voluminous skirt, I bury my face in it.

"Your Majesty"—Marie kneels beside me, and I can feel her hand on my shaking shoulders—"are you unwell?"

"Unhappy." The voice that speaks the truth is not my own. I look up. Yolande stands directly in front of me.

"Louis no longer loves me."

"Ridiculous," Elisabeth chimes in. "You are Marguerite of France; your beauty and piety are widely celebrated. At this minute artists are busy carving your likeness at Saint Germain-en-Laye at the king's request."

Yolande glances at Elisabeth with a combination of indulgence and disbelief. Her Grace is two years younger than Lady Coucy but always behaves as if she is the mother hen to both Elisabeth and me. "The important point, Your Majesty, is that the king prefers no woman to you. Well, no woman of his own age."

"What difference does that make?" I ask, allowing Marie to help me rise as I dry my eyes with the kerchief she offers. "He still favors the dragon, and she is quite as effective, if not more so, than any mistress in keeping my husband from me. And she has a powerful ally, God himself."

"It is true that His Majesty's increased piety is fomented by his mother *and* his confessor. But I would not suggest that Your Majesty try to reclaim the king from God. Moses's wife was not successful and nor shall you be," says Yolande grimly. "And if the king wishes to go about his palaces ill shod and poorly dressed, what can that matter to you so long as he urges no economies of dress upon you? You must turn your mind from bringing back the Louis of your wedding day and concentrate on securing your own position. And in this, the fact that you have no other young lady for competition will prove most helpful."

Elisabeth standing nearby pats the bulge at the front of her *surcote* meaningfully. She is six months gone with child. Her husband,

Raoul, brings her little offerings from the palace kitchens at odd times throughout the day. I wonder if Louis would be so agreeably attentive.

"A baby, I know," I snap, striding to the window and staring out into those same gardens, where Louis remains staring fixedly at the papers in his lap, even though the roses are beginning to bloom. "But as His Majesty forgoes his favorite foods for Our Lord, he has given up other things as well." The time is long gone when the slightest arching look from me was enough to inflame my husband's desire.

"But surely he has the needs of a man?" Elisabeth counters.

"At present he appears content to be nearly as celibate as a monk." My voice is bitter and I know it, but that is how I feel. I am sixteen years old; yet my husband forces me to live as if I were an elderly woman past the age of all desire. Yolande and Elisabeth cannot imagine what it is like to toss and turn night after night, longing for the touch of my husband's hand, dreaming that his legs and arms are wrapped around me in a lover's embrace, only to wake and find myself tangled in my covers, achingly alone. Then to receive letters from Eleanor hinting broadly that the King of England is not at all the grave, older man she expected and that his touch is her delight. It is nearly unbearable.

"Well, if he is not currently subject to a man's passions, he is still subject to a king's duties. Every king needs a prince. His counselors will remind him of this fact soon enough if they do not already," says Yolande. "Then he will be back in your bed. And when you bear the king a son, the court will buzz about you as bees circle a hive. Blanche's bullying of you and reign over the rest of us will be at an end."

I nod dumbly, less convinced of Yolande's words than she appears to be herself. And I feel tears sting my eyes again. How can

I explain to my companions that even if Louis returns to me more frequently by night, and even if the birth of an heir makes me queen in verity, I will not be content? I miss the Louis who was my friend; the Louis who played chess with me and walked in the gardens; the Louis who held my cold hands as we examined the progress of the building at whichever monastery or religious house held his interest at the given moment. If I tell my ladies that I am lonely, they will be confused. The palace teems with courtiers and others, never more so than now with the preparation for two weddings under way. This very month both Robert and Alphonse will be married. I will have two new sisters to wait upon me and join in my entertainments. Besides, if I confess to my ladies that I am lonely, they will be hurt. And I would not cause them such pain even to unburden my own heart, for truly they do bear me good company.

CHAPTER 5

My dear Eleanor,

    *His Majesty's brothers Robert and Alphonse are married
now. My two new sisters, though very different from each
other, are both excellent women. Yes, even Jeanne of
Toulouse (and I feel no small amount of guilt over all the
unkind things you and I imagined about her during our days
together in Provence). Either is better company than my
"dear sister" Isabelle. How I wish Louis would marry the
princess off and relieve our court of her dreary, overbearing
piety. But perhaps he does not notice it. He is seldom in
her company, being much engaged with the business of
governing. He has lately begun the practice, after his
morning Mass, of opening himself to petitions from those
with complaint either against his officials or any private
gentleman. He does not do this every day, but when he does
will sit for hours hearing matters and consulting with his
lords Peter de Fontaine and Geoffrey de Villette on what is
best to be done. I would not sound petty, but it vexes me
sorely that he spends more time with lawyers than he does
with me. . . .*

                Your loving sister,
                M

ELEANOR
SEPTEMBER 1237
PALACE OF WOODSTOCK, ENGLAND

I cannot imagine that I ever thought Henry old! Riding ahead of me, his goshawk on his arm, he cuts a very fine figure. He maneuvers his horse with confidence and virile firmness. Simply watching him kindles a desire in me to be with him. I give my horse a sharp kick and thunder past my ladies, giving my beloved Willelma d'Attalens, who came from Provence with me, a look of apology in response to her glance of unspoken admonition.

"There you are, Wife," Henry says with evident satisfaction as I reach his side. "I wondered at your lagging, you who so love to be first."

"First in your heart."

"That you are, madam, even when I ride out alone. No, I was speaking of your delightful thirst for life and adventure."

A sudden stirring in the underbrush ahead and to the king's right stops our pretty talk and draws our attention. Perhaps it is a rabbit or a quail? Henry, clearly thinking the same, prepares to throw his hawk. Then a man springs from the cover of the bushes. My horse rears in surprise and, as he does, I hear Willelma scream. I fight to bring my animal back under control. Henry, leaning precariously from his own mount, grabs hold of the beast's bridle and helps to bring its head down and forelegs back to the ground.

All this time the strange man stands not two horse lengths before us, shifting his weight from one foot to the other and muttering. With my horse firmly beneath me again, I catch my breath and look more closely at the man. His clothing is of good quality but filthy, as is his lank hair. He appears to be having a conversation and holding up both sides of it without need or notice of us. Every few words he punctuates his utterances by rolling his eyes, rocking back on his heels, and moaning pitifully. Some in our party snigger, but not my husband.

"Poor fellow," Henry says, speaking low, "I think he is mad."

As if to confirm my husband's surmise, the man begins to flap his arms as though fending off some sort of attack from above. My husband waits a moment longer until the wretch quiets himself and then, regarding the man with his customary half smile, says, "Good sir, you disturb our sport. We would ask you to stand aside."

But rather than removing himself from the path, the man rushes forward shouting, "Henry, scourge of England, poor pretender to the throne, resign your office and be gone like the pestilence you are!"

Every gentleman accompanying us is in motion at the same moment.

Uncle Guillaume and Imbert Pugeys reach the madman quickest. To my mind it is not coincidence that Savoyards are first to my husband's defense. My uncle strikes a blow with the hilt of his sword, knocking the villain to the ground even as he continues to rail against my husband. Then a multitude of men is upon him.

"Hold!" Henry has some difficulty making himself heard, for Imbert Pugeys and Simon de Montfort are thrashing the fallen fellow soundly and noisily. "That is quite enough!" The king's men straighten to their full heights, setting their clothing to rights as they do. My husband's insulter is left prone on the ground, sniveling.

"Forgive me, Your Majesty, but the man's utterances are treasonous! He should be flogged, hanged, or both!" Simon says, breathing hard from his exertions.

I follow Henry's gaze to the man on the ground. He is sitting now, rocking himself and singing some sort of childish song. Blood runs down his face from a gash where my uncle's hilt met his pate.

"Treasonous coming from any other man here, but this man's wits are out, de Montfort. Can he know what he says, let alone own it?" Henry shakes his head in the negative as if answering his own question. Turning to one of our attendants, he continues. "Take him back to the palace. See that his wound is tended and he is fed. We would do as much even for a beast, and surely he is little more." Then addressing me, he says, "Madam, it is not too late to have some pleasure from this afternoon's excursion. Are you in a mind and mood to ride on?"

I AM SUDDENLY AWAKE AND do not know why. Did I hear shouting or did I dream it? The room, my room, is dark. The last of the fire is gone, so it must well and truly be the middle of the night. I am about to close my eyes again, and then it comes, a cry, "Help! Oh someone, help!" Though the voice is terrified, I know it at once! It belongs to Lady Margaret Biset.

"Henry!" I sit bolt upright.

"What is it?" The voice is muffled and groggy from beneath my covers. The king is a heavy sleeper, but my voice never fails to rouse him.

Before I can answer, another shrill scream shatters the night, joined by hoarse cries and the sound of feet running on stone.

Henry, now fully awake, jumps from bed, stumbling in the dark. I can hear him pulling on his garments.

"Dear God, what can it be?" I know I sound hysterical. I feel hysterical and, at the same time, angry at myself for being so.

"Assassin! Assassin!" I do not recognize this new voice.

"To the queen!" This last shout is followed by a cry of pain.

"Stay here," Henry commands.

The door to my bedchamber swings open, and I utter a scream of my own. But it is only Margaret Biset. I can see her ashen face by the light of the candle she holds. The same candle offers me a glimpse of Henry as he pushes past. My lady closes the door behind him, bars it, and then places her back against it, though why she should think she will stand if oak does not I cannot imagine. Her gown is torn, her eyes wide with terror. A Psalter dangles from the hand not holding her candle.

"Margaret, in the name of God, what is happening?"

"A man with a knife—"

"Where?"

"He charged into your hall, shouting and cursing."

"Who is he?"

"I have never seen him before in my born days. Saints be praised that I was praying and not sleeping, or he might be here now!"

"The king, oh Holy Mary—he is not armed!" I jump from bed with no regard for my nakedness. "Help me dress."

"Your Majesty cannot go out!"

"I can and will. Now be quick." And to her credit Margaret is quick. After nearly two years in my household, she knows I cannot be gainsaid once I am determined. In a few moments, dressed but still barefoot, I crack open the door of my apartment. Not five yards away my doctor, Nicholas Farnham, squats over a prone figure. I can smell blood. I cannot see the figure's face, but a glance at his apparel quickly convinces me he is not Henry. I draw a sharp, sweet, breath of relief.

In the distance I hear the sounds of men—raised voices, grunts of effort, and the relentless pounding of something upon oak. I follow the sounds at such a pace that poor Margaret pants with the effort of keeping up with me. Suddenly there is a cracking noise, and I pass into the next chamber just in time to see men, carrying torches and with swords drawn, scrambling through a breached door. Henry stands just to one side of the opening with his chamberlain, William de St. Ermine, and John Mansel. For no reason I can think of I begin to sob.

I run to Henry without any thought for my dignity and throw my arms about his neck. He says nothing but puts one arm protectively around me as if to guard me from the sounds of struggle in the room just beyond. Then the commotion stops. My husband's men emerge. Two drag a man between them. His garments are torn and his face bloodied, but his expression is defiant. It is the man from the road this afternoon!

"What are Your Majesty's orders?" one of those holding the prisoner asks.

"Let him suffer; then let him die."

As soon as we are back in my bedchamber and alone, Henry pulls me into his arms. I am calm now, but he knows without asking that I will not be satisfied with merely being soothed. "You saw the villain," he says. "I thought to do my Christian duty in sending him here this afternoon. And my servants likewise, for after feeding him, they offered him shelter for the night in the stables. Apparently he is not mad, but very clever. He climbed through my bedchamber window and sought to slay me as I slept."

"God and Saint Edward be praised that he did not find you." I bury my face against my husband's chest and draw in the smell of him as a drowning man gasps for air.

"I am thankful, not only to God," Henry says, turning my face up to his and pushing back my wild hair, "but to you, Eleanor. You are my talisman. My need to be always with you has saved my life."

And I am surprised to find I can laugh just as easily as I cried earlier. "Perhaps now your brother will stop teasing you about your uncommon custom of passing the entire night with me."

"I doubt so. You know Richard's ambition. When he hears the news of this night, he may wish I conducted myself as other men do."

I AM WAITING BENEATH THE canopy covering my bath when the curtains part and Margaret enters, a triumphant look on her face. "The wicked man has confessed everything!" Though she is usually mild-mannered, Lady Biset's voice brims with loathing, and this suits me very well. In the two days since the attempt on Henry's life, my hatred of his would-be assassin has only grown stronger.

"Why then?" I ask.

Henry and I have pondered this question at length. Or rather I have pondered, and Henry has sought to soothe me. "It does no good to brood so, Eleanor," he said to me only last evening as I asked him for the hundredth time how any man could hate him so much, and more especially a man upon whom he had never laid eyes before.

"Not on his own accord," Margaret replies. She empties a bowl of rose petals into my tub while Willelma tests the water with her elbow. "He was paid by William de Marisco."

"The outlaw who preys on shipping in the Bristol Channel?" I find myself more, not less confused. True, the king is the source of all law, but a man sought for piracy can scarcely have hoped to escape execution by killing the king. I let my ladies pull off my shift and lower myself into the steaming water.

Picking up a sponge, Margaret begins to wipe my shoulders and arms. "The same. The de Mariscos are still angry that His

Majesty's grandfather gave their lands on Lundy Island to the Templars."

Disinheritance—here doubtless is a motivation for many things. The loss of land leaves a long mark on a family, whether it be lost at war, by law, or by king's command. My own husband has been shaped by such a deprivation. His father lost so many territories across the channel—Normandy, Brittany, Maine, Anjou. All of my husband's Angevin inheritance is gone, save Gascony and Poitou, with control of the latter much disputed. Henry dreams of regaining these lands. Not by assassination to be sure, for my husband is a man of great honor and piety, but he nonetheless brims with dislike for my sister's husband, the French King, whose father and grandfather took this portion of his birthright.

With understanding of Henry's attacker comes a surprising sense of relief. At last the questions plaguing me since that terrifying night are whisked away, and, closing my eyes, I relax fully into the warmth of my spice-scented water.

Later that afternoon, dressed once more and completely relaxed, I sit before my fire with my sister-in-law, Eleanor Marshal. It is another wet English day, precursor no doubt of another wet English winter. How I hate them.

"Eleanor, you must help me," my sister-in-law begs, looking up from her embroidery.

I want to help Eleanor. I like her very much, and she deserves to be happy, poor thing. Her first marriage was so unpleasant that she took a vow of chastity when she at last was free of it. But more than this, I want to help her gain her heart's desire, because the match she wants with Simon de Montfort, Earl of Leicester, serves our interests—my uncle Guillaume's and mine.

My uncle has been in charge of His Majesty's Council of Barons for more than a year now. He and Henry are on the firmest footing. I rejoice in this, for Henry will need help if he is to rise to the level of importance that he deserves, if he is to equal the reputation of Louis of France. But to make progress in that direction we must have the English barons in line, and too often Simon de Montfort and my husband's brother Richard lead them astray in pursuit of their own interests. If only Simon were not so capable and so charming! Then again, the same characteristics that draw other gentlemen of rank to him have drawn Eleanor Marshal. She is in love with him, and if a marriage can be managed, Simon will be family, tied firmly to the king and to the king's interests.

Yet I am hesitant to raise the subject with my husband. My security and the pleasant nature of my daily life rest entirely on Henry's good opinion of me as, after nearly two years of marriage, I remain stubbornly childless. So, I am learning the virtue of self-restraint, though I am sure my sister Marguerite would not believe me. If I am to risk a modicum of Henry's goodwill, I must be sure that my arguments are winning.

I shake my head to clear my thoughts. "Why not speak with your brother about the matter yourself?"

Eleanor blushes, "How can I speak to him of what is in my heart? He is a man."

"He will be no less a man if I speak to him. And surely men love as fervently as women do. Does not the Earl of Leicester protest as much to you?"

Apparently he does and very prettily, for Eleanor's color deepens further still and she looks down at her lap. Then, finding my eyes, she says, "Henry does not run over you the way he does me." I cannot argue with this. "Will you speak to him?"

"Yes, but it is best to wait until Michaelmas day when Henry is full of goose. Then I can have no doubt of his mood."

Eleanor puts down her needle and leans close to me, hardly

necessary as we are alone by design. "'Twould be better not to wait so long," she whispers.

"Do you mean . . . ?" For a moment I feel both sick and angry. It would be too unfair for Eleanor to be with child when I pray to the Blessed Virgin day and night to be so.

"No! I swear to you my courses come as regularly as yours. But"—and again she lowers her voice until I can barely hear her—"my vow is broken."

"You have let him have you?" I cannot believe what I am hearing. "Eleanor?"

She nods dumbly.

"I will speak to Henry as soon as I can. But until a wedding can be managed, you must not yield again. Not even I can help you if Simon puts you with child. You know Henry's sense of honor and his temper too well to doubt the truth of this."

The rest of my day is haunted by my conversation with Eleanor. Now that I must act—my hand forced by my sister-in-law's imprudent coupling with Simon—I am impatient to do so. But the marriage of a royal princess of England is hardly something I can bring up over dinner with the eyes of the court upon us. So I must bide my time.

In the evening Henry arrives in my apartment in preparation for taking me to bed. It is the first time we have been entirely alone since he left me in that same bed this morning. In keeping with our habit, we each take a glass of spiced wine and talk of the many little events and subjects that filled our day. The subject of Eleanor and Simon hums in my head even as Henry speaks of the English harvest. But still I wait, watching my husband's face as he talks, considering his posture. Then, when I am certain by these observations that Henry has had sufficient opportunity to shed the cares of his day and that his wine begins to relax him, I put the question of his sister's marriage to my husband.

As I finish, Henry's brow furrows. "Eleanor," he says, "de Montfort is a *preudomme*, but he is not English."

Standing with my back to my fire, looking at my husband seated comfortably before me, I feel my blood boil. I draw myself to my full height. How dare he make such a point! "I am not English, Your Majesty, and I was not aware you considered it a deficiency!"

"Eleanor." Henry's voice is pleading. He holds out a hand and beckons me to him, but I am not yet ready to go.

"Simon must wife. Would you not have him wife to your benefit? Already my uncles only narrowly prevented him from taking the Countess of Flanders for a bride by making sure Blanche of Castile heard of the proposed match. As it was no more in the interest of my sister's husband than it was in yours, that marriage was prevented. But what if Simon takes a wife allying him with France?"

"But my own sister? The barons will not like it. Already they complain that I favor Simon."

"And 'foreigners' generally," I say defiantly. My feelings sting still over Henry's earlier intemperate statement. The English are so provincial, so closed-minded. There has been just as much talk among the barons about my uncle Guillaume as there has about Simon. And all the talk is ridiculous since many of the complainers are of continental stock, and even those families who came with the Conqueror have been on this island only 150 years. "What have the barons to do with it?" I plant my hands on my hips and stare a challenge at my husband. "Are you not *king*?" I can never understand all the conciliation that Henry offers his vassals. My father would never have managed things thus, consulting with those who hold their land only by his gift or by the gift of his ancestors.

Henry looks sullen. I am making no progress in this manner, so I must try another. Henry may love me well, but, like most men, he does not like to be pushed. I must be consciously and purposefully the sweet and obliging Marguerite rather than bold Eleanor. I have been mimicking my sister on occasion as of late, and to great effect. I see now how she managed my parents with such ease.

Dropping my hands to my sides, I approach my husband and silently take a seat on the ground at his knee. I rest my cheek against Henry's leg, giving him the chance to calm himself. If I inadvertently trigger a fit of pique, all is lost. Henry can be as obstinate and stupid as a child when he is taken by such a mood.

When I feel Henry's hand on my hair, I at last glance upward to his face. "I am sorry, my love," I say softly. "I will never understand your English government. But I do understand a woman's heart. Your sister loves Simon."

"She does?"

"Yes."

"Loves him?"

"As I love you. And should not such love be honored?" I take Henry's hand in mine, offering him a soft look and a softer smile. "Besides, granting Simon this marriage will secure his loyalty in a way that aught else can."

"What does your uncle say?" Henry knows he is not the only one to consult with Guillaume on important matters.

"He wishes there were such an easy manner of taming your brother Richard." I can see that Henry's mind is turning to match mine. But he is not quite ready to concede.

"It will cost me money."

"Promise it now; pay it later."

"She made a vow of chastity, witnessed by Edmund Rich himself."

"She was led astray by Cecilia de Sanford. A girl's instructress always holds sway over her mind, particularly when, as with your sister, her mother is far away. Mistress Sanford ought to have stopped your sister from removing herself from the marriage market at sixteen, rather than urging it! The lady did you harm, depriving you of a valuable gift that might be used as a diplomatic tool. You ought to have been consulted."

"No one ever consults me." My husband's voice takes on a slightly whining tone.

"Eleanor does," I reply quickly, before Henry is carried away into a listing of his grievances. "She seeks your permission, your aid, your blessing. She has no mind to act without your approbation. Can you say as much of your barons?"

Henry is silent for a few minutes, unconsciously fingering my hair and staring into the fire. I neither move nor speak, marveling at how *I* have learned to patiently hold my tongue, a characteristic Marguerite urged upon me for so many years with no success. I must remember to tell her in my next letter, though I doubt she will believe me.

Finally Henry looks directly at me and smiles. Taking my hand, he pulls me up onto his lap. "Let my sister and Simon de Montfort come to see me," he says.

"Oh Henry! You will permit the marriage?" I throw my arms around his neck and give him a kiss on the cheek.

"How can I do otherwise," he asks, "when the happiness of my two favorite ladies appears to hinge upon it?"

"SHHH!" I TRY TO SOUND stern but cannot help giggling. It is the sixth of January, the Feast of the Epiphany, and Eleanor Marshal and I are making our way to the king's private chapel in the Palace of Westminster. We do so supposedly for no reason in particular beyond satisfying her urge to see her brother and mine to see my lord. But in truth, Simon de Montfort is waiting with Henry, and he and Eleanor are going to be married. This fact has been kept a secret even from my ladies. Well, not from Willelma, who shepherds us along from behind with a pained expression as if she were our nurse and we mere naughty children. The archbishop of Canterbury is expected to put up a fuss when he hears of the marriage because 'twas he who witnessed Eleanor's vow, but she will look duly penitent, and what will she care for Edmund Rich's words once she has Simon?

When we reach Henry's apartment, he is waiting to lead his bright-eyed sister through to his chapel and up to the altar. Having presented her to Simon, he takes his place at my side. As the ceremony begins, Henry's hand finds mine. It is a far cry from our own nuptials, but, as I approach the second anniversary of my marriage, I cannot witness the binding of any two people without happy tears. I hope Eleanor will be as content in her marriage as I am.

Henry absently fingers the wedding ring on my hand as Simon places one on his sister's, and I give his hand a little squeeze in return. Only one thing could make our happiness more complete— a prince. I must give Henry a son. Only this week my physicians prescribed a new tonic to awaken my slumbering womb. It tastes dreadful, but I take it without complaint—anything to conceive a child. Willelma thinks the tonic a waste. She is adamant that my womb will be fertile when the time is right.

"Women are like gardens," she insists. "They have seasons. You are still in winter, but spring will come, perhaps with your next birthday, and then you will bloom and your belly will swell like a good melon on a vine."

The thought of myself as a melon nearly makes me laugh out loud. *And why not?* I think defiantly. *Surely a wedding is a joyful occasion.*

ELEANOR AND SIMON HAVE LEFT us and gone off to their estates, but the rancor caused by their wedding more than a month ago lingers. There has been gossip among the court, talk among Henry's advisers, and tonight it appears we will hear from my husband's brother.

"The devil!" Richard bursts into the great hall at the Palace of Westminster after dinner. Henry and I were dancing, but Richard now bars our path. "Is it true?"

"Richard," Henry says, trying to put a hand on his brother's shoulder, only to have it shoved away.

"Is our sister married?"

"With our blessing." Henry's voice is cold, but the skin on his neck begins to flush as he grows hot with anger.

"To Simon de Montfort?"

"A good and faithful servant to the Crown."

"A Frenchman of middling fortune."

All the dancing has stopped now, and the music too. My uncle Guillaume glides over, a smile on his face. "Your Majesty, Earl Richard, perhaps you would be better met more privately."

"We would be better met a month ago before this nonsense proceeded," Richard growls, but he allows my uncle to turn him toward the outside aisle. Henry barks a command for the musicians to begin playing once more and then stalks after his brother. I trail behind, because who shall tell me I may not? Screened from the view of curious courtiers by one of the large pillars supporting the ceiling, the brothers face each other again.

"You had no right to marry our sister without consulting me— without consulting your magnates!"

"No right? Speak to me of rights, will you!"

"Yes, I will. You know, even if you found it convenient to ignore such fact, that custom dictated consultation with and consent from your council over such an important marriage. And as for my rights, am I not also the lady's kin? As near in relation as you? As concerned about her welfare?"

"Her welfare? If that is all that worries you, be done. Lady Montfort is quite abundantly happy with her situation." For the first time Henry glances in my direction. "Is that not so, Eleanor? Our sister writes to the queen glowingly of her new husband."

"This is not a fanciful troubadour's romance! It is a royal marriage! It ought not to be managed by women."

My uncle, silent himself, gives me a meaningful look, warning me to hold my tongue. He need not worry. Angered as I am by Richard's intimation, I am even more afraid to be drawn into this nasty quarrel. I move closer to Henry's side, between him and a large stone pillar.

"Get out of my sight." My husband spits his words at his brother with vehemence.

"I shall do better than that. I will away from London, to see the Marshals and hear what they will say that you marry the widow of their august brother to Simon de Montfort."

And with that, Richard turns on his heels and storms from the hall. For a moment or two Henry and I stand quietly. I can hear the music and the footfall of the dancers one aisle over, and also the beating of my heart.

"Pompous fool," Henry mutters under his breath. But I can see he is shaken. Then, in a falsely bright voice, he says, "Eleanor, come and dance with me."

I take his hand, but, as he leads me back to the assembled court, my eyes linger on my uncle, who remains unmoving in the shadows, lost in thought.

———

THE TOWER IS SO OBVIOUSLY a fortress, I think as we approach it this pale February day. I hope my husband and my uncle know what they are about. Will not the rabble of rebellious barons think we make more of them than they deserve by our change of residence?

Once I am inside my chambers, my mood lifts. How could it not, surrounded by hundreds of pink and white roses?

Uncle Guillaume enters late in the afternoon while my ladies are still unpacking. "Niece." He nods, and by his manner of doing so I know that he would speak with me privately, so we withdraw to my chapel where only God can hear us.

"This thing multiplies all out of proportion," he says as soon as we are alone.

"The number of earls and barons who have risen up in support of Lord Richard scares Henry even if he will not say it." I wonder, as I speak the words, if it is a betrayal of my husband to admit this. But no, how can it be when my uncle is the head of His Majesty's council? He seeks always to aid Henry in governing.

"These English are so fastidious about their rights and precedence. The points they choose to stand on, and perhaps to fight over . . ." Guillaume shakes his head again, this time in dismay.

"If this marriage makes the king stronger, what matter that they were not asked in advance?" I ask. "That was the union's purpose, to strengthen Henry."

"Yes, Eleanor, but against whom? Against the possibility of too much baronial power. You cannot expect Earl Richard, his cohort the Earl of Pembroke, or the other barons to appreciate that effect as we do. A letter has come, demanding that His Majesty dissolve the council that currently advises him, and submit matters of state to a new council of barons selected from among those who oppose him."

"Ridiculous! Why should any man, let alone a king, allow himself to be governed by his enemies?"

"Yet His Majesty considers it."

"What—?"

"You yourself said he was frightened."

And now I am frightened. This is not at all how I imagined it would be. My father has such power in his domains, and he only a count. My husband is a king, but his rule seems less absolute. I look up at the brightly colored saints in a window.

"What can be done?" I ask.

"Richard wants to go on crusade. Crusades cost money."

"You think the Earl of Cornwall can be paid to stop his protest against my husband?"

"In my experience, men can be paid to do or cease doing nearly anything so long as it does not trespass upon their principles, if they have them. Let us hope this is only a matter of wounded pride with the Earl Richard—pride that can be salved with silver."

THE EARL RICHARD IS ALL smiles as he pushes back from my husband's table with a satisfied expression. "Brother," he says, "my compliments to your cooks."

And Henry, who appears to have forgotten that it took a flurry of negotiation and more than six thousand marks to make Richard so jovial, slaps him on the back and says, "I hear that while you were out of the city you acquired a fine new horse to take on crusade."

Out of the city indeed! Oh Henry, how can you be so cavalier when he was out of London to raise mischief against you? I cannot take any more. Pushing back my own chair, I make for the door. Before I reach it, my uncle reaches me.

"Niece, why the sour look when everything is as it should be?"

"You do not find this playacting of brotherly love a little cloying for your taste?"

"Any show of fraternal harmony suits me admirably and ought to suit you."

"I know, considering how things stood only a month ago. But to pay for loyalty that ought to flow naturally from bonds of blood and family—"

"There are worse uses of money. And we have learned something important. The Earl Richard can be bought. A man who can be bought is never a serious threat. Remember that, Eleanor. It is a lesson that may serve you well while I am gone from these shores in answer to the emperor's call."

CHAPTER 6

My dear Eleanor, greetings and felicitations,

Your news was most welcome. I pray that you take after our grandmother, for, as Mother always said, she was a woman made by God to bear sons and to do so with remarkable aptitude.

As for myself, I wish I could tell you that I likewise expect a child, but I do not. I begin to think I never shall. Louis continues to be far more interested in God, in governing, in nearly anything, than he is in me. How can it be that after only five short years of marriage I have come to mean so little to him? The pain occasioned by His Majesty's behavior as a husband pierces my heart and tries my patience. Yet I feel guilty complaining as I am never mistreated but am always respected (by all save my mother-in-law). And what right have I to demand precedence over an entire kingdom of French subjects? I ought to be pleased that Louis strives ever to be a good king. How unfortunate then that my capricious woman's heart feels as it will, not as it ought. . . .

Yours,

M

ELEANOR
JUNE 1239
PALACE OF WESTMINSTER, ENGLAND

"I am huge!" Standing in my wardrobe while Colin, my tailor, makes an adjustment in my new gown, I regard my increasing girth with wonder.

Sybil Gifford, who joined my household the moment my condition was confirmed, summoned by Henry because of her great reputation for deftness in assisting women in childbirth, laughs gaily and says, "Never have I looked forward to attending at a confinement as I look forward to attending yours."

I place a hand upon my stomach and offer Sybil a blinding smile. I am the center of the known world just as surely as if I were painted on my husband's massive *mappa mundi*. I feel it to be so, and I am *thoroughly* enjoying it. And it is all because of my little prince. After nearly three years of marriage, the king had begun to think that, despite how often he planted my garden, I might never come up roses. Then in the autumn, my courses stopped. Henry had priests praying to the Confessor that we might not be deceived or disappointed. They are praying still, though my pregnancy is long past the point of doubt.

My fitting over, I make my way to my chamber to find new gifts from Henry—a bolt of golden cloth and a jeweled amethyst brooch that looks lovely laid against the fabric. I pin the brooch on immediately and run my hand over the expensive material.

"His Majesty asks that you commend him to your tailor and says he hopes to see you in a gown made from his gift very soon," Isabel d'Attalens tells me with a smile, while her mother, Lady Willelma, picks up the bolt of cloth to bear it away to my wardrobe. I am glad that these women who came with me from

Provence and who worried with me while I remained stubbornly unfruitful now share my pleasure in my good fortune.

Indeed, all my ladies, Provençal and English alike, seem to enjoy my glory as much as I do. Henry is very liberal with them in his current good humor, and the mood of the entire court is elevated along with his.

Never once has anyone dared to raise the question that haunts my nights once Henry has left me—it would no longer be seemly for him to stay the night in my bed; that he visits it at all we keep secret as best we can—what if this babe is a girl? Like everyone else, I abstain from speaking the possibility aloud. If Uncle Guillaume were here, I might share my fear with him, but he left England more than a year ago, right after the nonsense with Richard over the marriage of his sister to Simon de Montfort ended, and is now prince-bishop-elect of Liege. Several times in the last months, as the babe rolled and kicked within me, I considered writing to Marguerite to share my private fears. But how could I when my sister, married even longer than I, has yet to bear a child of either sex for her husband? So instead, I swallowed my personal worries and included a line of encouragement in one of my missives, pointing out that since I was thought barren and am not, it may, with God's grace, be so with her as well.

"Your Majesty, is anything the matter?" Isabel regards me quizzically, her mouth a flat line of concern. I must have allowed my own visage to reflect my thoughts.

"Nothing," I say brightly. "Let us go into the gardens and take some air."

I AM DELICIOUSLY SLEEPY. MY limbs are heavy. My eyelids are heavy. Even the air in the room seems heavy, slowing my every movement as if I were swimming in honey.

June has been remarkably warm this year, for England that is. The truly magnificent summers of my childhood will never be equaled by England's pale imitations. The late-afternoon sun worms its way through the vines hanging heavy outside my window, painting a fascinating pattern in light and shadow against the covers of the bed and Henry's naked back. I long to lift my hand and trace the pattern with my finger, but I lack the energy to suit my desire. We have been making love. Mortal sin or no, Henry's desire for me has not abated through all of the months I have carried his child. Even now, when I am past the time when Sibyl expected me to begin my confinement, my breasts swollen and my belly distended, Henry tells me I am beautiful. A soft, rumbling snore rises from Henry's form. He has surrendered to sleep. I let my lids fall closed and prepare to do the same.

Then I feel it—a powerful twinge. I am fully awake.

"Henry," I whisper, rising up on one elbow.

"Mmm," he mumbles, and rolls to his back without waking.

"I think it has begun."

Immediately Henry is fully awake too, his eyes wild. "I will call for Sybil."

I laugh out loud. "You might want to get dressed first."

"Yes." Henry scrambles like a dog with its tail on fire.

I rise ponderously and, as I do, I notice a rush of straw-colored liquid as if I have soiled myself, but I know that I have not. This must be the "birth water" of which Sybil has spoken. Before I can do more than put on my chemise, Henry darts from the room, calling Sybil's name as he goes.

But as the hours of my labor pass, I myself wonder why Henry was in such a hurry to find Sybil. The thought would be humorous if I were not suffering. Such pain—I have never known such pain. But oh the reward. A cry at last sounds that is not my own. *Laus*

Deo, I have a son! And I know as I look at his downy hair, his perfect miniature fingers, what it is to love fiercely. The memory of a boar with her brood that I once saw cornered by hunters comes into my mind. At the time her ferocity scared me, but now I am she. Let anyone try to hurt my Edward and they shall see my teeth.

London is going wild. No matter that it is the middle of the night. I can hear the drummers and the shouting in the streets. Henry arrives, and he is the most wild of all. After praising me and admiring our son, he races off to wake poor Walter de Lenche so that he may round up the clerks of the Royal Chapel to sing the *Laudes Regiae* as they did on my coronation day. Truly the man is mad, but mad with love for me and for Edward—named for the Confessor, of course; how could it be otherwise?

"Get me a pen," I tell Willelma, whose eyebrows rise at the odd request. "I must write to my sister the Queen of France."

"FOR MERCY'S SAKE, HENRY, YOU must stop turning back gifts." I run my hand playfully through my husband's hair as he sits in my hall, holding Edward who is nearly two months old. My son, in one of his increasingly long periods of wakefulness, is returning his father's earnest gaze.

"Why is that? Why should we accept anything unworthy of our little prince?"

"Because we are offending the givers."

"And they offend me by sending such trinkets."

I laugh. I know I should press Henry further. His rejection of certain of the prince's gifts is impolitic, but, I am beginning to sense, with some unease, that my husband has not the knack I might have hoped for things political.

A knock sounds at the door. "If it is the nurse, send her away,"

Henry says. "We are fine here, is that not so?" This last utterance is directed to Edward as Henry holds out a finger for our son to grasp.

"Enter," I call, expecting, like Henry, to see Edward's nurse, Lady Alice. But when the door swings open, it reveals the Duke of Flanders, coated in dust and clearly fresh from the saddle.

"Uncle! We did not expect you until tomorrow," I exclaim, both pleased and honestly surprised to see Thomas.

"The roads were good and my desire to see my great-nephew strong."

"Here he is," Henry says, holding the babe up, "the Lord Edward."

"Splendid," my uncle replies with real enthusiasm. And I can guess what he is thinking: the blood of Savoy extends itself to the throne of England.

"And how are things in Flanders?"

England and Flanders have always been allies, but never more so than since my uncle's marriage made him count there less than two years ago. My uncle is a very attentive vassal, visiting with us often, and my husband could not be more welcoming.

"Very well"—Thomas pours himself a glass of wine and takes a seat—"apart from being short of funds."

Henry laughs. "It is the same everywhere, whether a man be a count or a king."

"I told Your Majesty he need not expend so much on my churching." I am conscious that the event, to be held less than a week from now on the ninth of August, is costing hundreds of pounds, but Henry insists that everything, from the five hundred tapers to be lit before the Confessor's shrine, to the food and drink for the banquet following, be absolutely of highest quality.

"Nonsense. If I thank God for our prince, I must also thank you. No one is more deserving of celebration." My husband turns to my uncle with a ready smile. "Thomas, I shall instruct the exchequer to ready the money fief you are owed as my vassal. Will not five hundred marks in some part relieve your distress?"

"Most handsomely. But if Your Majesty would also consider paying those debts of the Earl of Leicester for which you stand as surety, I would be both grateful and obliged. My own debts incurred in support of my brother's candidacy at Liege are considerably more than five hundred marks."

Something is very wrong. Henry's face, a moment ago a model of friendly, open hospitality, has begun to color a deep purple. Instinctively I reach out and retrieve Edward from him.

"Debts of the Earl of Leicester?"

The change in Henry's tone is not lost on my uncle. "It is no matter, Your Majesty. Pray forget I made the suggestion. After all, I am not in England to collect money but rather, like all your other guests, to celebrate my dear niece."

"I, a surety for Simon's debts?"

"Yes, well . . ." Thomas looks at me helplessly. "Let us say no more of it."

"I fear, sir, that we must. What are these debts and in what amount?"

"I do not know the debts' origin, Your Majesty, as they were transferred to me by another with whom I had business. But the sum total is two thousand marks."

"Two thousand marks! That is more than thirteen hundred pounds!" Henry rises to his feet and strides about in great agitation. I withdraw slightly so that Edward and I might not be in his path. "And I am surety?"

"Your name was given."

"By Simon de Montfort?"

"You did not know?"

"I did not! And my sister's husband will wish it continued to be so!"

Once my uncle and I are alone in my hall, left by Henry in a huff and by Edward in the arms of Lady Alice, he says, "Believe me, Niece—I would not have intentionally created such trouble."

"I know it, Uncle." Poor Thomas seems despondent. I place a hand on his shoulder, then withdraw it. I may be a grown woman and a queen, but it feels odd to comfort one to whom I have always looked up. Taking my uncle's glass, I refill it. "But I think you make too much of this. Henry is angry, but Henry is often angry. His temper rises quickly, which is no good thing. But it falls just as quickly, and that ameliorates much. The Earl and Countess of Leicester will not be here for a few days. Henry loves Simon well and Eleanor more. I cannot believe our words here will even be recalled when he sees them."

"I pray it is so. I would not like to be the source of a family quarrel."

"I am only sorry that you must go away without the monies. If you are truly in extremis, I can look to my own gold."

"Henry lets you manage it then?"

"He does."

"That is well. A queen with favors in her gift is always better positioned to direct the Fates than one without."

"Would that you could stay and guide me. For having the ability to be of influence and knowing how to best use it are not one and the same. While Uncle Guillaume was here, I knew better how to direct my efforts."

"My responsibilities prevent it. But if Guillaume is not able to return soon, he and I shall consult upon who may come to your service. You have uncles aplenty." He offers me a smile.

"God be praised." I smile in return. "And all of them are welcome here. Whoever comes can count on His Majesty to be generous."

THE DAY OF MY CHURCHING has arrived.

"Your Majesty, you are the loveliest woman in Christendom," Margaret Biset effuses.

"How I wish I could see," says Emma. Margaret's daughter, who, like her mother, was selected by Henry for my household before I ever set foot in England, was blinded last year by a sudden illness, but I insisted she remain with me for her mother's sake. Margaret could not be easy were Emma not here.

"Come, I will let you feel my headdress, so that you may be amazed by how many pearls are upon it." And, good as my word, I tilt my head down to Emma's eager hands. When she is satisfied, I take a final look at myself in my mirror and say, "Shall we go to the great hall?" Henry has summoned all his richest and most influential magnates to London for my special day, and a grand party of their wives is assembling in the hall to escort me to Westminster Abbey.

"Ah, the Queen of England and of my heart," Henry exclaims when he catches sight of me. "And notice she is so modest that she colors to hear herself praised." He is in high spirits indeed.

The Countess of Devon and the Dowager Countess of Lincoln move forward, between Henry and me, and curtsy to me.

"Your Majesty appears well recovered from your confinement," the Countess of Devon remarks. "I am heartily glad to see it." She herself nearly died after the delivery of her second child, a daughter, two years ago.

"Have you seen the prince?" I am eager to hear praise of my son.

"Indeed, at his baptism," the Countess of Lincoln replies effusively, "and as fine a child as ever I laid eyes upon."

"We must have your Edmund for the Lord Edward's household."

The Countess of Lincoln opens her mouth to reply, but it is Henry's voice I hear. "Viper! Of all the unmitigated gall. How dare you show your face here?"

I look for Henry. He is no longer where he stood moments ago but is advancing through the crowd toward Simon de Montfort and his Eleanor, who, it appears, have just arrived. Simon's face is drained of color, and Eleanor looks as if she has been slapped.

"Your Majesty, were we not invited with everyone else to celebrate the birth of your son and the churching of his mother?" Simon's voice is cautious rather than dismayed.

"That is so, but I would never have issued the invitation had I known you were a thief."

"Thief, Majesty?" The color rises in Simon's cheeks. "Pray what have I taken that you label me so?"

"My very name! You used it as your guarantee. And, knowing that you have done so, even as I did not, you ought to have thought the better of coming."

"Henry"—Eleanor's voice is pleading—"however my lord has offended you, can we not speak of it in another, better, setting? No doubt his actions were error, not purposeful effrontery."

"He did not know he named me surety for a massive debt? Madam, perhaps *you* did not know, but he knew it certainly." Henry is only a few feet away from the couple now but continues to shout as if they stood at the other end of this great and cavernous hall. "Is it not enough," he continues, turning to Simon, "that I gave my sister to you against my better judgment and in contravention of the wishes of my council? Must I also stand liable for the bribes that you found necessary in securing a dispensation? As if a piece of paper could make your ill-begun marriage acceptable in the eyes of God."

I have no idea what to do. My stomach heaves. Fits of Henry's temper I have witnessed before, but never, no never anything like this. Part of me wishes to rush forward and stop this horrible entertainment before it goes further, but another counsels me to stay where I am, safely out of the range of the king's anger.

Eleanor is crying softly. Her husband puts a protective arm around her, which seems to enrage Henry further. He is now a horrible shade of purple.

"Your Majesty, whatever debts I have incurred, I swear that I will pay them and make this right," Simon says.

"The things you have done, sir, can never be put right! How will you repair the honor of my sister whom you seduced before you wed?"

Eleanor, looking past Henry, stares at me with disbelief. I would swear to her that I never told Henry of her surrender to Simon before their marriage, for it is the truth. But I cannot find my tongue, and even if I could, such a protestation would confirm what Henry already thinks as well as the rumors that doubtless gave rise to his thoughts.

"Your Majesty—" Simon's color is now as high as Henry's.

"Besmircher!" Henry prods the earl on the chest with one angry forefinger. Heaven help us if swords are drawn. I can see the Earl Richard moving in from Henry's right. Surely he must end this, but how with all the eyes of the court upon the quarrel? And suddenly, instinctively, I know what must be done. I let my knees go and collapse onto the ground.

"Your Majesty!" The Countess of Devon's distressed voice brings Henry's eyes to where I lie—a pile of expensive fabrics and jewels—and it is enough. He moves in my direction immediately, and all the court's eyes move with him. As I am helped to my feet by a concerned Henry and several other pairs of equally gentle hands, I see the Earl Richard shepherding Simon and Eleanor out of the doors at the far end of the hall. There is some satisfaction in that. But, I reflect miserably as Henry leads me to sit down, when I thought to be the center of attention today, it was certainly not like this.

CHAPTER 7

My dearest Marguerite,

Already you must know that I am safely delivered of my son, the Lord Edward, but I felt I must send a few lines by my own hand to assure you that I am well. Indeed, the king is so overjoyed by the pace of my recovery that he has awarded my attendant, Sybil Gifford, an annual pension for her good service in attending me through my confinement. He offers countless masses for our darling Edward, and such charity as has never been seen. I pray that you are well and may soon know the delights of maternity yourself. I tell you plainly there is no joy that can compare to it.

Your well and truly blessed sister,
Eleanor

MARGUERITE
AUGUST 1239
THE ROYAL HUNTING LODGE AT VINCENNES, FRANCE

Just once, I think as my women undress me for the night and rub my limbs to bring them to a rosy glow, *just once I wish we could enjoy marital relations as we used to—without praying.* I raise my arms reflexively so that Marie may slide my shift over my head; the time is past when Louis will take me naked.

After all, we are no fornicators. Louis is my husband. Our

marriage vows, now five years old, permit our activities, and the need for an heir to the French throne adds urgency to them. If I do not become pregnant soon, I may well be gone. Perhaps this thought is less worrisome to my husband than to me. Certainly my repudiation would delight the dragon of Castile. At the thought of delivering such a victory to my hated mother-in-law, my cheeks burn like fire, and my sisters-in-law, convinced it is a flush in anticipation of my husband's company, of his "attentions," titter irritatingly. Louis is still good-looking—*mon dieu*, there is no denying that. On the nights when he comes to me, it is easy to remember my first impressions of him—golden hair, golden armor, golden boy. Until he opens his mouth.

I know all too well what is happening to the man I married. He grows increasingly obsessed with things not of this world. And while penance and love of God are noble things, when they interfere with being king and husband, I cannot approve. Once hungry for my body and vexed only that, thanks to the dragon's machinations and the demands of his confessor, he must eschew my bed for Sundays and holy days, Louis now makes us kneel to pray before and after the act. Not that I might successfully conceive, but that we might be forgiven our carnal desires and any animal pleasures we experience—pleasures that he now considers wrong and self-indulgent. Pleasure of every kind has become his abhorrence.

Sometimes Louis even prays during the act. My ears burn with the memory of "mea culpas" that have choked from him as he enjoyed my body and censured himself for that enjoyment.

Tonight must be different. Holy Mary, Mother of God, you must help me to conceive a son. Eleanor has one. He is all she thinks and writes about now. He has made her secure, in her husband's love and in her kingdom. Surely I am no less worthy than she to be either queen or wife. Have I not been humbled enough by the pilgrimage that wicked Blanche made me take to visit the shrine of Saint Thibault? Being paraded by the dragon past the throngs lining the roads in all the villages on the journey to Saint-Thibault-des-Vignes so that all might see and pity my barrenness was so humiliating! Surely such pain will persuade you to intercede on my behalf and open my womb to my husband's seed? And if I conceive, I pledge I will have a silver reliquary made for the remnant of your Son's crown of thorns that Louis has just purchased from the King of Jerusalem, and I will offer the box to Louis as a token of gratitude for my fecundity.

Louis arrives. He undresses in silence, and I wince to see the raw flesh on his back where his whip with its five lengths of chain has flayed him. I must remember not to put my hands there as we couple. He sits on the edge of the bed.

I reach for the goblet I prepared before undressing and left on the small table at the bedside. "Husband, will you take some wine? It is watered." I know that Louis will reject the refreshment as part of his practice of self-denial unless he believes it is diluted. In fact it is not, save for the few drops of water I put in so that my statement would not be a bold-faced lie.

"Thank you." He takes a sip, and his eyebrows rise slightly. He is suspicious.

To distract him, I turn his mind in the one direction capable of holding it. "Louis, I have been waiting with great anticipation to ask how the plans for the Sainte-Chapelle progress. The Countess of Poitiers and I saw Pierre de Montereau with you. Surely if he has ridden from Paris, it was for the purpose of discussing the chapel?"

Louis's eyes illuminate, and his voice is warm when he speaks. "Every part of it shall praise the glory of Our Lord and of his saints. The stones themselves shall be adorned with likenesses of the martyrs." He relaxes visibly against the headboard, and I draw myself close to his side. Turning to face him, I wrap my leg over his. He does not draw away, may the Virgin be praised, but rather, as he continues to describe in detail all that was said this afternoon by his favorite architect, the excitement of his mind appears to spread to his body.

As my hand runs, unopposed, down his chest and he leans to kiss me, I offer one last prayer and allow myself to be transported by the anticipation of my own dear son.

"I feel a draft," Matilda says, turning her head this way and then that as if expecting to see the December wind where it seeps in. "Can you feel the chill, Your Majesty?" The concern in my sister-in-law's voice is sincere and sincerely gratifying.

"I am fine." I assure her. And indeed I am better than fine. It is Christmastide and I am nearly five months gone with child. *Joyeux Noël* indeed!

"I will go get your fur-lined mantle," Matilda insists, rising. As she moves away from the table, one of the dogs curled up at Louis's feet stirs itself to follow—animals love Matilda—attracting the king's attention.

"Where does the Countess of Artois go?"

"Merely to get my mantle, Your Majesty."

"That is most thoughtful of her. We ought to have positioned the table differently. Nearer to the fire. It shall be so." Louis stands up. The eyes of those gathered at the lower tables are immediately upon him, and the musicians stop playing.

"Please, Your Majesty." I reach out and put a hand on Louis's sleeve. "Do not disturb the assembled company on my account. I am fine." And when he hesitates, I add, "See, the servers begin to enter the hall with the peacocks. To disrupt their procession would be a shame."

"If you are sure," Louis replies, sinking back into his seat.

"Perfectly."

A gorgeous roasted peacock, redressed in its own feathers for a spectacular effect, is placed on the table before my husband. A servant rolls back the spiced skin of the bird, carves a slice, and moves to place the meat on Louis's trencher.

"Pray serve Her Majesty the Queen with the first cut," Louis instructs.

This is how it is of late. Everyone pampers me. Well, everyone except for Blanche. The dragon ignores me, but this is still an improvement. She no longer insults or slights me publicly. Perhaps she senses such treatment will no longer be tolerated by her son. The thought of the dragon tamed by my condition makes me smile.

I recall what Yolande said one afternoon early in my pregnancy, as she held a basin for me to retch into. "Blanche will not know how to feel, wicked woman." The duchess's voice brimmed with satisfaction as if the triumph were her own.

"This prince will be her undoing," I crowed, wiping my mouth on a cloth she handed me.

Now, looking across the figure of my husband at my mother-in-law, I say a quick *Ave* that my prediction may come to pass.

When the evening's celebrations end, Louis comes to sit with me in my rooms before I retire. Marital relations are now out of the question, of course. I wish this were not so, for while Louis does not seem to miss them, I, strangely, long desperately for his touch in my present state.

"Do you think the babe will be a son?" he asks.

"I pray so."

Louis looks so serious and so handsome with the firelight in his golden hair. I long to reach out and stroke his locks, but such an innocent and wifely gesture no longer comes naturally to me, so instead, I fold my hands in my lap. When he shifts to pick up his goblet of watered wine, I can see the top of a hair shirt peeking from beneath his tunic. I do not remark upon it. He is happy tonight, and I am happy with him. Why spoil things?

"And Her Grace the Duchess of Burgundy says the fact that I am carrying low indicates a son," I add. I do not mention to Louis that my nipples have also darkened, a change that Yolande assures me is further proof my little one will be a prince. Louis would doubtless find such a comment shocking, and even after five years of marriage, I cannot imagine sharing such an intimate detail about my body with my husband.

Louis sighs contentedly. "It would be very good to have a son, little queen." He has not used this endearment in a very long time, and I feel a surge of affection upon hearing it. *Yes,* I think, *I will give Louis a prince, and we will be happy as we once were.*

I AM DYING AND NO one will help me. Gasping, my wild eyes light upon the terrified face of my sister-in-law Jeanne, who is praying under her breath. Yolande places a damp, knotted cloth at my lips, and I pull water from it gratefully. And then the pain begins again. As it grips me tighter and tighter, I writhe and scream with all my might—howling like a rabbit caught in the jaws of a hound.

Where is Louis? Surely he can hear me. He has done this to me, and now he does not come. As the pain begins to ebb again, I hear the sanctimonious voice of Lady Elisabeth's detested mother-in-law, Madame de Montmirall, say, "Your Majesty should not scream so; it only spends your vigor."

With a strength I did not know I possessed, I struggle to raise myself semi-upright, grab the neck of the woman's tunic where she sits complacently at my bedside, and twist. I mean to choke the life from her before the pain takes me again, but I hear a ripping as her clothing rends and she escapes me.

"Out." Yolande's voice is firm. The midwife, taking advantage of the momentary lull in my agony, rips back my chemise, which has become hopelessly entwined about me.

Prying my knees apart, she barks to the women on either side of me, "Hold her!" Then she sticks her fingers inside me. I try desperately to twist my body away from those probing fingers, but my women have me trapped. The pain swells again. Holy Mary, Mother of God, how great must Eve's sin have been to justify this! And then I feel a pulling, a pressure as if the heaviest of stones is trying to force its way out of me. As the pain subsides again, leaving me limp and whimpering, the pulling remains.

"It is time," the midwife says.

Yolande takes my right arm just under my armpit and at my elbow. Robert's sixteen-year-old wife, Matilda, a squat, thick-waisted girl, takes my left arm in the same manner. Though she has yet to be delivered of a child herself, she assisted at two of her step-mother's confinements before coming to marry my brother-in-law Robert, the Count of Artois. Jeanne, my second sister-in-law, her hands trembling, follows Yolande's instructions and places a polished ivory stick between my teeth. Faithful Marie de Vertus and my dear Elisabeth each place their hands upon one of my knees. The bishop of Paris, the king's Garde des Sceaux, and an ambassador from my father's house are shown into the room. Surprisingly, I feel no shame before these men—no shame that they see my nakedness, and no embarrassment that they hear my screams, which begin again as soon as the next pain takes me.

"Push," the midwife commands, and no order could agree more with my own inclination. Teeth gritted around the stick, I struggle to force my child out into the light of day and stop my own suffering. Again and again with all my might I push. I begin to feel consciousness slipping away from me between my efforts—in those blessed moments when the pain withdraws, only to come back more cruelly than before.

"You must stay with us, Your Majesty," Yolande urges me. "Do you not wish to see your son?"

And I do, dear God, I do. I want a prince to reward me for my suffering; a prince to hold defiantly before his grandmother and to spare me the need of ever, ever, doing this again.

I shove with all my might. I can feel myself coming apart, tearing like a piece of cloth. Then something slippery slides from between my legs and I feel a blessed relief. A high long wail, not my own, breaks the air.

"Your Majesty," Yolande says softly, as if she would not have anyone else hear, "it is a girl."

I fall into darkness.

When I wake, the room is quiet and dark, and I cannot stop crying. A girl. In Provence, a daughter would be of some value. Our laws permit females to inherit and rule in their own right. But we are not in Provence. I have schemed and suffered for nothing. Louis will be disappointed, but will he also be furious? Will he be willing to repudiate me in my failure? Fear rolls over me in waves as pain did hours before.

"William of Auvergne," my voice croaks out, mimicking the sound of a crow on the wing.

Yolande rushes to my bedside and tries to put a cup to my lips. I push it away. I am thirsty, but there will be time enough to drink once he is on his way. "William of Auvergne," I insist.

"Get the bishop of Paris," Yolande directs Marie. As soon as I hear the door close behind my *chambrière*, I greedily gulp what I am offered. I am still tired, for I labored an entire night and morning. I must struggle to keep my eyes open until the bishop appears.

"Your Majesty," he whispers when he arrives a short time later, taking the stool beside my bed and leaning in kindly.

"Your Excellency, you must help me."

"Do you fear death, my child? For you need not; the midwife has no fear for you."

"No. But I fear the displeasure of my kingly husband. I thought to give him an heir, and I have failed."

"Your Majesty must not despair, for after six years of barrenness, your womb has been quickened. Moreover you have borne a healthy child. I examined her myself in case there was a need for immediate baptism, but there was none. You are not yet twenty. With the Lord's blessing, your husband may yet put you many times with child."

"Will you pray with me?"

"Of course."

"And will you do more? Will you go to His Majesty and tell him of my despair, of my contrition?"

"If it will calm Your Majesty."

"It will. Yolande, bring the silver ewer I keep at my table." Once again, I curse the limitations Louis has put on my ability to access and dispose of my income. It is hard to build alliances when one cannot make generous gifts. "Your Excellency," I say, placing the substantial piece of silver in his hands, "I wish to pay for some masses."

"For your child. It is understandable."

And I can hardly contradict him. Hardly tell him I want prayers offered that Louis will wake from the religious zealotry that stifles the man in him and leaves only the monk; that I will recover quickly and, yes, God help me, become pregnant again. So I merely nod. Then, squeezing the bishop's hand I plead, "You will see him?"

"As soon as we finish our prayers."

When Louis comes to wait upon me the next morning, his disappointment is palpable. Yet he sits beside my bed and takes my hand.

"His Excellency told me of your distress. Told me you sought spiritual solace the moment your eyes were open again after your delivery."

"It is true, Your Majesty." I lower my eyes humbly. I am still in bed, of course, but I trust I look much better than I did for my brief audience with the bishop. All my linens are fresh, and over my chemise I wear a fur-lined pelisse of pale blue—the same blue in which the Madonna is so often portrayed. I want to look pretty. I want to look pure. "Has Your Majesty seen our daughter?" The child is not with me now as the wet nurse has taken her to feed.

"I have."

"With Your Majesty's permission, I would like to name her Blanche." My sister-in-law Jeanne standing just behind Louis appears quite stunned by my pronouncement, and rightfully so. She knows I can have but little desire to honor the Queen Mother. Surely she must see, however, as a practiced courtier and wife herself, that my intention is not to please the dragon but to mollify my husband who adores the harridan even more than I loathe her. Besides, I think Blanche a perfect name for the mewling babe with her bald head and splotched skin. For who but a lady by the name of Blanche could ever have caused me such pain?

CHAPTER 8

My dearest Marguerite,

I have written to our uncles to assure each that the death of Guillaume is felt as keenly in England as it is in Savoy, in Flanders, or in Vaud. And while our dear uncle can never be replaced in my heart, I am eager that he should be replaced in my court and on His Majesty's council. I worry for Henry without such trusted guidance. His mind and moods are oft too capricious. And when his peevishness affects his politics, no good comes of it—either for kingdom or king. Yet I find urging a steadiness of temper and purpose upon my husband as frustrating as you must have once found urging that same virtue upon me.

I appealed to Uncle Thomas, who has always been a great favorite with Henry, to take Guillaume's place as royal adviser, but he tells me that affairs in Flanders make such a scheme impracticable. Uncle Peter, however, shows some inclination to make England his occasional home. I do all I can to encourage him, assuring him that, should he present himself at our English court, he will be received with great favor and a generosity that extends itself by more than words.

I wish with all my heart that, like me, you might have Savoyard support in France. It is too cruel that Blanche of Castile conspires to make this impossible and has kept your kin from you for six long years. Perhaps she knows that were

your family at your side, she could not treat you as badly as
she does. I know I have asked this before, but is there no
way to move Louis on the subject?

Yours,

Eleanor

———— · · ————

ELEANOR
DECEMBER 1240
PALACE OF WESTMINSTER, ENGLAND

Uncle Peter arrives at court on a cold, gray afternoon. Henry makes much of him from the instant of their meeting, slapping him on the back, making sure he is offered everything first at the banquet held in his honor. My uncle smiles unceasingly and praises everything he sees or tastes. Yet I can tell by the way his glance is in constant motion that he has critical eyes that see much they do not speak of.

My uncle is not alone. He brought with him a large party of gentlemen—men of Savoy to be sure, but also men of Geneva, the lands of his wife and her father. I notice how the Englishmen on my husband's council and those already swelling the ranks of our court in preparation for Christmastide regard these men with open suspicion. Perhaps they thought when word arrived that Uncle Guillaume had died suddenly on the slopes of Mount Cimini that the era of Savoyard influence in His Majesty's kingdom was at an end. They understand as little of the Savoyard nature as I often understand of their odd ways.

As dinner draws to a close Henry says, "Lord Peter, I grieved deeply over the death of your brother. You have come to lift the pall left upon my court and my heart by his passing, and you shall find me grateful for this. I think you must have a knighthood."

The Earl of Gloucester, sitting within hearing distance, nearly drops his goblet and only just manages to recover himself. But Henry ignores him.

"Yes!" Henry smacks the flat of his palm on the table before him, delighted with his own idea. "I will knight you on the Confessor's Day. And you must surely have land so that you may feel always at home here. Perhaps the Earldom of Lincoln."

Even I am astounded by this. Lincoln is rich land indeed.

"Your Majesty is *too* generous." My uncle's reply is gracious but also serious. He can hear the rumblings around him.

And though I love Henry and prefer his outbursts of extravagant goodwill to his outbursts of temper, I wonder why he can never see ahead to the consequences of his impulsive actions. He means to be good to my uncle, but, by the black looks of the men around us, may well do him harm—making him dozens of enemies before he is even a day among us. Praise God that the Earl Richard is on crusade, for I can well imagine his violent reaction to such an expensive show of royal favor.

"With Your Majesty's leave and indulgence, I and all my party are weary from the road and would retire early." Peter casts Ebulo of Geneva, who arrived with him, a meaningful glance as he speaks.

"Of course! We will have many evenings to enjoy your company. Pray take your rest."

As I have not had a single moment alone with my uncle since his arrival, when he begins to rise, I turn to my husband. "Henry, I would escort Lord Peter to his room and see that he is comfortable."

"By all means, madam." Henry smiles indulgently, placing his hand atop mine for a moment. "Doubtless he has letters for you from your excellent parents." Then leaning in and putting his mouth close to my ear he whispers, "Pray read quickly though, for I would be saddened to find you busy when I come to you this evening." Henry returned to my bed so immediately and so enthusiastically after my churching following the birth of our second babe, the Princess Margaret, that I half expect to be swollen with child again come summer.

Rising, I lead the way to the room given over to Peter's use while he is with us. Peter follows in careful silence. The things we have to say to each other are private. When we arrive, I am pleased to see that my uncle's things have already been unpacked and his linens placed upon the bed. Only a single servant is present, sitting at the fireside cleaning the boots Peter wore on the road. This man rises at the sight of me and, after an appropriate bow, departs without the need of an order on Peter's part. Such a well-trained man is a treasure.

"Is it true," I ask Uncle Peter the moment we are alone, "that Guillaume was poisoned?"

"The rumors appear to have reason." My uncle nods his head sadly, but his eyes, even in grief, are fierce. "Whoever poisoned him may have felled a mighty tree but cannot succeed in the end. We will put forward Philippe for the bishopric in Liege, and it shall come into steady Savoy hands as a tribute to Guillaume."

And in his stubborn unwillingness to be defeated, I see myself.

"But let us not dwell on unpleasant things." He takes my hand and kisses it. "I am honored, Niece, to be at your court. I bring greetings from your parents, of course, but also words of approbation from the entire family. You have done well. Two healthy children! His Majesty issuing eager invitations to your kin, offering a hand of friendship and his worthy patronage; and by all accounts you hold the respect and the ear of your husband. What will you do with it next?"

"I am not entirely certain." I look around my uncle's chamber as if the answer might be found there.

"If you will be guided by me, I can help you to see your interests clearly, and to assist His Majesty in achieving his own. Already I have news I think you will find interesting and profitable."

"Yes?"

"His Majesty's brother is a source of persistent unrest in this kingdom, is he not?"

"To be sure," I say, "though sometimes I think he makes trouble merely because his purse is light."

"He attacks Savoyard interests."

"He paints us as *estrangièra* when it is convenient. Never mind that England is more ably ruled as a result not only of the bishop-elect of Valence's former good service but by the efforts of dozens of other 'foreigners,' from stewards to clerks, who help to keep things in good order." Richard's attacks on my Savoyard kin and friends always sting as if they were attacks upon me personally.

"Well then, when he returns to England from crusade, let us give the Earl Richard better eyes," Thomas says. "It is to this that my news tends. The earl was a guest of your gracious parents on his way to the Holy Land."

"So I have heard by my mother's letters."

"But what your lady mother did not tell you, because such hopes are better spoken low into an ear than put on the cold, brittle page, is that he made much of your sister Sanchia."

"Sanchia?"

"Indeed. It seems that half a year as a widower left your husband's brother pining for womanly companionship. He was struck by your sister from the first, and her modest blushes, quiet speech,

and shyly lowered eyes drew him in completely. By the time he left
your parents' court in September, he was sorry to be parted from
her. I think with a little encouragement he would have her for a
bride."

To have a sister at court! Even if it cannot be Marguerite, such
a thing tempts me greatly. "But is she not promised to the Count
of Toulouse?" My eyes moisten slightly at this thought. When I
first heard that Sanchia had been offered as a sacrificial lamb to stop
the years of war between my father and that count, I cried in earnest. How bitterly I regretted teasing her and Beatrice as children
about the infamously fierce count. How terrified I imagined she
must be, facing marriage to a man who was both the bugbear of
her childhood and thirty years her senior. I still cannot believe my
mother would allow it.

"Marriage to Raymond of Toulouse would doubtless solve a
problem that dogs your father and his county, but it does not follow
that he could not be made to see Richard as a better groom."

"Do you not mean paid to see?"

Peter throws back his head and laughs. "The tutelage of my
brother shows well in you, Eleanor. We shall be good partners, you
and I, for we are both of a practical bent. Further, we shall be good
friends, for I will hold nothing back from you but tell you the
absolute truth, and you will behave likewise."

I smile. After all the times Mother and Marguerite have chided
me for my outspokenness and all the times it has surprised, nay
even shocked, my ladies, my sister-in-law, and even my husband,
I have at last found someone to praise and appreciate it. "Richard
for Sanchia. The earl could not be more tightly bound to our
family."

"He would also be beholden to his brother the king for for-
warding the match."

"Uncle, you are here only a few hours and already you lift the bitter cold and damp of the place."

"What this? Cold? Eleanor, I have lands in the Alps. What teeth can the English weather show that will compare to that? Now that the Earl of Cornwall is disposed of, if Your Majesty is not eager to be gone, I would raise another subject."

"By all means."

"Who is the most important figure in Your Majesty's life?"

"His Majesty, of course. No, wait." I lower my eyes for a moment and feel the blood rise to my cheeks. "If we are being entirely honest, I must say my children."

"You need not be embarrassed of such sentiments; they are natural. And more than this, they are politically wise, particularly with respect to the Lord Edward. He is the future of this realm, and who, I would suggest, is a better guard of that future than you, his most natural and loving mother?"

"I would kill for him and also die for him."

"Let us hope that neither will be necessary," my uncle replies, but he does not laugh or make light of my claim. "Who is charged with the care of the prince and his possessions until his majority should an untimely death take His Majesty?"

I cross myself, for I do not like to entertain the subject of Henry's death even for the sake of argument. "The Earl of Cornwall."

"Again Richard. Well, even if he marries Sanchia, we will not be secure enough in him to leave something of such importance in his keeping. Your Majesty is the obvious choice for the protection of all things appertaining to your son. You have the king's love, and his ear, and this then is how you will first bend it."

"All things?"

"Yes, starting with your son's household. Those who surround your son must be loyal to you and trustworthy beyond doubt. They must personify your willingness to live and die for the boy when you cannot be at Windsor. May I suggest Bernard of Savoy for appointment as keeper of Windsor Castle?"

"Because his ties are of blood, not only of county?"

"Precisely. Kinship is the best guarantee of good service."

And looking at my uncle, so serious and so obviously entirely ready to devote himself to me, I know he speaks true.

CHAPTER 9

Eleanor,

　　Summer has come. Knowing your love of gardens, I wish you could see these at Saumur. The views alone make them superior. This afternoon the air was so full of the buzzing of bees that I nearly fell asleep in the sun. Instead, I watched the creatures push their way into the blossoms of the eager, graceful flowers. Like the pear trees that will in proper time produce their sweet bounty, I long to find myself fruitful and swollen when autumn comes. I play the flower, dressing with great care, bathing myself in rose water. My mirror tells me that though I am twenty, my looks are as good as they ever were. But if Louis will have a son by me, he will need to be more of a bee and less of a monk than he has been since our daughter was born.

　　　　　　　Yours,

　　　　　　　M

———————————

MARGUERITE
JUNE 1241
SAUMUR, ANJOU

"Who is that boy with the king?" My choice of words is deliberate. By labeling the man a mere lad, I hope to convey all the appropriate disinterest that is at odds with the keen curiosity I feel.

"Jean de Joinville, Seneschal of Champagne." Elisabeth's tone betrays the admiration mine seeks to mask.

"He is attached to the court of fat Thibaut? How extraordinary." I mean this in more than one sense. It is extraordinary not only because of the obvious contrast between the tall, muscular young man with the dark curls and the ponderously sized Count of Champagne who has little hair of any sort left, but also because the men from Champagne appear to be in a fair way toward captivating the heart of the second French queen in a row. For, when Thibaut was young and an outspoken critic of my husband's father, rumors abounded of his amorous obsession with my despised mother-in-law. Did her heart leap like a stag as mine does now the first time she beheld her cavalier from Champagne? And if so, ought not such similarity soften my feelings toward her? Of course it has no such effect. I cannot, by my own experience of her, imagine Blanche young or soft or impressionable. And she is forever outside my sympathies, as I appear to be outside hers.

"He is writing the story of the Count of Champagne's crusade," Elisabeth continues.

"That does not sound very exciting. I understand the count fought only two battles, one of which was lost."

"I am sure the account of his exploits will improve mightily under de Joinville's pen."

"Ah, then he is a man of sense and knows how to flatter a patron."

"Yes, but also, from what I hear, a man truly gifted with words."

"Hm. Do tell."

"They say he has talent enough to make even Thibaut seem dashing." Elisabeth laughs as she speaks, and Yolande and my sister-in-law Matilda join her.

My eye casts about for the count and finds him standing with the man for whom all this grandeur has been orchestrated—my brother-in-law Alphonse, who will be invested with Auvergne and Poitou in the next days, though he has been styled "Count of Poitiers" for years. Thibaut's many chins waggle unbecomingly as he speaks, and I wonder that his wife is great with child by him again, her fifth by my count. She is a petite woman who looks totally incapable of bearing Thibaut's weight under any circumstances.

I am brought back to the present with force by the approach of my husband and the young Seneschal of Champagne. My ladies and I rise as if in a single motion and then drop low before Louis.

"Your Majesty." I know I am a picture of elegance and health in my tunic of white *cendal*, fitted ever so slightly in the bust to emphasize my breasts, grown larger since the birth of little Blanche. It is patterned with hundreds of my husband's fleur-de-lis devices and belted at my still-slender waist with a girdle of scarlet to match my ermine-trimmed mantle. All my garments are new and were designed to tempt Louis. His self-denial with respect to the pleasures of my bed has been strengthened rather than weakened by the additional absence he imposed upon himself after the birth of the princess. But today is neither a Sunday nor a feast or holy day, and so I am waging a campaign to draw him to me this evening. I put out my hand to my husband and he takes it. As he does so, I see the dragon take note.

"Wife, you and your ladies are a credit to this occasion, delighting the eyes of all."

"I hope Your Majesty knows well that it is only his eyes I care for, only his approbation that can please me." I flush slightly as I speak, conscious that at the very moment I make my claim, a portion of the sparkle in my eye and the toss of my head are directed to Jean de Joinville.

Louis is clearly delighted, as along with modesty he prizes loyalty greatly. He turns to his companion saying, "You see, sir, not only newly married men such as yourself hear pretty speeches from their wives." Louis turns his head back in my direction, and Jean de Joinville's gaze follows it. "Madam, this is the Sieur de Joinville, Seneschal of Champagne, and a gentleman of great piety." I wonder if the seneschal knows that, by referring to him thusly, Louis hints that he is already finding royal favor. When a man impresses the king, he is always quick to praise his piety—even if he knows so little of the gentleman that he must take that piety on faith.

"Sieur," I say, trying to smile with my eyes, "we hear from every direction that you are a fine writer and much sought to set forth tales for those who wish to be educated or amused." Do I imagine it or is de Joinville hanging on my every word? I wonder if he is breathing. His lips, slightly parted, seem better suited for other things, and I try to keep my eyes from lingering on them as I raise an eyebrow and continue. "Do your talents run to poesy, or only prose?"

"Only prose, Your Majesty." De Joinville's voice is strong, clear, and pleasingly without affectation.

"What a pity. In Provence we had so many poets. They were as common as red valerian along a roadside and so much taken for granted that I did not think to bring one with me when I came to France." The image of the minstrel who accompanied me from my father's court years ago passes before my mind's eye, causing me to question the motivation for my half-truth. "It seems I must continue looking."

"I am very sorry to disappoint Your Majesty." De Joinville clearly means it. The list of those wishing to see me pleased at the court of my husband is not very long, but perhaps this young man may make up for the absence of many.

THIS EVENING, TAKING A PAGE from Louis's book, I am on my knees upon reaching my bedchamber. I dismiss my women without letting them undress me and pray to the Virgin that Louis will come to me, for I am ripe. I can smell it.

When I was younger, I never noticed. But, after the birth of our daughter, in those first days of despair when I cursed God and my body, my dear Yolande, suspecting the cause of my great distress, offered to school me in the ways of my own flesh. She taught me how to detect the pungent change in my own urine. And now the scent pleases my nose, hinting at a secret source of power and pleasure.

I hear the door open, but I do not move. I know that if it is Louis, seeing me thus, dressed in the color of purity, hands clasped and eyes closed, will excite his feelings for me as little else can.

I am right, and, strangely, in the dark for a moment I forget the face of my husband, even his flashing blue eyes. Instead, I imagine a head full of dark curls, and I am startled when, reaching out to wind my fingers into them, I find Louis's lank, fair hair in their place. What will my confessor, William de St. Pathus, make of that?

I awake early the next morning, full of excitement and anticipation. My ears are alert to every sound, from the birds conversing riotously outside my window to Marie's soft steps beyond my chamber door as she consciously tries not to wake me while beginning the business of her day. As I stretch and roll to my back, the touch of the coverings on the flesh of my limbs sends shivers through me. I wonder whether I will see the Seneschal of Champagne today and if so, how soon? There are so many people gathered at court. Three thousand knights have come for Alphonse's investiture. But at the moment only one of them has the power to intrigue and divert me.

I close my eyes, trying to picture Jean de Joinville, and I am startled when his image comes to me naked. Perhaps I should not be. I may have lain with my husband last evening, but I am far from satisfied. In the last year, our "dear" mother Blanche moved from the Palais du Roi to her own residence on the right bank of the Seine. I was sure, with the dragon gone, I would have more success persuading Louis to pay me his marriage debt. I was eager to have him between my thighs again, not only so that I might have a son, but because my body harkened back to the early days of our marriage when it received pleasure from my husband. But I have been bitterly disappointed. Now there is none. No hands run eagerly over my body as he penetrates me. No lips suck teasingly at my pert nipples causing me to gasp with gratification. I am not certain that Louis even sees me as he satisfies his needs. His needs alone are considered.

I examine my imagined Joinville closely, running my mind's eye down his chest to the nest of dark hair above his member, hair as curly and irresistible as that on his handsome head. Almost unconsciously the fingers of my left hand rise to my nipple and begin to rub and pinch it in turn. My right hand finds its way between my legs. I am shocked to discover how sensitive I am to my own touch, and how my pulse quickens as I stroke myself. Imagining that the hands upon me are Joinville's, I give a little moan and another; then, fearing I will be heard, I put my left fist up to my mouth and bite upon my curled first finger. Strangely, even this brings pleasure. I hesitate for only a moment and then plunge the first two fingers of my hand inside myself. My hips writhe beneath the covers as I give myself all the pleasure that heedless Louis denies me. Lying back, satisfied at last, I feel a certain smugness. I have paid myself my own marriage debt, and whatever sin there may be in that, I cannot repent of it.

ALL AFTERNOON I WATCH FOR Joinville but do not see him. Sitting beside Louis, I receive dozens upon dozens of people. Blanche is with us in the hall, but she is indisposed and cannot sit for long periods. When she rises from her seat at Louis's other side and descends from the dais to walk about the crowded room, Louis twines his fingers in mine. The unexpected gesture of familiarity draws my full attention to my husband. Louis is enjoying all the pomp and ceremony of this gathering of nobles and knights, in spite of himself.

"Those who pay homage to us are the finest men in Europe," he says when we are momentarily at liberty. "Look at them." Then he sighs wistfully. "How much better it would be to see them in the field."

I draw my eyes away from the throngs of brightly dressed dukes, counts, seneschals, and bishops where I have been searching for Fat Thibaut in hopes that Jean de Joinville will be at his side. "In the field, Your Majesty?"

Louis's eyes burn with more heat than blue seems capable of emitting as he answers, "In the Holy Land, doing God's work."

Of course, crusade. Louis thinks about crusading a great deal as of late. He, I, and indeed all of Christendom know that Richard of Cornwall, brother of the English king and a powerful nobleman in his own right, is presently on crusade. His absence accounts for the timing of Alphonse's investiture. According to Eleanor's husband, the territory of Poitou is English, and King Henry has conferred it on the Earl Richard. My husband insists that the same lands belong to France because his father overran them shortly before his death, but Louis has only played the role of lord over them from a distance. Now he brings his brother here to sit above all the other noblemen in the region and receive their homage. It is a bold move—a gamble by my husband and the dragon to secure his power over this western territory and to open the possibility of converting it, at some later date, into a royal domain rather than a county held by a vassal. It would be bold almost to the point of recklessness were Richard of Cornwall within striking distance, able to defend his interests. Yet even as he moves to benefit from Richard's absence, Louis envies Richard and is jealous of his crusade. Every song, every story celebrating the Englishman's triumphs excites and chafes Louis.

"Your Majesty does God's work here in France. The city of Paris is ringed with religious houses that you have raised to Our Lord's glory and your own."

"For my own glory I care not a whit."

I am not fooled. Louis may be a very pious man, but man he is. He longs for military glory, for the prestige of being victorious on the field of battle. He longs to hear his exploits sung. And though I like crusade poetry very much myself, I would rather hear songs of love at present. A movement to my right distracts me from my reply. Blanche has returned, and Alphonse and Jeanne are with her.

"Your Majesty, I have just received word that Isabella of Angoulême, Countess of La Marche, has arrived." Blanche speaks very softly, stepping in close before Louis. Jeanne and Alphonse draw in as well. We form a tight circle, as if we are plotters within our own court.

"She is very clever," Alphonse hisses. "If you receive her before I am invested, she can avoid kneeling to me."

"She is not clever enough," replies Blanche with a derisive snort. "We and not she control the time and manner of her reception."

"Make her wait?" Louis sounds slightly dubious, and I am nearly aghast. Isabella of Angoulême is not only Countess of La Marche; she is also Dowager Queen of England, mother-in-law to my sister, a woman equal in rank to the dragon.

"Why not?" asks Blanche. "We have not come this far to have our work undone by a woman who steals her own daughter's husband. Any public insolence toward Your Majesty or the Count of Poitiers, any disturbance caused by the countess, could give others in your brother's territory courage to defy him. You know that Hugh of La Marche is popular among his peers, and so is his wife."

We *are*, it seems, plotters in our own court.

"Your Majesty," I venture, surprised at my own courage, not so much in having an opinion as in speaking it, "if she is so, might you not incite the Count of La Marche by treating his lady with discourtesy? Might not the countess urge her husband to be less compliant where you would have him more?"

Jeanne nods her head timidly in agreement, and I give her a grateful look.

"Ridiculous," scoffs the dragon. "Why would *any* man listen to his *wife* on such matters? Hugh of La Marche will no more listen to Isabella than His Majesty will listen to you." Blanche's last phrase is accompanied by a cruel smile. She turns to Louis expectantly.

"We shall do as you say, madam. Let the countess be kept waiting." Louis does not look at me as he speaks. Blanche, however, gives me a very meaningful glance before ascending the dais to take her seat at Louis's left. While Louis is turned toward her, I rise and flee.

My eyes brim with tears, so I keep them on the floor as I move toward the nearest door, eager to escape the lively room and its chattering inhabitants. As I reach the door, my steps quicken. Passing through it without looking, I run against someone.

"Your Majesty, my apologies."

It is Jean de Joinville. I recognize his voice even before I glance up into his mortified face.

"Sieur, the fault is mine. I found the great hall too close for my comfort and, in my hurry to get some air, did not look where I was going."

"It *is* warm," Joinville says solemnly, "much warmer than the weather I am accustomed to in Champagne this time of year."

He studiously ignores the implausibility of my statement—he knows I am from the south where it is as warm as it is beautiful— and I feel a rush of gratitude for the gesture. The seneschal's eyes have a remarkable depth when they are serious. Fearful of falling into them, I lower my own eyes again.

"Perhaps in the gardens you will find relief?" he continues. "With a breeze and a little shade. Would you like me to come with you?"

The last question is spoken so low and with such intensity that I cannot help but raise my face again. His arm is already extended, and his expression exhibits all the gravitas due me as his queen. But, do I fool myself, or do I see more than a desire to be useful in his eyes and in the way his nostrils seem to tense and relax with every breath as he waits for my answer?

"Yes," I reply, setting my hand lightly on his forearm. The sleeve fits very closely here, and despite its presence, I quiver like a vielle string at first contact.

We make our way outside. "Let us take the way along the parapet wall," I suggest. "The air will be fresh there and the views unmatched."

"As Your Majesty wishes."

Once at the wall, I release Joinville's arm and gaze down at the convergence of the Loire and Thouet rivers. The sky is blue and sown with white clouds. Our height above the town of Saumur is dizzying, and the greens of the flat valley beyond the city walls stretch to the horizon. I was not lying when I said the views are spectacular, but they are not *my* views. After seven years of marriage, my eyes still search for the rock-ribbed mountains and red earth of Provence. After a few moments in silence, de Joinville turns his back to the parapet.

"What a graceful château. It is hard to believe that the English built it."

Surprised by his comment, I laugh out loud. Then, recollecting that my sister is on an English throne, I cover my mouth.

Joinville appears to have the same realization, for he looks suddenly sheepish. "Pardon my impudence, Your Majesty. I forgot your relationship to the English queen."

"Yes," I reply, seating myself on a nearby bench and affecting great seriousness, "we ought to show more respect for the King of England's grandfather—particularly as *my* husband's grandfather took this lovely château from him. We can afford to be gracious to those we vanquish."

Now it is Joinville's turn to laugh. He has a beautiful laugh. Warm and melodious, it shakes his frame. "Then, His Majesty the Most Christian King of France has every reason to be affable." Joinville's eyes examine me where I sit. Giving an exaggerated bow he continues. "Our sovereign bests Henry of England at every turn, beginning with his choice of bride."

"Sieur de Joinville! It is very lucky for you that my sister Eleanor is not here," I reply in mock horror. "She would upbraid you roundly and with reason. I, however, know how to accept a compliment. You are in no danger from me. I merely protest that the Queen of England is exceedingly fair, clever, and charming, and were you to meet her, your opinion of my merits might alter."

"Impossible." The tone is still light, but the eyes are all conviction.

While it is perfectly chivalrous and appropriate for me to play at love as the ladies in song and story do, I know I am in danger here lest the game go too far. My morning thoughts of Joinville tell me as much. I must parry those serious eyes. "It is a great shame that this château will belong to my brother Charles when he is of age as he is the Count d'Anjou." I am surprised by my own candor the moment the words are spoken. It seems that, though I change the subject, I have a need to speak truth to the Sieur de Joinville.

"You do not like the count." It is a statement, not a question; yet I reply willingly enough.

"No one much likes him. He is a prating, pompous fourteen-year-old. I could, perhaps, forgive him that. But he is ambitious beyond his years. I do not trust him."

"But you trust me." One dark curl has fallen down over his right eye. It dangles, just grazing his eyebrow, which is raised slightly, awaiting my reply.

"So it seems, for I give you the power to do me harm. If you repeat what I have said, the Dowager Queen will make much of it, to my detriment."

"I would never lift voice or hand to injure Your Majesty." Join-ville pushes the obstinate curl back as he speaks. "I take your unguarded words as a pledge of friendship and return one of my own. Before coming to court, I heard that His Majesty cleaved too closely to his mother. These last days I have seen it to be true. The Dowager Queen treats the king as a boy, and thus unmans him. It is unseemly, and so is the way that she treats Your Majesty."

The seneschal could not have chosen more apt words if he wished to ingratiate himself with me. Yet I sense no fawning in him. His voice has a steadiness and certitude about it more gener-ally associated with age than with a youth first arrived at court. I gesture for him to take a seat beside me, and he does readily. "They say you are penning the story of the Count of Champagne's crusade. What was it like in the Holy Land?"

"I have no idea," Joinville replies frankly. "I did not travel with the count. I must write based on his report."

"You do not sound satisfied."

"Well, people often misremember things to their own advantage."

"You mean the count paints too flattering a picture of his deeds?"

"No." Joinville laughs again, lightly. "He expects *me* to paint the flattering picture. But, yes, he exaggerates. He is a good writer himself, and I wish *he* would tell this tale and spare my reputation. Perhaps he correctly judges that few men can tell their own story without being called braggart."

"Sieur, I do believe you worry over nothing. Surely it is not what you write but how you write it that will determine your reputation? All those who read your account will know that Thibaut's wishes directed your pen."

"The best writings, like the best men, tell the truth. I would make a name for myself as a man who can be relied upon."

CHAPTER 10

Marguerite,

. . . For shame! Are these the manners our mother taught you? To keep my husband's mother, a queen herself, waiting for more than a day! Is it any wonder then that her husband and her kin are risen in anger to defend her honor? I must conclude that your association with the French king is to blame, for is he not the same gentleman, and I use that term advisedly, who thought to pilfer another preudomme's lands while that knight was abroad carrying the banner of our faith? . . .

Eleanor

MARGUERITE

JULY 1242

THE FRENCH ROYAL CAMP OUTSIDE OF SAINTES, POITOU

And all this because we snubbed the Countess of La Marche. I wonder if the dragon thinks of that—of how certain she was that Isabella of Angoulême had neither the power nor the influence to start a rebellion. Doubtless she does. She has feared conspiracies against her beloved Louis for as long as I have known her, and in the end she created one involving both the English king and the emperor through miscalculation. How fortunate for my husband then that our kingdom is rich and his knights were ready. And now Louis has raised the oriflamme and achieved a victory in battle. Perhaps soon we can go home.

The tent is hot. And while I find it oppressively so, the baby slumbering against my chest appears to find it soothing.

"Shall I take her to her nurse?" Marie asks.

I am torn. The Princess Isabella, now four months old, calms me. But she also makes me warmer, so I nod and hand her to Marie grudgingly. Watching Marie disappear, I wonder again why it was so much easier for me to accept a second daughter than it was a first. Perhaps because there have been other causes for distress.

When I became Queen of France and Eleanor Queen of England, I never imagined our countries at war. Foolish of me, I suppose. I knew that Louis and Henry of England were rivals and disagreed over the ownership of certain territories, but I was used to the Savoyard way of thinking that families are best served by uniting. "When the members of a family fight among themselves, they are all the losers." This philosophy shared by my mother's brothers has allowed them each to grow rich and powerful without dividing the dominions of the House of Savoy, without ever giving my uncle the Count Amadeus a single sleepless night. But Louis and Henry are not brothers, though their wives are sisters. So I sit near the southern border of Poitou, bearing my husband company as he seeks to rout the English and their Gascon allies and subdue the rebellious Poitevin nobles.

Marie returns. She bustles about my tent with an amazing energy, apparently oblivious to the heat. Jeanne stares at her wanly from the couch where she reclines. She has been ill. At first it was hoped that she was with child. She and Alphonse have been married nearly five years and she has yet to breed. But it turned out she only suffered from that sickness of the bowels and belly so common in an armed camp. The illness is past, but Jeanne is still greatly weakened.

"Will Your Majesty take some refreshment?" Marie inquires.

"No. We dine shortly with the king. I will change now."

Jeanne makes an effort to rise and assist me, but I wave her back to her place.

"I wonder that you bother," she remarks listlessly. "You know that Louis will make no effort at finery."

"Indeed. But I will feel cooler in fresh clothing," I say. I am dissembling. Despite my estrangement from Eleanor, this war has had one positive effect. It has made Louis feel like a warrior. He may still dress like a monk sworn to poverty, but he has a warrior's appetites. He eats better than I have seen him do in years. He waters his wine less; using the heat and the exertion of battle as his excuse when Blanche turns an accusing eye in his direction. And he is back in my bed far sooner than I could ever have imagined. He will notice what I wear tonight, make no mistake.

The ground we tread on the way to the king's tent is dry and dusty. Men and animals have denuded the once lush patch where we camp. Jeanne trails slightly behind me. I can see the Charente River glimmering between the tents. The sun is in its descent, and perhaps within a few hours we will have some relief from the heat. The standards of Louis's knights banneret hang limp. There is no breeze to carry them aloft.

Knights and noblemen bow in acknowledgment as we pass. I cannot help but think of one who is not among them. Jean de Joinville is in Champagne, no doubt ably administering those territories while Thibaut is at his court in the Navarre. Sometimes I find it strange that a man with whom I passed not more than a dozen hours, and those hours more than a year ago, should be so much in my mind. But perhaps it is not *so* strange. It is no more uncommon to take an instant liking to someone than it is to take an instant disliking. My sister Eleanor used to brag that she could make up her mind about anyone or anything before I could say my alphabet. But I own it *is* unusual for me. I am a deliberative person. Not, as Eleanor liked to tease me, indecisive, but someone who likes to give every person and every question a fair chance to show their character. So the immediate amity I felt with the Seneschal of Champagne intrigues me and will not be forgotten.

When Jeanne and I arrive at Louis's tent, he and Alphonse are already present. They are glowing, not only with the sweat of the day but with the recent victory at Taillebourg. Louis is talking to his constable, Humbert de Beaujeu, doubtless about the next engagement. I see the marshal hovering nearby. The entrance of the ladies, or rather ladies other than Blanche who is already present and clearly part of the discussions, brings military matters quickly to a close. Louis approaches to lead me to the table.

"You prepare to lay siege to Saintes?" I ask, taking Louis's arm.

"In a day or perhaps two. You will be quite safe here."

"From all but the heat," Jeanne remarks, taking up Alphonse's arm.

Louis gives the Countess of Poitiers a withering look. He dislikes complainers.

"I am not the least concerned," I say lightly. "The English king, the Count of La Marche, and their allies stand no chance against Your Majesty."

"We do not know if Henry of England is still with the rebels. Rumors have reached us that he has broken with the Count of La Marche and already flees toward Bordeaux."

I say nothing, merely sinking into my seat between Alphonse and Louis, but I feel a great surge of relief. Eleanor is at Bordeaux.

With luck, albeit a commodity of which Henry of England seems to have precious little, her husband will reach her safely.

The basins are brought round. Hands are washed and wine is poured. I expect any moment to see food carried in. Instead, there is a great commotion just outside—feet scuffling, loud voices, the distinctive sound of blows. It is as if a battle has suddenly erupted. Louis and the other gentlemen are on their feet instantly, hands on sword hilts. Before they can charge out into the gathering darkness, however, the tent flap opens and a tightly drawn group of knights lurches and shoves its way through. At the group's center I can see two figures being dragged violently along as blows rain down upon them. They do not appear to be knights or even common foot soldiers, but are dressed in the manner of cooks.

"What is the meaning of this?" Louis barks.

The Count of Taillebourg breaks from the knot of men. "Your Majesty, we have uncovered great treachery." Turning back, he grabs one of the two servants by his hair, half lifting and half dragging him out where the king can see him better. The man's visage has aspects of a cornered beast. His glance darts about desperately as if searching for escape. His clothing is torn, and one of his eyes already begins to blacken. "This man and his accomplice were caught poisoning the food intended for Your Majesty's table."

There is a great and collective gasp from those seated. Blanche knocks over her cup, and the contents, red as blood, run before Louis where he stands, spilling down onto the ground. The count raises his arm and then lowers it with force, striking the miscreant on the head with the hilt of his sword.

"Stop." Louis's voice is calm. He walks the length of the table and then around it, halting in front of the count and his captive. "Who sent you?"

The man opens his mouth, but instead of speaking, spits full in Louis's face.

The count raises his sword, but Louis stills him with a gesture.

Lifting a hand to wipe his face, Louis remains composed. "Be warned, this is a serious business, and you will pay for it with your life. But if you are merely the instrument in another's plot, your passing shall be made easy and those responsible for your wickedness shall also be punished."

"Go to the devil!" the man replies with a twisted, defiant sneer. "I will tell you nothing, by Christ's cross and nails, nothing!"

Louis's face flushes scarlet, and I see the muscles in his jaw work and those in his arm tense as his hand clenches on the handle of his still-sheathed sword. "Get this man from my sight! He dares to blaspheme in my presence!"

I feel a need to laugh hysterically. "Dares to blaspheme"? And *this* is serious? The man dared much more! He dared to kill a king, to kill us all. Realization of the threat faced and narrowly escaped suddenly falls upon me forcefully. My body shakes uncontrollably, and the laugh that hung in my throat turns to a sob, which I muffle with my hand.

The count and a nearby knight drag the bold villain out. He continues to shout oaths as he is hauled away. Louis stands breathing heavily for a few moments and then, his face once more composed, turns to the second man still surrounded by French knights. In response to the king's beckoning gesture, he is pushed forward. This one is younger and slighter of build. He shakes as much as I do.

"And you, will you tell us at whose behest you came? We do not know your face, and we do not believe we have ever wronged you."

The man tries to speak and fails, then tries again. This time his voice emerges cracked with strain. "My mistress bid me hence."

"And who is your mistress?"

I take my eyes off Louis and turn them in morbid fascination upon Blanche. She is paler than bread when it lies resting before taking its turn in the oven. I know the answer to Louis's question before it comes. So does she.

"The Countess of La Marche."

I do not go to see the men executed. When Marie returns, she tells me that the small man, the one who trembled so terribly and told all, died swiftly by the sword. But, at Blanche's insistence, the spitter was fed a portion of the food he thought to serve us. He died in agony.

THE KNEELING WOMAN SEEMS SO much older than when I saw her last. Gazing down at her bowed head, I think that it is neither her more than fifty years of life nor the birth of fourteen children, including the English king, that have taken their toll on her. What ages her are defeat and capitulation. She does not cry. Nor does she look up while her husband, weeping openly himself, makes a groveling apology to Louis. She merely resolutely stares at the floor beneath her knees. I let my eyes leave the bowed head of Isabella of Angoulême, Countess of La Marche, and the two tiny daughters who kneel beside her and glance at Blanche. The dragon is beaming. No doubt she is thinking of all the castles and territories that the count lost in surrendering—lands and castles now ours.

My mind is on other subjects. This war is nearly over. Without Hugh de Lusignan, Henry of England cannot hold out against my husband. Even with the Count of La Marche, the English had little chance.

Louis allows the humbled family to rise. They move down the dais and stop before Alphonse and Jeanne, Count and Countess of

Poitiers. Slowly and elaborately the Lusignans pay homage for the lands they have been allowed to keep. Again my eyes find Isabella. This morning as she dressed me, Marie told me that two days ago the Countess of La Marche tried to take her own life. Can this moment of humiliation really be worse than an eternity in the fires of hell? Worse than the agonizing death that would have preceded damnation? For Marie also told me that Isabella planned to take poison—the same type she provided to her chefs before sending them into our camp to attempt our lives. I thank God silently that my sister Eleanor shall never know a moment such as this! Not at French hands. If I have to crawl before Louis in sackcloth and ashes, I will prevent it.

CHAPTER II

Sister,

Truly I do not remember when I was last so angry with you. How dare you employ such a tone in addressing me. It is not you but rather I who has the right to feel aggrieved and to express my displeasure. Have you forgotten that it was your husband, the King of England, who attacked my own honorable lord, joining with the insurrectionist barons from Poitou? When assaulted, Louis must defend the integrity of his territories, and I expected you to understand as much, rather than to accuse him of conduct unbecoming a preudomme.

But though mine is the side of right, still I beg you let us have no more of this. Let us not make personal what is essentially a political battle. To be at war with you, even through our kings and our countries, sits uneasily upon me. You are still my sister. I pray you will remember that no matter which of our husbands proves victorious on the field of battle.

I pray that when this letter reaches you in Bordeaux you are already safely delivered of your child.

M

Eleanor
July 1242
Bordeaux, Gascony

How can a duchy that makes such pleasant wine be full of such un-pleasant people?

I have been in Gascony for two months, and my husband's subjects do not impress me. I first settled at La Réole. But the people of that city, far from being honored by my presence, seemed to think my residence there might incense the French king to their detriment. Better they should have worried about incurring the anger of their own lord. Well, they will be sorry when Henry rides back from Poitou victorious and calls them to account! In any case, their ill manners drove me to Bordeaux where I now sit.

Yes, I am in Bordeaux and, I must admit, I am bored and sulky—a far cry from my mood when we sailed from Portsmouth on the ninth of May. Oh, my spirits were high as I went aboard the royal ship to begin this war—high despite my certain knowledge that there would be physical discomfort in traveling, as I was peril-ously near to delivering my third child. Neither Willelma nor Sybil wanted me to make the journey on that account. They begged me to give birth in London. When that failed, they tempted me to pass my time at Windsor with Edward and my little Marguerite, or Margaret as the English call her, who prattles away now more like her mother than the aunt for whom she is named. But I refused, vowing that I would not miss the war in Poitou even for the com-pany of my children. And Henry indulged me—to a point.

When we landed, I wanted, of course, to go right along with him to meet the troops from Poitou, Gascony, and Toulouse. After all, if my husband was going to teach Louis of France not to flout English territorial claims, I did not wish to miss the lesson. But

Henry forbade that. "A military camp is no place to give birth, Eleanor," he said. So ended the matter. Not even my wistful mentions of how much I longed to meet his mother, Isabella of Angoulême, or my praise of the lady as a great *virago* moved him.

He was probably right, though I have no plans of admitting as much when I see him. This lying-in was my worst. As if aware I am thinking of her birth, my new daughter, nearly a month old and named after my fair mother, grunts and snuffles in her cradle beside me. I rock her slightly to keep her from waking. Then I turn my gaze once more out of the window by which I sit to the flat, blue July sky. Now that I am not swollen in every limb, I long to fly like a bird to the battlefield and see what goes on there. I sigh.

Willelma, who sits nearby, perhaps hoping to cheer me, says, "Will Your Majesty not write to the Queen of France?"

I glance to the table where Marguerite's last missive lies. Willelma cannot know this, but it is an unpleasant letter. Perhaps I *did* complain when I wrote to her last, upbraiding her once again for Louis's audacity in provoking the English. But surely there was no need for her to get so angry. I have no desire to respond—at least not until I have some news from Henry. In his last letter he reported advancing to Tonnay-Charente. The French army was nearby and, as an exchange of letters between Henry and the French king had resolved nothing, battle was expected.

"Do you suppose they are fighting even now?" I ask Willelma.

"Who can say, Your Majesty."

Willelma's unruffled calm irritates me. I know *precisely* who can say—Marguerite. Her tent is pitched alongside those of her husband and his men. She will miss nothing.

Rising, I pace away from the window. Surely with the support of the powerful Count of La Marche Henry will be victorious. I suspect that Henry's mother, Isabella, has the strength of will to drive her husband the count to victory whatever the odds. I've heard that she barred the door of Hugh's castle against him until he vowed to punish the French for the insult paid her last summer! And if Hugh and his sons are not enough, the Earl of Cornwall is with Henry too. God's blood, Richard was angry when he returned to English shores to find that, even as he was rescuing French captives in the Holy Land, Louis had the gall to invest another man with his lands. His fury should make him fight like ten men.

Yes, Henry will defeat Louis, and then I will write to Marguerite. The high-minded tone of my response will nettle her, and that will serve her right, given her own recent, sanctimonious tone. This pleasant thought soothes me a bit, and I return to my vantage point at the window.

What if Henry does not win? I do not know where the thought comes from. Actually, I do. My ladies and I every day hear murmurings from the streets beyond these walls, talk of the prowess of the French king; reminders that the Lusignans have a history of fighting for the French and not just fighting against them. In fact, the Lusignan men who are now my husband's kin by marriage fought with Louis's father when he overran Poitou. My breathing begins to trouble me. I feel as if I am being smothered by my sudden doubts. I press my hands to my chest where it grows tight and try not to panic.

"Your Majesty?" Sybil speaks from the threshold. She moves quickly to set a tray she is carrying on my table, then rushes toward me. Willelma likewise stands and moves in my direction. I wave them off. What good can they hope to do by crowding me?

Closing my eyes, I struggle to draw in as much air as I can. Then, closing my lips as tightly as possible, I push the air out again against their resistance. The process makes a dreadful and embarrassing noise, and I am well aware that I must look like a great bloated bullfrog, but it has the desired effect. A moment ago I felt strapped round as with unbendable bands of iron like some barrel. But now the bands are loosed. I open my eyes, breathing cautiously and with measured slowness. Willelma and Sybil both appear stricken.

"The episode has passed," I assure them.

"Come away from the window, Your Majesty," Sybil urges. She always sees the air as author of my difficulties. "Take some nourishment." Walking to the table, she begins to uncover the dishes she carried when she entered. Their aromas are enticing; yet I rise reluctantly, fearing I will miss something. Sure enough, I am only just seated when the sound of horses at great speed can be heard. Rising, I knock over my chair and run to the window. I am just in time to see a last dust-covered rider pass through the wicket below.

"They wear the king's colors!"

"I will go and bring their leader here directly," Sybil says.

"You will do no such thing." The thought of waiting, even for Sybil to go and return, is unbearable. I move to my mirror, pinch both my cheeks, then, turning, say, "I will go myself."

My pace ever quickening, I move through a series of chambers, Sybil in my wake. By the time I reach the stairs, I am nearly at a run. I hurry down them in a manner hardly befitting a queen, and, opening the next door, reveal a much-bespattered John Mansel. His mouth is fixed into a grim and rigid line, and his eyes, while not seeking to avoid mine, have a deadness about them I do not like.

"Your Majesty." His perfunctory bow gives me a moment to steel myself. The news cannot be good.

I DO NOT KNOW WHICH is harder to bear—the dreadful troubadour songs about Henry's cowardice in battle or the weight of my sister's mercy. The year of Our Lord 1243 has begun very badly indeed.

"The treaty is just," Uncle Peter says. We are closeted together in my rooms in Bordeaux. "Urge Henry not to defer a moment longer. He must go to pay homage to Louis and sign."

"I know," I snap, "but can you blame him for delaying? To kneel before the French king as his man! It is an unpalatable thought."

"Louis has no desire to embarrass Henry. You know what Marguerite writes—Louis pushes aside the criticism of his own advisers over the lenient terms of the treaty on the grounds that Henry is his brother by marriage."

"Lenient? You call the sums we will be required to pay per annum lenient?"

"I do." Uncle Peter strides to the window and pretends to give the view some consideration, though I know for certain there is nothing to be seen, just an early-spring garden not yet beginning to bud. Turning, my uncle regards me narrowly with intense eyes. "Eleanor, you have to stop behaving like an angry child who has lost a game."

"I am not!"

"You are. It rankles you to lose to Marguerite, but put your feelings aside." Peter approaches me where I sit, and, leaning close, continues in a low tone. "Henry has a short memory; he was deserted by the Count of La Marche and already forgives him. Take a lesson— forgive the French king for being the better military commander."

"How can you say 'better'? You know that we were outnumbered and defeated by the count's mismanagement before Henry even set foot off our ship!"

"Mayhap. But Henry was also outmaneuvered. Louis of France gained nothing that he did not win fairly." My cheeks grow warm with a combination of anger and shame. I know my uncle speaks the truth. Henry fought badly at Taillebourg, then turned and fled.

But I bristle at any reminder of my husband's shortcomings. "The bigger loss in this campaign was Gascony," Peter continues, "which Henry gave away on a whim. We must concentrate on getting it back for Edward."

I cannot defend Henry in this. The grant of Gascony to Earl Richard robs our son. "How? When Henry feels that Richard saved him from capture."

"Richard *did* save him. And for this very reason we must bide our time. Richard returns from the campaign stronger than he left, both in Henry's affections and in the imagination of the average Englishman. Sting him now and his cries will raise the sympathy of too many. Let us make as much of him for a while as the king does."

My uncle moves away and takes a seat by my fire. For some moments both of us are silent. And then it comes to me. "No, we shall make *more* of him," I say. "I will urge Henry to finalize the marriage contract with my father immediately and to be generous in the financial terms. If we must pay Louis from the royal accounts, why not Richard? Then we will use the preparations for a lavish wedding to wipe away the traces of disgrace that dog the king. Give the English a spectacle and they will forget much else. The troubadours will have a new song to sing—a song of the women of Provence and their beauty."

"YOU LOOK LOVELY; IT IS foolish to fuss," my mother says, entering my cabin and passing behind me. Willelma holds a small polished bronze mirror a few feet away while I attempt to see myself in difficult circumstances. We are in the waters off Dover, and the November winds toss the ship most unpleasantly. It has taken me a long time to make my return from Gascony to English shores, and I intend to arrive looking my best.

"It is foolish not because I look beautiful, but because no matter what I do, I cannot measure up to Sanchia's loveliness," I reply. When my mother and sister arrived in Bordeaux to join Henry and me, I was completely taken aback by my sister's exquisite looks. True, she was always a beauty, but seven years ago when I saw her last she was but a child. Now she is a woman of seventeen with all the assets and attractions womanhood brings. She is so stunning that in my darker moments I wonder if it is wise to have her at my court. Surely every man will ignore me once she is in England. If I catch Henry glancing in her direction with any eyes other than those of a brother, heaven help her!

"Your sister will need more than beauty to make a success of this marriage." Mother takes the mirror from Willelma and gestures for her to leave.

It is amazing, I think, how quickly my mother and I resumed our familiar roles. All my worry that our prolonged separation might have left us awkward strangers disappeared within an hour after I greeted her in Bordeaux, but so too did my firm intentions to be treated as an equal. I will always be daughter to my mother, even if I am a queen, a grown woman, and a mother myself three times over.

"I see clearly how it lies between His Majesty and the Earl Richard. Your uncle, of course, instructed me on the topic while the match was being made, but I always understand better what I have seen with my own eyes." Apparently satisfied with my appearance and assuming that will be enough for me, mother flips the mirror over and looks at herself. She bites her upper and lower lip to bring the color, then smiles at her reflection.

"Then you understand the importance of reining Richard in. He thinks himself the more able of the brothers." I go to the window of my cabin and gaze out at the white cliffs that welcome me home. They are drawing close. It will soon be time to disembark.

I turn back to my mother. "Richard is not alone in his assessment. Too many of Henry's barons underestimate my husband in favor of his brother. If he cannot be checked, he is a danger to us."

"Sanchia knows she is tasked with bending Richard to the royal will."

"But is she equal to the undertaking? She is so reticent!" I find my sister boring. She is entirely pleasant, respectful, and attentive to me, but there is no spark in her.

"Not everyone can have your boldness, Eleanor. She may be timid, but she is loyal and, more important, she is dutiful. This is the one characteristic I managed to impart to all my daughters, however different their temperaments. So we may count on Sanchia to try."

"That is not entirely comforting, madam. My husband has spent three thousand marks and four manor houses to secure this marriage, and to try is not always to succeed."

"No, that holds true for *all* of us," Mother replies gently.

I feel my face growing hot. How dare she remind me of Henry's recent failure? But perhaps she does not; perhaps she only remembers and refers to some less than successful endeavors of my own. She is right, of course; if effort were the measure of success, my husband and not Marguerite's would be heralded as the greatest king in Europe. But even with all of my uncle's coaching and all my prompting and encouragement, Henry missteps again and again in governing.

"For a few weeks at least, we can guide her," my mother continues, ignoring my discomfort.

I feel vaguely cross with my sister for being as she is. Unfair? Perhaps. I have no other sister of marriageable age, so Sanchia provided the most direct and obvious way to tie Richard to my family, whatever her faults. And besides, he talked of her with such ardor after seeing her. But Savoyards are many. Another bride, less close in degree of relation but more apt for the purpose, might have been found had I known to look. Standing opposite my mother, I realize her interests and my own were not entirely the same in this matter. She wanted a wealthier and more prestigious husband for Sanchia than the Count of Toulouse, and she may well have thought it best not to apprise me of my sister's shortcomings before the marriage contract was executed. This thought fans the embers of my annoyance into white-hot anger.

"Let us hope Richard finds the coinage with which Sanchia pays her marriage debt as irresistible as he finds gold from my husband's purse," I snap.

My mother winces. "Eleanor!"

"A man will do much for a woman who pleases him in bed," I say petulantly. "If my sister has not the sort of personality to push her husband in the direction we need him to go, nor the cleverness to trick him, she may still manage him effectively through his lust."

My mother regards me for a moment or two without speaking. But if she thinks to cow me, she will be disappointed. A cry from on deck breaks our standoff. The sailors are making preparations to land.

"I will go and make certain of your sister. She will be nervous about being seen on English soil for the first time." My mother's eyes smolder, but her voice is even. She glides across my small cabin as if the ship were not even moving. Such an appearance of serenity despite the circumstances! At the door she turns briefly. "I think, Daughter," she says in the same mild tone, "you would do well to leave off preening and perfecting your outside appearance, and lavish more attention on matters of your character."

By the time the plank is dropped for us to disembark, I am thoroughly miserable. I wish I had not spoken as I did to my mother. Gazing down at the enormous party of noblemen assembled for our arrival, each splendidly dressed and beautifully mounted, I should feel proud. Only a few months ago, Henry's barons made him the subject of ribald jests, and now, here they are, looking grave and respectful and entirely appropriate to welcome me and my relations home. But I feel maudlin. I am disappointed that Henry is not among them, even though I knew he would remain at Westminster. Henry would make me feel better and tell me I have done nothing wrong—even if I have. Instead, Richard is at the head of the welcoming party, looking tall, grave, and stately. His height always offends me, though his being taller than Henry is no more his fault than my being taller than my husband is mine. Whatever lingering anger Richard feels over Henry's revocation of the grant of Gascony, it is certainly not on display at the moment. With any luck, the gift of my sister to this man will wipe away all his resentment over lands lost.

Richard saw Sanchia last more than three years ago in my father's house. My figure blocks hers at the top of the plank, but as soon as I begin to descend, accompanied by the sound of trumpets, I see his eyes widen. The fool, he is practically salivating! When my mother, sister, and I are all assembled on dry land, I make the introductions.

"Lady Cynthia."

From the way Richard says her name—or what she must become accustomed to answering to on this strange English soil—before he kisses her hand, you would think he was a boy of nineteen who had never been wed before. As he helps her to her horse, I notice his hand lingers at her waist far longer than necessary. I may be sorry for my coarse language with my mother, but it is abundantly clear to me, and doubtless to all the gentlemen standing close by, that Earl Richard is already imagining his bride naked. Perhaps this is not so surprising because his last wife, though he loved her exceedingly, came to him at thirty and as a widow. He has never had a young woman and a virgin. Well, other than his mistresses, some of whom have been young. I will not speculate on their virginity.

I roll my eyes slightly at my mother, but she studiously ignores me.

With my sister mounted, we move off. There is no time to waste; Sanchia is to be married before month's end. There are thousands of dishes and details to be seen to as everything will be done with utmost style. Henry promised me in his last letter that my tailor works from sunup to sunset to make certain that my every garment for the celebrations will be talked about for weeks by the English gentlewomen. Riding at the head of the party along a road lined with my subjects, I see their eyes pass from me to admire my sister, who rides at Richard's side just behind me, and I wonder if expensive gowns will be enough.

HOW A MONTH MAY CHANGE everything! My sister is a sweet thing, willing to oblige me in everything. She has my looks bested, but is so shy that despite her loveliness she often seems to fade into the background when in company. I like her better for the fact that she never tries to outshine me.

As for Richard, thus far his pleasure in her, and in being a member of my family, has made his relations with Henry the easiest I have ever seen them. At the rate he is bedding Sanchia—who is as open to my suggestions for this activity as she is to my suggestions on mode of dress or English customs—I am hopeful there will be a full cradle within a year to seal the marriage in the most satisfactory way possible.

And my mother! The lady has a head for politics I aspire to

match. She knows exactly whom to flatter and whom to ignore. Looking down the table to where she listens to Simon de Montfort, her hand on his arm, her easy smile encouraging his confidences, I forget for a moment my apprehension that this Christmas banquet hosted by my brother-in-law and sister comes uncomfortably close to rivaling the lavish nature of the wedding banquet in their honor that I presided over. Indeed, let Richard spend his money to feed Henry and our court for once. He has certainly had his share of our treasury.

Sitting beside me, Henry spreads his fingers contentedly over his stomach. "I am completely satiated."

"Completely?" I place a hand on his thigh beneath the table. With our little Beatrice eighteen months old, Sanchia's is not the only belly I mean to see filled in the next months. As Uncle Peter reminded me recently, one son, even if he be a very sturdy boy, is not sufficient hedge against an uncertain future.

Henry's sleepy eye widens a little at my insinuation. "Eleanor, have I told you how lovely you look?"

I am wearing a new gown made from the lengths of glimmering ruby fabric that Uncle Thomas brought for me when he came for Sanchia's wedding. He brought the same for my mother and sister, and all three of us are clad in his offering for this banquet. While I approved of the idea as a show of family unity, a part of me chafes at the very direct comparison that dressing so similarly is bound to inspire. "As lovely as my sister?"

"Pshaw," Henry replies, "she cannot compare to you. She is too skinny. Clearly, I do not remind you often enough of your beauty."

I laugh at my husband's gallantry. It is an endearing gesture. He need not compliment me extravagantly to be in either my good graces or my bed, but the habit of pleasing me begun in the early days of our marriage has never left him. "You tell me often, sir, but I never tire of hearing it."

Henry is in as fine a mood as I have seen since our return from the miserable mess in Poitou. Amenable, I judge, to nearly anything. I look again in the direction of my mother and give an audible sigh.

"What troubles you, Eleanor?" Henry is all concern.

"I am not troubled, only a little saddened that the countess must leave us soon. Of course, I understand that my father cannot bear to be without her longer when he is ill, but she is a good companion to me and, I think, an asset to our court."

"You can have no doubt of my esteem for the Countess of Provence. In fact, I was thinking of making her a gift. Would four hundred pounds per annum please you?"

"Henry!" I lean to kiss his cheek, and he beams.

"I shall have the endowment drawn. Shall we say half a dozen years?"

"More than generous." And I *do* think it generous. But such a gift was not the topic I had in mind when I raised my mother's departure. That lady has impressed upon me, with Peter and Thomas at either elbow, the importance of securing a loan for my father from my husband. Ill though he is, the count is engaged in a military matter and short on funds. It would hardly seem grateful to raise that issue now, but I will find the moment for it.

"WALLINGFORD CERTAINLY IS A FINE castle." Henry stretches out on his back in my bed, hands clasped behind his head. With the firelight glinting in his beard and hair, I think he looks much younger than his thirty-six years.

"I am sure he remembers that he had it by your hand," I reply, rolling on my side to see him better.

"He is a good brother."

"Yes." I can agree without dissembling at present. There is no purpose in reminding Henry of past instances of less than perfect behavior on Richard's part. And with the help of God and Sanchia, there will be fewer such instances in future. "A fine and loyal family is a prize beyond measure."

"True." Henry rolls to face me and cups my cheek in his hand. "And you are the great architect of my family and thereby my happiness. By your relations, I have gained loyal advisers, a caring mother, and now a new sister; and by your body I have been blessed with three healthy children."

I feel a lump in my throat. Leaning forward, I give Henry a gentle kiss. "You must not forget, Henry, that you are in part the author of your own contentment as well as the source of all my own. Did you not marry me, love me, and take to your bosom all my kith and kin as if they were your own? These were none of them preordained things. My own sister Marguerite has not a single soul at her court who shares with her bonds of blood and kinship." I think to myself that, did not the duty of sisterly loyalty forbid it, I might say more—I might say that it does not seem to me that my sister's husband loves her very much.

A heat born of our moment of tenderness is rising between us. Already I know that a second coupling this evening is inevitable, and I welcome it. But before I surrender to my passions and to those of my husband, I cannot let this moment pass. After all, there has been so much talk of family. "Henry, I am worried about my father."

"He is ill, I know." Henry's voice is sympathetic, but his attention, like his hand, is already wandering to my breast.

"Yes, but he is also in need of better defenses. Have you given thought to my mother's request for a loan?"

"I want to give her the money, Eleanor"—Henry dips his head to kiss the hollow between my breasts—"but my council is worried about the security for such a loan."

"Mother said today that we might have castles for that and might select them ourselves."

"I have a castle in Provence. Why do I need more?"

"Because"—I kiss the side of his neck just below his earlobe—"you are married to an heiress of Provence." It pains me to speak of my father's death, and I pray it will not be for many years, but every man is mortal. "And when that day comes, we may need to defend our claim."

"You mean from Louis?" Henry is clearly interested in this new line of conversation. He pulls back far enough to look me squarely in the eyes again.

"The French king will want Provence; that is certain. It is greatly to his advantage to expand his territories in the south." I stroke Henry's chest soothingly. I want to press my point, but I do not want my husband to become so agitated over Louis that I cannot conclude it, or that his present mood is spoiled. After all, I am nearly as eager as he to be done with politics and on to matters of love.

"Can we take possession of the castles your father will give us as surety?"

I wrack my brain to remember what Uncle Peter said upon this point during the light of day. Henry does not help the situation as, during the pause, he begins to rub his hand between my thighs.

"Of course." If that was not the case, I think, my uncles will now have to make it so. "But let us leave those details to my uncles and to another time."

"Agreed." Henry begins to lower his head to my breast once again.

But I cannot be easy until I clarify the point. I arrest his head in both my hands. "You will make the loan?"

"Four thousand marks, just as your mother asked." It is amazing to me that he can remember the amount. But so it always is; his moments of political lucidity come and go at the most unpredictable of times.

As for my own head, with Henry's promise secured, I have not another moment to spare for politics—English or Provençal. I desire nothing more this night than satisfaction of my desire at the hands of my husband.

CHAPTER 12

My dearest Marguerite,

Each day I hope to hear that you are safely delivered of your child. I have paid for masses that the babe might be the son you have prayed for these ten years. Surely between your petitions and my own, God and his saints must tire of hearing the subject of a French prince sounded, and they will be glad to put an end to our entreaties by giving your husband an heir. . . .

I remain your devoted sister,
Eleanor

MARGUERITE
FEBRUARY 1244
PALAIS DU ROI, PARIS

Louis, my darling Louis! In a single instant you have made me happier than I have been in many years, and more powerful. I look down into the face of my son, only minutes old. He has downy golden hair, so fair that it is nearly without color. His solemn blue eyes return my gaze.

"I think he can *see*," Yolande remarks in amazement from where she stands beside me combing my hair.

I hope he can also hear. The bells have begun to ring all across Paris. Ringing hours before dawn. Waking the city's inhabitants.

The King of France, the greatest and most respected monarch in Christendom, has an heir at last—my son. *My* son.

"The king is coming!" Matilda exclaims, bustling into my bed-chamber from the room beyond.

"Is *she* with him?" I dare to ask, because Louis's Garde des Sceaux and the other officials who were present to see me delivered have withdrawn so that I can be made presentable. All my ladies know precisely whom I mean.

"No," my sister-in-law replies, her eyes sparkling, "you were delivered so quickly that she has not yet arrived at the palace."

"Good." This is *my* moment of triumph. I do not wish to share it with the dragon. "Clever Louis," I say, touching his tiny cheek, "born at night while your *grandmother* slumbered. Born with so little suffering compared to your sisters. Do you come to make me a true queen at last?"

I hand the baby to Elisabeth, pinch my cheeks, bite my lips, arrange the coverlets, and then take the baby back, nodding to Matilda. She throws open the door, and my husband strides in.

"Your Majesty"—I incline my head acknowledging the king—"you have a son."

"So I have heard, God and the Virgin be praised." Louis moves to the side of my bed, and my ladies scatter, bowing as they go. "You have done well, my lady wife."

As he looks down on me, I see a ghost of the former Louis in his eyes—a glimmer of warmth and enthusiasm, even of fondness. I wonder how to feed the spark into a blaze. Will this prince bring Louis back to me?

"Will Your Majesty sit?" The offer is more than idle *politesse.* Despite the authority with which Louis entered, he is frail. A bad bout of the sickness of the bowels that struck his men at the end of the Poitevin campaign did not spare him. Even a year and a half later, he is not fully recovered. But Louis, usually so calm, is too excited to be still. He moves around to the other side of the bed, a vantage point that allows him to see the baby's face.

"He is very pale."

"No indeed, Your Majesty, only fair and handsome like his father." I smile upward. "Will Your Majesty hold him?"

Louis hesitates. To encourage him, I hold the baby up. Louis takes the child with great care—the sort of care with which I have seen him handle the precious relics for his Sainte-Chapelle.

As if reading my mind, Louis says, "How I wish the palatine chapel were ready for his baptism." He seriously considers the prince for a few more moments, brow furrowed and lips pursed in concentration.

"I must strive to be a better king, for now I am an example to the next king."

I feel my heart soften toward this man, standing in the flickering candlelight, his son in his arms. True, he often neglects and underestimates me, but he is never deliberately hard upon me. He is *every day* hard upon himself.

"Your Majesty is acknowledged by all to be a great king. And, Louis, you are a good man." I say the last very quietly, so as not to embarrass him in front of my ladies who have withdrawn to a respectful distance. I hold my breath wondering if Louis will take my words as I mean them—as a mark of compassion and affection— or if he will find them patronizing. His mouth relaxes into a little smile, and I relax in turn.

Handing me the baby, Louis says, "You have given me, and indeed France, a great gift. What can I give you in return?"

I do not think the question is asked in earnest. And even if it were, to answer it openly, to lay myself bare, is more than I have strength to do. Besides, I know that Louis loves me in his way. He cannot love me differently, just because I need him to. So I give the gallant answer, "What can I want when I have Your Majesty for my husband?"

"Perhaps a fine piece of samite to wear when you are churched? So fine that all will know you are the mother of a prince."

Smiling up at Louis, I hope the cloth will be fine enough to make Blanche jealous, or at least to remind her that *I* am queen. I have been patient. And after nearly ten years and three hard-gained pregnancies, my patience has been rewarded. No one and nothing can threaten my position now. I can hardly wait to write to Eleanor.

IT IS DECEMBER, THE GRAYEST of months, the grayest of times for France and for me. Louis is sick. Louis is dying. How can a year that began so well have come to this?

Someone is shaking me. My heart rises to my throat. Is this the dreaded moment when someone rouses me to say that Louis is gone? No, it is only Marie, waking me to resume my vigil at the king's bedside. I rise in the watches of the night, unable to give an accurate count of how many times I have done so since Louis was taken ill here at Pontoise. Yolande, bleary-eyed and not yet completely awake herself, stirs the fire and warms some wine for me. Marie and Matilda dress me in silence. No one comments on the slight but obvious swelling of my belly as they might have in happier times, but I feel a small kick as the babe in my womb stirs. The only sound in my bedchamber is a whispered undercurrent of prayer. As things have grown more serious, Elisabeth has taken to praying continuously under her breath. I am not sure she is aware of this.

We make our way like specters up the spiral staircase to the king's rooms. His antechamber is full of people—counselors, royal physicians, and priests. There are so many priests. Louis's Grand

Chambellan, Jean de Beaumont-Gâtinais, ushers us into the bed-chamber. We keep this room as warm as we can, though I cannot see the sense in it. The king is on fire, burning with fever. Either Blanche or I am always with him. In this one thing the dragon and I cooperate. We trade places at the king's bedside without speaking. Each of us grim faced. Each of us frightened of the same thing but for different reasons. If Louis dies, I will be lost, and I will lose my precious son. The king has named a council of regents against such an eventuality, and I am not on it. I can accept having no hand in the governance of France, but at the thought of being able to see my child only when and if his guardians deem it prudent, tears rise to my eyes. Why, oh why did I think that the birth of a prince alone would change everything?

My women take the seats at the foot of Louis's bed vacated by Blanche's ladies. The light in the room is too poor for embroidery, but they must do something, or at least appear to, so they pull close their frames, left behind from our last visit to the sick chamber. Elisabeth alone makes no pretense of being occupied but sits staring straight ahead, mumbling.

I move my stool as close to Louis as I can. The smell is overpowering and awful. Yet it is still a smell of life—sweat, urine, and that distinctive odor taken on by the breath of the fevered. The bile rises in my throat, but I swallow it down, leaning closer still. If I do not want the baby within me to be born fatherless, I must try to keep Louis with us. I take one of Louis's hands and marvel at how thin it has become. The skin looks like parchment. I press it to my cheek.

"Louis? Louis, can you hear me?"

My husband does not stir. As recently as four days ago he had periods of lucidity and was strong enough to lament his own condition with clarity before slipping from consciousness. Then delirium became his constant companion. When awake, he no longer seemed to recognize any around him but merely cried out to the Lord as a child awakening from a nightmare might cry out for his mother. But for the last two days, there has been nothing; he has not spoken and no longer opens his eyes.

Slowly and softly I begin to talk. I tell Louis anything and everything that I can think of—that his brother Charles was thrown from his horse but suffered nothing more than bruises; how many teeth little Louis has; about the progress that the builders are making on his Sainte-Chapelle. I talk until I cannot think of another word to say. Then I sing. This I do until my throat is dry. Nothing rouses Louis.

Dawn comes—a gray dawn. A tray is brought for me and consommé for Louis. A priest helps to lift Louis's head and shoulders. I try to give him some, but his lips are flaccid and my efforts without effect. He lacks even the ability to suck wine from a knotted cloth, though he must thirst, for his lips are cracked and dry.

Stiff from sitting for so long, I rise and pace the room. Matilda joins me. "Your Majesty should take some rest. Leave us to watch over the king. This constant worry is not good for you in your condition. You might lose the baby."

"I am more worried about losing my husband," I snap. Matilda looks crestfallen, and I know I am being unfair. Matilda is a good sister and is only showing as much by her concern. More than this, her anxiety for my child arises from a recent loss of her own. After seven years of marriage, Robert of Artois finally made her pregnant in the spring. But she took sick with rubeola and lost the babe shortly after she first felt it move. "Listen," I say, taking both her hands in my own. "I have slept and I have eaten. Do not ask me to leave Louis. You would not leave Robert."

"No," she concedes.

Around the time of Terce, Princess Isabelle glides into the room.

She is dressed so simply that she might be mistaken for a *béguine*. Going immediately to a small altar that has been erected along the wall behind me, she kneels in prayer. When she is finished, she rises in silence and sits beside me, taking my hand. For a long time we were not friends, and I am not sure that we are now, but we have come to an understanding. Nearly two years ago, surviving an illness as serious as that which now threatens her brother, she offered herself as an obligation to God. The dragon was entirely against the idea and ordered, cajoled, and ranted accordingly. A match was already being arranged for Isabelle with the emperor's eldest son—a match forwarded by the Holy Father. But Isabelle would not be bullied, and when I saw her stand up to Blanche in a way that Louis, ten years her senior, never could, she gained my admiration and support. She in turn has not forgotten that I took her part.

Some moments later Isabelle starts. A gasp escapes her lips. She turns to me, her eyes wide. "I do not think he breathes!"

Jumping up, I lean forward over Louis as all my ladies rush to the bed. His face is ashen. I can detect nothing—no rise and fall of his chest, no fevered-hot breath on my cheek as, hovering over him, I turn it to his mouth.

"A priest." I hear Matilda's voice as if she stood a league away and not merely by the bedchamber door.

Isabelle, who rose with me, takes my hand again in hers as I straighten up and look down into the vacant face of my husband. I feel a tear run down my cheek and then another. I must be crying. Yolande moves to the side of the bed opposite me and says in a low voice, "What shall we do? How shall we confirm it?"

I sense a commotion at the door. Turning, I see a priest as well as Jean de Soissons and several other noblemen. All appear stricken. None proceed more than a few steps into the room.

"Is he dead?" de Soissons stammers.

"Your Majesty, shall I cover His Majesty's face?" Yolande's voice is very calm. She lifts the edge of the sheet covering the king, waiting for my word to draw it up.

I cannot find my voice. I do not have to.

Louis sits up.

At the foot of the bed, Elisabeth collapses in a heap and is left where she lies.

"A cross." The voice is weak but it is unmistakably Louis's. "Give me a cross."

My entire body is shaking, but I move as swiftly as I can to Louis's altar and take up a cross of Poitevin silver lying there.

"Your Majesty," I say, holding the cross out to Louis. My hand shakes.

His hand, shaking likewise, rises slightly off the bed's surface, hovers, and then falls again. He has not the strength to lift it. Taking his right hand in my left, I raise it for him, just high enough that I may place the cross against his palm. His pale fingers curl reflexively around it. I place his hand, still clutching the cross, on his lap.

"He has taken the cross," exclaims Yolande's husband, Hugh, Duke of Burgundy.

"God, the Holy Virgin, and all the saints be praised," cries the priest, falling to his knees, hands uplifted.

Slowly all the men who entered at word of Louis's demise go down on their knees as well. Turning to the priest, Hugh of Burgundy asks, "Father, have you a cross for me as well?"

Yolande stares at me from the other side of the bed, across the miraculously reanimated figure of my husband. Both of us know without speaking what this means.

Crusade.

———

"NO, NO, NO, NO!" BLANCHE is apoplectic. I am stunned by her continued resistance to Louis's pledge. After all, *she* is the author of Louis's religious zealotry. And she was raised at the court of Castile during the *reconquista*, a holy war to reconquer territories on the Iberian Peninsula lost to Muslims—a war her father, Alfonso VIII, fiercely led.

It is two weeks since the king miraculously escaped death. Louis is well enough to be out of bed. He sits near the fire, wrapped in all manner of furs, and I sit beside him. Because his eyes tire easily, I was reading out loud to him when Blanche arrived.

"You cannot leave your kingdom ungoverned," Blanche says, pacing furiously. "You are needed here."

"It will not be ungoverned. You shall be regent in my absence."

This promise with all the power it encompasses does nothing to assuage Blanche. She stops in front of us, her cold, gray eyes narrowed to slits and her mouth turned fiercely downward. "You will not survive such foolishness. Look at you—you are too weak to read, let alone ride. Too weak to return to Paris to hold a Christmas court at month's end."

"I do not leave at once. There are preparations to be made. Mine will be the best organized and best provisioned expedition. What I do to fulfill my oath I will do wholeheartedly."

Blanche opens her mouth, but before she can say a thing, a timid knock sounds. "Enter." Blanche does not wait for Louis but gives the command herself.

The door opens to reveal the squat figure of Mincia, the dragon's ancient Spanish attendant. "William of Auvergne," she announces.

I am entirely surprised. Why would the bishop of Paris come

to Pontoise, a distance of more than ten leagues, in frigid winter weather? I can see by the look on Louis's face that he is puzzled as well. Blanche, however, does not so much as raise an eyebrow. She takes a deep breath, nearly a sigh of relief, then says, "Send him in."

A pleasant smile raises the corner of the bishop's thin lips at his first sight of Louis. He is genuinely fond of my husband. Then, as if he recollects something, the smile passes and he takes on a serious mien.

"Your Majesty, I praise God for your recovery. When I left Paris, thousands were offering similar prayers of thanksgiving."

"I am gratified to hear it, Your Excellency. I am thankful myself that Our Lord has seen fit to give me more time to do his work."

"Yes . . ." The bishop hesitates. "I understand that upon regaining your senses, Your Majesty took the cross."

"Indeed, it is so."

"And now you intend to fulfill your oath."

"Yes, sparing no expense, not of money, skill, nor even of blood."

I see the dragon wince visibly at the mention of blood.

"I must respectfully urge Your Majesty to reconsider." The bishop speaks softly, soothingly, as if Louis were still very ill.

"Oaths are not subject to reconsideration."

"With deepest humility, Your Majesty, let me suggest that you are mistaken. An oath taken under great duress, when a man is not himself, may be set aside without any compromise of dignity or any fear of divine disapproval. But if Your Majesty cannot be easy based on my word, I would be happy to write to the Holy Father at Lyon and ask him to offer you a release from your pledge."

"You think I was not myself?" Louis asks, his voice cold.

"They say, Your Majesty, that you had ceased to breathe. Your body was in the most extreme of circumstances, and your soul was very near to leaving it."

"I ask you again—do you think I was not myself?"

"I only suggest the possibility, Your Majesty."

"And I tell you"—a spot of color marks each of Louis's cheeks and his voice rises slightly—"that I was never *more* myself than at that moment! But I see that *some* will not be satisfied by my protestations." The king casts a withering look at Blanche. Then, turning back to William of Auvergne, he continues. "So I ask you now, while I am in full possession of my faculties if not yet returned to my full strength, and with these queens as my witnesses, to give me the cross."

The dragon blanches noticeably. She glares at William of Auvergne in a most intimidating manner. But what can the poor bishop do? Glancing about, he spots a crucifix on Louis's makeshift altar. Lifting it, he brings the crucifix forward and offers it to the king. Louis takes it in both hands and holds it fast.

"Your Majesty," I say, "I too would take the cross and share your work in the Holy Land as I share your life in France."

Blanche gasps. She has been outmaneuvered and knows it. She cannot possibly travel to the Holy Land with us. Now is my time and this is my battle—to use Louis's crusade to liberate not only Jerusalem but myself.

I smile sweetly as Louis turns to me with a beatific look and passes me the cross.

CHAPTER 13

My dearest sister,

Word of the King of France's miraculous recovery greatly relieves us all. I do not except Henry from that statement. Much as your husband and he are not on terms of cordiality since that business in Poitou, as Henry loves me and I love you, he could not be easy while Louis was in mortal peril. He has asked repeatedly for news of Louis in his letters from Scotland. What pleasure it gave me to be able to reply with news of the King of France's turn for the better and his resolution to undertake a crusade.

It is rumored that you will go to the Holy Land with your kingly husband. Tell me at once if there is truth in this. The Earl Richard has been, of course, and never stops boasting of his doings there, though he is back from crusade nearly three years. Still, if Richard's bragging is tiresome, his stories also paint pictures of countless wondrous sights. Should you really travel with Louis, you must promise to write to me with every detail of your journey so that it will be as if I am there with you.

Yours,
Eleanor

ELEANOR
DECEMBER 1244
PALACE OF WESTMINSTER, ENGLAND

Despite the bitter cold, I am out in the courtyard when Henry and Uncle Thomas ride in with their men. A war has been averted. This much I know, but I long to hear every detail.

"Eleanor." Henry's voice is filled with pleasure, and he kisses me despite the fact he is covered in dust. "How fine you look! How is my little son?" He pats my round belly with a possessive pride, heedless of the immodesty of the gesture when we are surrounded by men-at-arms.

"He is very well, sir, and glad, as is his mother, to have you back. I feared you would not return before I was delivered." Henry has been to the north, drawn there by the Scottish king's fortification of his border and by complaints from English merchants of Scottish piracy. Uncle Thomas marshaled a Flemish force in my husband's support and made a tidy sum by it. But, despite baronial complaints, his men were clearly worth my husband's money as a long war would surely have cost more than four thousand pounds. I give my uncle a blinding smile, and he offers me one in return. "Will Your Majesty and the Count of Flanders take some refreshment in my hall? I can have cold meats and every sort of good thing laid in my rooms while you refresh yourselves from the road."

"A fine idea." Henry rubs his hands in anticipation.

I myself can hardly wait, for surely when the three of us are closeted together we will discuss the treaty. I bustle toward my apartment, giving orders as I go.

The repast begins pleasantly enough. Henry has shed the dirt of the road and is in a fine mood. He starts to lay out details of the treaty with the Scots, punctuated with stories of its negotiation.

My uncle, content to play a supporting role, offers embellishments now and again, usually in the form of a fact or description showing the king to best advantage.

My husband clearly enjoys telling the tale and I enjoy hearing it, until he reaches a certain detail. I stare with utter disbelief at Henry as he sits at my table, a piece of fowl halfway to his mouth. For a single moment I allow myself to believe that I imagined his last words. Then he turns his eyes from mine to studiously examine the newly painted wainscoting, and I know by his discomfort that I did not mishear.

"How could you! How could you betroth Margaret?" Angry tears stream down my face. "She is only four years old. Just a baby." I slam my fist down on the table so hard that my uncle's cup goes over. Henry's eyes snap back to me.

"She does not go now," he replies. "We have agreed on the precise location of the line dividing England and Scotland. Scottish sieges along the border will stop. Alexander the Second will keep the York agreements. And in return, Princess Margaret will marry Prince Alexander of Scotland but *not for seven years.*"

"She is not a point in a treaty; she is your daughter!" I am so angry that my sentences come out strangely broken. Not a letter, not a hint did I have of this! How could such an important decision have been made without discussion?

"Eleanor." My uncle tries to place his hand over mine where it lies, still curled in a fist, on the table, but I shake him off. Undeterred, he continues. "Women marry. You know that. And they do so to the advantage of their families and their kingdoms, as you did yourself."

I have a nearly overwhelming urge to strike him. I know he is right, but all I can think of is my quiet, gentle little girl with eyes so wide and so blue one could swim in them. The thought of being parted from her is unbearable, whether now or in seven years. I bury my face in both my hands and sob.

"I thought this match would please you." Henry's voice betrays utter confusion, and the fact that he does not understand my feelings angers me again.

"Nonsense!" I snap, dropping my hands from my face. "You did not think of me at all." I bore my eyes into Henry's, wishing my gaze could shame him into repenting of his decision. He shifts in his seat and, when I continue to stare, rises from it and paces away from the table.

"On the contrary, Niece." My uncle's glance shifts from my husband's back to my face. His eyes are stern, a visual reprimand. "His Majesty raised your feelings at several turns. He was quite content to have the Princess Margaret settled so close on your account."

"How can you call it close when you rode nearly one hundred leagues just to get to the Scottish border?"

"But there will be no ocean between us." It is Henry who answers. He has turned back to face me. "Believe me, Eleanor—I have no more desire than you do to be a stranger to our child."

"But must His Majesty fight the Scots today over something that can be settled with a promise that need not be kept for more years than the princess has yet been alive?" asks my uncle.

I wipe my eyes and face with my napkin.

"We have seen the prince, Eleanor," Henry says, moving back toward the table. "He is a fine-looking lad, just a child himself, a year younger than Margaret." He comes around behind me and puts a hand on my shoulder—very lightly. No doubt he fears I will throw it off.

"And she stays with us until the wedding?"

"Yes." He squeezes my shoulder. "You really must try to calm yourself. Such agitation is not good for you or for the child."

My eyes drop to my swollen belly. Be this babe boy or girl, it too will have to leave me one day. That is the way of things and I must resign myself to it. Covering Henry's hand on my shoulder with my own, I look up into his face. "I want to go to Windsor."

"Eleanor, you should not be on the road in your condition. Let me send for the children. Let me have them brought here."

I nod gratefully; unable to speak for fear that I will start crying again. I do not want to miss another moment of my children's infancy, which now appears to me more fleeting than I ever imagined. I want to hold Margaret in my arms and tousle her curls. I will not mention Scotland or its prince to her—not yet.

THE CHRISTMAS COURT HAS BEGUN. The children, surprised by their father's summons, are delighted to be with us for the festivities, and their high spirits have restored mine. Edward is fascinated by the jongleurs. When it is his turn to ask a favor from his father the king in keeping with the season's traditions, he asks for a set of colorful balls of his very own. Margaret does not know if many of the entertainments delight or terrify her. This is particularly true of the mummers. She hides behind my shirts, frightened whenever they play for us, but when I try to remove her from the room, she pleads to stay. The entire Palace of Westminster glows. And more than the palace is alight at this darkest time of year.

"A thousand! A thousand candles before Saint Thomas Becket's shrine," says Sybil, beaming as she takes off my veil after another evening of revelry. "Day and night they burn."

"And the abbot at Bury Saint Edmunds has all his monks on their knees, praying for Your Majesty," Isabel adds, removing my shoes and rubbing my swollen ankles and feet.

As my fourth confinement looms, Henry wants a second son, and all of England knows it. What all of England does not know is that, in the last days, he has become fixedly concerned with my health. The obsession began in the wake of my violent reaction to the treaty with the Scots. After that sudden upset, I developed a fever, doubtless the result of crying for hours while I awaited the children's arrival from Windsor. I was put to bed and recovered in two short days, but the terror awakened in my husband by my brief incapacity dogs him still.

"If I should *lose* you, Eleanor," he fretted this evening as we watched the members of our court dance a *carole*. "If I should lose *you*."

And so he lights candles for a prince and for my safety.

My women leave me ensconced in a chair, my feet up on a stool and swaddled in furs against any possible chill, and Henry arrives in turn. He takes a seat beside me before my fire. When I mention my ladies' wonder and delight over all the fuss, he takes my hand. "The candles at Saint Augustine's are for you," he tells me, "for your safety alone." And I know that he does not say so to flatter, because despite his being only recently returned after a long absence, he has no congress with me. Yet every night he comes to sit with me, as he has this evening, and never fails to tuck me into my bed before leaving.

"Talk to me about the abbey," I say, leaning my head back against the chair and allowing my eyes to close. We have some glorious projects planned for this year, and a new prince is but the first. Henry will rebuild the abbey at Westminster. He made up his mind to do so before departing for the north and sent me many pages from the Scottish border filled with his ideas for the project. With his naturally discerning eye, the results must perforce be magnificent, and I am glad. There has been *so* much talk of the French king's half-built chapel and of all the relics my sister's husband has paid out a fortune to obtain for it.

"I have been thinking, we ought to secure a new relic for the abbey's rededication," Henry says. "Something to lie beside the bones of the innocents."

"A marvelous idea!" My eyes snap back open, and I turn eagerly to my husband. "But it must be an object of the most superior sort, something so stunning that it will make King Louis's piece of the crown of thorns seem nothing but a bit of bramble."

Henry chuckles slightly, then looks guilty. We both know my comment is hardly in keeping with Christian humility. But Henry wants the abbey to be grand, not only to honor the Confessor but to show that his piety is as great as any other king's—even Louis's. It is incomprehensible to me that his reputation on this point is not already secure. My husband hears Mass four times a day nearly every day, and lately has been feeding five hundred paupers daily as well. Why do the Benedictines at Saint Albans never chronicle that!

"I have appointed Henry de Reyns, as your uncle suggested," my husband continues.

"You got him!"

"He will arrive from France as soon as the weather permits. And when he is here, we will set about making Westminster everything. Not only a place where my son, his son, and so on for a thousand years will be crowned, but a mighty shrine to the Confessor and a place where English kings may lie in peace when their work is done."

I feel a shiver run up my spine. The tremor must be observable, for Henry asks, "Are you warm enough?"

"Yes." I squeeze his hand. "Only pray do not speak to me of tombs."

I regret the remark the minute I utter it. I did not wish to think of Henry's death, but his mind turns immediately to mine. "Heaven help me, I begin to regret you ever conceived this child!"

"Henry, you need another son," I say, trying to calm him.

"I know, but how shall I look upon him if he kills you?"

"I have a facility for giving birth. You know that. Sybil says I was made for it."

Henry mumbles something indistinct and crosses himself.

"When," I ask, trying to turn Henry's mind back to Westminster, "will the workmen begin to take down the present church?"

Henry's eyes continue to reflect abject despair, but he answers, "They will begin inside while it is still cold and breach the outer walls as spring arrives."

"Spring—now there is a glorious thought! I mean to spend the spring at Windsor, suckling this new babe in the shade of my gardens and directing the work there. You are not the only one with grand plans for a renovation, Henry."

"And in celebration of your safe delivery, I will pay for your renovations," Henry says, his looks lightening at last, "and you shall have another full-time gardener to order about. Will that please you?"

"Immensely. And when you come to visit, you can help me plant a tree for each among our brood. Trees that will by example inspire, with God's help, our children's little bodies to grow straight and true."

IT IS ACCOMPLISHED! WE HAVE a second son—an Edmund to join our Edward. My five-and-a-half-year-old prince, who returned to Windsor Castle immediately after Twelfth Night, sends a dutiful letter congratulating his father and me; or rather the head of my son's household writes and sends such a letter. It seems highly unlikely my son himself would be so effusive. With two younger sisters ensconced at Windsor with him, he is already savvy enough to know that babies take a while to make good playfellows, and until this baby is "good for something," Edward is not likely to show much interest in him.

I look down at Edmund, nursing vigorously at my breast. The time before he will be old enough to run and play in Windsor's gardens seems distant, but I know that it will pass with the speed of a hunter pursuing his falcon. What sort of boy will Edmund be? Doubtless he and Edward will be opposites. That is the way of children, no two alike, and already there is little in this second son that reminds me of my first. For one thing he is much smaller.

Well, never mind, I think, stroking the side of his tiny face with my first finger. *I am sure that all the milk I can give and the pure air of Windsor will soon cure that.* And in any event, being opposites is no bar to being boon companions or the closest of friends. Marguerite and I are proof of that.

CHAPTER 14

My dear Eleanor,

I begin to see the beneficial effects of our great undertaking. Not yet to the Holy Land perhaps, but to His Majesty. The king's full strength and vivacity are nearly returned, and all his considerable skills turn to the matter of raising armies, carrying them to the Holy Land, and keeping them in the field once they are arrived. Juste à côté de Montpellier he has begun to build a new port devoted entirely to our embarkation. It is most unfortunate that the name of some nearby marshes has attached itself to the project. Aigues-Mortes seems hardly an auspicious name for a place from which men will depart for battle.

And I? Besides being swollen nearly to bursting with this child, I am also very happy. Because I will travel with the king to the Holy Land and because I work hard now to help him recruit the necessary force of men-at-arms, Louis has more time and more patience for me than he has had in many a year. I feel certain that only two things are needed to secure my newly elevated position and perhaps, dare I hope, my husband's genuine affection: a second prince to secure Louis's line, and our separation from Blanche by a wide expanse of ocean. As one of these is a thing certain and the second is surely possible, as you have just proved by the birth of your darling Edmund, I view the

restoration of my early marital contentment as a thing within
reach.

Yours,
M

---·•·---

MARGUERITE
APRIL 1245
PONTOISE, FRANCE

I sit in the gardens, utterly exhausted. We have been recruiting,
Louis and I. Enthusiasm for his crusade burns in the king like a
flame. But it has been precious hard to ignite the same passion in
others. The Holy Father is more interested in crusading against
Emperor Frederick, and would have Louis join him. But all His
Holiness's cajoling has failed to turn my husband in that direction.
Louis will not be dissuaded from the Holy Land by anyone. So we
work to enlist the support of our vassals. *We* work. It seems that my
decision to take the cross is helping my husband. Men are more
inclined to go far from home if they can take their wives with them
as a source of comfort. A fact which, sadly, seems to mystify my
husband. But never mind that, as, since I am useful to his efforts, I
am much in favor at present.

I could be quite content if it were not for the English. In Louis's
eagerness to broaden the support for his crusade, he sent a call for
knights to my sister's kingdom. No one is coming. The English, it
seems, still sting from their defeat in Poitou, though two years have
passed. I cannot account for it, however I try, and it goads me.
After all I did to soften Louis's view of the English king and his
followers! I own I expected Eleanor to be grateful. But why should
I have? Eleanor has cared more for winning than any person I have

known since she was a slip of a girl. Control of her temper came only with age, and well can I remember lying facedown on a path in my mother's garden with Eleanor on top of me, fists flailing, because I had beaten her in some childish pastime. So, while the personal amity between Eleanor and me was restored shortly after the peace, my sister declines to push her husband or his knights to crusade with my husband.

I sigh, tired of worrying about my sister's obstinacy. Leaning back on the stone bench, I turn my face upward to the weak April sun and close my eyes. I imagine how much warmer the sun must be at Aix as I wait for Marie who has gone to get me a cloak and Yolande who will bring a small stool for my feet, insisting that, given my condition, they should be off the cold ground.

I hear a crunching on the gravel path.

"Your Majesty."

My eyes fly open and my head snaps up. The Seneschal of Champagne is standing not five feet from where I sit. "Sieur de Joinville!" I am normally known for my elocution, but the name comes out very haltingly indeed.

"Forgive me, Your Majesty. I did not mean to startle you. You are looking very well."

I am suddenly, horribly, conscious of my appearance. Only weeks away from giving birth, I am like a ripe pear, and no amount of finery donned for my meetings with visiting nobles can disguise the fact. I have not seen Jean de Joinville in four years, and now for him to see me like this!

"I am very close to my confinement," I blurt out, without considering either the appropriateness of my comment or its superfluous nature.

"So I see." De Joinville laughs. As the laughter is warm and lacks any touch of ridicule, it relaxes rather than offends me. "His

Majesty must be delighted. Sadly, I have not yet had the pleasure of being a father."

"What are you doing here?" I ask, again heedless of propriety.

"Well, I hear there is to be a crusade." His eyes sparkle teasingly. He is more mature now; his jaw firmer; his stance more confident. He is altogether charming.

"You will join us?" I feel my cheeks grown warm with pleasure. I could say they do so because every man Louis gathers behind his banner is important, but I would be lying.

"How could I fail to when I heard that my queen was going? I am at least as brave as she is."

"Then His Majesty and I shall see more of you."

"Most assuredly."

Oh, how I wish the *nefs* were ready at this moment. But as it is, even the port from which they will eventually sail is not completed.

Before either of us can speak again, there is a sound of someone approaching. Marie and Yolande round a nearby corner. Marie says nothing. She sees only a seneschal conversing with his queen.

Yolande, however, has wise eyes. "It seems we have left Your Majesty too long." She bustles forward and gives de Joinville a sharp look before continuing. "You ought to be inside where it is warmer."

Instead of putting down the stool tucked under her arm, she reaches out to help me rise. But I will have none of that. I am no invalid to be hauled up. I rise unaided and, I hope, gracefully despite my size and shape.

"You will excuse me, Sieur."

"Of course, Your Majesty." He gives a bow, then waits respectfully for my ladies and me to pass. Do I imagine it, or as we do so, does his hand brush the skirt of my gown?

THIS TIME I REALLY AM dying. It is not the pain that tells me so. The pain of birth no longer has the ability to either surprise or terrify me. No, it is the tone of the murmurings, and the expressions on faces around me that tell me something is wrong. Faces that include Louis's. Louis has never before been with me during my lyings-in. It is neither a man's place nor a king's. There is a false brightness in Louis's looks. It has been there ever since he entered. I wonder who summoned him.

At first all seemed well. I was struck with my pains midmorning and took to my bed around midday. My midwife rubbed my belly and the insides of my legs with oil, and all the women who faithfully attend me at such times gathered about. From that point it was expected I would deliver quickly. The milk was warmed for the washing of a new child. It is too early in the year for rose petals.

After what seems like an eternity of pushing, my baby still has not come. Lying limp in another short, blissful, lull between pains, I feel a sudden sting as the midwife opens a vein at my ankle to bleed me. Elisabeth is praying audibly to Saint Margaret. I close my eyes.

"What ails her?" The voice is Louis's, and the concern is gratifyingly real.

"Your Majesty, the child is prodigiously large. Much larger than His Highness the prince. The position is good, but Her Majesty's strength fails. I think we must pull the child forth."

"Then do so."

I can feel the woman's hand upon me and then inside me. The ordinary agony of such a thing seems oddly muted, though my eyes do spring open and find Louis's face. He looks pale as death.

Yolande and Matilda raise me from my prone position,

propping my back up against pillows at the head of my bed. The next pain grips me, they pull back upon my knees, and once more I strain to produce the baby. As I do so, I feel a sudden and excruciating pressure. The midwife has tied something around the babe within me, and she is pulling with all her strength. I can see the muscles in her sinewy arms shining with sweat and effort in the fading red-colored daylight. I scream wildly and stop pushing, but to no effect. The midwife is relentless.

"Push," she cries.

And when I do not, Yolande places both her hands on my belly and presses with all her might, while the midwife hauls the child out of me inch by agonizing inch.

Then I am gone.

When I regain consciousness, my first thought is that there is blood everywhere—all about me, on my legs, on my sheets.

Louis has hold of my hand. "We have another prince," he says, his blue eyes searching my face. What is he looking for? "I do not know if she hears me."

Yolande leans over me, and I try to focus my eyes on her. "She breathes."

"There has been much blood lost."

I cannot locate the figure attached to this voice.

Suddenly there is someone beside Louis. It is the dragon. Her voice I hear all too clearly. "Come away, Your Majesty. You can do nothing here." She has her hand on Louis's shoulder; he turns toward her. Again she admonishes him, "Come." He rises.

"No!" Without knowing how I got so, I am sitting up. "I see how it is! Whether in living or in dying you will not let me see my lord!"

Louis turns back, a look of panicked contrition on his face. I have won.

But then I know no more.

When I awake, it is dear Yolande's face hovering above me, not His Majesty's.

"Am I dead?" The sound of my own voice brings me an answer, for surely if I were a corpse being prepared for burial, I could not speak.

"No indeed," Yolande replies. "Though it was with greatest difficulty that the midwife brought you round." She sounds almost smug. "Once she did, His Majesty would not leave you but ordered his mother from your rooms in a tone I have never heard before."

I can remember none of this.

Perhaps sensing as much, Yoland continues. "You delivered three days ago." She offers me something to drink. "Prince Philippe is a magnificent child." She smiles again.

Philippe? Who is Philippe? She must mean my little Louis. Then I recollect myself. "Is that what the king calls him?"

"Indeed. After Philippe Augustus who was also a mighty thing."

CHAPTER 15

My dearest Marguerite,

Henry's letters sound much alike. He is grown tired of North Wales and of separation from myself and our children. Gratifying sentiments to be sure, as I do miss him terribly, but not what I most wanted to hear. His last, however, brought the news I have been waiting and praying for. A truce has been reached with Dafydd ap Llywelyn. The king and his men are on their way home. My heart celebrates, and I count the days until Henry can reasonably be expected, cheating in the king's favor by assuming nothing but good weather and good roads.

Yours,
Eleanor

ELEANOR
AUTUMN 1245
WINDSOR CASTLE, ENGLAND

"I love no place in the world so much as this nursery."

"No one doubts it, Your Majesty," replies Edward's nurse. She glances at me, sitting on the floor, with a slight shake of her head, but early in the prince's six years Lady Alice learned it was useless to suggest more dignified—or, as she liked to couch things, "comfortable"—arrangements. Beatrice sits before me, attempting to stuff a hand full of my skirt into her mouth. Her nurse, once my own, shuffles forward to extricate her.

"Leave her, Agnes," I say. "She does no harm." A mother four times over, I am too smart to wear my best things into the nursery.

"Why does Beatrice eat everything?" my little Margaret asks. At five she is such a solemn thing. She is pretty, but always wears an expression that suggests she is puzzling over something.

"Because that is what babes of two do."

"She looks like one of my dogs." Edward laughs, and so do the rest of us, which greatly assists me in removing the fabric from between Beatrice's teeth.

Now Edward is barking and racing up and down the room. Beatrice, standing up, toddles after him, yipping delightfully. Margaret takes the opportunity to claim Beatrice's place, sitting down and sliding close to me, until she leans against my side. "How fine and tall your brother is getting," I say.

"Will I be as tall as Edward?"

"No, my darling." I run my hand through her hair, even though I know that being tousled offends her juvenile sense of order. "Princes are taller than princesses."

"But you are taller than Father, and he is king."

This time I laugh so hard that I cry. She is right, of course. When I came to England, I looked up at Henry, but I have grown and he has not, and now I am the taller one. "It is time to learn the role of diplomat, my girl," I say, shaking my head slightly. "Some things we observe and keep to ourselves—women, I mean. Nothing good can come of reminding your father of my advantage in height. Men like to feel taller even when they are not."

Margaret turns this information over for a moment, her little face scrunched in concentration. "Do men like to feel wider too? Because Father is certainly that."

"I think I cut a fine figure." The voice from behind startles me.

"Henry!" I am on my feet in an instant, but my quickness avails me nothing. The children reach Henry before I do and are upon him like hounds on cornered prey. The king's eyes are alight and he is laughing. Then he glances at me and something changes. His eyes grow flat and his smile has a look of labor about it.

"Agnes, Alice, Mary, the children will tire His Majesty." The nurses rush forward, each to collect her own charge. Henry sends the girls off with a kiss and Edward with an exchange of solemn bows.

"Henry, the road home has fatigued you," I say with concern.

"Nonsense." But his eyes avoid mine when I try to find them.

I begin to feel uneasy. My stomach gives an odd little flip that has nothing to do with the babe inside it. In the nine years of our marriage, Henry has never taken up with another woman, but perhaps being so far away . . . I fight down the combination of anger and panic that rises in my throat like bile, threatening to choke off my breath. If I do not calm myself, I will have one of my breathing episodes.

"Shall we go out and visit your gardens? The sun is warm today." The invitation is correct in every particular—exactly what I would expect Henry to ask me and jovial in tone. But still I sense something. When I rest my hand on Henry's arm, the hand he places over mine seems tentative.

Windsor's gardens are a wonder. They are my favorite among all the gardens of the royal residences. But today, instead of seeing the new beds that have been added by my direction, my eyes are drawn to the patches of autumn leaves that have collected along the bottoms of the shrubs. "Edmund has begun to crawl."

"Has he! Well, the Confessor be praised."

Our second son, born at the start of the year, seems to be rather late in doing some of the ordinary things. His back is not straight. Henry and I are both concerned by it.

We walk in silence for a few moments. Then Henry says, "Eleanor, I have something unpleasant to tell you—something I wish for all the world I did not have to say."

I stare particularly hard at the withered foliage of my rosebushes.

"Your father has died."

My eyes rise to my husband's face to find his wet with tears.

"When?"

"August."

"But I have had no word!" I say in disbelief.

"That is my doing, I fear."

"Why?" My voice cracks as I speak, yet I do not cry. I am too stunned. My father has been dead two months, perhaps a bit more, without my knowing? How can it be possible?

"How could I let them tell you when I was not here?"

The sobs break loose from me with force. Henry pulls me to him, and I lean my head on his shoulder. "I have had masses said for the count every day since I heard. And I have dispensed alms."

I have not seen my father in nearly ten years, and I knew that he ailed. Many times before this moment, as he wasted ill, I thought that he must die. But now, in my mind's eye, I can only see him hale and hearty, dressed for my departure. "You will always be *my* Eleanor," he said, "even if you are also England's."

CHAPTER 16

My dearest Marguerite,

    I continue to ache. Not only in my heart, but in every limb. If I could but see you. See our sisters and our mother. If we could but be together at Aix. Surely in a place so full of Father and our memories of him, this burden of sorrow would be eased. As it is, I am wont to break into tears at the slightest provocation and then be regarded strangely for doing so, at least by some. I was glad that you wrote in such detail of the sepulcher you commissioned for Father. Though neither of us was present to see him laid to rest in it, it gives me a measure of peace to know that he lies at the Eglise de Saint Jean de Jérusalem in Aix in such splendor and dignity. I pray that it likewise comforts you.

Your devoted sister,
Eleanor

MARGUERITE
DECEMBER 1245
CLUNY, FRANCE

After four months I still cannot believe that my father is dead. He is dead, and has left me *nothing*.

All the grief I felt at his passing has hardened inside me, hardened into a tenacity of purpose as strong as the stone I selected for his sepulcher. By my father's bequest, the whole of the County of Provence belongs to my youngest sister, Beatrice, or will upon her marriage.

Well, I will not be deprived of my rights so easily! My father may have had the legal right to dispose of Provence and his unencumbered worldly goods however he wished, but what he had already promised to others he had no right to give, upon his death, to Beatrice. At very least, the unpaid portion of my dowry is therefore owed me as a debt, and I shall insist upon its payment. If my sister has not the ready money, then she can surrender the castles that secured the pledge. This is what I plan to press for presently, with Louis's help, but I want more; I want one-quarter of the lands in which I was born and raised.

My horse stumbles slightly, bringing my attention back to the road. I pull my dun-colored balandrana more tightly closed at the neck. We are passing through the gates at Cluny. Anyone bothering to look up from his business at the sound of our horses would see a party of nobles and suspect nothing more. We have ridden nearly one hundred thirty leagues in anonymity because ours is a secret delegation. Ahead, on a slight rise, I can see our destination, a massive abbey. I notice a distinctive octagonal bell tower standing in sharp relief against the slate gray winter sky.

Inside the courtyard, my uncles Boniface and Philippe are waiting. They arrived with His Holiness the Pope a few days ago. They are each archbishops now: Philippe of Lyon where Pope Innocent IV recently held his great Council of the Church, and Boniface of Canterbury in Eleanor's England.

Eleanor. A lump rises in my throat at the thought of my sister and the deception we practice upon her. She does not know of this meeting. Does not know that Uncle Boniface, whom her husband has promoted to such wealth and power, is here. I force the lump down. I am sorry that Eleanor was betrayed by our father, as I was. It smacks of injustice that her interests will be overlooked at this meeting, but it is up to her husband and not to me to press for what is rightfully hers. She will doubtless be vexed when she finds that Louis and I have taken possession of Tarascon, but it is not my fault that our father pledged the same castle twice, and my claim on it predates her own.

Besides, Eleanor knows as well as I do that Henry of England was prepared to take her without a dowry. From all she has written me over the years, I can hardly imagine he will put her aside now because there is trouble over her marriage portion. No, Eleanor has an adoring husband; she can well afford to let me have the castle at Tarascon.

Uncle Philippe comes over as I dismount. "Your Majesty."

"Your Grace." Despite the bone-chilling cold and my fatigue from the road, I cannot resist giving my uncle a smile.

"May I escort Your Majesty to your rooms?"

"Please." I place my hand on my uncle's arm, eager to be out of the weather and to hear what he will tell me. Perhaps the Holy Father has agreed already to endorse French demands.

We make our way quickly to the chambers set aside for my use. I have no patience with the servants who carry in my personal effects and wish to begin making up my bed. I dismiss them by gesture, and even turn away the boy sent to bring me refreshment, unburdening him of his tray at my threshold. The niceties of arranging this place for my physical comfort can wait until I have heard what my uncle has to say.

"His Majesty wants Beatrice for his brother Charles d'Anjou."

"If he can get her. My sister is the most sought-after bride in Europe, thanks to a few strokes of my father's quill." I know that I sound unbecomingly bitter, but who would not be resentful in my place? "Thirteen and endowed with all of Provence. Men would take her were she ugly as a crone. And, as she was a pretty child, I suspect she is not."

"No. All my nieces are women of great beauty." Uncle Philippe hesitates for a moment. Regarding me oddly, as if something is out of place on my face and it puzzles him, then he says, "Louis will have to pay the pope to get her for his brother, and so will you."

"Me?" And though I sit in front of a roaring fire to restore some warmth to my frozen limbs, the flames have no effect. The cold I feel at the moment cannot be dispelled by fire. How could I have failed to foresee this? "Do you mean my ten thousand marks? My castle?" The thought of forgoing the portion of my dowry still owed me raises an icy anger in my blood.

"Boniface and I would not have you blindsided."

"But Louis promised to insist upon the payment of my marriage portion. He is prepared to help the Holy Father in his struggles to unseat Emperor Frederick. Surely that will be enough." I feel as if I am pleading.

Uncle Philippe shakes his head. "When your mother made the pope Beatrice's guardian, she likely saved Provence from being torn to bits. Even if His Holiness might consent to a division of Provençal holdings, we must take actions here to see that the county stays whole. It is in the Savoyard interest. It is in Your Majesty's interest."

"How can it be in the interests of *our* family to allow Provence to come into the hands of a member of the French royal family? Especially one as ambitious as Charles? Safety for Provence, for my mother and Beatrice, through an alliance with France by all means, but the surrender of Provence? It has always been an imperial fiefdom. The Holy Roman Emperor may tolerate our family's bonds with the Capets, but surely he will not like to see the French king's brother seize possession of imperial lands."

I suppose it would anger my husband to hear me speak so, and anger Blanche of Castile even more. But the dragon has herself to blame for my divided loyalties. Her behavior over the years of my marriage, more than any other thing, has impressed upon me time and again that my interests and France's are not the same. She has, more than any other person unrelated by blood, strengthened my sense of myself as a Provençal and a Savoyard first and foremost.

"You misunderstand me," my uncle replies. "There is no question of that. If we Savoyards are to give our imprimatur to this match, it will be on the condition that Provence remain an independent county. The county may pass to Beatrice's heirs by Charles but never to Charles outright. And I will personally make certain that the emperor knows as much."

Beatrice's heirs. My uncle could not be more clear. Not only is my promised dowry being set aside, but I will be expected not to contest my father's will. How dare all my nearest relations treat my claims, my wishes, so cavalierly? I rise from my seat, pull myself up to my full height, and, giving my uncle what I very much hope is an imperious look worthy of Eleanor, say, "With all due respect, Your Grace and the archbishop of Canterbury are being played for fools."

"How so?" My uncle's voice remains quiet and without anger. "If you fear His Majesty will not abide by an agreement of his own making, an agreement stating outright that Charles may not inherit, it is best you tell me now."

And like that, my momentary flare of anger at Philippe passes. He cannot understand the workings of the French court as I do, and he does not know my detestable brother-in-law Charles. "No. You will have no difficulty with Louis. Where he gives his word, he will follow it to the letter. But you do not take into account the groom himself. Charles is as unlike Louis as day is unlike night.

He is pompous, rapaciously ambitious, and capable of disregarding everything, even the commands of his king, to pursue his own aggrandizement." I stare at my uncle intently as if willing him to understand as I do that Charles will take Provence for himself whatever terms are negotiated.

My uncle presses his palms together, almost as if he is praying, and rests the first fingers of his hands against his lips, contemplating. Then, letting his hands fall to his lap, he says, "If that be the case, it is better to have the count tied to the family than not."

I sink back into my seat, exhausted with the effort of trying to make Philippe see the situation with the same alarm that I do. "It will be like having a wild animal. We may keep him in our menagerie, but we will never tame him."

"I will expect you, Marguerite, to work with Beatrice; to school her, and keep her mindful of our interests. She in turn shall work on the Count d'Anjou."

FOR A DOZEN YEARS I have longed to see Aix again—to be welcomed into the embrace of its many towers, to find myself in the arms of my mother. This is not the homecoming I imagined. Charles has been strutting around like a peacock, styling himself as Count of Provence for days, though his wedding took place only moments ago. I can hardly look at my mother! She appears as smitten with Charles as my sister Beatrice is. Apparently both are so relieved that he is neither the Count of Toulouse nor the Prince of Aragon that they are blind to the size of his nose and his spoiled, demanding, bad temper. *Well,* I think with satisfaction, looking at the guards in the square struggling to push back an angry crowd of my countrymen, *I am not alone in my distaste for Charles.*

"Smile," my uncle Thomas instructs, putting one hand under

my elbow and raising his other hand to acknowledge the crowd as if they were cheering rather than jeering. The Count of Flanders inspires respect. It is for this reason that he braved the January cold and traveled to Aix for Beatrice's wedding. The Savoyards, united and glamorously attired, attempt to give the union of my sister and my brother-in-law gravitas and legitimacy—to prevent anyone from getting the notion that my sister was bundled up and handed over to the highest bidder.

"By God's blood!" he declares under his breath as we stop beside my horse. "You would think we were in Marseilles."

And I know what he means. Never in my father's lifetime did any, save his subjects from that brazen port city, complain of his rule or protest his actions. Yet now as the bridal party rides in close formation and heavily guarded, from the cathedral to the castle for my sister's nuptial celebrations, the crowd along our route jostles like a pack of vicious dogs. They do not like this match—not at all. I wonder if Beatrice, riding behind me, sees them and understands their mood? I suspect not. I suspect she has eyes only for Charles riding beside her in lavish silver and vermillion robes.

The wedding banquet is sumptuous and, like the five hundred knights Charles brought to rescue and secure my sister, Louis is paying for it. Still, as the last of many courses is cleared, Charles leans in the direction of his mother and says, "This is nothing compared to what I might have had at Paris."

I see my husband's jaw tighten, but he says nothing.

"You have a fine county," Blanche responds. "Pray be content." The dragon is generally very indulgent of the last of her sons. But her look now is far from loving. No doubt she turns over in her mind the cost and effort required to bring him to this moment.

"I do not see why I do not merit as fine a wedding as His Majesty had," Charles continues, unchecked by his mother's tone.

"Because you are not a king." The words are out before I can stop myself.

Charles regards me across the stiffened form of his brother as if I were not a queen. "Well," he drawls, "I am the son of a king as my brother was not."

I feel as if I have been slapped, but Charles pays no mind, turning to his stony-faced mother for support. "Is that not the case, madam? My grandfather reigned still when His Majesty was born and our father was yet a prince."

Blanche looks as if she would do murder. Charles leaves her in a most uncomfortable situation. She would never willingly take my part, but the Count d'Anjou insults her darling Louis. "Why not dance with your wife?" she says quietly.

"Yes, I may as well make the most of these festivities, meager as they are." Charles extends a hand to my sister Beatrice.

She either has not heard the words exchanged or is not discomforted by them, for her cheeks show no stain of shame and her eyes only a bright delight at being the center of attention.

I refrain from commenting upon Charles's behavior for the rest of the evening, though on more than one occasion I must clench my teeth to do so. However, I cannot help casting frequent glances at my mother and uncle to see if they are as irritated as I am by the new count. When at last I can escape the great hall, it saddens me to be so eager to flee a room that was the scene of so many happier occasions in my childhood. As I am prepared for bed, I remind myself that if I cannot think better of my brother-in-law, I ought to at least reserve judgment of my sister. After all, Beatrice is young and doubtless as in love with the idea of being a bride as she imagines she is with Charles. I drift to sleep, promising to make a concerted show of kindness toward the new Countess of Provence.

The next morning, setting aside our inequality of rank, I call on my sister. Charles is not a stickler for doctrinal niceties, so it is certain that he had Beatrice on her wedding night. Remembering my own first experience of the marriage bed, and in keeping with my vow of the night before, I wish to be a support to my sister.

Arriving at the rooms of the Countess of Provence, I find her talking gaily, surrounded by her ladies. I am reminded again, and with force, that my sister is a stranger.

"Your Majesty." Beatrice dips a curtsy, and then her bright, hard blue eyes devour me, going over every item of my apparel from my golden pearl-studded crespine to the toes of my patterned silk slippers. "We are so behind the fashion here! Before Your Majesty's arrival I did not know it, but now I can hardly wait to bring the fashions of Provence into line with those at the court of France. I see no reason we should be behind anyone."

Elisabeth, who accompanied me on my errand, shifts uncomfortably beside me, and I find myself unable to think of any fitting response. My silence has no effect on my sister.

"My husband says that everything in our county must be as in France, and he has brought so many Frenchmen with him that we will soon be as French as you are at Paris."

"No one could be prouder of the Kingdom of France than I, but are there not many fine Provençal traditions and customs worth keeping?" I long to say more, to ask her what our mother would think to hear her speak so, dismissing as old-fashioned a court that has long set a standard for grace, hospitality, and artistic accomplishment. And at that very moment, before Beatrice can utter another inanity, Mother enters with Romeo de Villeneuve at her side. Her face is pinched and my father's counselor . . . Can this be the same man who promised Louis Tarascon and set me on my way as a bride? I realize with a start that de Villeneuve must have been well into his prime a dozen years ago, though as a girl I would not have noticed. If he seems old now, it is only the natural order of things. I wonder for the first time if the years have left any unbecoming marks on me.

"Marguerite." Mother embraces me for a moment, then steps back and looks me pointedly in the eye. "Sieur de Villeneuve and I have been speaking with my new son."

I give a quick glance in Beatrice's direction, but she is completely occupied displaying to her ladies a particularly fine piece of baudekyn silk she received as a wedding gift. "The Count d'Anjou is a very singular prince," I say, nodding slightly.

"With very singular ideas for how Provence is to be managed."

I feel my stomach sink. Why would no one listen to me at Cluny?

A week later I have had the same thought recur to me so often that it begins to have the sound of a refrain from a familiar song as it rises to my mind unbidden. Not once, however, to my credit, have I allowed it to pass my lips. Pointing out my prediction that things would go badly will not lessen the pain that Charles is causing my family and my beloved homeland.

"It seems in addition to his knights, the count brought an army of lawyers with him."

My mother and I are in my room—not the room I am lodging in presently, but *my* room, the room I occupied with Eleanor during the countless childhood hours we passed at Aix. I sit on the edge of the bed I once shared with Eleanor—Eleanor who does not yet know that Beatrice has married into the house of Capet—and watch my mother pace.

My mother is sick of Charles already.

"How can our manner of governing, which has been the model for our neighbors, suddenly be so totally deficient?" she exclaims. "Our trade and our revenues are the envy of many."

"Ah, Mother, but therein lies the problem. Charles will not be happy until he controls them."

"He will cause unrest among our lords, and then heaven help him." The weak morning sun gives my mother a complexion of ashes as she stops in its rays.

Or, heaven help the noblemen, I think.

"And the insults!" Mother resumes her pacing. "Only last night at dinner he said such things to His Grace the archbishop of Arles."

"My husband's brother has never been known for his charm. When he was a boy of seven, I watched him insult the King of Navarre as if he were that sovereign's equal."

"He knows nothing of our ways and thinks nothing of them."

"What will you do?"

"Under your father's will, I have the use and possession of substantial properties in this county for the rest of my life. I will establish my own court at one of my castles and do whatever I can to preserve this county as your father left it."

CHAPTER 17

Marguerite,

Never did I truly believe such a thing possible. Although our father expressed an intention of bequeathing the entirety of the County of Provence to Beatrice when his illness first fell upon him, I hoped that the approach of death would inspire more just action. I hoped in vain.

In my more charitable moments I tell myself that, to his mind, swayed by his longstanding habit of favoring Beatrice and the fact that she alone among his daughters remains unmarried and unsettled, this decision seemed necessary. And in my less charitable moments, well, I do not trust myself to say what I think in my less charitable moments, though only you will read my words. They would not reflect well upon me.

And the insult to you and me goes beyond being deprived of a rightful share of the county. Imagine pledging the same castles to more than one king. I am so furious that I half hope the Count of Toulouse arrives with his armies to claim Beatrice by force before the Holy Father can safeguard her. I know it is unchristian to wish our sister to pay for the sins of our father, but I simply cannot help myself. I urge you, my sister, in the strongest terms, to appeal our father's testamentary bequests. We shall certainly do as much.

Yours in shared grief,
Eleanor

ELEANOR
FEBRUARY 1246
LONDON, ENGLAND

I am reeling.

"How can this be?" Henry's voice shakes with anger. "We have only just dispatched our letter protesting the terms of your father's will to His Holiness, and Louis of France already has the Countess of Provence married off to his brother!"

Henry waves the pages in his hand at me. His breath rises, ragged and visible in the cold air. We are having a bitter winter; even indoors one cannot keep warm a dozen feet beyond the fireside. There was ice on the water in my ewer this morning.

I have seen Henry angry before, many times. I have even seen him angry with me. Yet the look on his flushed face unnerves me. "The French push their borders southward while I, like a man sleeping, continue to offer alms in honor of your dead father! I feel the very fool." He pauses again to peer at me. His eyes are full of mistrust. "Madam, do you mean to tell me that you had no inkling? You who hear from the Queen of France so often?"

"Henry! How can you think it?" The accusation that I glimpsed in his eyes now hangs in the air. My tears flow, but they are angry tears. We have been betrayed. *I* have been betrayed. By my family!

"And the four thousand marks I lent to your mother, monies we could ill afford, what is to secure that loan when Charles d'Anjou has my five castles?"

I have no answer. I am too angry to speak in any event. How *could* Marguerite and my mother! Did they actively plan this treacherous marriage or merely attend it? And my uncles! Besides word of my sister Beatrice's hasty wedding, my husband's agents brought rumors that Uncle Boniface attended meetings at which our rights—we his greatest patrons—were effectively destroyed. My Savoyard kin have thrown themselves onto the side of France and into disfavor with my kingly husband, disregarding everything I have done to forward them. Well, I cannot worry about them. I must act to save myself lest I be lumped with the rest of my family in Henry's fury.

As if reading my fears, Henry says, "When this weather breaks, madam, I suggest you take yourself to Windsor. I look at you and see a Savoyard."

A Savoyard—this term was never an insult before. My relationship to the house of Savoy was one of my great attractions when Henry sought to marry me. Since then he has benefited by my connections, most recently in a treaty with my uncle, the Count Amadeus of Savoy. And suddenly I am both inspired and enlightened.

"Well then, see the Count of Savoy, your newest vassal," I say. This must be the reason that Uncle Peter worked so furiously to secure that treaty—to give Henry something even as something, unbeknownst to us, was being taken away. I cannot approve of such duplicity, but I can and do grudgingly admire it. "See our new castles in the Alps, with all their advantages.

"If the Queen of France and her husband injure you, surely I am not guilty. I swear she is no sister of mine when she brings Your Majesty grief. I shall not send her another letter!"

Henry knows what such a pledge means, for he has watched me write countless missives to my sister these ten years and teased me as I waited impatiently for Marguerite's replies. He remains silent, but I see a softening in his eyes. As he looks at me, I feel certain that he sees the wife who loves him rather than a woman whose family has behaved so shockingly.

I press my advantage. "I see that Your Majesty is determined to judge and condemn me by the sins of others. I will go then and tend to our sons. They may be young, but they are wise enough to recognize that I place them always before myself. It is unfortunate that their father does not accord me the same credit." I rise from the fireside, letting the fur throw I had tucked over my lap fall to the ground. I have covered less than half the distance between my seat and the door when Henry steps in front of me.

"Eleanor, my heart, I know you are loyal." He reaches out a hand to me and, when I lay my own in his, pulls me into an embrace.

CHAPTER 18

Eleanor,

What is this new sorrow heaped upon me? The sudden break in our correspondence was most unexpected, and I pray it will be of short duration. Believe me when I say that the loss of my dowry is as nothing compared to the loss of your goodwill. My fireside seems empty without your letters to bear me company of an evening. . . .

M

MARGUERITE
MAY 1246
MELUN, FRANCE

"If only I could forgo this investiture," I say, wincing slightly as Marie crosses my plaited hair at the back of my head with more vigor than usual.

Yolande hands Marie a crespine amply studded with jewels, then gives me a wicked smile and says, "Would you miss the Count d'Anjou kneeling before you and the king to pay homage for Anjou and Maine?"

"No indeed, Lady Dreux, that will be the most pleasant moment of the affair. You well know I will delight in seeing my brother on his knees. If only we could devise a method of keeping him there."

Yolande and my ladies laugh. I join them, but inside I am seething. To see my detested brother-in-law Charles knighted—made Lord of Vendôme, and Vicomte de Laval and de Mayenne—and to celebrate him is like putting salt in a wound, particularly as the titles are belated wedding presents. And to see my sister Beatrice is like poison. Her marriage cost me dearly, and I do not think of my lost ten-thousand-marks dowry, monies that the new Count and Countess of Provence have made clear they have no intention of paying. No, I have forfeited something far more precious than silver. Because of Beatrice, I have lost Eleanor. I have not had a letter from her in four months.

I cannot blame Eleanor; I know how it looks. I have written reams. Written until my hand cramped, trying to explain that my personal claims in Provence have been set aside along with hers; that I am not to blame for the reports we receive—reports of Charles stealing castles and diverting fees that are rightfully property of our mother. These reports sicken me. But I am sure that all Eleanor sees and hears is that France will have Provence and that the Capets reach their grasping hands into Midi.

I watch with satisfaction in my mirror as my crown is placed on my head, and I hold out my hands so that Yolande can slide on my most impressive rings. Unlike Eleanor, I am not known for extravagant habits of dress, but a lesson must be taught. I will use the occasion of her husband's knighting to show Beatrice her place, not only in the hierarchy of the French royal family but in my heart. I will use this gathering in Charles's honor to repudiate my sister.

After the ceremony I sit beside the king in a hall full to overflowing with the most important nobles in France. Doubtless our guests are looking forward to the first of a week's worth of lavish banquets and entertainments. Louis is distracted, talking with the

Count of Sarrebruck about crusade preparations. I can never see the count without thinking of his cousin, the Sieur de Joinville. There is something about the mouth of the first that reminds me of the second. But today I am in no mood to be pleasantly preoccupied.

Turning to Beatrice, under cover of all the noise and motion I say, "Well, Countess, here is pomp enough to satisfy even the insatiable Count d'Anjou. And an opportune moment for him to be out of Provence as well—I hear that he is not very popular there."

Beatrice looks up at me with vicious eyes. She is fuming over the fact that the dais on which we sit was deliberately constructed so that she sits considerably below me, and below Blanche of Castile. I had surprisingly little trouble suggesting this arrangement to the dragon. She loves both her sons; like me, however, she is wise enough to see that Charles will take every opportunity to infringe on Louis's rights and good humor. "It is only those rebellious tradesmen in Marseilles. Your Majesty knows well they are content with no one."

"Only Marseilles? How then can you explain the expulsion of His Holiness the Pope's nuncios at Arles and Avignon? Uncle Philippe wrote to say that the Holy Father was not leastwise pleased."

Beatrice colors. She knows I am needling her, but what can she do? My tone is pleasant and I am queen.

"Well, never mind," I continue. "All men cannot have my husband's facility for ruling. Louis is beloved wherever he goes. How fortunate that Charles will never be a king, given his deficits."

I can actually see Beatrice's teeth grinding. How I wish the noise of the crowd were a little lower so I could hear them.

Tired of my company, Beatrice rises and moves into the crowd, seeking the arm of her swaggering husband. No matter. My dear

Yolande approaches, shepherding the new wife of Hugh of Châtillon, Count of Saint-Pol. Rising to greet them, a distinction I did
not show my sister when she came to take her seat earlier, I am all
smiles. I have a message to send in the course of these events. The
little countess will be the first of my couriers, but I will employ as
many as necessary, and speak often and loudly until my words reach
distant shores; until they reach my sister the Queen of England.

Having accepted the ladies' reverence, I draw their arms
through mine as if the countess had the same claim on my friendship as Yolande. "I sat too long at this morning's ceremony," I say.
"Let us walk awhile."

Saint-Pol's wife is the daughter of the Count of Guines, a vassal
of my uncle Thomas, Count of Flanders, and master of territory
very close to the English Channel. I dearly hope she repeats to her
father all that she sees of my treatment of Beatrice over the next
days, and all that she hears. "Countess," I address the girl with all
the solicitude I can muster, "His Majesty is so pleased that your
husband has taken the cross, and I am happy you will be part of my
collection of ladies when we set sail for the Holy Land." In truth I
have heard she is the last sort of woman I would wish to spend time
with—a childish, petty thing with a talent for gossip. Luckily she
is also precisely the sort of girl whose head is easily turned by royal
attention.

"Your Majesty is so kind," she simpers, positively glowing and
glancing about to see who is close enough to notice us walking
arm in arm.

"Not at all. Are you feeling settled at Blois? It is difficult to
marry so far away from one's relations as I well remember. For
many years I felt the absence of my family keenly." I hold my
breath, wondering if she will say what I wish her to. But, of course,
the comment is so very obvious, surely it must come.

"It must be a great pleasure for Your Majesty to have your sister the Countess of Provence married to the Count d'Anjou, for now you will have her with you often."

Leaning in, I lower my voice as if taking the countess into my confidence. "Not at all," I reply. "The Countess of Provence is not the companion I would have chosen. I much prefer my English relations."

Moments after she leaves me, I glimpse the countess across the room, deep in conversation with several other ladies of rank. When I see their eyes turn in unison to Beatrice, I know that rumors of my denouncement of her will be spread throughout the court before the sun sets.

CHAPTER 19

My dear Eleanor,

    *I have scorned Beatrice publicly and treat her with so
little kindness or respect that I might be reasonably mistaken
for my husband's mother, and yet you will not be placated.
How long, Eleanor, can you remain angry with me? Surely
you of all people know how little sway I have over events in
the court of France. I was not the author of our sister's
marriage, nor am I the benefactor of it. . . .*

                    Your sister,
                    M

ELEANOR
JUNE 1246
BEAULIEU ABBEY, ENGLAND

My goodness, the bishop of Winchester drones on. The new abbey buildings are impressive, and they have cost Henry a good deal of money, but is it really necessary for his lordship to comment on the laying of every stone? Glancing past Sanchia at the Earl Richard, I wonder if his long looks are, like mine, induced by the endless speeches or by the fact that his first wife is buried not ten yards away just before the altar? Glancing to my other side, I see that Edward's eyelids are drooping. I ought to give him a stern look or nudge him, but I haven't the heart. After all, if I were only seven, I would be asleep already. I reach out a hand to settle him comfortably against me and find his skin touched with fire.

Fever! I have no more time to waste on the bishop, and no thought for what is appropriate or polite. Rising, I lift the prince, wrapping his legs around my hips. His little arms naturally rise and clasp round my neck, but his head lolls back frighteningly and his eyes are unfocused as they seek my face. Henry gives a puzzled look as I start down the long aisle out of the church.

Outside, I glance about in panic and then realize that faithful Willelma has followed me. "Get the physician!"

"Which one?"

"All of them."

Responding to the urgency in my voice, she leaves at a run. I still have no idea where to go. Everyone is at the dedication.

"Mama," Edward whimpers. Panic rises in me, pressing my chest and closing my gullet. And then Henry is there behind me.

"Eleanor?"

"He's burning with fever." I do not mean to shriek, but my voice sounds unnaturally high as it escapes my throat.

Henry reaches out a hand to Edward's head, then draws it back as if burned. Wordlessly he takes the prince from me and begins to stride toward the living quarters of the Cistercians. I have to run to keep up. And all the time I can hear Henry murmuring reassuringly to Edward, talking about his favorite dog, the goshawk he got for his birthday, and how they will go hunting soon.

We install Edward in the abbot's room. He is bled, but the fever shows no sign of abating. Physicians buzz around him like bees as I sit at his bedside holding his little hand. A few yards away the prior buzzes as well, like an angry hornet. My jaw clenches as I look at him. He is talking to Henry.

"I understand, Your Majesty, the queen's desires to stay with

Lord Edward. Her Majesty's feelings are becomingly maternal. But there are the rules of our order to consider. We cannot appropriately house women underneath our roof."

"Cannot or will not?" Henry's voice is as cold as my Edward's cheeks are hot.

"Please, Your Majesty. I assure you the prince will be cared for day and night with the utmost skill until such time as he is well enough to be moved."

"Listen to me." I am on my feet and striding toward the prior. "His Majesty's father built this abbey, and His Majesty can take it down." The prior's eyes open wide and his jaw drops. "And that is what will happen if another word is said about my leaving—down it will come, stone by stone, and I will help with my own hands."

"Your Majesty!" The stunned cleric turns to my husband for relief.

"Mansel!" Our Lord Chancellor separates himself from a small knot of counselors standing near the door in response to Henry's summons. "Her Majesty will be staying with our son. Please make the necessary arrangements."

The prior sputters like a drowning man pulled from a river. Henry turns to him, raising his eyebrows slightly as if to invite further challenge, and says with great deliberateness, "Stone by stone."

"why does the fever not break?"

"Your Majesty, we are doing all that we can." It is the fifth day since Edward was taken ill, and the prince's physician's eyes are bloodshot with lack of sleep.

All that you can is not enough, I think furiously. I know I am being unfair. The prince's physician, the king's physician, my own Peter de Alpibus, and indeed the abbey's simpler are all doing their best. They try remedy after remedy, but my Edward continues to burn, by turns shaking and delirious, and then stuporous. I never leave him, sleeping on the floor beside his bed, much to the distress of everyone but myself. How could I sleep elsewhere? At least as things are, when I wake in panic, desperately listening for the sound of his breath, I have only to reach out a hand to find him and reassure myself that he lives still.

Turning to the king's physician I say, "I wish you to list for me every herb and tonic you have tried thus far." Listening to his litany, I realize that most of the English remedies are unfamiliar. The medicines of my own childhood are missing.

"Have you no borage?" I ask. Henry's physician looks back at me blankly. "Starflower?" Perhaps it is known only by its common name here.

"Your Majesty, I am sorry, but I am not familiar with such a plant."

Turning from the doctor, I put my hands to my face in pure exasperation. I must admit that I myself have never seen the star-flower growing on these shores. If only we were in Provence, where it grows thick this time of year. I would make a tea of its petals and leaves. Nothing is better for fever.

Henry slips into the room. He looks as wild as I feel, with dark circles under his eyes and hair unkempt. He has every monk not otherwise engaged in the day's business praying for Edward. But, like me, I know he feels it is not enough. Both of us would *do* more, but there is nothing to be done.

"Eleanor, you must get some air. You begin to look ill yourself."

I nearly laugh despite the horror of our situation. Being lectured on my appearance by Henry at the present moment has a touch of the ridiculous about it. "Henry, I am fine."

"You are not fine."

"No."

"Nor am I." He rests a hand on my cheek for a moment.

Henry has come to sit with his son, but I do not rise. It is not necessary. Henry always sits on the bed itself, as close as he can to Edward. His physician is not pleased by the practice. He worries the fever is catching. But Henry does not care. He takes the basin from a monk who has been laying compresses on Edward's forehead. "I will do it," he says firmly.

"Do you know what I saw in the field outside the gates this morning?" Henry begins speaking softly to Edward. The prince's little eyes pop open at the sound of his father's voice and search, with a painful fogginess, for his father's face.

I feel damp upon my cheek and am surprised when my curious fingers find a tear. I must be crying. But just as Edward's eyes *look* empty, I *feel* empty—not calm and removed, but hollow in a way that aches desperately. *Dear God, please do not take my little Edward. He is such a beautiful thing, long limbed, fair, bright. I realize he seems uncommonly good for this life, but even if he would make a perfect angel, please, please leave him to his father and me.*

Children die. I know it. But until this moment I never *felt* it. My own mother lost two sons before Marguerite was born. Marguerite herself has lost a child, little Princess Blanche. Blanche was only a year younger than Edward. What would my sister say to me now in my terror? Would she hold me in her arms as she did when as a girl I woke her from a sound sleep to tell her of my nightmares? No, it will not do to dwell on Marguerite; there is no comfort to be found in that quarter. In keeping with my declaration to Henry, I do not write to my sister. And the letters she sends me, offering excuses, do not move me. She will not admit that she plotted against me, instead insisting that we are equally robbed by our sister Beatrice's marriage. Her stunning lack of contrition rankles me. Even recent rumors of a public declaration that she prefers me to the Countess of Provence leave me unmoved.

I reach out my hand and touch Henry's sleeve to get his attention. Then I hand him a cup so he can offer Edward a drink.

"I cannot comprehend why none of the usual medicines induce sweating." The prince's physician stands at the foot of the bed, shaking his head.

Willelma lays her hand on mine. When I turn, her wise eyes regard me with urgent meaning. It is clear that the physician's last statement triggered some important thought or memory. "The sweating tea!" she exclaims.

And at once I feel a fool for not thinking of this remedy from my homeland myself. "Do you know how it is made?"

"*Plan segur*, who do you think brewed it for you when you were a child?"

I scramble to my feet, eager to be in motion now that there is something useful to be done. I am in the alley along the cloister in an instant with Willelma behind me. Monks flee before us, but I have no patience for their delicate sensibilities. "You"—I stop a wispy young man with my voice—"where are the kitchen gardens?"

"Good Heavens," I exclaim to Willelma when we arrive. The herb garden is prodigiously large. As we search frantically in the late-afternoon sun, the monks working in a nearby vegetable patch scuttle away like beetles. Willelma secures a basket from one as he goes. The catswort and mint are quickly found. We are careful to keep them apart as we pick, lest their similarly shaped toothed leaves lead to confusion. The egrimoyne, however, is nowhere in evidence. I try not to panic. The heat and the pollen-laden air are beginning to make my breath labored. I concentrate on breathing slowly. At last I spot the characteristic yellow flowers along a low stone wall at the garden's rear. We go straight to the kitchens with our supplies, but no sooner do we cross the threshold than our path is blocked by a round monk with more chins than he has folds in his cowl. His hands are tucked under the front flap of his long sleeveless apron and remain there even as he makes a smooth bow.

"Your Majesty, with respect, this is no place for you."

"And you are?"

"Brother Geoffrey de Middleton, cellarer of the abbey."

"With respect, Brother de Middleton, Lady d'Attalens and I have medicine to prepare. Where else do you suggest we find knife, pot, water, and fire to brew it?"

"Confide the recipe to me and I will see it prepared."

"You are a very brave man. If the tonic is not efficacious, are you willing to be responsible for its failure? Even with the life of the heir to the throne at stake?"

De Middleton's chubby face colors. As I suspected, he is *not* a brave man, merely an officious one. "This way," he says, leading us to a scrubbed wooden worktable. "Our kitchener, Brother Gilbert, will get you whatever tools you need."

With the officious cellarer out of our way, it does not take long for us to prepare the herbs and steep the tea. I am soon back in Edward's chamber, sitting on his bed. I pull my son onto my lap, supporting his head and shoulders against my breast. Willelma hands me a cup filled with our handiwork.

"Edward," I say, dipping my head to whisper in his ear, "Mama has something for you. Something to make you feel better." I put the cup to his lips and slowly tip some of the liquid into his mouth, praying that he will swallow. He does! Willelma and I smile at each other in a moment of intense satisfaction. When the cup is empty, I relax against the wall at the head of the bed, with Edward leaning against me. Henry, sitting on my customary stool, takes my hand. We sit in silence. The sun is setting and I am bone tired.

"Lord Edward must have one cup every hour for the next three," Willelma instructs the prince's physician, though such instruction is entirely unnecessary for neither she nor I have any intention of leaving.

After the penultimate dose, I doze off. Even the rough stone wall behind me is pillow enough in my present state. I awake with a start, feeling unpleasantly damp. Looking down on Edward in the candlelight, I quickly see that his hair is moist and his skin glistens. He is sweating—sweating profusely. The back of the fever is breaking.

Willelma hands me the cup, and I administer the last dose carefully, concentrating on not spilling a drop with my shaking hands. My job accomplished, I begin to cry—to cry as I have not since I was a child, in huge gulping sobs.

Henry shoos the physicians and attendants from the room, then returns to join me on the narrow bed, lying on his side and curling around me as I in turn curl around Edward. Gradually my sobs subside, and I drift to sleep, bathed in Edward's sweat and pressed tight between my two great loves.

CHAPTER 20

Eleanor,

    . . . Soon I will leave for the Holy Land. The steps of my journey will take me to places that you know well. To Beaucaire to see our mother, to Avignon, to Marseilles. In all these places I will expect to see you. To catch your former self out of the corner of my eye. Before I reach Aigues-Mortes where my ship stands ready to bear me to unknown lands and perils, I ask two things of you. Forgive me for whatever acts, large or small, childish or womanly, you in your own judgment believe I have trespassed against you. And write to me, so that I may not leave these shores burdened by the silence you have maintained for so long.

                        Your loving sister,
                        Marguerite

———————

MARGUERITE
JUNE 1248
CORBEIL, FRANCE

It has been a season of good-byes. My good and faithful friends Elisabeth and Yolande, whom I thought to take to the Holy Land with me, left me in quick succession. Elisabeth was carried away by plague, and Yolande in the bearing of a child, a child delivered so many years after her last that nothing good could reasonably be expected from his mother's confinement. My grief over their deaths is profound.

And always the loss of Eleanor is there, waiting like an unreliable tooth to pain me just when I have forgotten it. I had not seen my sister for years before she turned from me; yet she never felt absent from my life. She was with me daily, in a phrase spoken by others that reminded me of her, in a thought of my own that was undeniably shaped by our growing up together, in a place or a person seen through the filter of her imagined opinion. Now, after such a long silence on her part, I cannot bear these once reassuring reminders. I train myself not to think of her, not to mention her. I am as a cloistered nun where it comes to memories of Eleanor. Yet rather than bringing me pleasant calm, my self-denial leaves a bitter feeling, and I fear becoming as one of those whose withdrawal from the world has not left her graceful, but rather withered and rigid.

I try to tell myself that time will bring me other friends and that by it all things are healed. I notice that a new Lady Coucy, Elisabeth's replacement, is part of the party standing apart and a little to one side on this summer morning, more than three years after Louis and I took the cross, as the real leave-taking begins. I promise myself that I shall endeavor to be kind to her, but that will be difficult since her very existence reminds me that my darling friend is gone.

"Say your prayers without fail," Louis instructs our small brood with a serious face. My little Louis regards him with solemn attention. The prince is lean and a goodly size for four, but still not as tall as three-year-old Philippe. Philippe, who is constantly in motion, pays the king no mind. Instead, he drops to his knees to examine something in the dust that has caught his eye. Princess Isabelle makes an attempt to hoist him up but fails, and his nurse takes charge, swinging my second son to her hip with practiced ease.

Blanche stands waiting to be given charge of my babies. Her face is expressionless as I kiss each on the cheek. Little Louis throws his arms about my neck, even though I did all I could last evening to prepare him for this moment. His nurse scuttles forward to remove him from me, but I hold up a hand. Louis *is* the golden prince I mistook his father for at first sight. He is a warm, open, little soul, and, unlike his father, his affection for me equals mine for him.

I put my mouth to his ear and whisper, "Three months is not so long. Isabelle will help you count the days."

Then I hug him fiercely before passing him to the nurse. My husband seems vaguely embarrassed by my show of affection. But I do not care. This is the moment I have dreaded most since we took the cross. I know that Blanche understands the sudden emptiness I feel, even as she refuses to offer me a look of reassurance or commiseration. She will be parted from her sons today too.

The children are whisked away. My eyes sting as I fight to keep from crying. Robert of Artois and Charles d'Anjou come forward in turn and take their leave of the dragon. Solemnly she offers them her blessing, but I notice that her left hand has seized a portion of her mantle, fingering it and twisting it in a most uncharacteristic manner.

Then Louis steps forward. He embraces his mother, then says, "Madam, I leave all that is of importance in your hands, my children and my kingdom, knowing that you will manage things as you always have—to my good and my glory."

Blanche's face collapses—an event without warning and without precedent. She looks old and frail. "I fear," she begins, but her voice breaks, and in the silence that descends I sense weakness. She begins again. "I fear, Your Majesty, that we will not meet again in this life." Then gathering herself together, she is issuing orders once again. "I admonish Your Majesty, as the woman who gave you life and loves you like no other, to behave always in a manner that safeguards your immortal soul. Seek God's glory in the Holy Land rather than your own, that I may see you in heaven if never again in France."

Never again in France. The excitement this possibility kindles in me is indecent, and I know as much. It is impossible, much as I hate her, that I could pray for another Christian's death. Imprudent too, for I leave my children in her care. Yet, as we ride off in the direction of Beaucaire, some part of me hopes that I will return from battle with the infidels to find that my chief battle at home has been won in my absence.

AFTER BEAUCAIRE, I BEGIN TO look for the Sieur de Joinville. This might seem a foolish waste of time as knights by the hundreds join us from every direction, but I feel certain that when he reaches the royal party, Joinville will find a way to make himself known to me.

We move slowly, as we must with so many men, but I am glad of it, for at every turn in the road I find the scenery of my childhood. The weather too, with a warmth that my husband's northern kingdom is never able to match, puts me in high spirits. When Avignon comes into sight, I am struck by the thought that fourteen years ago I waited at its gate for the French to arrive. Today, at twenty-seven, I *am* the French.

Beatrice rides beside me. I wonder if she remembers that long-ago day. I doubt so. The hours I have passed with my sister in the two years since her marriage have convinced me that her mind is occupied nearly entirely with herself. In this she is perfectly matched with her husband. Still, for the sake of the crowds, I treat Beatrice with marked cordiality these days. The public tableau of family must be preserved. I learned this at my mother's knee, and the rule applies equally whether the family is Savoyard or Capetian. In truth, it is hard not to feel a little sorry for my sister, prideful though she is, because she is carrying her first child and is very ill. As if to punctuate my thought, she directs her horse to the roadside and, clutching the animal's neck, leans over to vomit.

"Do you need to rest?" I ask.

Louis looks displeased. Unlike me, he finds our ever-slackening pace maddening.

"Surely the countess will recover better in the city than by the side of the road."

The impatience in Louis's voice needles me. I long to point out that we might have sailed already were it not for his insistence on stopping at every religious house along our route to solicit prayers and feed the inhabitants at royal expense. But I remain silent. My newfound empathy for Beatrice is not as strong as my desire to be on the best of terms with my husband during this trip. I give my sister an encouraging look as one of her ladies offers her a linen kerchief to wipe her mouth.

"Your Majesty is perfectly correct. The count and I"—she appeals to Charles by glance—"anticipate the greatest pleasure in having Your Majesty and the queen as our guests. And I will rest best in my own castle." Beatrice gives a little triumphant smile, and I am reminded that though this may have been the land of my childhood, it is now my sister's and hers alone.

Our arrivals at every city and village have been well attended, and Avignon is no exception. As we draw near, the road begins to be lined with people shoulder to shoulder and several bodies deep. But something feels different. Instead of jostling for position, the people are still, almost sullen. I notice few women and even fewer children, though in other cities youngsters littered our path with summer flowers.

I glance at Louis, riding just in front of me between Robert and Charles. But he is either not aware of anything out of the ordinary or not concerned by it.

My sister Beatrice too seems oblivious. "How do I look?" she asks Matilda who rides between us. "Can you tell I have been ill?"

Matilda shakes her head.

As I am about to dismiss my unease as silly, Matilda pulls her horse closer to mine and says in a low voice, "These are not, I think, the faces of subjects joyfully welcoming their sovereign lord and his lady home."

A sickening thud prevents me from replying. It takes a minute for me to realize what has happened. There is a second thud and Beatrice shrieks. A splatter of something dark red and thick stains the front of my sister's *surcote*, as if her insides have come out. For a panicked moment I think she has been wounded, and then the smell reaches me. Dear God, someone in the crowd is pelting us with offal. The royal party draws together. All manner of waste showers upon us. I seem to have whatever was left of someone's trencher scattered across my skirt. I twist this way and that, trying to see everything at once. The mob, for now it is clear that is what they are, presses in from both sides. Some of the men have staves; some are better armed. For the first time in my life I know what it is to be afraid for my safety at the hands of men. Then, as my throat tightens and my heart races, I hear a voice from the mob.

"Go back to France," somebody yells, "and take your brother with you."

"There he is," another voice screams. "The Count of Provence took my land."

I feel a sudden all-consuming rage, a rage strong enough to overcome my fear and force it down. Charles! This is all because of Charles. Because of his greed and his disrespect for my father's people and for our Provençal ways!

Men have begun to fight where our party meets the one by the roadside. Some of Louis's knights dismount, and at least one rides out into the crowd. I can see him striking blows with the butt of his sword. How long, I wonder, until he uses the blade? Giving my horse a vicious kick, I push my way to Louis, disregarding the startled face of Robert of Artois as I force his horse aside.

"Call off your knights before someone is hurt," I plead.

Charles d'Anjou stares at me incredulously. "This rabble attacks us," he says with a sneer. "A lesson must be taught."

"These men attack *you*," I reply. "Perhaps you ought to ask yourself why." I turn again to Louis. "Your Majesty, it is unseemly for knights well trained and well armed to turn blades meant for killing Saracens upon Christian tradesmen and farmers."

For a long, dreadful moment Louis looks out over the scene. I can hear blows from every direction, voices cry out in pain and anger, and somewhere a woman sobs. Then, to my great relief, he stands in his stirrups and calls to his constable, who is near at hand.

"Bring the men to order! Make it clear to all that I will tolerate no violence against the crowd. We are not some collection of street urchins to be incited to riot by a few pieces of rotted fruit or a coarse word. Run them off by all means, but do not hurt them."

It takes time for the whirl of jumbled motion around us to slow. But at last, the mob begins to yield to the wall of my husband's mounted men, scattering back toward the city. Some, injured, are carried or dragged by others. I feel something wet on my nose and raise my hand, wondering who can be throwing something at me now that the crowd is departing, only to realize that it is the first drop of a summer shower.

A moment later I am drenched. The downpour speeds our attackers' retreat. Shouts and curses fade, and then without warning a sharp cry rings out, a wail that rises and then settles into a steady keening. The little Countess of Saint-Pol, whom I never gave thought to other than as a pawn in my denouncement of Beatrice, is off her horse not twenty yards from where I sit. Off her horse and on her knees in the rain, pulling with small white hands at the sleeve of a figure on the ground. It is Hugh of Châtillon, her husband. The people of Provence have made her a widow for the second time in her short life.

"Why?" Beatrice's shaky voice startles me. I turn to her, dirty and sodden, and raise my open palms as if I too seek an answer. The fact that she asked the question is all the proof I need that she would not understand my answer, even if prudence did not dictate that I remain mute.

CHAPTER 21

LET THERE BE NO STRIFE, I PRAY THEE, BETWEEN ME AND THEE . . . FOR WE BE BRETHREN.

GENESIS 13:8

ELEANOR
JULY 1248
CLARENDON PALACE, ENGLAND

Usually I enjoy my garden. But today, despite the gorgeous blooms of my roses and the fact that English sun shines as if it has forgotten that this is a country of rain and fog, I am not having a pleasant time as I sit on the stone bench and watch Henry pace in short steps before me.

"Eleanor," he says in exasperation, halting for a moment before me, "have you not taught me that family is everything?"

My own words and deeds turn on me. Of *course* I have preached family to Henry these dozen years. But I meant *our* family. And *my* family. Not his half brothers. But I can hardly say that!

"But they do not behave as family ought," I reply, trying to distinguish the Lusignans, who have arrived on English shores like an invading horde, by their behavior from my own kin. "Rather than supporting your reign, they upset everything, riling the barons and spending your money like water."

Henry pouts. "I seem to remember expending considerable sums on your kin when they arrived. Did I not make your uncle

Peter the Earl of Richmond as soon as his feet touched English soil?"

There is no use reminding him that Peter himself saw the danger in that hasty gift and worked hard to quiet the angry murmuring that Henry's impetuous generosity stirred. "Henry, you have been exceedingly gracious in your favors to my relations. But have they not in turn given you good service?"

"Of course, Eleanor, and so shall my brothers."

"They are off to a bad beginning!" I try to keep sarcasm out of my voice because it is the quickest way to anger Henry, but I find it *very* difficult. Henry can be resolutely blind to the truth of a situation when he wants to be. "You know that your barons were not in the least pleased when you gave the Countess of Pembroke to William as a bride. They complained about such a plum title and such lands going to a foreigner—"

"Just as they complained when we married Alice de Saluzzo to Edmund de Lacy," Henry interrupts defiantly. "They are only greedy and want all the best heiresses for themselves and their sons."

Henry is right; the English complain about every "foreign" marriage. But, unlike my husband, I believe that the recent vituperative nature of such protests is very directly related to the appalling behaviors of his Poitevin kin, so I return to that subject. "We are agreed then that your barons objected. But, had William shown proper humility and behaved like a true servant to Your Majesty, they might quickly have forgotten. Instead, your half brother throws his weight and your name around everywhere."

Standing up, I stalk off to the nearest rosebush. I try to pick a pale yellow blossom for myself, but, though I bend and twist, the cane will not break. Instead, I succeed only in pricking myself until my fingers bleed.

I round on Henry who has remained standing silently by the bench—perhaps hoping I am finished. "You know he is whoring about openly while Joan de Munchensy sits in misery at Hertford Castle, growing large with his child!"

"Eleanor!" Henry's face colors. I am not certain whether he is embarrassed by my language or angered by my accusation.

"Yes, whoring!" I repeat, tossing my head. "And as if *that* were not enough, he behaves like a common criminal, breaking down locked doors and taking what belongs to others. The poor bishop of Ely was at his wits end when he wrote to Uncle Boniface. The doors to His Excellency's cellars forced, his servants threatened, his best wines poured out to your half brother's servants or left to run upon the ground. And what punishment have you meted out to the perpetrator? None. Instead, you secure nomination to the bishopric at Winchester for Aymer, a man equally debauched."

"They are my *brothers*, Eleanor."

"*Half* brothers, the sons of a man who betrayed you and opened you to mortification during our campaign in Poitou." I have never forgiven the Count of La Marche for beginning the battle in Poitou prematurely, before English troops arrived, or for abandoning Henry and surrendering to the French precipitously after Taillebourg, even if my husband has.

"They are also the sons of my mother, Eleanor. My *mother*."

Henry's voice drops, and I see the pain in his eyes. I cannot understand his sentimentality over his mother, which has only increased since her death. Isabella treated him pitifully while she lived—deserting him to remarry and flouting his interests whenever they did not correspond with her own. I hate her for how she neglected my husband, and for how she played upon his loving nature. But right now I hate her even more for the brood of noisome, oafish sons she allowed Hugh of La Marche to breed from her.

"How can I turn on my brothers? Would you want Edward to turn on Edmund?"

Henry's question brings a sudden flash of clarity. Henry *wants* these brothers, and he needs to believe they are good and that they love him. This complicates things—not the least among them my feelings. I know how Henry ached for family before I came to him. He has said it to me a thousand times—how sorry he is that he and Richard grew up strangers; how he would have our family be as close as the one I came from; how much he wants to know his sons as his father never knew him. Now it is my turn to feel the sting of tears.

Henry walks to my side and, in a single deft motion, breaks the stem I was struggling with and hands me the flower. "Invite the Countess of Pembroke to court," he suggests, looking sheepish, "and I will suggest to William that if he cannot abstain until his wife is delivered, then at least he ought to be less public in his activities."

I know this will not be the end of our troubles with the Lusignans. Yet what is damage to the stores of the bishop of Ely, or any of the damage caused by William de Valence's bad behavior for that matter, compared to the serious heartache Henry will suffer if I press my point? Surely my own people can work round the Poitevins or just ignore them, as can I personally. And should they do something to more directly damage me, there can be no question as to the winner in such a battle. The Savoyards will not be bested by some drunken riffraff no matter whom they are related to.

UPON RETURNING FROM THE GARDEN to my apartment, my first order of business is a letter to Uncle Peter. He is stopped at

Windsor to settle a matter with Edward's tutor and will be waiting for a report of my conversations with the king. To be honest, he might have resolved the issue that takes him to Windsor by letter, but with the Lusignans' sniffing around for everything they can get, it is more important than ever that Peter and I assert control over matters pertaining to the Lord Edward.

Protecting my son's lands and interests is the great work of my life. In fact, in addition to discussing the Lusignans with Uncle Peter by letter, I must write of Edward's Gascony. My uncle and I are supporting the candidacy of Simon de Montfort for seneschal there. It is our opinion that he is the perfect man to put that critical but ever-troublesome part of Edward's appanage in order. But, despite my ongoing attempts at persuasion, Henry does not, at the moment, see things as we do. Henry wants to send Richard, but I know that gentleman will have Gascony for himself if he can. He has always angled for it, and all the more so since it was given him and then snatched back five years ago.

No, Peter and I must continue to press most firmly for de Montfort. Simon will wish to be paid, and paid handsomely, but he will not poach the territory itself. This suits me as I will never rest until Edward is invested with those lands and holds them secure from threat.

I sit down at my writing table and look down on the garden I just left, but, instead of thinking how best to set things forth for Peter, I find myself distracted by my new windows. My eyes follow their delicate silver-gray grisaille pattern. I wonder if I might have something similar done in fabric for a patterned gown. Perhaps in the lovely gold and warm pink of my new tile floor—or am I too old at twenty-four to wear pink? I get up and, ignoring the inquisitive glances of my ladies, hurry to my bedchamber to consult my mirror. No, by God's coif! My looks are as good as they ever were.

Moving to my dressing table, I eye the finely carved casket I keep there. I need not open it to know what is inside—every letter that Marguerite has written me since Beatrice was married. Although I have not answered a single one, I have not had the heart to dispose of them. Running my finger over the box's top, I think how strange it is that before I broke with Marguerite, I felt no pressing need to keep her letters. A few, to be certain, are tucked away, but most, once answered, I simply burned.

I take out Marguerite's last letter. Like so many before it, it pleads for an answer. And in its closing lines, my sister posits that perhaps I do not read her missives at all anymore—that they are sent in vain. *Just because I do not speak, Sister,* I think, *does not mean I have not been listening.*

Family. Henry forgives his *everything*, and I am the loser by it. I, on the other hand, am more wary of clemency. I have repaired my relationship with Boniface because practical and political necessity demanded it. And my relationship with my mother is mended as well, a task materially assisted by a recent visit during which she assured my husband that, whatever the rumors to the contrary, she did not surrender the rights to castles pledged to us to secure Beatrice's marriage.

Yet I have not forgiven Marguerite. Perhaps I cling to my anger at my sister because her betrayal hurt me more than the others and deep cuts are not easily healed.

I have not forgiven Marguerite, and who is hurt by it? Marguerite to be sure. She makes no attempt to hide it. But I am also. *"Stubborn Eleanor. You are too stubborn for your own good."* I can hear Marguerite saying the words as if she were in the room. And why not? She has sounded some variation on this theme countless times over the years. And now, if her *nef* sinks at sea, if she is killed or captured in the desert, if not a single word of hers ever reaches me again, what stain will I carry on my soul? Who will mourn her more than I?

Taking her letter with me, I return to my writing table. The garden no longer has the power to draw my eye. Uncle Peter can wait.

CHAPTER 22

Marguerite,

. . . We are sisters. People have been wont to tell us since infancy how different we are. But in truth, Marguerite, when compared to those not of our blood, we are more alike than different. Too much alike to be unforgiving of each other's faults. Whatever part you may have played in the marriage of our sister Beatrice, it is forgiven. Can you forgive likewise my stubborn obstinacy in neglecting you for so long? I have been foolish, but I have learned from my error. I swear to you there is no act of yours sufficient to permanently harden my heart against you. This I learned, and I will not forget it again. . . .

Your sister,
Eleanor

MARGUERITE
AUGUST 1248
AT SEA

I have my letter! It arrived yesterday, on our very last afternoon in France. Standing on the deck of the royal *nef*, near the ship's castle, I say a prayer of thanksgiving. Marie, at my elbow, thinks I pray for the safety of all the thousands of souls at sea since this morning. And I will do that too, but later.

Moving away from my lady, I open Eleanor's pages again. I have plenty of room and quiet for my reading and reflections. A majority of the ladies on board have not yet become accustomed to the effects of being at sea, but it agreed with me from the very first moment the anchor was drawn up. The wind feels good, and the sun on the crests of the waves sparkles like diamonds. Having finished Eleanor's letter for a third time, I gaze out over the water and begin to count ships. I can see thirty in addition to our own. I wonder if the Sieur de Joinville is aboard one of them. Having failed to catch sight of him on land, it will be some weeks now before I have any hope of seeing him. And in truth, I had very little hope of glimpsing him at Aigues-Mortes, though I could not stop myself from closely examining every knight who passed.

With the sound of the seabirds in my ears, I recall the day we arrived at Aigues-Mortes. Louis was ecstatic as the city came into view, for though he planned it, and paid for it, before the moment it rose on the horizon, the king had never seen the result of his labors save in his own imaginings.

"Look at it!" he exclaimed with enthusiasm. "Out of nothing we have built a city with a single purpose—to launch the crusade that will take back the Holy Land." And I knew I ought to admire Aigues-Mortes—that Louis was waiting for me to comment on its fine wooden wall and imposing towers. Ordinarily I am sure I would have, but all I could see at that moment were the tents. Hundreds upon hundreds of tents of every size and color girdled the city walls. When I asked how many men had gathered, how many stood ready to ride and march into battle behind the oriflamme standard, Louis's constable, Humbert de Beaujeu, reported that more than two thousand knights were already present, with more arriving. More astonishing still, two times that many archers had been assembled, and twice again as many men-at-arms as archers. For the first time I grasped the full magnitude of our undertaking. I found myself wondering whether the many ships and crews that my husband commissioned from Genoa and Sicily would be enough to carry so many to the Holy Land.

I am called back to the present by the touch of sea spray on my face. I tuck Eleanor's pages into the bag at my waist—it is Eleanor's *aumônière*, the one covered in poppies that she gave me all those years ago. The new letter joins the last she wrote me before Beatrice was married. I've been carrying that missive as a talisman to bring me luck—luck in the form of the letter that will now displace it. It is time for me to go to my cabin, not to eat, as Marie has been urging for hours, but to begin a letter to Eleanor. I will tell her of the great city that Louis and I built in the marshes, and how we make first for Cyprus where the stores that we purchased for our army lie waiting.

"TO WASTE SUCH WEATHER IS a sin. We should never have left Limassol and come to Nicosia." Louis's voice is soft, but it brims with dissatisfaction. I slip silently into the room, unwilling to interrupt the discussion.

"And I say again, Your Majesty, we do better to act as we have—to wait for all the ships that have not yet landed and the men who have not yet arrived." The voice of Humbert of Beaujeu is equally composed and equally urgent.

"Even with the hand of God upon us, it is prudent to have the largest possible force at Your Majesty's disposal when we go into battle," adds Philip of Nanteuil. "If those knights and armed men who were separated from us at sea do not find Your Majesty here, in Cyprus, there is some chance that they might come to harm trying to join us in the Holy Land."

I can see at a glance that Louis has called together his good knights, those half-dozen or so *preudommes* in whom he places the most faith and respect. When we landed at Limassol last month, Louis was as excited as any child to see the massive stores we had paid for heaped in fields and waiting according to plan. Having worked for three years, and spent more than one and a half million livres to be ready to fight, Louis is eager to be in battle. It was with difficulty that his noblemen persuaded him not to set sail immediately for the Holy Land. And the greater part of him needs to be convinced of the wisdom of that decision again regularly.

"I would not abandon any of my men," Louis concedes. "But it is already October—" Noticing me, my husband stops abruptly. His eyes seem confused and his mouth sets into a straight line. "What do you do here?"

I hesitate for a moment, biting my lower lip, embarrassed by his reception. I thought to be a partner to Louis in this undertaking, as I was when we were recruiting knights, but the closer we get to the Holy Land, the more I am treated as a distraction. "Your Majesty, the Countess of Provence has been delivered of a fine, fair son, and she and the count have named him in Your Majesty's honor."

The king starts visibly. In his obsession with Egypt, it seems he forgot that my sister has been laboring for two days. I know that he did not miss me in bed last evening, for since we left French shores he has chosen to keep himself pure, but I am surprised he did not notice my absence from High Mass this morning.

"This *is* good news." The Count of Artois shows all the warm enthusiasm his brother lacks. After eleven years of marriage, he became a father for the first time before we left France. Matilda, good soul, pines daily for the daughter she waited so long to have and was then forced to leave behind to be with Robert on crusade.

"Indeed," Louis says, his eyes still on me and still disinterested. I wonder if he notices that my eyes are bloodshot. They are not so only from bearing my sister company. I have been crying with frequency these last days. My foolish heart believed that Louis the crusader and Louis the golden prince whom I met at Sens as a bride would be one and the same. The disappointment of my hopes is hard to bear.

"Shall I convey Your Majesty's pleasure in the event? Perhaps a small gift?" And then, as Louis's expression remains vacant, "Some masses?"

"Masses, yes, the very thing." For a moment his face is enlivened and then, like that, he turns from me. I am dismissed—forgotten entirely. I feel my eyes begin to sting again, and I slide toward the door. Louis speaks to the Lord of Nanteuil. "When we dined yesterday, I overheard Erard of Brienne say that the Count of Sarrebruck and his cousin have arrived."

I stop in my tracks. The "cousin" of whom Louis speaks must be the Sieur de Joinville.

"Yes, Your Majesty, I believe *les deux* are in the city."

"Send word to the Sieur de Joinville. He impressed me from the first, and I would have him as my man."

JEAN DE JOINVILLE IS WITH the king. I have stationed Marie outside Louis's rooms. When Joinville comes out, she will bring him to me. If Yolande were alive and here, she would know better than to do so, but Marie is devoted without feeling that she dare try to influence me.

I am in a small courtyard at the castle in which Henry I, king of Cyprus and regent of Jerusalem, so kindly installed us. I found this spot while exploring. It is removed from the main rooms—an interior courtyard space, narrowly pressed by white stone walls and distinguished by a single twisting tree at its center. I believe I am the only one who knows of it. Its weathered door is off the kitchen garden, and I myself opened it expecting to find nothing more than gardener's tools.

In my solitude I allow myself to relax. The weather is *calfar*, like the autumns of my long-ago home. As warm as a Parisian summer. I am comfortable in Cyprus. The clear blue sea at Limassol and the outline of the Troodos Massif in the north, seem familiar. This is a land with some of the same languid grace of Provence. Yet it is exotic too, and the very newness of its sights and smells excites my curiosity and my senses.

There is a soft rapping at the door, and it opens to reveal the Sieur de Joinville. He is so *bèl*, more handsome than I remembered him, and not because of the finery he wears in honor of seeing the king. He looks directly at me, in a way that Louis never does anymore—making me feel a person of interest and importance.

"Your Majesty." He gives a bow as I sweep forward to greet him.

"Sieur de Joinville, I had begun to think you lied to me."

"Lied?" The bridge of his nose furrows slightly.

"Three years ago, when you told me you were coming on crusade."

"And here I am."

"Yet I did not see you in Aigues-Mortes."

"Did you look?"

I search Joinville's face for any touch of amusement or incredulity, but instead I see only an earnest desire to know. "Of course."

"My cousin and I hired a ship in Marseilles."

Marseilles. My mind's eye sees its port, the sea glittering in the sunlight. "His Majesty has retained you?"

"Fortunately. I have nine knights dependent upon me and

awoke this morning with less than three-hundred livres in my purse."

Joinville does not ask why I wanted to see him; nor does he question that we are alone. This is just as well, for I have no satisfactory explanation. I only know that from the moment I learned yesterday that he was in Nicosia, seeing him became a thing so important that I did not sleep last night.

"I gather," Joinville continues, "that, despite His Majesty's wish it might be otherwise, we will pass the whole of the winter here in Lefkosia."

"Lefkosia?"

"A servant, a Greek, told me that is what his people call this city."

I like that. I like that Joinville is interested in this place as more than a delay in our expedition. I too am on this journey not merely to conquer, but to absorb. To taste, touch, and see that which is different. "I believe, Sieur, that we will stay because, *enfin*, His Majesty's common sense is stronger even than his desire to be in Egypt."

"What do the ladies do to pass the time?"

"My sister complains bitterly about everything that is not like home. And the rest are content to behave as if we were at home, embroidering, gossiping, dining."

"But not you." He makes the statement with a certainty bespeaking far closer acquaintance than we have.

"If I wanted to be in France, I could easily be there. I am in Cyprus, and I would see something of it."

It is clear that Joinville is thinking. We stand in silence for more than a moment, but there is nothing at all awkward about it. Then he says, "Would Your Majesty allow me to take you to see the monastery at Politiko? I am eager to see it, as Saint Paul once preached there." His eyes shine. Do they do so at the prospect of being with me, or, as my husband's would in this situation, at the prospect of beholding a holy site?

I laugh. "A monastery! My Lord of Joinville, I am a very pious woman, but I visited enough monasteries *en route* to my ship to satisfy me for a very long while."

"Where shall I take you then?"

"To Curias, to see the ruins."

"So far as that?" Joinville's eyes open wide. In this shaded place they are dark almost to blackness, but they are far from dead.

"His Majesty has given me permission to take a small party on such an expedition, so long as sufficient knights can be found to safeguard us, and so long as he is not required to go himself." I had hoped Louis would be enthused for the journey, and proposed it for the purpose of having him more to myself for a few days than I do here in the city. When he showed no interest I dropped the idea, but at this moment I find myself quite as eager to go as I was initially. "I should think Curias would suit you as well as Politiko, for Saint Paul preached at both."

It is Joinville's turn to laugh—the same rich, warm sound I remember from the gardens at Saumur and at Pontoise. I believe I could listen to him laugh all day long. "Curias will suit me *better*, so my men and I will act as your guides and guardians if His Majesty can spare us."

MY SEA IS EVEN MORE beautiful from here at Curias; stretched out to the horizon, bluer than the sky.

"Your Majesty, take care." The Sieur de Joinville ascends the last few risers to where I stand at a run. "What will I tell the king if you fall?"

That I died happy, I think. I offer Joinville a smile. "I am in no danger, Sieur; I am very sure-footed." We are in a massive theater of white stone, stone that shines in the sun to blinding effect. Our Greek guide insists that his ancestors built it, but the Lord of Coucy says that the Romans did. Portions of the magnificent structure have collapsed, but I have climbed to the very top of what remains so that I might look down on the Mediterranean. While Joinville may fear my falling, I fear nothing. My heart is so light that should I slip, I am convinced I would take flight as a bird and glide off over this splendid scene.

"Please, Your Majesty, let us go back down." Joinville gestures to where the balance of our party wanders beneath the brilliant autumn sun. He reaches out his hand, and I cannot resist placing mine upon it.

In the fortnight since Louis retained Jean de Joinville, I have seen more of him than in all the years since Saumur put together. Each moment a delight, each moment more precious, whether we are dancing, exploring the markets of Nicosia, or conversing. We can talk of everything, and we do. Things I have not told my husband of fourteen years because he showed no interest I speak of easily with the Seneschal of Champagne—particularly things of my childhood and my family.

Leading me carefully downward, testing every step before I take it, Joinville says, "Our guide tells me that there are some very fine mosaics nearby. Shall we see them or have you had enough for the day?"

I tighten my grip to make a small jump, realizing with regret that in a few more steps we will be on level ground and I will have no further excuse for keeping hold of his hand. "Oh, I would see them, by all means."

Only the Sieur de Joinville and I are interested in the mosaics.

The others, tired of sights, choose to remain behind, seated on large blocks of stone at the amphitheater where they may partake of refreshments. I am not at all disappointed to leave them as I raise a hand to wave good-bye to my ladies.

We do not go far, and the house, when we reach it, is unlike any I have seen. One side has fallen, but the central portion looks sound. Having led us this far, our guide stops at the threshold, gesturing for us to go in.

The Sieur de Joinville exchanges a few words with the man and then tells me, "He insists it is safe, but I will go first to espy any rough places."

Leaving the Greek behind, we pass down a short corridor and into a large room, graceful despite its decay. Four elegant columns form a square at its center, holding the edges of a crumbling tile roof where it opens to frame the sky. Beneath this aperture, the floor is sunken to form a pool.

"Beautiful," I say.

My voice disturbs a pair of birds somewhere, and they flutter up, a flash of gray and white, through the open ceiling. The movement surprises me, and I instinctively move closer to Joinville. My eyes travel to the walls. They are not tiled but painted, and whatever scene they once showed is faded and missing in patches. Then I look down. Geometric patterns, *fantastiques* in their complexity and involving numberless tiles, give way in the near distance to spaces peopled with figures. Moving forward in silence, I find myself standing before two men in combat. These are not knights such as I am accustomed to seeing. They wear helmets and some sort of curved metal over their shins but are elsewise largely naked. A tight tunic, girdled at the waist and sleeveless, rides up on each man's legs where he crouches, revealing the flesh of massive, tensed thighs. Bare arms, muscled in tiled detail, heft short swords and shields. One of the warriors has been stuck, and blood pools at his feet.

"Your Majesty," Joinville says, his hand tugging slightly at my sleeve, "come away. This is not a scene fit for your eyes."

"Why not?" I know Joinville is merely being chivalrous, but I am tired of being excluded and sheltered by Louis. I will not allow Joinville to treat me in the same manner. After all, I have been on campaign before. I put my hands on my hips and, tilting my head, look him boldly in the face. "Are my eyes fit only to gaze upon the flowers and animals that we saw portrayed in tile this morning? Sieur de Joinville, we are off to war. Surely in the Holy Land I will witness battles where the blood that is shed amounts to more than colored tile?"

"My God! You have a lion's heart inside a lamb's breast! Why His Majesty does not value you more I cannot say."

I catch my breath at this strange, blunt exclamation. I have never thought of myself as a lion. Eleanor, yes; she is all fierceness and daring. Could there beat at the center of me a heart that is likewise brave, even reckless? Whether by this question or by Join-ville's candor and the frank admiration in his tone, I find myself emboldened.

"And you? Will you not admit how you value me?"

Joinville takes two steps away and when he turns back, his eyes are on fire. "I would admit more if I dared."

"You are a banneret with men at your command. You are on your way to do battle against the Saracens. What should you fear?"

"Dishonor."

"Mine or your own?"

"Yours. No, that is not true." Joinville must see my hurt sur-prise for he hurries to continue. "I fear to bring evil upon your head, *c'est sûr*, but more than that, I fear your disdain. Your rejection might prove blow enough to fell me as surely as any Saracen sword."

I ought to rebuff him, but there is no decision to be made. The moment for sensible action has passed, not in the present silence as Joinville's eyes search my face, but the very first time we were alone when I sensed more was at stake than courtly love and play-acting. "My heart has sought yours since the moment I first laid eyes upon you," I reply.

And then I am in Jean's arms and his lips are on my lips. Such a kiss I have never had—soft, searching, expressive. It is almost as if we are speaking to each other without words. I feel dizzy, but I also feel something else—the strongest desire I have ever experienced in my life. I close my eyes and see Jean in the short tunic of the tiled warriors—I see his muscled thighs and imagine them between my own. I need Jean to touch me, to take me as a man takes a woman, but how can I possibly say so? I have not that much boldness in me.

When Jean takes his mouth off mine he is gasping and wild-eyed, like a fish drawn up on shore. "Oh my sweet love," he says. "We must be very careful."

I reach up and put a hand into his dark curls, something I have dreamed of doing for so very long. "No one is here but the guide."

Jean smiles down at me and gives a warm laugh. "I was thinking more broadly."

"Of course." I feel my cheeks warming slightly at my own eager abandon.

"I am not content merely to kiss you in this ruined place, though God knows I will do so again." And keeping his promise, Jean lowers his head, thrusting his tongue once more between my hungry lips. I put my arms around his waist and lean into him with a fierceness that threatens to throw us both off balance, as if I would melt into him and be consumed.

"God's coif," he moans, withdrawing his mouth again. "We had better go, before I lose all control and strip you naked on this spot."

I rest my cheek against his chest, knowing I will not have the courage to say anything if I must look him in the eye.

"Why not?"

I hear his breath catch against the background of his beating heart. His arms tighten around me. Then releasing me, he steps back and offers a devastating smile.

"Well, for one thing, we would not be very comfortable," he says, gesturing to the surroundings, all tile and stone. "And for another, I meant what I said—if we choose this path, we will be in grave danger. It is treasonous—"

"No!" I say sharply. "Surely to love cannot be so serious a crime." But of course I know he is right.

"I told you once that I would be known as a man who speaks truth. We must speak and hear it now, however painful. We stand at the precipice, and if we would plunge over it, let us do so with eyes open so that we may take all possible care, and so that never will we have cause to curse and say, 'If only we had thought.'"

Again I feel the soundness of his words, even through the haze of my lust. If I am to take Jean as a lover, it ought to be because I choose to follow my desires, not because I am overwhelmed by them. But taking what I want is out of the ordinary for me. I have ever governed myself by reason and by a compulsion to do what was expected of me—to behave as a model daughter and then a model wife—a compulsion driven by my desire not to be called impetuous and headstrong as Eleanor was. Standing and watching Jean, his breath still irregular as if he has run a long way, I realize that my lifelong devotion to what is proper has not made me happy. Like my sister, I shall choose to have things my own way this once and see if that brings me joy.

"Treason then," I answer. "I can accept that. I must accept that, because to turn from you now is something I cannot accept. I can love France and also you."

"And I swear that I love France better because I love you." Jean's words come out slowly and softly, as if he is thinking them through even as he gives voice to them.

"Then let me give myself to you. Let us find a way. Not here, I concede, but soon. My heart is so full I cannot wait." I do not mention that not only my heart but my entire body aches.

"Tonight. There is no one to disturb you once your ladies are dismissed."

He does not mention Louis, but I know what he means. As my husband does not travel with us, there is no one to visit my bed; no one but Jean. "Yes, tonight. Come to me from the garden."

OUR PARTY RETURNS TO LIMASSOL in the late afternoon. This is where we are lodging while we see the wonders of Curias and other sights along the Cyprian coast—staying in the same castle that Louis and I made our home immediately after arriving from France. It is a castle built by the Knights of Saint John. I cannot wait for the sun to go down.

"Your Majesty has seriously overexerted herself," Marie chides at the table where my ladies and I take our evening meal.

"In truth I am too tired to eat." I am amazed how easily the lie slips off my tongue. I who have always prided myself on veracity. "I was selfish today, keeping you all in the sun so long, but I am chastened. Tomorrow we will stay in and rest."

Matilda looks at me with concern. I offer her a reassuring smile. It would be too terrible for her to worry that I am ill and insist on sleeping at the foot of my bed tonight. "Shall we have music or games to pass the evening?"

Finally night comes. I admonish Marie not to disturb me until I call for her. "I am certain," I say, as she tucks me into bed, "that I will sleep as one dead." Another lie, and just as easy as the last. When she is gone, I make myself count to one hundred before getting up. I creep to my door and, holding my breath lest I make a noise, fix the bolt. Then, I go to the other door, the one opening onto the garden. This door Marie has fastened for the night. As my hands fumble with the lock I wonder if Jean is already waiting.

I am not left long in suspense. The moment I ease the door open, Jean is inside and turning to fasten it behind himself. He catches me up in his arms and kisses me. Then moving his mouth to my ear, he asks, "Are you certain?"

By way of answer, I turn from him and, stepping before the fire, pull my shift over my head to reveal my nakedness.

"By all the stars in heaven, you are the most beautiful thing I have ever seen."

Even at the start of my marriage, when Louis indulged in me with regularity, he never gave voice to such admiration. I feel giddy with the delight of being thought lovely; yet at the same time I am aware that my body reflects the children I have borne. I wish Jean could have seen me when its contours were more girlishly perfect.

I recall the morning that I first paid myself my own marriage debt with images of Jean swimming before me, and all the times since that I have pleasured myself while imagining his nakedness. "I want to see you," I say simply, surprised by the low, broken sound of my own voice.

Without a word Jean begins to disrobe, dropping his clothing carelessly to the floor. I find I am touching my own breasts as I watch—rubbing them, teasing the nipples into a state of alertness. And when he is as naked as I, I cannot believe the beauty—every limb well muscled; the dark curly hair on his head tousled and childlike from pulling his tunic over his head; and, nestled among the dark curls of his groin, his member fully engorged. Slowly he approaches me. Rather than kissing me, he buries his face between my breasts, replacing my fingers upon the nipples with his own. He takes one nipple between his lips, kissing and sucking by turns, and I nearly swoon. My hands, which in all my years as a married woman have never touched my husband's bare member, find his swollen organ, stroking it. The skin is like velvet, fascinatingly soft beneath my fingers. All I want is to pull it to me and impale myself upon it. But Jean stops me. Sweeping me into his arms, he carries me to my bed and lays me upon it. I draw up my knees, knowing what comes next. But Jean appears to have no intention of mounting me.

Lying beside me, stroking my cheek, he whispers, "Marguerite—my God, how many times I have imagined saying your name, how many times I have heard myself speak it in my dreams—from this moment I live for you." He begins to kiss me again, every part of me—lips, neck, shoulders, breasts—and as he does, his fingers move between my legs, searching tenderly for a place that will give me pleasure. When he finds it, I cry out softly.

"Jean," I beg, "take me or I will die."

"You will not die, I promise," he replies with a slight laugh, "and I will take you. But I would not just receive pleasure from you; I would give it."

I turn toward him, again trying to pull him into me, but he gently resists, dropping his mouth to my breast again and suddenly thrusting a finger inside me. I abandon all control and all thoughts of control. Waves of pleasure roll over me like the waters that break on the beaches of Limassol not far from where we lie. My hips move without effort to meet his finger and then, deep inside me, something begins to spasm. I bury my face against Jean's shoulder to muffle my gasps of pleasure. Just as it begins to subside, Jean slips himself inside me and I thrill again. Rolling him on top of me, I wrap my legs about his buttocks and my arms about his neck, drawing myself up to him even as he plunges into me. He is groaning, and the sound gives me a feeling of delight and power. I long to make him lose control; to make him tremble as he has me. I feel my muscles begin to tense again and then, without warning, Jean withdraws from me and begins to thrust against my belly. Looking down along my own nakedness, I reach with both hands and desperately try to pull him back inside, but he will not be moved. And a moment later he spills milky white seed across my stomach. I begin to shake with sobs both of joy and frustration.

As if he understands perfectly, Jean cradles me in his arms, pushing the hair back from my face.

"*Si non caste tamen caute,*" he whispers.

And then I know, this is one of the prices I must pay. If I cannot be chaste, I must, at least, be cautious. Because Jean is not my husband, he cannot let himself run inside me. He cannot risk quickening my womb.

LOUIS APPEARS HAPPIER TO SEE Jean than he is to see me upon our return. Far from being rankled, I take pride in the favor the king shows Jean. He is mine now, and I would have everyone recognize how glorious he is.

At dinner our first night back in Nicosia I am seated between the two. To be so close and not touch Jean is maddening. As the first course is carried away, I wonder if I might brush my hand across his knee beneath the table without anyone noticing.

"Was it exhilarating to stand where Saint Paul preached?" Louis asks Jean, taking a sip from a glass of such a strikingly dark red liquid that I wonder if he has stopped watering his wine.

"Your Majesty, there was much about the journey that was both exhilarating and humbling. I am beholden to Her Majesty for suggesting the trip, and to Your Majesty for honoring me with the commission of escorting the queen."

I misswallow some of my own wine and am left coughing. The double entendre in Jean's answer causes a small spasm inside me. He is toying with me.

"I am very pleased that you and Her Majesty have become friends," Louis says, wiping his mouth.

I hope I do not color at this remark, and I pray if my cheeks *are* pink, those around us attribute the fact to my having just recovered from choking. I am remembering what Jean did to me among the sand ridges of the salt lake at Akrotiri—the flawless blue sky framing his head as he took me, and how the beautiful pink birds rose up in a cloud, disturbed by my cries of ecstasy. These were not the actions of a mere friend. I believe there is sand in my garments still.

"Come and hear Mass with me tomorrow morning. Afterward we will have a good talk. I want to show you an extraordinary tent that I received by way of a present from the King of Armenia. There is some fighting in that country, and the king sends word that any of my knights who are bored waiting to sail to the Holy Land may do service with him and earn a profit."

"Will Your Majesty permit such an excursion?"

"I am of mixed mind on the subject. I hope every day to see the last of my ships arrived so that we may proceed to the Holy Land. Any delay once they are landed waiting for knights to be recalled would be insupportable. But at the same time, some of the men are finding distractions far more dangerous to their mortal souls than honest combat."

Louis glances to see if I am paying attention. I take care to appear as if I am looking down at my trencher while watching him from the corner of my eye. Apparently convinced that my attention is fixed on my food, my husband mouths the word "prostitutes."

"Reprehensible to be sure, Your Majesty. Men serving their God and their king ought not to debase themselves so. But perhaps it is also understandable. Not every man has the comfort of a wife upon this journey."

When Jean departs for the evening, I retreat to my rooms. Though it is early, I have my ladies undress me and then dismiss them. Their chatter will only distract me from the one entertainment that can satisfy me—thinking of Jean. Of course, remembering the moments of our travels together is no substitution for having him with me, and I have no expectation of seeing him in my bed this evening. Now that we are returned to court, other arrangements must be made. So, knowing I will see Jean again in the morning at Mass, I say my prayers and climb into bed, eager for sleep.

Then Louis arrives. He has not touched me since we boarded our ships at Aigues-Mortes; yet tonight he comes. I feel nauseated at the sight of him, not out of guilt or fear that he will discover what I have done, but at the thought of his touching what Jean has touched.

"Wife," he says, nodding curtly to acknowledge me where I lie trembling as if I were a new bride beneath the covers. He puts out his candle, slides in beside me, and immediately presses his frantic mouth against mine.

I am glad that it is dark and he cannot see my face; glad too that he has not sought or required any sort of reciprocation from me in many years. With his tongue still pushing invasively into my mouth, he thrusts himself between my legs. Over and over he stabs himself into me, pinioning me against the mattress. I feel as if I am being violated. Hot angry tears flow down my cheeks. Louis grunts like an animal, "Uh, uh, uh," in time with his thrusts.

I want to cry out, to pound on Louis's back with my fists and make him stop, but there is nothing to be done. He is my husband and has rights over my body. I squeeze my eyes shut and pray for it to stop. Yet on and on it goes, and with it my mortification. At last Louis experiences release. After a few moments, he withdraws from me, swings his legs over the side of the bed, and, adjusting his shift, rises to leave.

"Good night, Wife, and God save you," he says from the threshold with ludicrous formality. As the door falls closed behind him, I begin to sob openly. How did I bear this for so long? And then I realize that before Jean touched me, I had come to expect nothing from the marital act but an opportunity to conceive a child—to make myself more indispensible to my husband and more secure in my position as queen.

CHAPTER 23

My dear sister,

*Cyprus is the most wonderful kingdom in the world.
The people, like the weather, are warm; the markets are full
of goods from the east unlike any I have before seen. I find
myself thankful for the storm that separated the king's fleet
and set us to overwinter here (though I would certainly never
own as much to His Majesty).*

*I am recently returned from a journey to the south coast.
Such a trip. I walked for hours upon the beaches near
Limassol—some covered in the finest sand as white as the
snow that falls in France in winter; others, closer to the city,
covered with a coarse, gray mix of pebbles. I saw a lake filled
with salt water as if it were the sea. It was frequented by
birds of a shade of pink I have only ever seen in the rising or
setting of the sun. I saw the great ruins at Curias. Everything
delighted me, including the company, for my party was made
up of my favorite ladies and the finest and most gallant of
His Majesty's knights. As each day drew to a close, I slept,
wrapped in soft, salt-filled breezes. I have truly never been
happier since we were children together. . . .*

Your sister,
Marguerite

Eleanor
January 1249
Palace of Westminster, England

I pick Marguerite's letter out of my lap and read it once more. She is a different woman, as if the air in Cyprus has blown away all the cares in her life. Perhaps we are merely light and shadow, the two of us. We cannot both tread an even path at the same time. For years while my marriage to Henry was as smooth as the undisturbed surface of a pond, I could tell that Marguerite, though restrained in her complaints, was unsatisfied with Louis. And now, I find my husband increasingly either distracted or argumentative and Marguerite—scanning the pages, I suddenly realize my sister has mentioned her husband but once. Singular. And who are these young men in whom she takes such a sudden interest? The half brothers of Uncle Peter's wife? This might be reason enough to recommend them to Peter's favor. But what can Geoffrey de Joinville, Simon de Joinville, and William Salines be to Marguerite? I remain puzzled, but my sister can twist my arm from a very long way when she wants to. They *are* family. Uncle Peter will surely help me place them and it will please my aunt as well as my sister, so why not?

A servant comes to put more wood on the fire. I stir and stretch contentedly like a cat safe in the warmth of the blaze from the reach of winter cold. I finger the front of my pelisse; it is made of the most beautiful siglatoun and lined in gris. What satisfaction it gives that I can have such luxury in a garment that few eyes will ever see—that, in fact, is intended solely to cover my chemise and keep me warm while I wait for Henry to come to me for the night.

A knock sounds, startling me. If it was Henry, he would simply enter. My ladies have gone for the evening, so I merely say, "Come," rising as I do to greet the unexpected caller.

Uncle Peter strides in, looking exhausted. "Henry has just presented the living at Flamstead to his wardrobe clerk."

"What?"

"To Artaud de St. Romain." Peter flops down on a stool before the fire.

"But I gave that benefice to William of London a fortnight ago. I, not Henry, have wardship of those lands."

"Is that what you plan to tell His Majesty if he comes this evening?"

"If?"

"The king is very angry, Eleanor. Angrier than simple misunderstanding over authority warrants."

"There is no misunderstanding," I reply, pacing away from my uncle. "The authority is *mine*."

"All right," Peter says, shrugging. "We can take that position, and we can likely defend it successfully. But what I want to know, Eleanor, is *why* Henry challenges your gift so fiercely."

"How should I know, Uncle?"

"You have not quarreled?"

"Not about Flamstead."

"What then?"

"A dozen little things and nothing at all." It is my turn to shrug. I recall in a rush a disagreement of the evening before over some behavior of my cousin, Gaston de Béarn, in Gascony. As if I could control all my relations however far-flung! "Believe me, Uncle—I am as mystified as you, both by this particular action of the king and by his general mood of late. It used to be that I was perfection in his eyes and excepted from his reproachful tongue. But now he questions my expenses and inquires into every mundane household decision I make. The other day, without warning, he accused me of thinking more of your opinions than his."

"Then he had best not find me here." Peter rises wearily. "What shall I write to William of London?"

"That he must stay where he is. He is the rector of Flamstead, and he should pay no mind to whosoever says otherwise."

Uncle Peter goes and I resume my seat, but I no longer feel comfortable or content. I now dread Henry's arrival; yet at the same time I would have it over, for nothing else will give me such a clear idea of how things stand between my husband and me at present. My suffering is not long. Scarce have I tucked my slippered feet up beneath me when the door swings open and Henry walks in.

As is my custom, I rise to pour him a goblet of wine. When I am halfway to the decanter, his voice stops me.

"I am not staying."

"No?" I work hard to keep my face open, as if I have no reason to suspect he is angry.

"I saw your uncle on my way here."

I do not take the bait, merely remaining mute.

"Is it true you conferred the living at Flamstead on your chaplain?"

"Yes," I say with a deliberate lightness, "I am surprised that you only hear of it now, for it was done more than two weeks ago. He is already in possession."

"Well then, you can dispossess him!" The color rises in Henry's face, leaving it blotched and red. His normal eye narrows until it nearly matches his drooping one.

"Does Your Majesty have some objection to the conduct or reputation of William of London? For if not, why would you wish me to withdraw my favor?"

"By nails and by blood, Eleanor, it is not the man who offends me but the favor itself. Flamstead was not yours to give, any more than is the money in my purse." He grasps the bag at his waist to emphasize his point.

"How so, Husband, when you yourself gave me the wardship of Roger de Tony's lands until he reaches majority? Does not the rectory at Flamstead sit upon those lands?"

"Call your lawyers, lady—a grant of wardship does not convey the power over advowsons."

"So we have the need of lawyers between us! Here is a pretty pass." Henry's flare of temper ignites mine. If he thinks to humble me by his behavior and force my capitulation, then he needs to be reminded that I am not so easily thwarted. "I do not believe I was outside my rights, but if I was mistaken, why, sir, do you seek to embarrass me and undo what has already been done?"

"Will you recall your man?" Henry's mouth is tight as he speaks, and his words come out in a growl. Ought I to be afraid? Perhaps, but I am too angry that he attempts to bully me to properly fear.

"I am not of a nature to be intimidated by glowering," I reply, lifting my chin. For a dreadful moment I fear Henry is going to slap me. In fact, I see his hand rise slightly before he drops it again. In all the years of our marriage he has never struck me. That he considered doing so now only redoubles my resistance.

"How high does the arrogance of woman rise if it is not checked!" He virtually spits the words.

"However elevated, sir, it cannot approach the height of your own."

Henry spins on his heels and storms from my room, calling for his chamberlain as he goes.

The next morning, John Mansel slips into my antechamber more like a mouse than a former Lord Chancellor and a man covered in the favor of both his king and queen.

I shoo my ladies to the other end of the room and motion for Mansel to take the seat beside my own.

"Your Majesty, I thought you would wish to be apprised that His Majesty has sent the sheriff of Buckinghamshire to compel the bishop of Lincoln to evict William of London from Flamstead."

"The bishop would not dare."

"He may be sorely tempted, Your Majesty, when his alternative is to appear in court to explain why he does not."

"Thank you for coming to me. This is news I must have even if it saddens me."

"There is more. The king this morning dismissed William of London from your household. He is your chaplain no more."

I see red. How dare Henry! I am not a child whose household needs to be managed for her. The time for lawyers may have come indeed. Struggling to control my rage or at least to keep it from making itself obvious by my voice, I say, "My Lord Mansel, William of London is a worthy soul. I thought to reward him for his faithful service by this benefice, but it seems I may have ruined him instead. You know the laws of this land, both church and civil, better than I. How can I best mend my friend's fortunes?"

"Write to the bishop of Lincoln and urge him to follow his conscience in the matter. He is a man who is possessed of one where many are not, and by granting him leeway to use his own judgment where the king orders him, you will likely obtain an ally."

"THIS IS YOUR DOING!" HENRY yells, not caring that my ladies are present.

"What is my doing?" I ask meekly. If we are going to have witnesses to our conversation, I will use that fact to my advantage.

"The blasted bishop of Lincoln has excommunicated Artaud and placed the church of Flamstead under an interdict."

I had not heard this, and, being blindsided, must struggle mightily to keep my delight from showing. Writing to the bishop of Lincoln has proved more effective than I dared imagine. "What has this to do with me?"

"Did you not write to the bishop? Come on woman, do not dissemble. Admit it!"

"I do not deny it." Turning, I address my sister. "Lady Cornwall"—Sanchia starts at the sound of her name, no doubt unwilling to have the king's attention drawn to her—"run to my clerk and ask for the copy of the letter I sent last month to the lord bishop of Lincoln."

While Sanchia is gone, Henry taps his foot triumphantly. But he will soon discover I have been too clever for him. Taking the letter from my returning sister, I say, "Your Majesty, when I learned you had ordered William of London turned out from the parish to which I sent him, it became clear to me just how deeply my innocent actions had offended you. Knowing myself to be far less knowledgeable than Your Majesty in the laws of this land, I took the first opportunity to write to the bishop and assure him, whatever his decision in the matter, he was in no danger of making an enemy of me. That, in fact, I relied on his good judgment in an area where my own could not be trusted to be sound." My voice could not be sweeter. I extend the letter to Henry, who snatches it from me.

He reads it through, then thrusts it back in my direction. He must know there is nothing in it that, to anyone else's eyes, would justify his laying the bishop's actions at my door. But this only makes him more angry. "I shall take the matter to court."

"Be assured, Your Majesty, that no one will be more pleased

than I to see it settled, for the estrangement it causes between us is a source of great unhappiness to me."

Henry is not moved. He merely grunts and departs without taking any leave. But my ladies are much affected, especially when I loose a torrent of tears as the door closes behind the king. By this evening there will be no one at court who has not heard of Henry's reprehensible behavior. My husband thought to embarrass me, but it is he who shall be shamed instead.

Standing at the foot of my bed that evening as my ladies undress me for the night, I am surprised I do not feel more triumphant. As I anticipated, I was the object of much solicitude during dinner. The whole assembly seemed to pity me. Henry himself avoided me as best he could. Whatever the legal decision in the case, I am the winner. If they find in favor of William of London, it shall appear to be through no effort of mine, and if they find against him, my show of dismay and contrition this day assures that none may suggest that I acted in open defiance of the king. All are placated except the king. Henry is fuming. And I am, quite inexplicably really, feeling a bit low.

As I slide beneath my covers and the tapers are put out, I realize that Henry has not come to me in more than a month—not since the argument over Flamstead began. This is the longest that he has eschewed my bed since our marriage. Not that Henry would be good company in his present mood. Still, the absence of his familiar form is nearly as oppressive as his anger. Lying in the dark, I shiver. Henry's square, familiar body usually quickly takes the chill off my sheets. This silliness has gone on for too long. I toy with the idea of seeking him in his chamber. But even should I manage to reach his rooms without being spotted by dozens of people, my pride rebels at going to him when *he* is at fault. I want reconciliation and am even willing to bend to get it, but not so far.

Perhaps I ought to withdraw to Windsor to be with my lambs, I think, rolling about in the vast empty bed, unable to get comfortable. The domestic tableau there would surely soften Henry's heart when he grew lonely and followed me. I try to picture the castle, the nursery, my children—but all I can see is Henry's face at dinner, cold without a single smile for me. It is not a comforting image. A man capable of such looks might well *not* follow me. The only time I had his attention all evening was when I danced with Geoffrey de Langley. There was no mistaking the black looks Henry threw our way. Well, Henry needs to be reminded that he loves me; perhaps I might use de Langley for that purpose. The thought surprises me. I turn it over in my mind, staring into the dark corners of my room. De Langley is younger than the king, well formed, and known for his shrewdness and ambition. If I draw him on to make Henry jealous, he will certainly play the courtly lover in return.

No! I thrust the thought away with vehemence. I am not capable of such cruelty. There is a special circle in hell for women who cuckold their husbands!

CHAPTER 24

Marguerite,

In my last letter I recounted how Henry and I were very nearly at war over the gift of a church living, and my disbelief that it should be so. I wish I could say that, with that argument at an end, our relations were improved, but they are not.

As vexing as it was when Henry ceased to be easily charmed by me, snapped at me, and disagreed with me over the smallest of matters, things are now even worse. I am overlooked. It is as if I am a stool or a tapestry. I am in the room, but I am not of interest. Last night, alone in the dark, I spent hours searching for some failing of mine that would justify this ill use, but I simply cannot understand what I do to displease Henry and turn him from me. I am very much as I ever was—and you must concede that one asset of a stubborn personality is that it seldom changes. I am older to be sure, and a little plumper. But if my waist has thickened these dozen years, 'twas the bearing of his four children that has worked the change, and he would do well to remember it.

My sole consolation presently is that I have heard no whisper that the king pursues other women. . . .

Eleanor

MARGUERITE
APRIL 1249
LIMASSOL, CYPRUS

"We are back where it began," Jean says. We sit, side by side, our horses drawn so close that our knees touch, looking down upon the city of Limassol. Yesterday the court returned to the coast in preparation for the voyage to the Holy Land.

"Did I love you this much then?" I ask teasingly. Then shaking my head I add more seriously, "No, I could not even imagine such a love."

Jean has taken me riding. As one of Louis's closest intimates he is trusted with everything, and *certainly* with my safe conduct. For appearances I have Marie with me. She sits on her own mount at a respectful distance. How glad I am now that I trusted her with my secret on the morning after I first took Jean to my bed in this very city. I remember how I feared her censure; how I dreaded telling her. But I had no choice—I needed her to take charge of my linens, which would betray my having lain with a man to any woman not virgin herself. And I knew also I would need her assistance if I were to have any hope of continuing my intimacy with the Seneschal of Champagne. How surprised I was when, after I made my confession, she threw her arms about my neck saying, "Bless you, lady! At last you will be loved as you deserve."

"Are you ready to go to the Holy Land?" Jean asks, calling me back to the present.

It seems an odd question. That is why we set forth from France, and already we have been away from home twice the time that I promised my little Louis. "Of course. And surely, despite the pleasures Cyprus has afforded"—I run my hand along the top of his thigh and leave it resting there in comfortable familiarity—"you are eager to be in battle? You are like all the others in this, like the king himself, spoiling to spill the blood of the Sultan of Cairo and his men."

Jean laughs. "You are right. I came to fight. But I dread two things about our departure from Cyprus—the weeks we must spend on separate ships without sound, sight, or touch of each other, and being as sick at sea as I was coming here."

"And which is worse, Sieur, being sick or being lonely?"

"I cannot make a fair comparison"—he gives me an easy smile—"as I have scarce gone two days without seeing you in the last four months."

The sun is setting off to our right. The water in the bay is touched with shades of pink. I am lost in my own thoughts and Jean in his. When we return to the palace, we will make love in the little walled garden where I first received Jean on the day Louis retained him. The air, already warming, will kiss my skin as Jean does. Then I will retreat to my rooms with the smell of him on my flesh, and Jean will go and sit with Louis until it is time for him to return to his lodgings for the evening.

As if reading my thoughts, Jean turns to me and says, "There was never a more pious man than His Majesty; I am convinced of it. Nor a better teacher."

I incline my head, noncommittally. I believe Louis's piety to be both very great and entirely sincere; however, unlike Jean, I am not swept up in it.

"Last night we spoke on the duty of a Christian knight to embrace the articles of faith without allowing a moment of doubt. And His Majesty offered an illustration that made all clear to me." Jean is most earnestly pious himself, and always striving to perfect his religious understanding. Yet, perhaps because he treats me so very differently than my husband does, his quest for religious certitude never rankles or annoys me.

"What did Louis say?" I am only mildly curious about the answer, but as it is clear Jean longs to tell me the rest of his story, I have no objection to hearing it.

"He asked me how I know that my father's name was Simon. I told him that while I was not so fortunate as to know my father, my mother had told me much of him, including his name. 'Well then,' His Majesty replied, 'if you have such faith in your mother, surely you will grant as much faith to the words of the apostles as represented by the Credo.'" Jean shakes his head in amazement. "Such a simple, clear, explanation. It did me much good."

We are quiet again, but I am no longer easy. While the continued and ever-growing closeness between my lover and my husband has many good effects—keeping Jean often in company with me and elevating him to the prominence that I feel his merit deserves—I cannot observe it without some misgiving. For it has a darker side. The more favor Louis shows him, the more Jean's conscience bothers him.

As if he is again privy to my private thoughts, Jean looks at me with a sudden, agonizing, seriousness. "Who am I?" he asks.

"You are a knight of great courage. His Majesty's faithful servant, and my own beloved friend."

"No." Jean's voice is rough, and he pushes my hand from his leg. "I am a traitor to my king and my queen's debaucher."

Now the guilt is mine—not guilt for betraying Louis, for I have not been bothered by that emotion for a single instant since giving myself to Jean—but guilt for Jean's tortured feelings. And something more—I feel ashamed. If Jean harbors regrets and I have none, then what am I but a lascivious woman and a temptress?

Pressing to my mouth the hand he expelled so violently, I begin to weep.

"Oh God," Jean says, his face falling, "I am sorry."

"You told me," I say, sobbing, "that once begun, we would not look back with remorse. But Louis bewitches you with his talk of God."

"No!"

"Yes." And suddenly I am angry. "But mark me well, my lord; Louis is no more perfect than I am or than you are! He is just as single-minded and selfish in the pursuit of his desires as we; just as possessed by his own sort of lust. Yet he is excused everything because his obsession is with God."

"Marguerite—"

"I do not want to hear it." But I *do* want to hear something. I want to hear Jean say he loves me and that my love is worth the discomfort he feels in Louis's presence, worth even the mortal sin we heap upon ourselves day after day. *How did this happen?* I think. How did our beautiful afternoon end in raised voices?

Jean appears stunned. He gives an odd, stiff, inclination of his head—almost a bow. "I will take you back," he says.

We ride in miserable silence. At least I presume Jean is miserable. I know I am. I cast a sidelong glance, hoping to read Jean's eyes, but he is staring straight ahead. As we come to the outskirts of the city, he pulls up his horse and looks directly at me for the first time since we left our vantage point.

"Forgive me," he says simply.

And I want to. Oh, how I want to. But my pride is stung. Jean has made me feel like an adulteress for the first time.

"Only when you forgive yourself."

Jean sighs. "I love you more than all the world, but do not look for me tonight."

I RISE AND DRESS THE next morning with nervous energy. I want to send away the *surcote* my ladies bring me and ask for the best I brought with me, but how can I possibly make such a request without raising suspicions? Jean likes to see me in pale blue—and not because it makes me resemble the Blessed Virgin. Gazing in my mirror, I see dark circles beneath my eyes, the product of the hours I lay awake worrying over our exchange of words. Others can see them too. Marie, who knows their cause, says nothing. But Matilda asks kindly, "Are you ill?"

"Perhaps like Lady Coucy, she expects a crusade baby," Beatrice quips saucily, leaning past me and helping herself to some of my rose water.

I feel a sudden surge of nausea, not because I am with child, but at the thought of Louis making me so. Thank heavens, after a revival of interest in such deeds, the king has not touched me in more than a fortnight. "No, no," I say, "bad dreams are all that is the matter with me. I slept ill."

"Bad dreams?" Matilda repeats, her brow furrowing. "I hope they are not omens. Did they have anything to do with ships?" She crosses herself. Matilda despises being at sea and dreads the next leg of our journey.

I smile reassuringly at her. "Not a single ship."

I am eager to arrive at Mass. Will Jean appear haggard, betraying that he too has passed a night without finding rest? But as I take my seat, I notice that the Seneschal of Champagne is not sitting in his customary place among the king's favorites. Where can he be? Surely our argument was not enough to keep him away.

Back in my rooms, with the window flung open to satisfy my desire for spring air and a small fire in the grate to accommodate the other ladies' constant fear of taking a chill, Marie raises the subject that I dare not. "The Seneschal of Champagne was not with us this morning."

"Perhaps he *overslept*," Beatrice answers in an odd tone. She lowers her voice conspiratorially, "Despite playing the saint before the king, Charles believes the seneschal kept a woman in Nicosia. Perhaps he has another here."

My ears burn, but I do not credit what my sister says. Charles is jealous of anyone who has more influence with Louis than himself. "I have not heard the seneschal's name mentioned among those debauching themselves," I say sternly. "And you know that His Majesty is constantly giving Giles le Brun the names of men to be reprimanded and urged to see their confessors."

"Oh heavens," says the Countess of Jaffa, "a face as fair as the Sieur de Joinville's can do better than a common prostitute." All the ladies save for me chuckle, for I am not the only woman who can and does appreciate Jean's beauty. "I would not be at all surprised if he partook of some of the local noblewomen."

I wonder what her serious-minded husband would think to hear her talk so, but I am certainly in no position to chastise.

Matilda tucks her needle into her embroidery and pushes back her frame. "Shall I go and see what Robert can tell of the seneschal's absence?"

She is not gone long and I am relieved at her return. Now all this nonsense will be at an end, and we will hear that Jean has a toothache or a sick horse.

"Well," says Matilda, beaming, "here is something for us to mull over in earnest. His Majesty received a message last evening from the Empress of Constantinople. She is stranded at Paphos and asked that Erard of Brienne and the Seneschal of Champagne be sent to her aid."

"Oh, the empress has an excellent taste in men! Two dashing knights to her rescue." Beatrice laughs.

"For heaven's sake, Beatrice," I chastise, "Lord Erard of Brienne is the empress's *cousin*."

"No doubt that is why she asks for him," says Matilda, "but why the Seneschal of Champagne? Does she know him?"

"Perhaps she would like to." Beatrice gives a not so subtle thrust of her hips. Vexatious to me at the best of times, she is truly becoming intolerable.

"I am sure, Matilda, that you misapprehended. His Majesty thinks highly of the Sieur de Joinville, *with good reason*." I give Beatrice a look. "No doubt the king suggested him for this commission." I am startled by how much my voice sounds like my mother's when I give a lecture. And I appear to be entirely convincing. But even as the other ladies nod and go back to their handwork, I wonder myself if it is true.

EMPRESS MARIE OF CONSTANTINOPLE ENTERS the hall with Jean at her elbow. It is the first time I have seen him since our quarrel; since his departure to collect the empress. His eyes meet mine, but there is little they can say in such a public setting. Yet, though I know as much, his face and figure hold my glance, and I look away with difficulty as the empress begins to speak.

"Your Majesties."

She is lovely; tall, with eyes as dark as Jean's. The hair showing beneath her veil and crown is likewise as dark as a raven's wing.

"I have come on behalf of the emperor to beseech Your Majesties to support him as you did before, lest Constantinople be lost."

Money and men; that is the empress's errand then. She is certainly dressed like a woman who comes begging. I wonder that she did not change before coming before the king. The mantle she wears shows every sign of the road. Well, this will do her no harm with Louis.

"Will you dine with us tomorrow?" Louis asks rather than commands, in deference to the equality of rank between us, though, given what the Emperor Baldwin II asks, my husband might be as imperious as he likes.

"With great pleasure, Your Majesty." Is it my imagination or do her long dark lashes flutter?

"We will discuss what is best to be done, and perhaps I can persuade the emperor to join us when we march on Egypt," the king says by way of dismissal.

Then she withdraws, Jean leading the way.

How I long to run after them.

Instead, I sit like stone beside my husband. I remain even after Louis, saying something by way of parting that I do not hear, takes his leave and goes about his business. My ladies mill around the now-otherwise-deserted hall, but I have not the energy to dismiss them. I observe with but half attention as Lady Coucy takes matters in hand and sends them off. She herself withdraws a short way with my dear Marie. I can hear them murmuring like water over small stones, and then, with a curtsy, Lady Coucy is gone as well. Marie takes a seat at my feet.

I continue in silence and in a state of strange suspension, unthinking, unseeing, but not unfeeling. As the shadows shift across the walls, I half expect Jean to return and find me where I sit like the carved effigy of a queen, but he does not. Finally as those same shadows lengthen incontrovertibly, I rise, saying simply, "I will dine alone and then retire early."

I seriously doubt that I shall either eat or sleep well. But better the possibility of nightmares than the certainty of bad thoughts.

Or so I tell myself as Marie leaves me in my bed for the evening. The disappearance of her candle as the chamber door shuts behind her seems symbolic—a reminder that the light in my life has gone dark.

The next morning Louis calls upon me in my rooms, startling not only my ladies but me as well.

"I am here, madam, to seek your advice."

I am dumbstruck. "My advice, Your Majesty?"

My husband paces back and forth. "I have been neglectful in my treatment of the empress, and I hope, with your help, to rectify my failing."

My mind travels back to Marie de Brienne's brief audience. It was completely unremarkable. How can Louis imagine he offended? "Whatever help I can offer, Your Majesty, I give gladly."

"The Lord of Nanteuil has just left me," Louis continues, taking the stool opposite my own and lowering his voice. "It seems when the empress abandoned her wind-torn ship, she had nothing but the clothing upon her back. I invited her to dine with the court without ever once considering that she might not be in a position to dress herself for the occasion!"

"Your Majesty could not have guessed her circumstances."

Louis looks into my eyes. It has been a long time since we have sat this close. A long time since I have had his full attention. "But I *ought* to have asked if she needed anything. Fortunately, there was one among our party who behaved better than I. Joinville sent the empress all the makings of a dress and *surcote* this morning. But surely such garments cannot be assembled by this evening?"

And with that sentence I cease to hear my husband. Jean has made a present to the empress. Perhaps he selected the fabrics himself yesterday afternoon when he was again absent from court. The image of Jean's hand running over a length of luxurious samite invades my mind. He has not the money for such things! Why did he not suggest she write to the king?

I realize that Louis is looking at me expectantly. He has clearly asked me something. Dear God, what was it? Marie, who hovers by habit just behind me, comes to my assistance. "I observed, Your Majesty, that the empress is willowy like you. Might you not make a present to her from your wardrobe?"

"Excellent!" Louis clasps his hands delightedly. "Surely there can be no insult in such a gift from the Queen of France."

Still dazed, I force a smile. "Indeed, Your Majesty, I will send her something of my best so that if we are *en retard*, we will not be outdone in quality. Marie, bring out my new gown made from the damask the Countess of Jaffa helped me to secure, and my pale blue *surcote*. It will look lovely with the empress's dark eyes."

Marie's jaw drops slightly. She hesitates. I nod dismissively, and she bustles off to my wardrobe. A short time later Louis leaves with the *surcote*. It is Jean's favorite, and he will never see me in it again.

My day passes slowly. No matter what my occupation, my mind is disturbed with regularity by two equally unsatisfactory images—first, the empress clasped in Jean's arms wearing a beautiful tunic of his choosing and second, the empress likewise embraced but wearing my very own *surcote*. The smile on Jean's face as he strokes her dark hair causes me much agony, though I chidingly remind myself the entire vision is woven of my own foolish fancy.

At dinner I keep my attention assiduously on Louis and our guest. I am unfailingly gracious to the empress, though the fact that she looks so lovely in my clothing, as lovely as I imagined she would, rankles me. As the meal comes to a close, I see Jean from the corner of my eye, trying, and not for the first time, to gain my attention.

Smiling at Louis, I say, "Shall we have dancing?"

Louis has always been a most excellent dancer. I long for Jean to watch my husband lead me to the floor; to see me flirting with him as our footwork is admired by all the court; to be jealous. True, the king has not danced since we left French soil, not even when the King of Cyprus held a banquet to welcome us. But now surely he will feel the call of duty—the duty to be a gracious host. And sure enough he rises. I do likewise, expecting him to offer me his hand. Instead he says, "Madam, with your indulgence, I would lead our guest to the floor. I am sure the Seneschal of Champagne would be honored to partner you."

I suppose I ought to have foreseen it. Louis, who is so supremely unconscious of his own rank, was bound to be scrupulously sensitive to the rank of our visitor. *Well,* I think, watching Jean come forward for me with a hand outstretched, *I can manage a single dance without falling to pieces.*

The musicians play a *nota,* a dance suited to conversation, but for the first moments we are silent. Then as we make a pass, Jean says quietly, "When can I see you?"

"You are seeing me now."

"To talk."

"Mercy, I had the impression that was what we are doing."

He gives me an exasperated look as the pattern parts us. Then I see his glance wander to the empress. Even now he cannot keep his eyes off her.

When we draw back together he begins again. "Why?"

"Why what?"

"Why that *surcote*?"

"You admire it and you admire her. Is it not fitting then that she should wear it?"

I watch the play of emotions on Jean's face. "This is about the empress?" His voice sounds oddly relieved, and his relief irritates me. "Then it is nothing."

Nothing! The cruelty of his words stings me. Here is another man who considers my feelings nothing—or rather something to be dismissed out of hand. I am grateful the dance is over. Louis comes to retrieve me, giving his partner's hand to Jean in the process. The next dance is an *estampie*, too complicated and quick for conversation, which is just as well for while I can feign a smile, I doubt I could manage a word. At every turn I seem to be confronted by the image of Jean and his pretty partner. I feel as if a great weight presses upon my chest. Is this what Eleanor feels when, in the heat of summer, she finds herself unable to breathe? When the music stops I say, "Your Majesty, I have a sudden headache. Do you think I might slip away to nurse it in solitude without giving offense to our guest?"

"Alone?" Louis seems genuinely concerned, and my conscience pricks at this lie though it has lain quiet through so many others.

"I would not have an indisposition of mine spoil the festivities in honor of the empress."

"Your consideration is laudable." Louis unexpectedly draws my hand to his lips. Only a few months ago I would have been thrilled at such a gesture, but now I only hope it makes Jean jealous. "Go and find relief. I will offer your excuses when your absence is remarked."

The music begins again. With so many bodies in motion I feel certain I can steal away without being noticed. But at the door of the hall, I glance back and find Jean's eyes upon me. In the corridor, I pick up my skirts and run toward the staircase. Surely, if I am quick I can reach my rooms.

I am not quick enough. At the bottom of the steps he catches me, pulling me out of the circle of illumination created by the nearest cresset and into the shadow of the steps.

"My Lord of Joinville, I must ask you to let me pass."

"You are being ridiculous!"

"Ridiculous?" I twist, trying to free myself from his grasp.

"Yes, ridiculous." Jean pins me against the wall, effectively thwarting my attempt to escape.

"I am not the one making a fool of myself over the Empress of Constantinople."

"The empress is here to gather knights—"

"And *you* were her first acquisition!"

"I gave her a letter pledging to go to Constantinople should Louis choose to send a force. Nothing more than she will get from many of the others."

"And did the others send her vair and *cendal*? I think not! Did you send her a fine linen shift as well?"

"Stop, please. The empress is nothing to me. Do I need to swear it?"

"The empress is nothing you say, but it is I who feel like nothing. Four days without word. You left me to think the worst."

"And did I not also think it?" Suddenly I see the pain behind Jean's exasperation. His eyes are nearly hollow with it. "When I waited in vain for Marie to bring a summons from you once you knew of my return? Tonight at dinner when your glances and smiles were only for Louis, a man who deserves them better than I? As for being nothing, you are everything—light, breath, food, drink—I am starving without you."

"But with me you are ruined. You said so yourself. You betray your king and your better nature."

"My king, yes, but myself, no. I am the man who loves you, body and soul. I can be no other. If I have learned anything during these last agonizing days, it is that. You need be jealous of no woman, not now, not ever."

I know he is not lying. I know it from the fierceness of his look, from the tone of his voice. I raise one hand up to the side of his face, and he turns to kiss my palm. Then a noise from above reminds us where we are. The shadow suddenly seems too shallow to safely contain us.

"Go," he whispers hoarsely. "I will follow."

And I want to run, to scamper to our garden, to seal our new understanding with a meeting of bodies, but suddenly I remember the look in Louis's eyes as I left him and I feel his lips upon my hand.

"The king," I say, "I cannot say why, but I know he will come to me tonight."

Jean moans. "I cannot bear to think of it."

"No"—again I reach up, this time to stroke his cheek—"not for that. He thinks I am ill. He will come to see how I fare." I feel Jean's muscles relax with relief. And then I am gone, my feet given wings by my happiness.

CHAPTER 25

My dear Eleanor,

It saddens me deeply to learn that you and your lord are no longer in accord. Your marriage seemed, like our parents' before it, a union of minds, hearts, and purposes. There were prickles and stings to be sure, and you were not shy in complaining of them, but always they seemed kept in check by a deeper affinity.

Oh Eleanor, who can say what causes a husband's regard to fade or what precisely will bring it back again? Perhaps constancy of affection is beyond some men. The renewed attention and affection that Louis showed me when we were gathering knights for crusade waned considerably once we were surrounded by those same knights and on our way to the Holy Land.

So I offer no advice. I will, however, remind you of the proverb "A bad peace is better than a good quarrel." This wisdom has oft helped me to moderate my own marital expectations.

M

MARGUERITE
JUNE 1249
OFF THE COAST OF EGYPT

Praise God we have come to Egypt at last, though there are not as many of us as there should be. While we were still within sight of the Point of Limassol, a great wind, like the breath of a fierce beast, came up, driving many vessels from our fleet to whence God alone knows and we do not. It is hard to understand why the Lord should see fit to blow so many of Louis's good knights off course for a second time. Everyone on the royal *nef* wonders at it.

Looking at the remaining ships, perhaps half of those that departed from Cyprus with us, I myself wonder but one thing— not what God meant by this second storm, nor whether we have enough knights left to meet the infidels, but is Jean's party among them? It is the question that has been dogging me for nearly three weeks—keeping me from resting as the rough waves have kept others. The image of him cast up on some strange shore discomforts me, but strangely, I do not fear him lost at sea. Surely, if he were gone from this world, my heart would know it instinctively.

And now in a short time I will know if he is among the missing. Louis has sent word to the other ships anchored around us in the open water calling those of rank and status to the royal *nef* so that the first battle of this campaign can be discussed. While I wait for the arrival of this august group of knights, and for the one among them the sight of whom will banish all worries in an instant, there is something to distract me.

The land mass that this morning was merely an indistinct sliver has grown to a distinguishable shore. The outline of a city is clear as are the figures of men on the beach. Such men! They glisten more golden than the sun that sets them on fire. And rising from their number, a constant beating of drums and sounding of horns render the air alive with the anticipation of battle. I feel it as keenly as the knot of men surrounding the king. Beatrice and I are the lone ladies on deck. The same drums that excite the men terrify the rest of my companions. We sisters from Provence, it seems— much as we are dissimilar in other ways—are made of sterner stuff than the Frenchwomen.

"So few!" Beatrice says. "If this is all the mighty Ayyüb can muster, we will be in the Holy Land less time than we were in Cyprus."

"I hope so," I say, thinking of my son Louis still counting the days at home, and Beatrice's little Louis left behind with a nurse at Limassol. Besides, an army conquered with ease would mean fewer dead and fewer injured.

Then a sailor in the riggings calls out, *"Le barche,"* and Beatrice and I join the rush to the opposite side of the deck. The water is littered with an assortment of ships' boats approaching from every direction. Just below, so close that he must step aside as the rope ladder is dropped, is Jean.

He smiles up at me mischievously, as if he enjoyed worrying me all these weeks. He is up the ladder in an instant. How I wish I could clasp him to me when he reaches the deck, but instead Louis does. Jean's greeting to me is limited to a slight bow as he moves away to make space for other knights scrambling aboard.

He and his cousin are quickly drawn into a group including Louis's brothers. Though everyone talks at once, Jean remains silent, gazing in my direction. I know he pays no more attention to what they are saying than I am paying to Beatrice who continues to comment on each new arrival. He looks wonderful. His skin has a warm glow imparted by many hours in the sun. I cannot detect any loss of weight, which would suggest that he avoided seasickness on this journey despite his fears.

There are too many men to fit comfortably in Louis's cabin, so when the last of the small boats is moored, the knights merely stand near the forecastle to begin their discussions. I wonder if the sultan's warriors on the shore can see them, but as most do not have their armor on, I doubt they glitter despite the brilliant sun.

"I would attack at once," says Louis, "using every boat available with hull shallow enough to approach the shore."

"Your Majesty," rejoinders Philip of Nanteuil, "would it not be more prudent to wait for your men and arms that were blown off course?"

"You urged me to wait at Cyprus, and I did wait," Louis replies, "but this is the second time God has seen fit to scatter some of my forces asunder. There is a message in this. God wishes my troops to be as they are—not one man more, not one man less. Besides, we greatly outnumber them as we are. What honor could there be in waiting for more overwhelming numbers?"

"None, Your Majesty." I thrill at the sound of Jean's voice. "But what of those of us who have no galley available to go ashore?"

"Here is a man after my own heart, eager to be slaying infidels," says Louis, his face flushing with pleasure. "My Lord of Beaumont, see that the Seneschal of Champagne has a galley at his disposal." Erard of Brienne slaps Jean on the shoulder in delight. The two have been inseparable since they traveled to Paphos, and no doubt he thinks to row to shore with Jean. "What do you say, Beaujeu?" the king asks, turning to his constable expectantly.

Beaujeu did not rise to his office by fighting losing battles. "Your Majesty speaks with reason. In addition, unsheltered as we are in this place, it would only take another surge of strong winds to scatter the rest of our ships."

"Tomorrow then, at dawn, we will teach the Sultan of Cairo what Christian men may do with the blessing and in the name of their God."

Dawn. Must I then send Jean into battle uncaressed and uncried over? So it would seem. The leave we took of each other in Cyprus will have to see us through this greater separation.

He lingers till the last, till only half a dozen men remain to retreat to their boats, then gives me a peculiar look over Louis's shoulder as they embrace in parting. Even as I have profound confidence in him, I wonder, when I see him next, will he be alive or dead?

IT IS THE PROVINCE OF women to wait. I feel as though I have been waiting my whole life—waiting to bear a son, waiting for the dragon to surrender her hold on the king, waiting for Louis to realize he can love God and love me. I excelled once at patience and acceptance, swallowing my disappointments; counting on perseverance and time to change what I could not. But, having finally been granted the heart of a good man, time and fate now have the power to take away as well as give. So, as the boat bearing my husband and his standard makes for shore, my heart beats faster than the rowers' oars. I pace back and forth along the ship's rail, heedless of the stares of my ladies.

I can have no hope of spotting Jean and his men among those heading to battle. Other than Louis's boat, the only vessel distinguishable belongs to the Count of Jaffa. This boat is so thoroughly covered with his coat of arms that no man on shore or at sea can doubt whom it carries. Then, as the landing party nears the shore, a vessel crammed with men and horses passes the boat carrying the king and his royal standard. I know with a certainty of the heart if not the eyes that the boat that has taken the lead is Jean's. It draws up to the shore and men begin to pour from it like ants.

"The king!" Matilda cries, and my eyes snap back to Louis's boat. It is not yet to the beach, but someone is in the water, waves lapping at his breast, arms over his head. When I see the royal standard in those upstretched arms, I know my sister-in-law is right. Louis has jumped from his boat.

"Eager fool!" I clutch Marie, thinking of the weight of Louis's armor. "He will drown himself."

But as I watch, Louis struggles to the shore, standard still in hand. Boats are falling thick upon the beach. Frenchmen set their shields into the sand and their lances as well, creating a deadly and pointed wall between themselves and the sultan's men who ride forward. And like that, the battle begins—we can see horses in motion, lines of French bowmen making easy shots across the sandy expanse, men falling—yet at this distance it all seems strangely unreal, down to the muted cacophony of drums and horns, cries, and grunts.

I cannot say if the time is long or short, so fascinated am I by the constant motion of the fighting. I am trying to find Louis among the fray when my sister's voice sounds.

"The cowards run!" she shouts.

Deo gratias, I believe Beatrice is right! The forces of the sultan have turned, and with our knights in pursuit, they move at break-neck speed toward the outlines of Damietta. As quickly as it began the skirmish is over. The beach so full only moments before is largely empty. Only boats and the bodies of the fallen mar the golden tan expanse. I wonder how many we have lost and, more important, if any I knew or loved are among them.

"SOMETIMES IT IS A BLESSING that Louis neglects you."

This is the first moment I have had alone with Jean since I sighted him on the deck of a galley rowing out to the royal ship. Louis, it seems, cannot waste his time bringing me ashore, and delegates the task, even though it means another has the pleasure of announcing the victory.

Throwing my arms around Jean's neck, I give him a long kiss by way of reply. We are in my cabin, alone save for Marie who is packing my things. My other ladies are readying their own belongings. It is three days since Louis's boat rowed to the beach. The city of Damietta is his, and soon we will be escorted to it.

"Don't you want to hear about the taking of the city?" Jean asks.

"No," I reply, reaching up to put both my hands in his curls, headless of the sweat and dust that cover him. "All that I needed to know of the battle I knew when I saw you alive and whole."

"And I was counting on an opportunity to spin tales of my bravery."

"I promise to hear every word of your stories, only save them for a time when I am better able to attend. Marie, get me some water and a clean cloth, so the Seneschal of Champagne can wash."

"Ought we to be so publicly alone?" Jean asks as the door falls shut behind my retreating companion.

"No one will notice. Everyone runs back and forth preparing to disembark. Besides," I add longingly, "what can we do in a few moments anyway?"

"Not what I want to do, that is sure." Jean smiles. "Every moment of the three weeks since I held you last I have thought of nothing else." Then, perhaps seeing my skeptical look, he adds, "Well, every moment except when I was in battle."

Marie returns bearing a basin and a length of linen.

"Food and wine," I say. "Surely, even with all the tumult of packing, a man fresh from battle can be fed."

Then, walking Marie to my cabin door, I add under my breath, "Do not hurry."

I help Jean remove his tunic, then the coat of mail and the padded pourpoint underneath. Seating him before my mirror, I dampen the cloth and begin to wipe the dust from his face and his neck. He sits completely still and silent. There is something oddly reverential and deliberate about my washing of him, and at the same time something painfully erotic. I kneel to remove his chausses and then, when he sits in nothing but his silk *gamboised cuisses*, I begin to wipe his chest. He moans with pleasure, watching my every move in the mirror. Dropping the cloth, I unlace the front of his *cuisses*. In a single fluid movement I lift my skirts and lower myself onto his engorged member. We sit face-to-face and, as I raise and lower myself rhythmically upon him, Jean devours me, kissing my face, my neck, my ears.

"Oh God, how I've missed you," he murmurs, his arms entwined around me, pulling me against his damp chest.

The abstinence imposed upon us by the voyage to Egypt assures that all my sensations are exaggerated. Each time I settle upon him, the feel of his flesh sliding against mine nearly overwhelms me. I cannot pull him in deep enough, nor hold him there long enough. Yet, even as I experience this pleasure, I dread the moment he will break it off and pull himself, unsatisfied, from me. I stop moving.

"What is the matter?" Jean asks, his eyes wild.

"I want you to give me your child."

"Marguerite, you cannot ask it." The words come out in a shocked gasp.

"But I do ask it. The battle for Damietta was but the first. We will be parted again and again, and each time I will fear your loss every moment until your return. Give me a part of you to hold in my arms and as a talisman against your death. Give me your son."

"If someone should guess."

"Why would they?"

"Louis hardly touches you, and if no one else knows that, he certainly does."

"The day I know my womb is quickened, I will do whatever is necessary to bring Louis to my bed. He will never deduce the child is not his, while I will have the joy of knowing for certain that it is yours."

"My son . . ." I can see the longing in Jean's eyes—not a sexual longing, but the same desire I feel, to create something solid and beautiful from our love, damnable though it may be. "Yes," he says simply.

Slowly I begin to move my hips once more. Jean's lips are upon mine. His organ, which had started to subside in our pause, hardens again to stone. As I begin to gasp with pleasure, glad that his mouth dampens my moans so that no one but he can hear them, I feel a change in his breathing. It is rapid and ragged. Then his arms pull me to him and, with his face buried against my shoulder, he cries out into the fabric of my dress and lets himself go.

I find myself praying for the first time during the act of love. *Holy Mary, most blessed of all mothers, forgive me my sins and bless me with the child of my beloved.*

I SIT ON A BENCH in the autumn sun, waiting for Jean. Now that it is obvious I am with child, we meet alone quite openly. It is beyond the imaginings of the noblemen and ladies surrounding us that anything improper could take place between the king's favorite and the king's pregnant wife. Nor has there been a breath of scandal about the babe itself. Louis is quite inordinately and surprisingly delighted to be the father of a child destined to be born in the Holy Land. As for the real father, Jean could not be more tender or attentive.

I run my hand over the arch of my belly, enjoying the curve of it. The late-afternoon sun no longer reaches my seat, but the rays that bathed it for most of the day have left the stone warm. It amazes me to think that in Paris they shiver already. For the second winter in a row I will be where the cold cannot touch me, but, as wondrous as my life has been since my eyes last lingered on the French coast, I cannot reflect on the passage of so much time without a touch of sadness. My little Louis will be six in February. The fluttering of a new life within me makes me think more often of my golden prince. Can he still remember my face? Is he counting the days as I asked him to, even though their number are now five times what he ever thought to tally before I came home again?

I cannot help but think that Robert, usually the favorite of my brothers-in-law, is the reason we are not home victorious already. After Damietta fell, an offer came from the Sultan of Cairo to exchange the holy city of Jerusalem for it. Imagine! Jerusalem in Christian hands after only a single battle! Jean and I were sure Louis would accept, as were any number of the king's advisers, but Robert of Artois set himself against it, arguing that the sultan would make such a trade only if he felt Jerusalem likely to be lost in any event. He painted pictures of a broader triumph, and Louis, flush with confidence in God's blessing after finding the gates of Damietta open and the city largely deserted before him, listened. Installing the court in his new city, Louis, so eager to fight when we first sighted shore, resolved to wait for the ships that had gone astray and for the arrival of Alphonse and Jeanne, who had initially remained in France to assist the dragon in establishing her regency.

So, I have lived in Egypt nearly as long as I did in Cyprus. The memory of the battle on the beach has become distant, replaced by the reality of daily raids on the camp surrounding the city walls—of men left beheaded in their sleep; of our crossbowmen picking off Saracen riders at a distance—juxtaposed with long stretches of time unbroken by useful activity for the majority of Louis's troops.

Then two days ago, the sails of a ship on the horizon brought the promise of change. The Count and Countess of Poitiers have arrived at last on Egyptian soil, so Louis's council meets to decide on battle plans.

Jean arrives, rounding a clump of low palms and looking cross. "Well, the Count of Artois continues *much* in favor!" he says as he approaches. Whatever was decided at the meeting, it is not to Jean's liking.

"What is the matter, love?" I pat the bench next to me, but he either does not see or is too agitated to sit.

"We are *not* going to Alexandria." Jean runs a hand through his curls in exasperation.

"What? But I thought all agreed? Only yesterday at dinner I heard the Count of Brittany and the constable discussing the fine harbor there and how it would make supply of our armies an easy thing."

"His Majesty, as you know better than anyone, has no interest in easy things."

"True."

"The Count of Artois has convinced him to march against Cairo, saying, 'He who wishes to kill the serpent must first crush the head.'"

"But Cairo is inland." My mind runs over the vast stores of supplies we spent so much time and money collecting at Cyprus. Some of them have of course been ferried ashore during the last months, but the majority of our supplies lie safely still in the bellies of our ships—waiting for a trip to Alexandria that will not be made.

"We must depend on the river." Jean sits at last and puts his head in his hands. When he looks up, he says, "More than thirty-five leagues of river and we will have to control it all or risk being cut off from resupply."

"God help us."

"He will have to. This is what His Majesty counts upon—the divine righteousness of our cause."

"And you?"

"I believe in the power of Christ and his saints, but I do not understand why it is necessary to make our victory in God's name less certain and more difficult than it need be."

"When do you go?"

"The king would depart at the beginning of Advent, and it is providential."

"Let us pray so."

I HAVE BEEN CRYING MOST of the day—not sobbing, but breaking into tears without warning and over the oddest things. I am not alone. Earlier, as she finished a shirt that Robert will take with him, Matilda's cheeks were tracked with tears. Even my sister Beatrice, usually brassy in her confidence, is subdued, but she blames her melancholic turn on the babe in her belly rather than on any fear for her husband in battle.

Tomorrow they go. All the men, or nearly all. Louis leaves five hundred under the command of the Duke of Burgundy to hold the city until his return and to safeguard me and the other wives.

My ladies have left me, each to pass a last evening with her husband according to her own nature, some in forced cheerfulness and others clinging and solemn. I do not believe there is a single one among us who does not fear or dread the rising of tomorrow's sun.

Louis made it clear that he will pass the whole of the night in his camp outside the city walls, praying. He took his leave of me after we dined. And though I am a faithless wife in the eyes of the Lord, my heart ached to see him go. But when, overcome by a sudden feeling of tenderness, I urged him to take care for himself, his reply reminded me that my concern is wasted. *"Deo adjuvante non timendum,"* he said. "God helping, nothing should be feared." His tone was so nonchalant, as if Our Lord's help was a thing certain. Not for the first time I wished I had a little more of his faith, and he a little less of it.

Jean left with Louis. It would have been unseemly for him to linger behind. But he swore he would find a way to return to say the farewells we had not the luxury of before the last battle. I sit at my dressing table, carefully examining my face for any evidence of tears. I would send my love away with an image of my beauty, not of my sadness, etched in his memory.

A knock sounds. I am surprised it is so bold. It must be other than Jean. Marie rises from her place before the fire and goes to the door. It opens to reveal a guard I do not know.

"A messenger from His Majesty the King," he announces.

Jean stands just behind him, looking very officious. I nearly laugh in spite of myself.

"I cannot stay long."

I take his hand and silently lead him to my bed. Fully clothed, we lie face-to-face, drinking in the sight of each other.

"Promise me something." I reach out a hand to touch his cheek.

"What?"

"Promise that you will confess before you go into battle."

"No." Jean's voice is fierce. "The danger is too great. Do you believe for a minute that any confessor is above being bribed, or merely using what he knows to his own advantage?"

I drop my hand.

"You know I speak truly," Jean continues. "You do not even trust William de St. Pathus so much. You do not confess our sin. You carry its full weight upon you day after day. This is the burden we agreed to when first we came together. I do not flinch from it now."

"You never flinch from anything," I say, taking his hand and placing it on the swell in my belly. "That is why I love you." I put my other hand behind his neck and kiss him.

Mine is not the sort of kiss to incite passion but rather the sort that is beyond passion—a kiss that is a seal, that says, *"You are to me as holy ground."* And I feel in his lips, in the hand that cradles his unborn son, the same sort of love returned, a love that puts the other before everything.

"Do you not know," I say, drawing away and regarding him solemnly, "that I will worry every minute you are gone that you have fallen under some Saracen's sword?" Jean opens his mouth, no doubt to reassure me, but I place a finger on his lips. "That worry alone will be nearly unbearable. Would you heap upon it the fear that with every exchange of blows you risk eternal damnation on my account?"

"What can I do?" Jean asks.

"What has the king complained of endlessly while we waited for the last of the ships to arrive? That the men have fallen into evil and idle ways, just as they did at Cyprus. Into gambling, into drinking, into *fornication*." Jean looks puzzled; clearly he does not understand where I am headed. "Go to your confessor and tell him that you have had carnal knowledge of a woman not your wife." Jean raises his eyebrows. "It is the truth. Not the full truth, but I think you may do penance for the sin without confessing the lady's name."

"The priest will think I have been with a whore!" Jean's face reddens. He sits up suddenly, leaving me to look at his back. "That very thought defames you, Marguerite, in a manner I cannot bear."

I rise slowly from my own side of the bed and move round it to his to stand before him. "If I can bear the worry and the waiting, surely the ill thoughts of a priest who does not even know whom he insults can be nothing to me."

"Does it mean so much to you?"

"Yes."

He swallows hard. "Then I will do it."

I lean down and kiss him again.

"And will you do something for me?" he asks. "Will you give me something of yours to carry with me over the many leagues that lie ahead?"

I nod and then retreat to my wardrobe. I have so many things—costly things, among them brooches and rings of great value that might preserve Jean from want in some faraway city. But when it comes to imbuing luck and to the protection that love can provide, there is only one object worthy of my knight.

Returning to my bedchamber, I hold out the much-worn *aumônière*, the crimson and orange of its poppies faded. A true gift of the heart—first Eleanor's and now mine.

As if he knows as much, Jean says, "It shall be sewn into my pourpoint over my ribs as a reminder that as Eve was Adam's rib, you are mine."

CHAPTER 26

My dearest sister,

. . . I am grown tired of searching my character for shortcomings and heaping blame upon myself for my present marital unhappiness. It occurs to me that when your husband failed to show you the affection you deserved, you were not in the least to blame—for you tended your marriage as the most careful gardener. So why have I presumed that some failure on my part must account for the sudden neglect I suffer?

No, I declare it boldly, Henry is the root of our marital ills. They are, it seems to me, a natural outcropping of his capricious nature, grown ever more so as he ages. I know I have oft recounted stories of his changeable temper, sanguine one minute and peevish the next. But before these last wretched months, I was, if you will recall, generally a witness to his fits of pique rather than a victim of them. That has altered. Now Henry is likely to see me as someone wholly apart from himself and his interests, when he notices me at all. Therefore I am as likely to bear the brunt of his sudden anger as anyone else at court, and I do not like this change at all. . . .

Eleanor

ELEANOR
AUTUMN 1249
LONDON, ENGLAND

"Henry, will you not come with me to Windsor? It is so beautiful this time of year, and the children would be happy to see you."

"Eleanor, I have work." The words come out in a tone of admonition, not regret. As if to punctuate my husband's thought, John Mansel and a clerk carrying a sheaf of documents enter.

"Beg pardon, Your Majesties," Mansel says, spotting me and preparing to retreat.

"No, no, come ahead," Henry replies. "The queen is leaving." His eyes move in my direction as he speaks, but I do not have the feeling that he truly looks at me.

"What shall I tell the children?"

"I will ride out next week or the week after, as my business allows."

"I will be very sorry not to have your company on my journey." I am not even rewarded with a smile.

Closing the door behind me, I turn to stare at its oaken length. The man who sits behind this door is not the same man who thirteen years ago took me as his bride, called me his treasure, and meant it. He is not even the same Henry as two years ago. That autumn Henry ordered a bower woven through with colored leaves and late-blooming flowers built in a corner of my garden at Windsor as a surprise for me and then ravished me inside its shadows.

The marital contentment I took for granted for so long has vanished. I cannot say precisely when it started to fade. I suppose it began to diminish so gradually that at first I did not notice it. Certainly by the time the fuss over the living at Flamstead arose, I was aware that something was wrong. But, foolishly, I thought Henry and I were only experiencing a small episode of rough weather and things would right themselves of their own accord. The last months have disabused me of that notion and left me far less sanguine. Nothing I do pleases Henry anymore, at least not for long. Nothing I say charms him.

Turning on my heels I return to my apartments. My ladies are packing my things. *They* look up and smile as I enter. *They* are very much as they ever were. But the rooms themselves seem suddenly faded. The color has drained from the pink and white roses on my walls. Doubtless sunlight has faded them, and fixing them would be easy enough if I had the energy to order it. An artist could come in and touch up the paint while I am at Windsor. I wish it were as easy to understand the fading of my husband's love for me and that it were as easy to fix.

In the evening Henry comes to my rooms as is his habit. Henry, the King of England comes, not *my* Henry. His face is sullen from the moment he enters. He takes his glass of wine from my hand with no thanks and no smile.

"Henry, what is the matter?"

"The matter?" My husband pauses where he is undressing beside my fire. "Other than my being overwhelmed by complaints from the Gascon barons about de Montfort's rough treatment of them? He has disinherited William de Solaires."

"I do not want to talk about Gascony."

"Really, madam, well, here is a first. You have badgered me about securing Gascony ever since we took it back from Richard."

I am on the verge of demanding whether it is wrong to care for the fortunes and possessions of our beloved son, but I stop short, letting my hands drop from my hips. Such a remark will only set us upon a political discussion and a contentious one at that. Ever since I pressed my point over Flamstead and won, I have been nagged by the growing conviction that the cost of my victory was greater than my pleasure in it and that, in fact, I made things worse for myself.

As I stand looking at my husband—his posture indicating that he is waiting, perhaps even wanting to fight—I think back to a letter Marguerite sent me, to the proverb "Better a bad peace than a good quarrel." Perhaps that is correct. Perhaps being right and proving as much to Henry is not as important as being in his good graces. I promise myself I will not say another word, and then I do.

"I am less worried about Gascony than I am about us. You will not come to Windsor with me tomorrow; you scarcely seem to notice me anymore—"

"I did not come here to be nagged." Henry cuts me off. With a defiant look he picks up his tunic and pulls it back over his head.

"Henry, please, why are you so quick to be angry with me?"

"I might ask why you are so quick to criticize. God's blood, nothing I do suits you. You would do well to remember that *I am* the husband here; *I am* the king. It is not my role to please; it is yours." With a vicious tug Henry tightens the girdle at his waist. "I believe I will sleep better tonight if I sleep alone."

After Henry goes, I sit on the edge of my bed and cry. Tomorrow morning I leave for Windsor. To leave on such a note! Why oh why did I say anything at all this evening about our relationship? I could have talked of little things and allowed Henry to exhaust himself in my bed. Had I done so, I would have nothing to keep me awake this night but his snoring. Now I fear I will be sleepless with worry.

When Uncle Peter comes to take a private leave of me shortly after sunrise the next morning, he is quick to notice the dark circles beneath my eyes.

"Niece, I am glad you are leaving," he says. "The country air will bring you better sleep."

"I seriously doubt so. And though the river smells particularly bad this season, it is not London, its noise, or its filth that disturb my rest. I fear, sir, that I am losing the king."

"Why, because he no longer comes when you crook your finger?" Peter seems vaguely amused by this, and I cannot reconcile it. After all, he is always first to remind me of my position at the pinnacle of Savoyard power in the English court. Surely it cannot please him that my influence wanes.

"It is no light matter. If I am diminished, Uncle, many will make the descent with me."

"Eleanor, you must learn to distinguish between Henry the king and Henry the man. It would be troubling indeed if your power to influence the king politically were to seriously lessen, but that is unlikely in my estimation. Henry has surrounded himself with your kith and kin and continues to listen to their advice, even in the face of competition from the Lusignans. Of course, that could change, but I will do all I can to prevent it, and that includes pointing out to you what should be obvious." My uncle Peter pauses for a moment to shift in his seat and take my hand. "Henry the man is not young anymore, nor is your marriage. You are in the middle of things. The time of grand passion may be past, but the time for hard work is not. If you can reconcile yourself to courting respect and not adoration; if you can keep your eyes and your energies focused on our projects, I believe all will be well."

I feel my face warming. "Do you mean I must accept Henry's diminishing regard? Accept it, though I have given him all a husband could want?" My voice catches. What I really mean and cannot bear to say aloud is that I have given Henry my whole heart and cannot imagine surviving the pain of having such a gift set aside as if it were a tunic that no longer fits. Can this, I wonder, be what my dear sister has felt for most of the years of her marriage? Lonely and abandoned? How horrible. And though I have been sympathetic to her complaints, I suddenly wish there had been a deeper compassion in me as I listened to them. I understand them at this moment as I never did before.

"A husband's wants change. Cannot a wife's expectations do likewise?"

"No."

My uncle sighs. "Come, Eleanor. I will escort you to your horse. The ride to Windsor offers you an excellent opportunity to think. You are always quick to know your own mind and slow to change it, but I have every faith that you will see the sense of what I say in the end. You are too practical to risk all we have built—patronage and power, your son's legacy—merely to chase after the romantic stuff of troubadours' tales."

Each day I pass at Windsor I expect to receive a letter from Henry saying he is coming. When I am gone from London a week complete, I give orders that I am to be notified immediately, day or night, should the king arrive. When I am with my children a month and the trees in my garden are bare, I cease waiting for a servant to come running with word that Henry has arrived. Then, just as I begin to believe Henry will stay in London and I will not see him until I go to Westminster for our Christmas court, Margaret Biset returns to my chamber shortly after I have been put to bed. The king is here. I am on my feet and giving orders in an instant.

"Eleanor?" Henry looks up with surprise as I enter his apartments. He is seated. While one servant unclasps the cloak from about his neck, another begins to remove one of his boots. "I did not expect my arrival to wake you."

"I had only just gone to bed, Husband, and I asked to be roused."

"Is something wrong?"

"No indeed, now that you are here everything is right." I smile in the sweetest manner possible. "I was only eager to see you and to make sure that you want for nothing after your ride. Are you hungry?"

Henry's eyes drop to the platter I carry, filled with cold meat and other tidbits.

"I am."

I bustle to Henry's table and begin to lay a place for him while his second boot comes off. Uncle Peter was right; my ride to Windsor gave me time to think, as did the time I passed here without my husband. But my conclusions were not, perhaps, those my uncle predicted. I will not abandon the project of recapturing Henry's love. I merely mean to wage my battle by stealth rather than bold action. I will be charming, agreeable, even diffident, as mild mannered as my sister Marguerite, even if it kills me. And while some part of me knows that this effort may be futile—after all, Marguerite's docile nature did not bring her a happy marriage—I cannot think what else to try.

Henry dismisses the servants with a nod, takes a seat at the table, and tucks into the food. I say nothing, though I am eager to pepper Henry with questions about the capture of my cousin Gaston de Béarn in Gascony. Instead, I stand silent, waiting table for my husband and making certain his goblet remains full.

Henry swallows a mouthful of bread. "How are the children?"

"All well. I cannot wait for you to see Edmund. I think the new course of activity the doctor prescribed for him is making a difference, for it seems to me he stands straighter."

"Marvelous."

"Tell me about your journey."

There is not much less engaging than an account of a ride over the same English roads I traveled myself six weeks ago, but, to my credit, I manage to keep my eyes upon my husband and feign interest and attention as he talks of his trip.

As he finishes his account, Henry reaches out for my hand. "I am glad you came to greet me." He pulls me into his lap.

"Shall I stay the night with you?" My offer is contrary to our habit, which is to spend those evenings we pass together in my apartment, and the novelty appears to spark my husband. He answers me with a kiss, somewhat sloppy from the wine he has consumed. But no matter, a kiss is a kiss. I murmur appreciatively, making more of the gesture than it deserves. Flattery and feigned delight may not be palatable to me, but they are easier to stomach than estrangement. Marguerite was right—a bad peace is better than none at all.

"LISTEN TO THIS. 'THE INFIDELS turned and abandoned the fray, though they were mounted and His Majesty's men on foot.'" Marguerite's letter from the Holy Land arrived this morning, proclaiming a magnificent French victory at Damietta. As soon as I finished it, I came to Henry's apartments, believing that within its pages I might finally have found an event, an aspiration, strong enough to completely restore the affinity between my husband and me.

We are at Westminster in preparation for Christmas. My campaign of sweetness and liberal praise has done much to keep us from arguing openly, and the approach of the festivities attendant upon the season has put Henry in a jovial mood; yet I remain unsatisfied. We still lack the fire of the first decade of our marriage and also the easy accord. We need a project to unite us. I had hoped an addition to our family would do the trick—Henry has always been adoring and attentive when I am carrying his child—but our coupling is as infrequent now as it was frequent for so many years—infrequent and also uninspired. Is that, I wonder, why I have failed to conceive? Must I be satisfied to be fertile? There can be no other explanation as I am only twenty-six, certainly not yet past an age for the bearing of babies. Whatever the reason, if a child is not forthcoming, another undertaking must be found.

Perhaps if we go to the Holy Land, all will be well for us. My sister is happy there, just as she was in Cyprus. Her letter shows it. She is happy despite having been dissatisfied with her husband for many years. I have been discontented with Henry for a much shorter time, so surely my happiness will be more easily restored by a dose of crusading? Seeing the excitement in Henry's eyes, I feel my hopes rise.

"Go on," he urges, looking up from his table spread with drawings and notes in the clear, distinctive hand of Henry of Reyns concerning the ongoing work at Westminster Abbey.

" 'The sultan's troops ran past the city, neglecting in their haste to sever the bridges. And so His Majesty reached the city walls without inconvenience or molestation, and, finding the gates of the city left open when its guardians who, no braver than their fellows on the beach, fled before our armies, the king entered the place and made it ours.' "

"Magnificent!" Henry says thumping his fist with satisfaction upon the tabletop and sending a sketch floating to the floor. "Such a victory." For a moment he forgets that Louis is a rival. He sees not the man whose father once nearly stole the English throne but only the dramatic events in which the King of France has recently taken part.

"Henry, you should go to the Holy Land," I say, coming

forward to scoop up the fallen paper and place it back before him. "Do you not long to see it, and to hear your prelates sing *Te Deum Laudamus* at the site of a triumph in battle?"

"By God I do, Eleanor." Henry beams. Then his face falls suddenly. "Do you think I would have the support of my barons? They deny me their backing and thwart me in so many other endeavors."

"They are a pack of obstinate fools." I take Henry's face in my hands and kiss him lightly on the end of his long nose. I wonder when the touch of gray appeared in the hair just at the center of his forehead. "But surely we can get fourscore or so to take the cross with you. And as for the majority of your subjects, they will surely be excited to see you follow in the footsteps of your uncle the Lionheart. When you come home covered in glory, those barons who make so bold in their criticisms of you now will be more careful in their talk and respectful in their tone."

"You know, Eleanor, I do believe you are right." Henry takes both my hands and squeezes them. He crumples Marguerite's letter in the process, but no matter, it has already done its work.

"Louis of France's crusade enhances his reputation. Why should not such an expedition also elevate mine? Am I not as brave as Louis? And as pious? Surely God will grant me the favor and success he has given the French king."

"Let us take the cross! At Canterbury in grand style."

"You will take the cross with me?"

"If you permit it. I would by no means miss the opportunity to see you riding across the desert sands, banners raised high and armor shining in the sun, like the great knights of the crusade poems."

"Shall I bring you an infidel's head as a tribute?" Henry asks, pulling me onto his lap.

I cannot help but imagine the scene: reclining under a golden tent, high on some hill where I can see the armies clash below; Henry, storming back to me after routing the Saracens, carrying the turbaned head of an infidel general on the saddle before him.

"By all means. And reclaim the holy city of Jerusalem in the name of God and the Confessor so that poets will sing your praises for a hundred years," I reply with excitement. What pleasure there would be in that! The unhappy lyrics of those dreadful songs composed half a dozen years ago when we failed in Poitou still haunt me but would be driven from my mind completely by such new tales.

A SCANT TWO MONTHS LATER I sit in my rooms writing to my sister of the transformation that preparing to crusade has wrought upon my husband. As I dip my quill into my ink to sign my letter, I remember when, not so many years ago, she wrote a similar missive to me. The day is bright presaging spring and lifting the spirits of all my ladies to giddy heights.

I do not need the good weather to make my heart light. My own personal crusade conducted on English soil has been victorious. Lured by some combination of my changed behavior and the excitement of working together to prepare for our travel to the Holy Land, my husband's attention and admiration have returned to me. I am once again not only the Queen of England but also the queen of his heart.

I give my letter to Willelma to dispatch, wondering how long it will take to reach Damietta, or to find its way into Marguerite's hands if she has already moved on to other cities and other victories. Months, that is certain. What new adventures will she have in the meantime? And what exciting experiences has she had already in the time it took her last letter, announcing that Louis and his troops were to depart for Cairo, to wend its way to me?

Maude de Lacy bustles in, carrying something large wrapped in fine linen. "It is here," she proclaims, "the book His Majesty bid the Master of the Temple to send you."

I am on my feet in an instant, carefully unwinding the cloth from around the volume while my ladies crowd in from every side. The *Chanson d'Antioche*! Henry thought of it last night as we were going to bed and ordered it brought for my pleasure this morning before Mass. I open it to a collective gasp of appreciation from my companions. The illuminations are marvelous. On the page before me I see a knight, armored in gold and seated on a magnificent white warhorse, skewering someone atop the city walls of Antioch.

"My, he is very handsome," I say, laying a finger upon the figure.

"Shall I tell His Majesty you are looking for a handsome knight?" Maude jokes.

Christiana de Marisco gives a deep throaty laugh and pretends to be shocked.

"No indeed," I insist, pretending likewise to be scandalized. "His Majesty *is* my handsome knight." Of course, I am not at all shocked. My acquaintance with Maude stretches back several years, formed over the course of my residences at Windsor, a castle her husband managed for the Crown. I like her mischievous sense of humor. I like her generally. And I particularly like that she can be useful to my current plans.

"It is you who lacks a husband at present," I continue, adopting a softer and more serious tone. "Do you not grow tired of keeping Windsor Castle all alone?"

"My late husband was a good man—"

"I'll not say nay, as he was relation of mine," I quip. Maude was married to Peter of Geneva who came to England as part of my retinue when I arrived as a bride, but she has been widowed for more than a year.

"I do not want to tempt divine providence by asking for another."

"Ah," I say, drawing her arm through mine and leading her away, leaving the others occupied with my beautiful book, "but what you will not ask for you may receive nonetheless."

"What nonsense you talk." Maude squeezes my elbow.

"Not at all. I am expecting the arrival, once the sailing weather is dependably good, of a kinsman of my uncle Peter's, Geoffrey de Joinville. I have heard he is more handsome than any knight in that book."

"And will it please Your Majesty for me to marry him?" Maude looks unsettled. When I try to meet her gaze, she lowers her eyes to the floor.

"It would please both the king and myself very much." Of course, I have not discussed the matter with Henry, and it is sure to displease his barons even if it pleases him. Maude has a good deal of territory in both England and Ireland that will go along with her hand if she marries again. No, my plan is to persuade my friend to the match first and then tell Henry, when the young de Joinville is on English soil and introduced at court, that Lady de Lacy fell in love with him at first sight. Henry is still a man much moved by tales of love.

Seeing that Maude has not raised her eyes, I add, "It should please you too, for he is a strapping young gentleman of barely twenty-one. Who would not want such a man in her bed?"

"You think to scandalize me out of my surprise," Maude says, shaking her head with a slight laugh.

"I will assure you, my dear friend, that if you accept Geoffrey, you will find him possessed of more assets than youth and vigor. His Majesty will see to it that he has an office worthy of your hand. You have my word."

Maude is practical. She knows that, given the importance of her possessions and the fact that her son by Peter died, she will not be allowed to remain widowed indefinitely. I feel sure she would rather have my choice of husband than the choice of my husband's advisers. Sure enough, she squares her shoulders, takes a deep breath, and says, "Let it be as Your Majesty pleases."

And I am pleased—pleased because I will be able to tell Marguerite that I have found a handsome fortune for yet another one of those de Joinville brothers in whom she takes such an interest. I give Maude a kiss on the cheek. We return to the others, and I call out, "Who will be the first to read aloud?"

BY MID-MARCH, ONE OF MY chambers at Westminster is full of ladders and men with brushes.

"Since you love the *Chanson d'Antioche* so much," Henry says, holding a candle aloft to see the painters' progress one evening before we retire, "I thought it only fitting you have some of the stirring deeds it recounts to decorate your apartments."

"I cannot wait to see you astride your warhorse," I say, putting my arms about his waist. We are standing directly before a figure modeled on the same besieging knight I so admired from the book.

"I will be astride you much sooner than that," Henry replies, dropping his mouth to the place where my neck meets my shoulder.

It is as if we are newly married again. I need only glance at Henry to spark the king's lust. I am ecstatic. Marguerite must be nearly ready to give birth in the Holy Land. With any luck I will be with child myself before the babe my sister now carries is weaned. Henry takes my hand to lead me back to my bedchamber.

"No," I say, my voice coming forth as a hoarse whisper though we are entirely alone, "take me here, beneath these images that I may imagine we are already on a far-off shore, conquering the Holy Land together."

My dearest Marguerite,

  Christians everywhere rejoiced at the news of the King of France's victory at Damietta. I felt particularly lucky to have a firsthand account of the battle, for surely the details in your letter must have come from Louis. Am I to suppose from this that his victory has placed him in excellent humor and that his corresponding munificence extends to you, dear sister? I certainly hope so.

  As for my own husband, things are much better between us, and what was already mending was nursed to full recovery by your letter. Truly, your tale of victory had the effect of a good tonic upon Henry. He is as a young man again. He and I have both taken the cross. Of course, we cannot set sail at once. You know full well the vast amount of labor and expense necessary to assemble a crusading army. But I do so hope we reach the Holy Land before all the fighting is at an end.

          Your loving sister,
          Eleanor

MARGUERITE
SPRING 1250
DAMIETTA, EGYPT

I can barely rise from my bed in the morning. My ladies think it is because I am so great with child. Matilda chides me for not beginning my confinement, for still climbing to the battlements every day, looking in the direction of the river and hoping for the sight of Louis's messenger, of Louis's colors.

But it is neither the babe inside me nor "too much exertion" that causes my malaise. I am no fool. I have had no word from the king in nearly four months. No word from Jean. Something terrible has happened. And the weight of not knowing how terrible bends me nearly to my breaking point. For all I know, both men are dead and all my children are fatherless. Is it any wonder then that I am weary?

Leaning on the stone in front of me, surrounded by archers, flanked by a concerned Marie and my sister, I look at the river winding into the distance and see a sinuous and treacherous serpent. Somewhere along its length between myself and the French army, the Saracens must command it. I wonder what happens to the supply barges I send. What do the men eat if provisions are not getting through? Then I am seized with terror almost to the point of panic at the unwelcome thought that dead men need no nourishment. I want to scream, but if I become hysterical, what and who is to hold my court of women or the larger city together? Only alone, in the deep watches of the night, when like a child I demand every candle be lit to drive out the unseen monsters of the dark, do I cover my face with a pillow and scream until my throat is raw.

Descending from the tower, I find my sisters-in-law and the other noble wives waiting in utter idleness in my chambers. They no longer look up hopefully at my return, nor does every knock at my door as each long day unwinds cause them to start in hopes of a royal messenger. We have become old and broken women, even as the air is filled with the sounds and smells of spring. The only soul oblivious to our torture, I think as I find my seat, is Beatrice's little daughter lying in her cradle. She waves her tiny fists in the air as Matilda, now beginning to show with child herself, rocks the cot slowly with her foot.

I cannot write to Jean. If I could, if I could pour out all my worry, all my thoughts of him in his absence, how the picture of the pink birds of our afternoon at Akrotiri comes to me at unexpected intervals catching me off guard, what sweet relief it would be. But such candor in writing would be misplaced, even under extremis. Thank God I can write to Eleanor. I call for my escritoire and bury myself in the letter I started yesterday.

When the door opens, I do not look up. It is Marie's exclamation, "Your Grace!" that captures my attention.

The Duke of Burgundy stands on the threshold, smiling. Smiling!

"Your Majesty, soldiers in the south tower believe they have espied our troops."

I am on my feet in an instant, large as I am. "Show me."

I take the duke's arm and make the climb with all my ladies, babbling like excited children, trailing behind me. When we reach the top of the tower, soldiers and archers make way.

"You see, Your Majesty, coming along the right bank of the river." The duke points out over the landscape to guide my gaze.

The sun is just past its apex overhead, so there is nothing to hamper our view save the distortion created by distance and heat rising off the ground and water in waves. I can clearly see Louis's standard and a number of others that I recognize.

"God be praised, God be praised," Matilda says with a sob from behind me. She continues to repeat the phrase over and over as the ladies embrace one another, wild with joy. I alone stand unmoving. I will know no relief until it is clear who has returned. The number appears significant, but not as many as left us. And where are the litters? Surely if Louis was still among the living he would never abandon the wounded; yet I see not a single man carried or even assisted among those who march ever nearer.

"Stop!" I command sharply, and the celebration of my women abruptly ends.

"What is it?" my sister-in-law Jeanne asks, moving beside me and laying her hand on my arm in concern.

"Your Grace, something is wrong, I sense it," I say, looking at the duke.

The duke stares back at me as if I were an imbecile or a small child to be indulged. "What could be wrong, Your Majesty?"

"The queen is right," replies a nearby guard, shading his eyes with his hand. "Look at their clothing."

The duke and I peer out again. The first ranks of men are much closer now, and though they wear the tunics of French knights and carry their shields, they have the swarthy complexions of Saracens and the footwear as well.

"Dear God, they are infidels." The duke's voice is quiet, yet its message, so horribly unwelcome, carries to all the ladies in my party. As if with one voice, a great wail rises up to replace the laughter and embraces of a moment ago.

I feel my legs giving way beneath me and clutch the wall to keep from falling. A Saracen bears the oriflamme of France. Louis has been defeated, that is sure, but where is he? Where are my brothers-in-law? Surely all of Louis's army cannot be dead. Jean cannot be dead!

"Send to all the gates of the city," the duke barks to a nearby knight, "that none may be deceived by these men and grant them entrance. Your Majesty, I must get you and the ladies inside before their archers reach the edge of their range."

I know he is right; yet even as I let him lead me back down the stairs I wonder if the instant death provided by an arrow might not be a blessing.

"Find out all you can," I say, "then come to me and we will decide what is best to be done."

"PRISONER?" I AM SEATED BESIDE a window, out of sight of those on the plain between the city and the river but where, even with an imperfect view, I can glimpse the tents of the enemy as they go up.

"That is the message from Sultan Turan-Shah." The Duke of Burgundy looks grim, but not panicked. There is something in that anyway. Nearly everyone else seems to be. "He warns us to lay down our arms and retreat to our ships or risk being taken as His Majesty was. Or worse."

"Do you think he speaks true?" Both the duke and I wonder about this new sultan. We wonder what happened to Sultan Ayyüb. If he was killed in battle, then the victory of the Saracens may not have been overwhelming.

"Who can say with an infidel, Your Majesty." The Duke shrugs and opens his hands expansively.

"I agree," I reply, nodding. "All that the sultan's message tells us is that he considers it to his advantage that we believe His Majesty lives." I shift in my seat, momentarily distracted by the sound of weeping from somewhere nearby. "Can we defeat his forces?"

"Not with five hundred knights, Your Majesty." The duke lowers his eyes as if embarrassed by this fact.

"They are so many, the Saracens?"

"They continue to arrive even now."

"Can we hold the city?"

The duke looks up again, his eyes narrowed and his brow furrowed. He clearly did not anticipate my desire to stand our ground. "Your Majesty?"

"Can we hold the city?" I repeat slowly and distinctly.

"I believe we can."

And suddenly I feel it, that distinctive tightening in my abdomen. *Oh God,* I think, *must it be now?* I shove all thoughts of childbirth away, and, staring directly into the duke's eyes, I say, "Then hold it. Hold it as if it were the most important thing you have ever possessed, because if in fact the king lives, it may be."

The duke bows and starts for the door. As he reaches it, a second pain spurs me to make a request. "Your Grace, I would be pleased if you would send me one of the most venerable of the knights under your command. He need not be young, but he need be a *preudomme* who knows his duty to his queen. This man I shall make my personal guard."

As soon as he is gone, I call Marie and tell her to make my chamber ready, not for confinement but for birth. "Do not shutter the windows," I say. I must know what goes on in the city and without its walls or I will go mad with terror. "And let no one but my ladies know that my time has come."

Those who have attended me through delivery before gather, their eyes red and their faces tear-streaked. I walk about my chamber, stopping to lean on a chair or the bed as the pains take me. When the knight sent by the Duke of Burgundy arrives, Marie shepherds him in. He has lived more than sixty years if he has lived one, but he has kindly eyes and a strong chin. I nod my head to acknowledge his bow.

"You see, good Sieur, that your queen has great need of you at present. I labor now to bring forth a prince or princess of France. I have no choice in the matter, though the timing be ill; God wills it should be so. Yet things are so uncertain that even as I bring forth this new life, the Saracens may breach the city walls and storm this place. I command you that should that happen, you must draw your sword and have it at the ready. Delay as long as you can to give my child a chance to be born and spirited away, but under no circumstances let me be taken. At the first sign that the infidels have entered this palace, you must strike off my head with a single blow."

Matilda gasps and, pressing her fist against her mouth, begins to sob.

The knight's face, however, remains strong. "I shall strike without hesitation, Your Majesty. You have my word. Never would I see a queen of mine subjected to the hands and whims of an infidel."

Another pain takes me, stronger than those before it, causing me to cling to the post of my bed. When it passes I say, "Marie, place a chair for this good gentleman. It is time."

I do my best to labor in silence. Had anyone told me such was possible, I would have denied it, but my fear is stronger than my pain and my sense of duty is stronger than both. Louis may be dead. Jean may be dead. I may, therefore, wish I were dead. But I am not dead and I am Queen of France. The men and women brought to Egypt by my husband who live still, whether within the walls of this city or captive God knows where, need me to be a queen first and a woman second. So, when the pain takes hold of me, I bite my lip till I draw blood, I moan low and long, but I do not scream. Somewhere in the agony of it all there is a loud knock on the door of the room beyond. Marie departs and returns with the Duke of Burgundy. When he sees me, knees drawn up, straining, he starts and looks away.

"He insisted on speaking to you," Marie says in a low voice as the pain subsides and I relax back onto my pillows.

"It is nothing, Your Majesty," the duke stammers, without turning his head in my direction. "It can wait."

"No," I gasp. I hold up my hand to bid him to wait, then push through another dreadful pain.

"I can see the head," the midwife declares with satisfaction.

"Be quick," I command the duke. I am nearly beyond listening thanks to the unbearable pressure in my loins, but I fight to keep my mind focused.

"The Pisans and Genoese pack to depart."

Even in my present circumstances I recognize the serious nature of this threat. Without those men and their boats, the city will have no source of supply; nor will we have means of retreat. The ability to come and go by sea is a necessity.

"Oh Holy Mary, Mother of God, pray for me," I moan. The pain is rising. I close my eyes against it and against the light of this impossibly cruel day, pushing with all my might. I know the babe is born before I hear it cry; I know by the blessed relief that descends the instant it is free of my body.

"Praise God, our king has another son," the midwife declares.

A son! I have given Jean a son. And now I must find out what happened to him, to Louis. I must trade this city for them if they live. I must have Damietta; without it I have no hope.

"Your Grace," I say, eyes still closed so that I can see my own thoughts clearly, "I will speak with the leaders of these men—"

"But Your Majesty—"

"In one hour."

MY ROOM IS FULL FROM wall to wall. Either these men are curious to see a queen in her childbed or the number of those who lead equals that of those who follow. On the whole, they look uncertain, and that is a good thing for I would have them change their minds.

"Gentlemen"—I glance round, trying to catch the eyes of as many as I can—"I understand that you think to depart. I beg you not to leave this city. We cannot hold it without you, and if we lose it, His Majesty and all those brave warriors taken captive with him will be lost as well." I pause, expecting a response of some sort, but no one speaks. "If this does not move you," I continue, "think of my ladies and of me, in no condition to even rise from my bed, mother of a babe not two hours old. What horrors shall be our fate if you desert us?"

"Your Majesty," a man in his prime with the skin of one who has been used to the sea speaks from the foot of my bed, "what choice have we? We have neither food nor the funds to buy it."

I do not know if they are truly hungry or merely greedy. I do not care. Gold and silver I have; more of it than I have men, that is sure. Louis showed me the many chests on our ship with pride. "And if I keep you at His Majesty's expense, ordering all the food in the city to be purchased in my name?" The Duke of Burgundy standing just to my left looks stricken; I can see his knuckles whiten on the hand resting on the hilt of his sword. Likely he disagrees with my decision. I do not care.

When the men are gone, persuaded to stay by my bribe, I call for my son. The midwife brings him in trailed by Marie. With them is a nurse I recognize as the same who suckles Lady Coucy's daughter, who is now nearing her first birthday.

My baby is quite marvelously perfect with an abundance of dark curly hair so similar to Jean's that under other circumstances I might worry that others would notice. Presently, however, I have other cause for concern. "You must take him to be baptized at once," I admonish Marie. "Ask Jeanne to stand as godmother and the Duke of Burgundy as godfather. Or, if the duke cannot be spared, ask whatever nobleman you can conveniently find, but on no account delay. There is more peril to threaten this prince than a mother need ordinarily fear."

Marie nods. I hand the child back to the midwife reluctantly. "Bring him back to me directly from the font," I plead. Then turning to the nurse I add, "Though you may have the charge of him, I will suckle him myself. If I cannot know where his father is, I will keep the son as close at hand as I can." Of course, the nurse thinks I mean His Majesty, as should Marie, though perhaps she is too clever to be fooled.

"And the name, Your Majesty?"

I hesitate. 'Twould be safest to name him after one of his uncles or, perhaps, my own father. But I cannot be wise. If, God forbid, one Jean has been lost to me, moldering somewhere in the desert sun or suffering at the hands of his Saracen captors, I must have another. "Jean Tristan," I say, "and we will call him Tristan for he has been born into great sadness, and it is only by the grace of God that this prince, and indeed any of us, shall live to see happier times."

"A BARGE MOVES DOWN THE river, Your Majesty." The Duke of Burgundy brings this news himself. "It is very large and appears to be loaded with yet more men."

We have held the city for three weeks, watching every day as towers and pavilions are erected outside its gates. One tower in particular fascinates me. It is taller than all the rest and, like the elaborate tent beside it, bears the standard of Sultan Turan-Shah. Sometimes when I go to our battlements late at night and peer out at the Saracens' camp illuminated by hundreds of fires, I glimpse a shadow at this mighty tower's top and wonder if I have seen the sultan and if he can see me.

"I will have a look." I hand the slumbering Jean—for whatever I have instructed others to call him, I think of my son by the name he shares with his father—to Matilda, and make my way to the battlements.

"Do you see it?" His Grace points, and I do indeed, pulled along by at least one hundred oars. I cannot say why, but my eyes leave the river and scan the top of the great tower. I can see no one there, but if the tower is occupied, surely whoever stands at its apex is on its other side watching the river and the progress of the barge as I do. "Can such a conveyance hold enough men to tip the balance of the siege?"

"We will count them as they unload," the duke replies, evading the heart of my question.

I am on the verge of turning to descend when I am stopped. My eyes, sweeping the infidels' encampment with a parting glance, see something most unexpected—a column of dark black smoke rising beside the tower.

"It burns!" I cry, returning to the wall.

And sure enough, at the tower's base I can see flames licking it greedily—flames stoked by dozens of men. I do not understand why they would destroy their own tower.

"Mamlūks," the duke says, the tone of his voice betraying that he is as bewildered as I am. Then suddenly he gestures wildly. "My God!"

A magnificently dressed man has emerged from the tower's base preceded by two soldiers. He clears a group of armed men near the doorway, even as his two companions fall holding them back from him, and he sprints toward the river. A dozen Mamlūk warriors chase after him. There is nowhere for him to run. And he must know it, for at the river's edge he turns to face those who pursue him. Without hesitation one among them knocks him to the ground. For a moment he is obscured from view by a mass of warriors. When they part, he lies motionless, limbs oddly askew, his splendid white and gold robes stained red with blood. I wonder who he is, or rather, was. Could it be the sultan himself lying lifeless in the dust?

"And these are the men who hold the king," I say, finding my voice once I am safe in the shadows of the tower stairway.

SOMETHING OF GREAT IMPORTANCE WAS clearly begun by the death I witnessed on the riverbank. Seven days crawl by during which the infidels no longer seem to pay any attention to us. Their small forays toward the city wall by night to see if my archers sleep at their posts have stopped. The drums and horns, once sounded to frighten us, are silent. The barge remains moored in the great river without troops coming ashore. And all the time the corpse lies where it fell, scavenged by birds, but otherwise unattended.

I spend a curiously large amount of time thinking about the dead Egyptian, not so much pondering who he was as wondering why no one mourns him. Surely he had a loyal friend? A devoted servant? A wife? Perhaps none of these felt as they should for him. Was this his fault? Was it theirs? These are not idle questions. For, after my initial relief that Louis and his army were not destroyed, I am finding it hard to worry for him as I should—or at least as the other wives worry for their husbands. I pray that the king is alive, and for his deliverance. But my words come from a sense of duty and a fear that if he is dead, my little Louis, too young by far to rule, will be destroyed by his uncles or dominated by his grandmother. When I try to muster tears for the *man* who is my husband, they do not come. It seems not enough fondness remains in my heart to weep for Louis, and the guilt for what I do not feel is oppressive.

The eighth day after the tower burned is the Lord's day. On my knees at Mass, I find myself unaccountably praying for the fallen man, infidel or no. When the service ends, my ladies stay where they are to offer yet more prayers for their missing husbands and our missing knights, but I rise. If God does not know my heart by now, another litany of its hopes will not help.

The light in the courtyard is blinding after the dim of the chapel, so at first I sense rather than see that something extraordinary is going on—there is a sound of snorting horses and running feet—and then a group of noblemen becomes clear, crowding around a man on horseback. The rider's face is down because he speaks to someone standing beside his mount. The Duke of Burgundy and several others, who must have exited the chapel just behind me, rush past, jostling me slightly as they go. The rider looks up, his face is as gaunt as that of a beggar in the street; yet I would know it anywhere—it is my Lord Geoffrey de Sergines! Lifting my skirt, I run to join those clustered around him. And while the others do not immediately notice me, de Sergines does. Climbing with difficulty from his horse, he staggers forward on unsteady legs to bow before me.

"Your Majesty."

"My lord," I say, taking him gently by the shoulders and helping him to straighten up, "have you come from the king?"

"I have. I have been at His Majesty's side since we were taken captive together. And I would not have left him now did I not think my commission might see him freed."

France still has a king and I a husband. The verifiable knowledge that Louis lives moves me unexpectedly. A feeling of great relief and thanksgiving surges through me. Yet it is imperfect. I must have news of more than Louis to wipe the final traces of dread from my heart.

"Sir, we must get you out of the sun and off your feet."

"Lean on me." The Duke of Burgundy slides Sir Geoffrey's arm around his shoulder.

We make our way painstakingly toward my apartment. By the time we reach it, the crowd following us is prodigious. I can see my ladies scattered throughout, no doubt drawn from the chapel by word of the knight's arrival. Eager as all are for news of the king and the other captives, because theirs is a story of defeat, some of that news is doubtless bad and therefore best confined to the smallest possible number. I hold the door so Sir Geoffrey, still leaning on the duke, can pass, then slipping inside, pull it shut behind me. The duke settles de Sergines into a chair, and I pour out a goodly measure of wine for the gentleman, though judging by his looks, he would be better served by a meal.

"In God's name what happened?" The Duke of Burgundy's voice is rough with emotion.

"We lost." The statement is so simple. "I could tell you how, where, and when, but all such a recitation would do at present is leave the king longer a prisoner."

I nod my head in understanding. "You have come with terms."

"Yes," de Sergines says wistfully.

"I will hear them, but first, pardon a woman's weakness and tell me how many good knights have died."

"Better to ask how many live. The fighting took a fearsome toll, and our imprisonment carried off yet more. Your Majesty is, God be praised, not a widow, but among your ladies there will be *many*. The king's brother the Count of Artois is dead. The Lords of Coucy, Orleans, Coublanc . . ."

As his voice trails off, my thoughts fly to these men's wives, clustered outside the door. Their fear will end not in relief but in desperate misery. Yet even as I grieve for them, a voice inside my head shouts, *What of my Lord of Joinville?* It is a question I cannot ask aloud, for Jean is neither husband nor kin to me. So I turn to a question I can ask. "What must be done to ransom those who still live?"

"The surrender of this city and a payment of four hundred thousand livres has been agreed upon. Then His Majesty and the knights shall be freed."

"Four hundred thousand!" The duke's eyes bulge like those of a hunting dog held too tight on its lead. "Your Majesty, such a sum is unconscionable. You must not pay it."

"Shall I tell the king when he is free that you did not think his life and the life of his fellows worth so much?"

"That is unfair," the duke says, blanching. "These are not Christian knights, Your Majesty! To hand over so great an amount to men of no integrity may be to throw it away."

It is my turn to be stung, for the duke is right. Whether the word of an infidel sultan should be trusted is a matter fairly open to debate. I turn to de Sergines. "How are the moneys to be paid? And how can we be sure that if we do pay them, we will not do so in vain?"

"His Majesty and other gentlemen of rank will be released upon surrender of this city. They will be allowed to board ships brought into the mouth of the Nile, but not to leave the river. When half the moneys promised are paid, the ships will sail for

Acre, to which city we will be allowed to withdraw without molestation. The final two hundred thousand livres may be dispatched under guard from the safety of that city. As security that it shall be paid, some number of lesser knights as well as the common prisoners—archers, foot soldiers, and the like—will remain in the hands of the Saracens."

"We will weigh out the initial two hundred thousand beginning this hour and finish if it takes the whole of the night—"

"Your Majesty, I must protest!"

"And I must pay," I retort sharply, rounding on him. "If your dear dead wife and my dear friend Yolande sat in your place to advise me, she would not question me as you do now! She would understand that as a wife and a queen I must take whatever risks are necessary to save my kingly husband."

"And if the infidels blockade His Majesty's ships?"

"At least I will know I have tried."

I LEAD EVERYONE TO THE ships myself, with baby Jean in my arms and my eyes fixed on the chests of counted gold and silver being borne before me. As it turned out, two full days were needed to weigh the first half of the ransom. I could never have imagined that. Nor could I imagine I would still be in ignorance as to whether Jean lived after such a time. But Geoffrey de Sergines had bound himself to return to his captors forthwith with my answer as a condition of his being allowed to come. I could not even persuade him to rest long enough to have a meal, for he feared that if the Egyptians thought he had made his own escape, they might hurt the king. Had he dined, I would have begged him to make a list of all men of rank still among the living. As it was, he departed within moments of having my commitment to pay, telling me only the names of the ladies among my train he knew for a fact to be widows, and leaving me as hungry in spirit as he was in body.

Dawn is just breaking. The flickering light of the torches illuminating our way, along with the notable absence of noise other than the shuffling of feet, gives our procession a funereal atmosphere. Matilda staggers along just behind me, supported by Jeanne and Marie. I would that the ransom could buy her husband back for her. And yet, though the thought is cruel, it seems somehow fitting that he of all my husband's brothers should die. After all, was it not on his account that Louis pursued Cairo rather than Alexandria?

"Just think, soon we will be going home." Beatrice's bright voice is jarring. Now that she is sure that Charles is alive, my sister, inappropriate as always, is all high spirits, as if our ordeal were over, when in truth we are in the midst of it.

I ignore her, looking instead toward the Genoese galley waiting next to my own ship to receive the two hundred thousand livres in coin and plate destined to free my husband from Saracen hands. It will row to a point farther inland along the river where a pavilion has been erected. This is the place at which Louis and his remaining knights will board the ship. Only one galley is needed as de Sergines estimated that little more than one hundred knights remain. Holy Mary, Mother of God, did we not leave Aigues-Mortes with at least twenty times as many? If a score of men rot in the desert or float bloated in the Nile for each knight who boards that ship this afternoon, how can I continue to hope that Jean has survived?

Once we are on board the royal *nef*, most go below immediately, but I stand at the rail with ever-faithful Marie, watching the surrounding ships take on passengers. The Duke of Burgundy is nearby. Neither of us speaks, perhaps because words seem useless at present.

The boards are pulled up, and a man who looks oddly familiar approaches the duke. It is the sailor who spoke on behalf of the Pisans and Genoese on the day my baby was delivered. He seems to be the captain of this vessel. "Shall we make sail, Your Grace?"

"Can we not wait until His Majesty's ship is ready to sail?" I ask.

"Impossible, Your Majesty," the duke, not the sailor, responds. "The infidels may want the ransom weighed out again. Would you hold us ship-bound for days? Besides, we are not safe this close to shore now that Damietta is out of our hands."

"All right then," I say, nodding curtly.

I turn from my present position and cross the deck to face the open sea. I will have to take Louis's sailing on faith. *How unfortunate,* I think as the sail is unfurled and the first tear rolls down my cheek, *that I have so little faith left at present.*

AS SOON AS LOUIS'S SHIP is sighted, I order my people—all who made the journey with me from Damietta: knights, ladies, even servants—to make themselves ready in their finest array that we might meet the king as if he returned victorious. Many nobles of the city of Acre, where we have found refuge, join us on our way to the wharf, bringing Palfreys to carry the returning French knights up the hill to the castle that has been given over to the king's use. Jean Tristan is with me, but safely in his nurse's arms. I feel too unsteady to trust myself with him.

The deck of the galley is crowded with figures notable at a distance largely for their odd costumes. Many are dressed more like infidels than knights; some appear as nothing more than bundles of rags. Then, as the gap between the galley and the shore closes, comes the moment when faces can be recognized. Frantically the ladies gathered around me begin to search for familiar features. I look to the center of the deck, expecting to see Louis, but he is not there.

Having done my duty, and looked for the husband whom I know lives first, my eyes begin to search for the face I most want to see. Figure after figure fails to belong to my seneschal. Not that determining as much is an easy task. The men are, all of them, changed so greatly. And with every knight who proves to be other than Jean, my search becomes more frenzied. It seems no matter how many times I cautioned my heart over the last days that my love is likely dead and I will see him no more, my foolish heart heard without believing. I wonder, when Jean fails to get off the ship, will I fall dead where I stand?

Near the right end of the railing, my eyes alight on Philippe of Nemours, his face so dirty that, but for the fact I have seen him a thousand times, I might not have known him. Next to Nemours stands a figure, draped in a blanket tied at the waist with a bit of cord, who searches my face. When the dark eyes meet mine, I can no longer hear the calls of those on shore hailing those on the ship, nor feel the jostling of my ladies as they twist and shift to see better. It is Jean! Without volition I fall to my knees, overcome by a thanksgiving such as I have never known. Dear God, I know at last the meaning of grace. For only by my Savior's largesse could my love be alive and carried home to me—I do not deserve such mercy. Praying in the dirt of the pier, I swear that never again will I doubt, but while I breathe I will trust the cross.

Without meaning to do so, I have set an example. The ladies around me begin to sink to their knees with hands clasped in prayer. The noblemen follow suit, and we are hundreds on our knees as the plank is laid to the ship to allow its passengers to disembark. For a moment nothing happens.

"Where is the king?" someone murmurs.

A ripple moves through the crowd. Can it be that Louis was not released or expired on the voyage? Then the men nearest the top of the ramp part and make way. A figure, so thin and frail that a gust of wind might toss it overboard, emerges. Clad all in black satin and fur, his garments cut like those of a sultan, my husband stands and surveys his subjects below. But if we expect some pronouncement, there is none. Making his way down the plank on shaky legs, Louis prostrates himself cruciform as soon as he reaches dry land. After a moment he struggles to push himself up to his knees. His actions are painful to watch. They might belong to a man of fourscore years; yet Louis is only six-and-thirty. Once kneeling, he cannot rise alone and reaches out. The Duke of Burgundy rushes to assist him. Rising, I follow. Upon reaching my husband, I curtsy before him.

"Your Majesty, how we have prayed for this moment."

Louis extends a hand and ever so tentatively touches my cheek. His form is withered and wasted past even what it was when he returned from death to take the cross. His hair is so dull and matted, it would be impossible for anyone who did not know him to imagine that once it glittered like spun gold. His eyes are hollow and so sad that I find my own tearing in response.

"Surely not this moment, lady wife. For I come to you in defeat and greatly ashamed of it."

"What need is there for shame when you have given God your best? And while it is certain all here would have been gladdened by a victory, we give praise nonetheless to God and his saints for Your Majesty's preservation and return."

Instinctively I offer my arm to my husband as one might to an elderly person. He takes it with a look of gratitude such as I have never received from him before. A strange thought flits through my mind: *might I have an opportunity to love Louis broken, as I was*

never allowed to love him when he was possessed of certitude and strength?
Is God giving me a second chance to be a good wife and a blameless woman?

But as Louis is helped to his horse by a dozen eager hands and I to mine, I find myself searching the crowd for Jean. It seems it is not in my nature to cleave only to one man, though I make an oath to myself as our horses are in motion that I will nurse Louis with all the tenderness I possess.

THE GREAT HALL LOOKS LIKE a hospital and smells like a barn. I have seen my husband to his own apartment; ordered his dinner; called for his bath to be drawn; undressed him for that bath with my own hands; and burned his clothing. Leaving him in the care of his servants, I made my way to this place, trying with every step to force the image of Louis's poor naked figure from my mind—the ribs jutting out from beneath stretched and sallow skin, the bites of countless fleas, the dirty matted hair in his most private region, and everywhere dust and dirt on a man who always kept himself meticulously clean.

I am here to find Jean. But, in order not to seem too obvious, I offer a kind word to every gentleman I recognize and encouragement to every wife come to claim and lead or carry away her returning husband. What seemed like so few survivors when we heard their number seems overwhelming now that I must search among them. As I leave yet another group, a voice sounds behind me.

"In all my dreams the angels had only one face."

Bursting into tears, I turn. Jean, or what is left of him, stands before me. His hair, uncut since God knows when, is long and wild like a hermit's. Dirty curls brush his shoulders and mingle with the thick, curly, matted beard that obscures his face. He is incompletely covered in the rough blanket he wears, and the naked limbs that protrude are streaked with dirt. His right calf is scarred, clearly from a wound that festered before it healed, and I wince, wondering where else his beautiful body has been pierced and slashed. His feet are bare.

Yet Jean smiles. How can he smile in such a condition? "Angels ought not to cry."

I wipe my eyes on my sleeve. "You look terrible." It is the truth, but it is not what I want to say. I want to throw my arms about him and tell him that I love him.

"Thank you." His slightly mocking bow very nearly undoes me. "I hope to find something more suitable for court when next I appear." Then becoming serious he says, "You were safely delivered of your child?"

"A beautiful son." A tear escapes Jean's eye, leaving a track in the dirt that covers his face and disappearing into his unkempt beard. "I will introduce you when you have had some rest."

"I must find lodgings."

"No." Putting a hand on his arm, I turn him toward a window. In its recess there is no one to hear me. "Rest, love," I say, touching his shoulder as he sinks to the stone of the window ledge. "Let me care for you. Is that not what angels do?"

Leaving Jean, I set off with purposeful step, plunging back into the crowd. I know whom I am looking for—the bishop of Acre, who is present, condoling with the sick and offering last rites to those whose conditions seem to make that prudent. The bishop is a countryman of Jean's. *Surely,* I think, *he will help.* And I am not disappointed.

Returning to Jean, I find he has fallen asleep leaning in the window's corner. For the moment I do not wake him, but instead examine his once-familiar face and form more closely. Like Louis, he is but a shadow of the man who left me—underweight and covered in dirt. But unlike Louis, when his face is in repose it seems very like his old self, not transfigured by grief and loss as my husband's is.

I want to see to his dinner and to gather some fabric for clothing, but I am loath to leave him, fearing irrationally that he will disappear again for as many months as he has been gone. So I take a seat on the opposite end of the window ledge and watch my love slumber. The hall is clearing. Most of those who have returned have been claimed by wives, servants, or friends. A middle-aged servant approaches me where I sit, or rather, I realize as he draws closer, approaches my lord.

"Who are you?" I ask as the man quietly takes a seat on the ground beside Jean.

"Caym of Sainte-Menehould, Your Majesty. I am in the service of this seneschal."

"Then serve him well," I say, smiling.

The man nods.

I explain that the bishop has offered Joinville lodgings and bid the man go to the kitchens in my name and bring back something for his lord to eat. I know I must return to Louis soon; duty commands as much. When I see Jean's servant returning through a door at the other side of the hall, I put my hand gently on Jean's and call his name. His eyes flutter open.

"For once I do not dream."

"Did you dream of me often in your captivity?"

"Constantly."

"Listen, love, your man is coming with something for you to eat, and after this he must take you to the priest's house in the parish of Saint Michael."

"When will I see you again? It may be some days before I am ready to present myself before His Majesty."

A few days would be an unbearable separation when I have just had Jean restored to me. Nor would a public meeting where I must share him with Louis satisfy. I have a thousand things large and small to say to Jean. I would examine every inch of his body until I am satisfied that he is whole and sound, and I would hear the story of every moment since he left me.

"Do you trust your new man?"

"Yes."

"Then I will find your house after nightfall."

"Ought you to be abroad after dark?" The thought that Jean worries for me in his present pitiful condition is unutterably touching.

"'Ought' has never entered into things where you are concerned."

"MY DECISIONS WERE FAULTY FROM first to last. So much blood and death, and it is all on my head. Can even God forgive such failure?"

This is *not* my husband. That is my first thought as I sit near Louis listening to his confession, as it were. He has always been a man plagued by guilt—but a man who doubted God? Never.

"Your Majesty, you have oft said yourself that God can forgive the truly penitent heart anything. And, if you will allow me to be the judge, whatever faults were yours in this campaign, you do not shy away from shouldering them. In fact, you accept the blame for everything; yet surely, as you are only one man, not all that went wrong can be laid at your door or at any one person's. Luck and fate must also have played their parts."

"But I am not just one man—I am a king. I must be held to a higher standard. I wish I had died in the desert."

Rising, I go to Louis, crouch before him, and take both his

hands in my own. "Louis, you must not say such things. You are perfectly right, you *are* a king and therefore you have a duty to live and reign. The security and prosperity of France depends upon that, as does the well-being of such persons who remain with you here." Louis does not respond. He will not even meet my eye.

I return to my seat, searching for something to talk about that will at least distract my husband from his misery. It is far too early to relate to him all that passed at Damietta or to tell him that I have written to the dragon asking her to gather the remaining monies necessary to discharge the terms of Louis's surrender. "The Seneschal of Champagne will dine with you tonight."

"Joinville? Where has he been?"

"In the care of the bishop of Acre."

"I must chastise the seneschal for keeping away so long. He is a fine companion, and loyal. Madam, if only you knew."

"Your Majesty, it is less than a week since your ship landed. Think how many of the hours since then you have passed in sleep. No doubt it was the same for the seneschal." I find oddly humorous this shared devotion that Louis and I have to Jean. But it is providential for me as well. The fact that Jean is a known favorite of the king makes the items I have sent him in Louis's name—camelin, fine soap, ointment, meat—seem entirely unremarkable. Even my personal visits, should they become known, might plausibly be explained. But they will not become known, I tell myself, shaking off the idea. Jean's man, Caym, has proven as trustworthy as Marie. Last night he came for me, waiting in an alley near the castle gate, so that I would not have to walk to Jean's alone.

"Yes, you are right. Have we any word how Joinville fares? He was very ill on our sea voyage, very ill indeed. Yet never did he complain. He thought only of my comfort, trying to find me a bit of food, seeing a bed was made up for me as my people were useless and had not done as much. He was mortified when his illness forced him to leave me to go to the rail."

Hearing such a tale of Jean pleases me abundantly. Louis has told me several grim stories in which other knights failed to behave as their duty and their nobility demanded, but apparently Jean was true to his nature even in extremis.

"I understand the seneschal is weak like Your Majesty, but is expected to recover," I reply. Jean is frail—nearly as frail in body as Louis, but not as weakened in spirit. When I kiss him now, I do so gently, as if the force of my lips alone could break him. "He was delighted to hear of the birth of a new prince."

"He must see Tristan when he comes. What a fine child. Really marvelous." Though Louis spent little time with our children in France, he is greatly attached to this new one. The baby is the sole thing sure to rouse him when he sits in a sullen, fitful stupor. And even when Jean Tristan cries, Louis will not let me send him away.

Reminded of the prince, Louis rises and walks to the cradle at the other side of my chair, staring down with obvious pleasure at the swaddled form sleeping there. "What a fine man he will be."

"A fine man," I echo, "like his father."

I AM BEING READIED FOR dinner when the knock sounds. Marie alone attends me as of late. Those among my ladies whose husbands returned I have granted leave to be with them as they convalesce. Those whose husbands will never return I have granted leave to grieve as they see fit, instructing them to attend me only when they feel that they would not be alone.

"My Lord of Joinville!" I am as surprised as Marie sounds. Jean has always been the soul of caution about visiting me when and where others might come to know of it. He slips in, beautifully dressed in garments made from fabric I had sent to him.

"I had to come," he says, looking sheepish. "How could I bear to meet him first before fourscore pairs of eyes? To see him but not hold him?"

And then I understand. Jean has come not to see me but his son.

"Of course," I say gently.

Rising, I go to the cradle and lift Jean Tristan from it. Though he is sleeping, I lay him on the bed and unwind his swaddlings. The activity awakens him and, apparently satisfied with his freedom, he kicks his small legs and grunts with pleasure.

Unlike poor Louis who always must be asked or urged, Jean sweeps the baby up into his arms, burying his face in the child's round pink stomach. Then, raising his head again, he cradles the babe in one arm, touching the various parts that make up his son—tiny toes, hands, ears, dark curls of hair. "By God, he is the most beautiful thing my eyes have ever beheld. And so big!"

I laugh. "He never stops eating." And hearing my voice, our son makes my point for me by rooting against Jean's chest, making a smacking noise with his mouth. Jean hands him back to me, and seating myself on the bed, I unlace my gown, and the drawstring at the neck of my shift in turn, then put the babe to my breast. Jean sits beside me and places his arm about my shoulder.

Catching a glimpse of us thus in the mirror of my dressing table just opposite, he says, "We are a handsome family." And I own that he is right—or we would be had the Fates permitted my hand and my heart to be bestowed upon the same man. Would that it could always be like this! Then I remind myself that only a handful of days ago I promised God I would never again ask for anything for myself.

I lean and give Jean a quick kiss. "You had better go. Louis will be waiting for you. He is eager to see you."

"He is much changed," Jean says, his face growing suddenly solemn. "When I was captured, I was held first with those other knights taken with me upon the river. The king, however, was held with those captured upon land. When my party was brought to that dreadful camp outside of Mansurah to join His Majesty and his fellow prisoners, I almost did not recognize the king."

"He is not the same man," I agree, "and it is too early to say whether he will become himself again." I do not add that I would not have the old Louis back completely; that this Louis, sad as he is, has a touch of humanity about him that his former incarnation as God's fearless and unbending warrior lacked.

Jean slips away, and I see him next in a far more formal mien and setting when he presents himself to Louis and me before dinner. My husband is genuinely delighted to see the Seneschal. When Jean finishes bowing, Louis reaches out a hand to him.

"It is good to see the signs of recovery already upon you." Louis takes Jean's hand in his own and squeezes it. Then looking about him at his brothers and the surviving *preudommes* who are well enough to join us at table, he continues. "Here at least is some proof of God's mercy. I did not leave all my best knights dead in the desert."

At the end of the meal, Louis takes Jean away with him for what I presume will be a long discussion of politics and theology. *No matter,* I think as Marie tucks me into bed, for while Jean risked a visit to my chamber to see his son earlier, he is not fool enough to return to my apartments by night.

Someone does come to me, however—Louis. It is a strange thing that he should recover his desire as a broken man, when at the height of his powers he often lacked it completely. Stranger still that, because I have resisted Jean on the grounds of his health when he tries to begin such activities, Louis will be the first man to enter me in more than half a year.

The king is so unsure of himself, so tentative, as his lips seek mine that I find myself helping him. Stroking his hair, his face. Kissing him when he is hesitant. And then the most extraordinary thing happens. Louis whispers, "Thank you" as I help to guide him between my legs. I find that I am crying—for Louis, for myself, and for this glimpse of the tenderness we might have known had things been different.

"I love you," I whisper fiercely in his ear. And I mean it, though I surprise myself. I would heal him with this act of love if I could. I can tell he is tiring, his weakened body unable to follow through on his sexual need. Gently I roll him to his back. He weighs so little that it is easily done. His eyes open wide as I climb on top of him and continue what he began. If he wonders at my boldness or at my knowledge of such a position, he says nothing. Instead, I watch with satisfaction as he relaxes into the pillows, allowing me to stroke his gaunt chest where the ribs show. Slowly, tenderly, I rock up and down on him as if I would soothe him by the action. As his excitement grows, his arms rise and his hands clasp my waist. When he experiences release, the pleasure on his face harkens back to the first days of our marriage. He is asleep before he can remember to leave, and I do not wake him.

I DRIFTED TO SLEEP LAST night contented and awoke this morning refreshed, but my day is souring rapidly. Jean is in agony. "You withheld yourself from me, but gave yourself to him?" The expression on his face is both despondent and accusatory.

My face warms as if mine were an act of betrayal, then colors further still as I realize that it was. *Why,* I think to myself, *why did*

I find it necessary to tell him? And I cannot answer the question. I am used to being honest and open with Jean, yes, but when I arose this morning, I felt, instinctively, that what had passed between Louis and me was something secret. I woke my husband with a kiss and saw him off to his own rooms to dress with a smile. I reveled in his smell even as I washed it from myself. And I had no intention of telling Jean. None. But as I stood watching Jean eat the meal I brought for him, the confession slipped from me unbidden. Perhaps I knew I needed forgiveness.

"I am sorry," I say.

Jean puts his hands over his face. "Go," he mutters.

"He is my husband, Jean." My voice pleads for understanding, but I do not understand myself. Why do I find myself thinking of Louis in tender terms?

He looks up. "I know, and I hate him for it."

"You do not hate him any more than I do," I protest. I try to kiss Jean, but he holds me away.

"What. Will you let me have you now? How can I with his traces still wet inside you?"

"Please," I whisper.

"Go away, Marguerite. Leave me alone."

Turning, I run from the house as if it were on fire, barely able to keep my composure in the street.

I GO TO LOUIS'S ROOMS to see him take his meal. His physician tells me when the king dines alone, sometimes he entirely forgets to eat. He holds out his hand to me as I enter; when I offer mine in return, he kisses it.

"I thought you told me that when you called upon him two days ago, the Seneschal of Champagne was well."

"So he was." I have not been to see Jean since he ordered me out of his lodgings on the occasion of that visit, thinking that his wounded pride might better be salved in solitude.

"Well, we have not seen him."

"If Your Majesty desires his company, send for him. I am certain he will come. After all, he is such a friend."

"He is indeed."

Louis falls into staring ahead. I gesture to his bowl and he takes a spoonful of broth. Then he stops again.

"On the day my brother the Count d'Artois passed from this world into paradise, I and the knights under my command faced furious battle. We were between the river and a brook of goodly size. One party of infidels was at us from the direction of the river and a second thought to strike us from behind. But Joinville, seeing the little bridge they would use, understood its importance and set himself to defend it with a small party. All afternoon they held that bridge, though Joinville himself took five arrows."

I do not know what to say to this. Jean has never related the story of the bridge to me. More often than not, when I ask about his scars, most still angry and red, he brushes off my questions. "It does not matter how I got the wounds," he tells me. "I am content that none was so grievous as to prevent my coming back to you."

Shaking his head in wonder, Louis continues. "At nightfall when my crossbowman reached his party to offer relief, they found him joking with the Count of Soissons about how useful tales of their exploits might be in charming the ladies, as if the situation were not grave and their service not important. But I tell you, Wife, had the bridge been lost, I would very likely have been lost as well."

Louis finishes his soup as I watch in silence. Then, placing his spoon down upon the table, he says, "Perhaps you should go

have a word with Joinville for me, and take some of this consommé. The Sieur told me when he dined with us that Lord
Peter of Courtenay was refusing to pay four hundred livres the
seneschal is owed. Joinville may be in difficulty without the
monies. Tell him that I will pay him and deduct it from some
money I myself owe de Courtenay. Let Lord Peter complain to
me if he will."

With the story of Jean's bravery fresh in my heart, and the prospect of bearing such news to him as he will be glad to have, I make
up my mind to go. If he is still vexed with me, I will remind him
how many months he longed to see me and could not and how silly
it is to hold a grudge now over something that neither of us can
prevent nor control.

When Marie and I reach the little house leaning against the
ancient and venerable Church of Saint Michael, no one answers
our knock. I try the door, but it is locked. It seems odd that Jean
should be out and about in the city when he is not yet strong and
stranger still that if he felt up to going out, he did not come to sit
with us at court.

"If Caym is with the Seneschal," I say to Marie, "surely that
creature Guillemin is at home." I do not like Jean's other new servant. He has a shiftiness about him that puts me on my guard.

"And no doubt he is napping when he should be working, Your
Majesty," replies Marie, no more impressed with the man than I
am. "Pray knock again."

I pound for several minutes but to no avail. Having come this
far, I would not go away again without leaving the broth Marie
carries or a note. Besides, I feel a strange unease, an instinct really,
that something is not as it should be. Then I remember something
Jean told me on one of my early visits—that he took great solace in
the ease with which he could pray day or night in his new lodgings

thanks to their communication directly with the church by way of a small vestry.

Rounding to the front of the church, I push open the heavy door. As it is time for neither a service for one of the hours nor a Mass, the place is deserted. The mosaic scenes from the life of Saint Michael that cover the walls glint in the light from a series of small high windows. Behind the altar there is a door that surely must connect to the living space. Opening it, I am surrounded by the vestments and accoutrements of the Mass. I am greeted by the smell of aging fabrics and incense, but underlying this there is another smell—one of sickness and decay.

Throwing open the next door in frantic haste, I am confronted by a fearful sight. I stand just at the head of Jean's bed. He is in it, eyes closed, lids translucent, face as white as death. Beside the door on which I knocked so futilely and at the foot of the bed lie Jean's servants, looking no better than their master.

For a moment I am frozen where I stand. Surely, oh Lord, Jean did not survive so much in the last months to die at Acre? The door drops shut beside Marie and, taking in what horrified me before her, she lets out a little cry. At the sound of it, Jean moans and shifts fitfully beneath his covers.

This proof of life frees my feet. Moving to his bedside, I lay a hand upon his forehead. "He burns!"

"The smell!" Marie sets down the broth on Jean's small table and covers her mouth and nose with her hand.

"Yes." Turning back Jean's covers, I find him lying in his own filth. With all who serve him suffering from the same illness that felled him, there was clearly no one to help him to the stool.

"Heat some water," I bark at Marie, "and find new linens if you must run out to the market to buy them." Ignoring the stench, I lean in and say, "I am here, love. You will be well now."

Jean mutters something through cracked lips, but I cannot make it out. I find wine, pour a small amount, and lifting his head, urge it upon him. He swallows greedily.

Finished kindling the fire and putting the water on as I asked, Marie is rummaging around in a trunk near the wall, pulling out the few items of clothing Jean has managed to accumulate since his return. I am happy to see that a shirt is among them. Taking the neck of the shirt Jean wears in both hands, I rip it open, continuing to tear down its whole length. Untying his soiled braies at the knees and unrolling their waist, I try to tear them free of him as well, but the fabric will not cooperate. Taking my knife from my girdle, I use it to carefully rend the fabric at one hip, then tear furiously until the undergarment too falls away.

"Help me roll him," I call to Marie who is closing the trunk again. We turn Jean on one side, thankful in this one instance that his frame is still underweight. I am conscious of the great heat of his skin beneath my hands. While I hold him in place, Marie pulls away the remains of his shirt and braies and casts them onto the fire. But the linens beneath him are dirty as well.

"There were no sheets among his things and no doubt the straw is soaked through," she says grimly.

"Go home. Bring sheets, a feather bed, and a blanket."

"From where, Your Majesty?"

"I do not care. Take them from my bed if you must. But be quick."

I cannot stand the thought of laying Jean back in filth, but there is nothing for it at present, so, placing him on his back, I draw up the fetid cover again. Pulling a stool beside the bed, I sit and take his hand.

"What am I to do with you?" I say, talking merely to break the silence. "Ever since we set foot in the Holy Land, I cannot let you out of my sight for a moment without your finding trouble of one sort or another." I am surprised to see Jean's eyes open weakly.

"It would be better then if we were not parted." His voice is faint and tremulous, but I can make him out clearly nonetheless.

Putting a hand against his burning cheek I reply, "It would be better. Take care to remember that before you think of doing anything foolish such as dying."

"I feared I would—lying here, when no one came—would die without seeing you."

"Well, I am here now, so lie quiet."

Like an obedient child, he takes another sip of the wine I offer, then closes his eyes and drifts to sleep.

When Marie returns, the real work begins. Supporting Jean from either side, we struggle to move him to a stool. Though he is awake again, his legs are of no use to him. Once there, he cannot sit on his own. I put my arms around his chest from behind and struggle to keep him upright while Marie removes his soiled sheets and straw-filled mattress and then makes the bed anew. Then she holds him in turn while I clean him with basin and sponge, dumping dirtied water again and again out the window. It is a blessing that Jean is sensate only part of the time or he would be mortified. When his eyes do open, they struggle to follow my movements. Satisfied at last with my handiwork, we slide a new shirt over Jean's head and bear him back to his bed. I am utterly exhausted.

"We should send for a physician."

"And so we shall, only let me feed him first."

While I warm the broth, Marie checks on Jean's servants. I must own in all the time I labored never once did it occur to me to wonder whether these men lived. I know this is unchristian, but it is the truth. Both, as it turns out, are still of this world. Marie does her best to bathe their faces and give them each a drink, while I lay

Jean's head in my lap and, gently rousing him to consciousness, ply him with broth from a cup.

"It is my own fault," he says, resting between swallows. "This illness flows from my sin."

He is becoming agitated. I try to soothe him by stroking his face, and I put the cup to his lips again, but he pushes it away.

"When you were here last, I was so jealous. Jealousy is a special sin in my case, as I am jealous of the king for loving what he has every right to love."

"Louis does not love me. He is fond of me to be sure, but love me as you love me? No."

I do not think this a lie. There has been a thaw in my relations with my husband, but does Louis love me? I do not believe or even hope as much. Nor am I love struck and foolish as I was as a bride. But even as I reassure Jean, I wonder what might be if Louis continues to behave as he has been since returning.

"I think you are too hard on yourself." I bend to kiss Jean's forehead. "Is not God a jealous God? Why then should you be above the emotion?"

"Ah, but the Lord is jealous only for what belongs to him by right. I am jealous for what I have stolen."

"Fool," I reply, kissing his brow again, "you steal nothing, for I give you everything with the greatest of pleasure."

CHAPTER 28

Dear Eleanor,

The news that you are back in your husband's favor came as a balm to me, and verily I am in great need of one. I am glad that the victory at Damietta proved useful to you. It no longer provides any comfort to me, even when it is eagerly urged upon me by my ladies as proof of the French troops' military prowess and God's favorable disposition toward them. I have had no word from the king in too long—far too long to suppose that things go well for him. I am filled with such terror. The weight of it is heavier than the child I carry, and it drags me nearly to the dust. If something has happened to the king and to his knights, what shall become of my child? Of my ladies? I rest here at Damietta with scarcely five hundred men, many of whom are not soldiers but sailors and foreigners. I do not like to think what would happen if we were attacked. Of course, we have the ships at our back, waiting off shore. But the thought of retreating to them, a collection of women and children without our men, is scarcely more palatable.

Pray for me, dear sister, and do not be too eager yourself to leave English shores and come to these. There may be glory to be had in the Holy Land, but I fear there is also death.

Your sister,
Marguerite

ELEANOR
JUNE 1250
WINDSOR, ENGLAND

"God preserve us, can this be true?" Henry sits in his customary chair at his council table, but only Uncle Peter and
I are with him. He is speaking of what, doubtless, all of Europe
talks of—the stunning report that Louis of France left most of his
magnificent army dead in the desert.

"Disbelief was Blanche of Castile's response, Your Majesty,"
Peter says. "I have heard she hanged the first messengers to bring
her the news as liars and blasphemers. Poor souls."

"And Marguerite?" My body trembles all over as I ask the question. Does my sister's lovely head decorate the walls of an infidel
city somewhere? My vivid imagining of such a thing threatens to
deprive me of consciousness, and I must reach out and clutch the
back of the chair before me.

"I have precious little news of Marguerite, but we know she
lives, for it *is* reported 'twas she who gathered and meted out payment of the mighty ransom necessary to see her husband freed."

"The sum promised"—Henry looks down at the letter from
one of my uncle's contacts in the French court that Peter has laid
before him—"is so large that to speak it aloud would seem an
obscenity. The King of France will return much weakened by
this." Then, glancing in my direction, Henry shifts uncomfortably
and says, "Sorry, my dear."

I leave the council chamber at a run and go straight to the
chapel—not to my gallery, but to the aisle before the great altar.
Prostrating myself, I begin both to cry and to pray. *Holy Mary,*

Mother of God, watch over my sister. How mortified I am that I envied Marguerite her travels. I imagined it all so clearly—as a story— forgetting that tales of honor and glory are just that, tales. And now the illuminated pictures from the *Chanson d'Antioche* are wiped from my mind by the thought of my beloved sister surrounded by blood, by death, and by danger. *Dear God, forgive my sin of envy and guard me from it better in the future.* I know, even as I think the words, that this would be miracle indeed. I am an envious creature by nature, at least where it comes to Marguerite. And if I am so fortunate as to be granted a miracle, I would not waste it on improving myself, which ought to be my own toil. The miracle I want now is my sister home safe to France, even if she be the only survivor of her husband's ill-fated endeavor.

Slowly my fevered thoughts, tears, and murmurings are quieted by the stillness of my surroundings. The cold of the stone floor rises up through me and, far from being uncomfortable, eases my distress. As I lie, facedown, I hear footsteps upon stone. Oddly, I am not curious enough about who approaches to even lift my head.

"Mother?" It is the voice of my Edward. "Father is looking for you."

I draw myself to a seated position, arms around bent knees, and gaze up at my son. He is a tall boy for eleven and even taller from my current vantage point. "Goodness," I say, rubbing my eyes on my sleeve as if I were the child, "I pray he has not alarmed the entire palace on my account."

"No. He looks very quietly. He came to the nursery first and was going on to your gardens. I came here because it seemed the next most likely place." He puts out his hand to assist me in rising, and then, seeing I am not inclined to do so, sits down beside me drawing his own long legs up so that he is sitting as I am.

"The King of France was defeated in Egypt and taken prisoner." The starkness of my statement nearly brings me to tears again.

"You worry for Aunt Marguerite."

I nod dumbly.

"I wish I could rescue her for you. I am good with a sword; everyone says so."

Edward has begun his training in arms and, though I say it myself, shows his Savoyard blood. "Did I ever tell you what they called your great-uncle Guillaume?" I ask my son. "A 'second Alexander.'"

"Really?" Edward's eyes blaze.

"Yes. When he went to fight with the emperor near Turin the spring before you were born, not one but two horses were killed beneath him in a single battle, but he never stopped fighting. You will be just like him." I reach out and stroke my son's hair. "Only not too soon. For my sake."

"Mother!" Edward bristles slightly, but he moves closer and leans against me. He is still, thank heaven, more boy than man.

We sit quietly for a moment. I am pondering how fast the years have flown since I held Edward as a babe in my arms while he is doubtless envisioning himself in armor.

Then he says, "It is a good thing for a man to be brave."

"Yes. And also a good thing for a woman."

"But you have men to protect you."

"I see. You would protect me from everything?"

Edward nods determinedly.

"And what about when I am in London and you are here? While your uncle Louis was in the hands of the Saracens with all his knights, did not your aunt Marguerite have need of bravery?" I have picked an example I think Edward can understand. I do not mention all the times in ordinary life—in the delivery of a child or in the nursing of one when he is sick—that I have found bravery necessary.

"If Aunt Marguerite is brave, then why do you weep and worry for her?"

"Because she must also be lucky. The brave may die as well as the cowardly."

CHAPTER 29

Marguerite,

. . . Say only that you are safe, that you are whole. Our uncle assures me that you are and, more than this, that you rose to the occasion of your husband's defeat and rescued all by firm action. If that be so, it is to your credit and to the benefit of your husband and his kingdom, but do I admit too much by saying that I care nothing for such larger things? Your survival and that of your family are more important than any kingdom. You must remind yourself, surrounded as you are by tragedy, that so long as the corpses piled in the desert do not include any of your kin, all else can be borne. . . .

Yours,
Eleanor

MARGUERITE
JULY 1250
ACRE, KINGDOM OF JERUSALEM

"You were playing at dice again!"

Louis is so angry that he is shaking. I am angry too. The king's brothers *know* how he feels about gambling; yet against his wishes and despite the fact that his recovery has been hard fought and is by no means secure, Charles and Alphonse show no regard for His Majesty.

"We were not cheating," Charles replies cheekily. "And none of the knights who took our money is complaining."

Louis's complexion, still pallid from captivity, grows whiter still. "We are on holy ground with a serious purpose—"

"We are waiting for Your Majesty to recover sufficiently to go home," Charles interrupts. "Is there any good reason we should be bored while doing so?"

My husband appears too stunned or perhaps too pained to speak. I look to my sister, hoping, for the sake of my husband, that she will restrain hers. But Beatrice pays no attention to my pointed glance. Jeanne, on the other hand, nudges Alphonse with her foot under the table.

"Your Majesty," the Count of Poitiers says, rising, "I apologize for any offense given and shall endeavor not to repeat it."

"Meaning he will take more care where he plays and with whom to avoid being called out," I whisper to Matilda.

We dine, as a family, in the king's apartment. For his convenience, but also, I presume, so there will be no one to witness his dressing-down of his brothers. These reprimands have become increasingly frequent. The Counts of Anjou and Poitiers came back from captivity in relatively good health when compared to their fellows. They apparently expected the royal court to be just as it was before, with the same entertainments we all enjoyed in Cyprus. They seem completely without regard for the memories of so many, their own brother Robert included, who died, or a thought for the hundreds of common soldiers, some of them their own retainers, still held prisoner by the Saracens!

Alphonse reseats himself and we sit for a moment or two in

uncomfortable silence, except for Charles and Beatrice who carry on a low conversation between themselves. As the bowls have already come and gone after the meal, each of us expects the king to dismiss us. My sense is that all eagerly anticipate being free of Louis's critical eye and going off to seek more pleasant company. I myself anticipate a stolen hour with Jean before he is expected with the king.

Sitting back in his chair, Louis looks us over and says, "I received a letter from our lady mother this morning."

Suddenly the sullen brothers are all attention. Even at a distance Blanche commands in a way that Louis cannot.

"She has dispatched the monies that Her Majesty"—he nods appreciatively in my direction—"so presciently wrote to request on our behalf the moment the terms of my surrender were known to her."

It was, I think, the one time in my sixteen-year marriage that I have ever written to Blanche with honest and bold language. I knew our chests here could not supply the balance of the ransom and knew as well that the dragon would do everything in her power to assist Louis.

"Our mother earnestly entreats me to return to France with haste on the grounds that my kingdom has need of me and that my truce with the English king soon expires. She is also particularly eager for you, Alphonse, to claim in person the county of Toulouse, which became yours upon the death of your good wife's father."

"I will go home most willingly the moment Your Majesty is ready!" Alphonse replies with real eagerness.

"Hm."

The tone of Louis's voice, not entirely approving, shocks me into wariness. Surely we are going home as soon as the last monies are paid? I've written to little Louis and told him as much.

"After receiving our mother's letter, I summoned the noblemen who live and hold possessions in this land. Unlike you, Brother, they show little zeal for my departure."

"What?" Charles blurts the word out without thinking. Then, recalling to whom he speaks, he sits up straight in his chair and in a more careful tone says, "Pardon me, Your Majesty, but surely you do not think of staying in this forsaken place. With so few knights left, what would Your Majesty propose by it?"

"The barons here seem to think this land will be lost in its entirety if I withdraw. But"—Louis puts up a hand to stop Charles who shows every sign of interrupting—"I make no decision on the point at present. No, I will hear advice before deciding such an important matter."

Charles looks momentarily relieved; then his face clouds again. "Whose advice?"

"Yours, Brother, to be sure, but also the advice of my councilors and of the *preudommes* who survived the desert with us and have ever given me excellent counsel even when I would not hear it. And, of course, I will hear the opinion of the Holy Father's legate."

I can guess what Charles and Alphonse are thinking. As soon as they leave this room, they will seek the very men whom Louis names and secure their opinions. I would do the same had I the purse or the political connections for such action. Next month it will be two years complete since we set sail from Aigues-Mortes. We have exhausted what supplies we did not abandon in Damietta, and our mighty army is largely dead or imprisoned in Egypt. There is nothing for it but to swallow our pride, accept our defeat, and go back to France. Why not do so at once so that Louis can continue to recover his health in his own kingdom?

"I ask you, Brothers, to join me tomorrow with those others whom I have enumerated. What better day than the Lord's day to consider and discuss such a weighty business?"

"YOU WILL ADVISE THE KING to go home," I say confidently.

Jean and I are once again reduced to meeting in odd places—this afternoon a small shed in a field of olive trees with Marie standing guard nearby. For some weeks after his dreadful illness I had an excuse to visit Jean. But now that he is completely and magnificently recovered, it would look suspicious for me to hang about his lodgings. *How unfortunate,* I think, feeling his arms tighten around me, for after watching him sweat off the fever and convalesce in his bed, we could now make much better use of it. And who knows for how much longer? Jean does not know that my womb is quickened, but I must tell him soon or risk his spotting the evidence of it himself. I fear his reaction, however, for the child is Louis's, sown in me during those weeks the king touched me and Jean did not.

"You sound like the papal legate," Jean says, beginning to unlace my dress.

"You have already seen His Excellency?" I ask with difficulty, for Jean's mouth is closing upon mine.

"You want to talk about the legate?" Jean gives me a mocking look. "That is rather damaging to my feelings."

"I *do* wish to talk about the legate. But I suppose talk can wait since it is obvious such serious subjects do not have your full attention at present."

"No." His eyes laugh. Having pulled my tunic off, he fingers my nipples through my chemise. "And in another moment they will not have your attention either."

When we are done, we lie for a while on the pile of large nets used to catch olives during the harvest that made our impromptu bed. The weather is balmy, and, had I not more serious issues on my mind, I would be content to rest until Jean recovered enough to take me again. Knowing his thoughts likely run in the same direction, I pull my chemise back down to cover my hips, rise grudgingly, and begin to dress.

"The legate?" Jean asks teasingly.

"The legate."

"He came to me even before Louis's summons for the morrow. Whomever he pays for information in the king's household, the legate gets his money's worth. His Excellency knew Queen Blanche calls the king home. He is of the opinion that Louis, being out of money and nearly out of men, should go and asked me to opine as much when His Majesty sought my counsel. He offered me my passage back to France on his ship, along with my board on the journey in return for such advice."

"That seems a magnanimous gesture, to reward you for saying what you surely would have said anyway. But promise me not to travel with His Excellency, for I feel certain Louis will offer you a place on our ship."

"Marguerite, I cannot advise Louis to withdraw to France."

"What!" I could not be more shocked. "Why ever not?"

"Because of advice given me by my cousin the Lord of Bourlé-mont before I came to the Holy Land."

"And what, pray, was this sage advice that it requires you, and indeed all of us, to continue in this land not our own?"

"He urged me to remember that a knight's honor rests on more than his bravery in battle. 'Recall,' he said, 'the words of the Lord, "As ye have done unto one of the least of these my brethren, ye have done it unto me."' No man can return from the Holy Land without shame if he leaves the humbler people who set out in his party in the hands of the infidels. How can the king return to France—how can *I* return for that matter—while the Saracens hold hundreds of archers, foot soldiers, and the like?"

I want to be angry, to disagree vehemently, but I cannot. Instead, I feel as if my heart is breaking, and I begin to sob. Jean pulls me against him.

"You are right," I say, suddenly finding my anger and pounding my fists against his breast even as I continue to weep. "But I hate you for it. How much longer can you expect me to sit in this desert? Do you want little Jean to grow up here, in hardship? With no ken of his native land?"

"No. You know I wish neither of you to suffer. But nor would I have my son grow up to realize that his father, either the man he calls by that name or the man who owns it, was a self-centered coward who abandoned the very men he marched into danger to languish and die."

I have no answer for this, and merely lay my cheek against his chest.

"I will speak to Louis," Jean continues. "I will urge him to send envoys home with a call for more troops in case the Mamlūks need to be held to the terms they agreed upon at swords' points. And I will urge His Majesty to select noblemen for this errand so that they can accompany the wives and children back to France and safety. If Louis and I cannot go home without dishonor, it does not follow that you may not."

"No!" My heart beats wild at his suggestion. "Do not ask me to leave you."

"Why not? It is sensible and surely, with you to assist the Queen Mother in raising reinforcements, we will follow you before long. Only let us wait for the arrival of the balance of the ransom from France and let us celebrate the release of the remaining prisoners that the transfer of such monies to the Saracens ought to occasion—"

"What makes you think that task will proceed more smoothly than did the march on Cairo? Nothing in these wretched lands goes as it is planned. Besides, can you know so little of Louis, you who are every day closer to him and first among his knights? He will do *anything* by way of penance for his failures, even die here. Mark me well—he does not stay merely to ransom prisoners. You have heard him say yourself that he will not leave the Kingdom of Jerusalem to be lost. And if he remains, I must remain to remind him—to remind both of you it would seem—of his duty to the Kingdom of France."

Jean places a tender hand upon my cheek. I shake it off.

"But do not ask me to be happy about it. And do not ask me to concede the point yet. There are others besides yourself who will offer advice to the king. They may well recommend he go home. His brothers certainly will."

"Now it is you who ignore His Majesty's essential nature," Jean replies. "He is a good king. He will not abandon those who serve him to rot in prison. Such a thing is not in his nature."

"Nor is it in his nature to defy his mother," I reply. God help me, but for the first time I am glad that the dragon is a bully and thankful that she exerts an unnatural pull over my husband.

THE COUNT AND COUNTESS OF Poitiers and the Count and Countess of Anjou stand on the deck of their ship. Beatrice shed many tears over me at the bottom of the plank before she went aboard and Charles affected a long face, but I am not fooled. They are delighted to go.

As I expected, they advised Louis to return to France as did nearly everyone else. Only Jean and the Count of Jaffe urged him to stay, and their fellows lambasted them for doing so. And when Louis proclaimed that he would not desert the Kingdom of Jerusalem, his brothers—treacherous, disloyal brothers—declared that they felt their crusade oaths fulfilled and would go to France with or without the king. As a departure against His Majesty's wishes would be embarrassing to Louis and demoralizing to those who did intend to stay, my husband immediately announced he was ordering the counts home to assist Blanche with her regency and to raise an army and return. I suspect Louis even believes they will come back and bring more troops with them so that he can continue to crusade, but seeing Beatrice's smug little smile as the plank is drawn up and the anchors weighed, I know we are being deserted.

I feel despondent. Not only are my royal brothers-in-law departing, but the sea around their vessel contains a veritable fleet. Despite Louis's promise to dispense royal funds to allow those who wished to stay to do so, his surviving knights by and large have had enough discomfort and defeat and are going home. Even the royal council is depleted. Only the chamberlain, Lord Geoffrey de Sergines, and Louis's new constable, Giles le Brun, stand at his side as the ships begin to pull away from shore. And, of course, Jean is also beside the king, more in favor than ever and newly retained for a further term in Louis's service at a price of two thousand livres.

"It is sickening," Jean says, moving to my side. "As if the Count of Poitiers passing out coinage and jewelry as he went aboard were not spectacle enough, he and Charles had the audacity to beg me to watch over Louis in their absence. If they were truly so concerned with the health and welfare of the king as to be moved to tears and entreaties, why not turn back at the dock and repent of their decision to go?"

Louis and his retinue turn their backs to the sea and make their way toward the city. He will not miss me if I do not trail along. With his frailty diminished and a new plan for redeeming his losses in battle by improving the fortification of Acre consuming his energies, I find the king increasingly his old self—the self that neither needs nor appreciates me. This saddens me, but it has not the power to reduce me to tears as similar behavior did when we arrived in Cyprus two years ago, for now I have Jean whose love and friendship for me never falter.

"And if you are truly concerned with the welfare of His Majesty," I say, turning away from my husband's receding back, "do what you can to push matters along here. For mark me, those departing will never return, and if we tarry too long in concluding our business here, we may arrive in France to find one or the other of the counts king in all but name."

"Not while Blanche of Castile draws breath," Jean replies.

For the second time in recent memory I find myself grateful for the dragon's fanatic devotion to Louis. Jean is right; she will not allow him to be usurped.

"And, while those knights who leave us seem unlikely to return, I would not be so certain that other men-at-arms are not forthcoming," he continues, nodding idly to a knight who passes. "The Counts of Poitiers and Anjou may lack enthusiasm for raising an army for His Majesty, but the Queen Mother must surely understand that it is in her interest to send reinforcements."

I try to feel cheered by his confidence but cannot. And Jean, who knows me better than anyone, sees as much.

"I will do all I can to press His Majesty forward while we wait. The Mamlūks agreed to surrender the lesser prisoners as part of our treaty. Perhaps a timely reminder. I could go to Cairo—"

"Not you." The only thing worse than continuing on here for an indefinite period would be doing so in fear of Jean's safety.

"I forget," Jean says gently, "that while His Majesty and I still have a circle of companions, this departure leaves you nearly alone."

The memory of the second Lady Coucy's tearful farewell this morning rises before me, but I push it from my mind. "I still have the Countess of Jaffa, Marie, and the *béguines* in my service." I wipe angrily at the moisture gathering in the corners of my eyes; then looking up into Jean's face add, "It is worth the loss of many simply to be rid of Beatrice with her frivolous nature and fatuous conversation."

Jean begins to laugh. I am about to join him when a wave brings a dead fish to shore close to where we stand. The odor overwhelms me and sends me retching. Jean's eyes open wide and his laughter stops at once. "By God's coif! You are with child!" His voice is more concerned than incensed, but when I nod my head, his anger breaks through. "Why did you not tell me?"

"You would have put me on the ship."

"So I would have." Jean considers me, his eyes dropping to my stomach as if testing himself to see if he should have noticed something and did not.

"His Majesty does not know." It is a statement, not a question. "If he did, he would have put you on the ship as well." Jean puts both hands to his forehead; then, remembering that though most of our party has disbanded, we are in a public place, he drops them again.

"He would not," I say, feeling slightly defiant. "His Majesty will be delighted."

Jean and I part. I see him next when those few and faithful who remained with His Majesty gather to dine. The challenge I read in his eyes spurs me to tell Louis about the baby. So, after dinner, I seek a private moment in the king's oratory and reveal my condition.

His Majesty is *not* delighted. But nor is he displeased like Jean.

Looking up from his knees where he was arranging himself to pray he asks, "Are you sure?"

"Perfectly."

I continue to stand where I am, waiting for happiness or even recognition to spark in Louis's eyes. I myself am surprisingly happy to be carrying his child, perhaps because I feel, after his delight in Jean Tristan, he deserves to celebrate a son born in the Holy Land who is really and truly his own. But Louis continues to look at me blandly. After a few moments he says, "Was there something else?"

"No. Shall I leave you to your prayers?"

"Or stay and pray with me if you like."

If the request was warmed by even the slightest touch of real feeling, I would be tempted. But the man before me bears no resemblance to the man who lay with me to beget the child I carry. A few months after hobbling off a galley in the harbor, that man, I conclude, is gone just as surely as if he had boarded one of the *nefs* this morning and sailed for France.

CHAPTER 30

Dear Eleanor,

I cannot contemplate the marriage of my niece, your darling Margaret, without being overcome by memories. I am certain it must be the same for you. I recall all the ideas I had about being a wife and a queen; how I thought myself a woman grown as I left Provence to become a bride. I realize now, of course, that I was a fool. No, not a fool, only foolish, and that is both the nature of youth and its saving grace. When we are young, we must be hopeful, fanciful even. We must believe that all that is new holds the possibility of being good. Were it otherwise, leaving home would be unbearable. Life would be unbearable. And if we learn later that husbands, that crowns, that indeed all of life is not as we supposed it would be, it does not follow that we will be discontented. Perhaps true happiness can only be recognized and claimed once one has suffered some of life's disappointments.

So, as you say good-bye to your daughter full of love and pride but also touched by sadness and misgivings, know this, Margaret is what you made her and therefore far better suited for the life that awaits her than you can imagine. I have great faith that she, like her mother, will be a wise queen and, in her turn, a tender mother.

Your devoted sister,
Marguerite

ELEANOR
DECEMBER 1251
YORK, ENGLAND

Eleven-year-old Margaret, always so reserved and decorous like the aunt for whom she was named, clings to me, crying.

"I do not understand," I say, though I understand perfectly and would cry too if I did not think it would make matters worse. "You were fine throughout our journey. And only look at the beautiful rooms His Grace the archbishop of York has prepared for us." I sweep out a hand to encompass our surroundings, so lavish they nearly rival the best of my own chambers. But the gesture is wasted because Margaret will not raise her head from my breast.

"I do not want to be married," she says, sobbing. "I want to go home to Windsor with you, Papa, and the boys."

There is nothing I can say to that. Some wild part of me wants to slip away to the stables with my daughter and ride for home before anyone notices we are gone. The Eleanor who was a bride herself fifteen years ago might even have done so. The Eleanor I am now knows the gesture would be both useless and foolish. *At least,* I think, stroking my daughter's waist-length hair to soothe her, *I need not frighten her further with talk of the marriage bed. That is a mercy indeed!* Alexander of Scotland is forbidden to touch his wife, my daughter, until she attains her fifteenth year. Henry and I insisted on this, and hope by it to preserve her childhood just a little longer and guard her from the dangers of too early a pregnancy.

"Mother," says Edward as he bursts into the room without ceremony, trailed by his friend, a rather more timid Nicholas de

Molis, "can my friends and I have our leopard tabards now?" Then, suddenly aware of his sister's distress, he adds, "What is wrong with Margaret?"

"She is only a little homesick."

Edward regards his sister as if she were insane. "But we have just arrived and everything is splendid! There is a fire eater in the courtyard; would she like to see him?"

"Perhaps later." While I speak, Margaret raises her mournful eyes to me, clearly wishing her brother gone. "For the moment it is enough that you and your companions should enjoy him. Why not go along and explore the rest of the archbishop's palace? But do not go out into the streets." There are multitudes in town for the wedding, and with Scots and Frenchmen mingling among the English, there is bound to be violence along with boisterous celebration.

"What about the leopard short coats? Nicholas, Bartholomew, and Ebulo have not seen them yet."

"I'm sorry, but your friends will have to continue waiting to admire them. You know those tabards are for the wedding banquet."

"Oh Mother." Edward sighs the words as if I am denying him his birthright.

"Edward, enough! You have a trunk full of beautiful new things. The tunic you are wearing was new this morning."

"Fine. But when I get married, I will wear whatever I want in whatever order I like to wear it."

Though I cannot think what to say to this remark, Edward turns and races out, obviating the need for response. De Molis bows and edges out, drawing the door shut behind him. As soon as he is gone, I disentangle myself from Margaret and lead her to the washbasin. Pouring out some cool water, I wipe her forehead and then clean away the traces of tears from her face. Finally I wring out the square of linen and, bending her over the basin and lifting her hair, lay it on the back of her neck to calm her. Should any of my English ladies see me do such a thing in December, they would no doubt cluck their tongues and predict a dire chill for the princess. But I, who grew up hot-blooded, know that with agitation comes overheating and without relieving the latter the former cannot be eased.

Sure enough my daughter's breathing slows. I remove the cloth and lead her to a bench where we can sit side by side.

"Margaret, you cannot doubt that your father and I want the best for you. And though you do not believe it now, being the Queen of Scotland is a very good thing indeed. Nor do we send you alone. Did you know that when your aunt went to France these many years ago, she was left entirely alone—without a single blood relation, without her nurse, or even a lady-in-waiting from her own country?"

Margaret shakes her head solemnly. She has heard many stories of my sister before, but not this one. No, until now I have confined myself to the pleasant and diverting tales of my sister's girlhood and my own. But as Margaret leaves her own childhood behind, she is ready for the sterner stuff of life.

"You, by contrast, will have Lady Cantilupe and Sir Geoffrey de Langley who have been appointed by your father especially to see that your rights and privileges are respected at all times in your new court."

"Will you write to me every day?" Margaret asks, eyes welling again.

"If you like. But I imagine you will have more to tell than I. You go to see new places and make new acquaintances while I return to all the familiar scenes and people." And with that single phrase I am transported back to a different chamber, a different leave-taking. "I know," I say, "I will give you something of mine—something to take with you and to wear when you are feeling far from home." I wonder, did my sister take my *aumônière* to the Holy Land with her? Does she still wear it as frequently at thirty as she did at thirteen?

Two large casks of my jewels and other finery sit on top of several of my larger trunks. The first cask does not yield what I seek, but in the second I find it—a fine gold belt patterned with shields made of pearls. I paid a fortune for this piece. It was intended to dazzle the eyes of visiting dignitaries when Henry knights the Scottish prince. I slip it around my daughter's waist and fasten it. Then we both break out in peals of laughter as it slides down and over her hips. "It will need some adjusting," I say, "but I am sure His Grace knows a good jeweler. He knows everyone in York."

TWO EVENINGS LATER I PUT Margaret to bed, singing to her as if she were a tiny baby. As her eyes fall shut and she surrenders to sleep, I turn to her nurse. "Sit up beside her tonight. I would not have her wake alone."

The good woman nods, and I notice a tear escape from her own aged eye, dropping onto the embroidery in her lap.

Returning to my own room I seek distraction. "Willelma," I call, "Christina, let me see all my garments for the wedding."

At once there is bustle; there is finery. I am holding a new mantle, fingering the heavy gold braid and ermine trim when Henry enters. I expect him to look pleased, for no one loves the display and pageantry of state occasions more than my husband, but he looks concerned.

"Yes," I say, turning to Christina, "it is all perfect. Pray remove

it now and cover it for the morrow." She and Willelma scurry off
with my other ladies in their train, each bearing an item to the
room that has been designated my wardrobe for these festivities.

"Henry, will you take some wine?"

He nods, and I hurry to pour for him. After a deep gulp he says,
"The streets are impassable. Already people take their places along
the route to the Minster with more shoving than it pleases me to
see. Can you imagine how they will behave after a night spent
drinking to stay warm?"

"Can we get through safely?"

"Perhaps, but why attempt it? I have spoken to Walter de Gray,
and he advises we marry them here at dawn."

"Here?" I will be very sorry to miss the pomp of a larger ceremony; yet I suspect Margaret will not. And surely I will not enjoy
myself at all if my child is terrified en route by obstreperous crowds
in the streets. "Will the Scots agree to it?"

"The boy's guardians are smart. They know the largest part of
the crowd is English, so they have more need to worry for the
safety of their charge than we do." Suddenly Henry chuckles. "The
boy is smart as well." Having been a boy-king himself, my husband
has an affinity for his soon-to-be son. "After you withdrew with
Margaret this evening, I asked him whether, since he is here on
English soil, now might not be an opportune time to pay homage
to me for Scotland. And he avoided the question like the most
polished diplomat. 'Your Majesty,' he said, 'I came here in peace
to become your son, not to answer difficult political questions.' If
he is this clever at ten, he should be as silver-tongued as de Montfort before he is twenty." Henry laughs again; then he looks sober.
"If he is not good to her, all his cleverness will be to no avail. I will
march across his precious border and bring her home."

———

I FINISH READING THE LAST line of my letter from my daughter the Queen of Scotland and lay it in my lap. Four months into her marriage, Margaret writes daily, as do I, in obedience to both my promise and my inclination. Though she is homesick, there is nothing in her letters that causes me to repent of her father's decision to wed her where he did. The politics of the marriage appear sound, and, surely, as the couple is very young, affection will follow from being raised together side by side?

I am at Reading this fine spring evening with another marriage much on my mind. I have just dispatched Adam Marsh to Odiham with a message for the Earl and Countess of Leicester. Sometimes I do not know why we bothered, Uncle Guillaume and I, to work as we did to marry Henry's sister Eleanor to Simon. The marriage was meant to secure a smooth relationship between Henry and Simon, but its efficacy was short-lived. And I fear much of the blame lies with my husband, though that is something I was careful not to say in my letter—not even between the lines.

A man can be tied to a family or to a king by matrimony, but if you would keep him loyal and content, you must treat him with constancy and justice—train him to your service as one trains a child. But Henry is not good at consistency. He sets those who would do his bidding in one direction and then lambastes them when he finds them where he set them! Ever since he sent Simon de Montfort to Gascony, he has done nothing but complain about the earl's management of things there. To be sure, de Montfort has not been as effective as any of us would have wished, and his methods—well, they would not be mine. But to withdraw royal support from the earl would be disastrous for our son Edward.

Edward *must* have Gascony. Yet at the time of Margaret's marriage, there was a great danger that all the castles de Montfort had captured for my son would be lost again because Henry would not pay the cost of their defense, though he clearly promised to do so before de Montfort set out. I pressed as hard as I dared to get Henry to pay those monies. Though I was successful at last, I do not think Henry has forgiven me yet for taking the earl's part.

So I am not sorry Henry is not with me here but is in London. My evening will be quiet without my husband's company, but at least it will not be contentious. I will move to Windsor tomorrow. My ladies think this relocation a result of my desire to see my children. And so it is. Edmund's last letter was accompanied by a tooth, the first he has lost, and he longs to "frighten" me with his smile, which he says resembles that of a beggar on the street. But I am also deliberately closing the distance between myself and London. Uncle Peter says that additional Gascon lords arrive in the capital daily, each complaining loudly of abuse at the hands of the Earl of Leicester, and there is talk that the next parliament will bring the earl to an accounting for his actions. If Simon de Montfort is to be tried, it behooves me to be close enough to receive reliable reports of the proceedings.

Reliable reports are overrated, particularly when they bring word that my husband has made a fool of himself. The examination of Simon de Montfort before the parliament, which dragged on for more than a month, has just ended. My Franciscan, Adam Marsh, wrote me pages describing the trial itself—the accusations by the Gascon lords and my brother-in-law's able and restrained defense of himself. It was left to family to bring the news of Henry's ill-thought-out and awkward conduct.

I am in my hall at Windsor with all the windows full open to allow in the June sunshine and air, but I am not enjoying the fine weather. No, my pleasure in the day was spoiled the moment my uncle began his report.

"It is just as well that you were not there to witness Henry's outburst," Uncle Peter says, pacing before me. "He ranted at the barons like a disappointed child."

My uncle knows I cannot bear to see Henry embarrass himself. I can never reconcile the errors of judgment in governing and the stubborn stupidity of the king's public actions with the good-natured, attentive behaviors of the father and husband whom I love deeply. *Oh Henry,* I think, *what can you have hoped to gain, either in dignity or in authority, by denouncing and defaming Simon de Montfort in front of your parliament after a collection of those same magnates exonerated him of all charges?*

"So that is that. Simon is exonerated, but he is also finished in Gascony. Yet the job he attempted there is not completed. What can be done?" I pick up a bird's nest that Edmund brought me from the garden off the small table beside me and turn it over in my hands. My eyes are drawn to the bits of down meant to line it, evidence that, like myself, the mother bird was interested in the comfort and security of her young.

"His Majesty is resolved to go to Gascony himself and attempt its pacification."

I suck air in through my teeth and shake my head. I have as much call as any to know Henry is not possessed of overwhelming military skills. Still, he has a personal interest in holding Gascony that goes beyond any other man's. It is his legacy to his son. "When?"

"He cannot go at once," Peter replies. "Funds must be raised. And while His Majesty is gathering silver and troops, we can use the time to author a diplomatic strategy. If money is to be spent and men are to die, let us be as certain as possible of success."

"Can we not work on Gaston de Béarn?" It is most inconvenient to be related to one of the chief rebels in Gascony and even more so because I mistakenly intervened with the king to get him released when Simon de Montfort had him captive.

"We can try, of course." Peter shrugs. "But it is a foolish master who trusts a dog that has bitten him once already. Gaston may plead shared blood to save his own skin, but he has never shown any inclination to obey calls for family loyalty in support of our interests. He likes Gascony in a state of relative lawlessness, for then he and the other barons may take for themselves the power and revenues that should belong to the Crown." Peter pauses for a moment, stroking his beardless chin. His eyes lose their focus; then with a snap they are back on my face.

"I think," he says, "we would do better to send envoys to the King of Castile."

"But Alfonso of Castile accepted homage from the rebel barons not three months ago; he suborns their rebellion against English territorial claims and English rule of law, and seeks to claim Gascony for himself."

"Yes, but he is chary and knows that neither his attenuated claim to dominion over Gascony nor any military victory there are things certain. He will talk and he will *listen*."

"Then we must send someone who speaks well. Will you go yourself, Uncle?"

"If the king sends me. But, with humility, I might be better by the king's side as he steps off his ships."

"He will certainly make sounder steps by your presence. What about Mansel then?"

"I can think of none better. But before we, or more precisely His Majesty, sends anyone, we must have something to propose. We must offer Alfonso of Castile something to persuade him that an alliance with England will be more profitable to him than marching his troops around Gascony in the hopes that he might be its next duke."

My uncle takes a seat. I put down Edmund's nest and, as I do, my eyes wander over the collection of other trinkets presented me by my children—a stanza of poetry beautifully copied out by Beatrice; a small withered nosegay gathered for me by Edward. Edward is thirteen now and taller than I am. I look up. "It comes to my mind that Alfonso of Castile has a half sister approaching marriageable age."

"By the auspicious name of Eleanor," my uncle replies with a smile.

CHAPTER 31

My dear Eleanor,

    . . . How long will I be kept from my home?

    When His Majesty proposed staying in Egypt two years ago so that those lesser soldiers whom he lost into captivity might not be forsaken, I could not in good conscience fault him. But I feared then and I know with certainty now that his commitment to seeking their freedom was but the smallest part of what held him here. Louis cannot bear having lost. He hopes still, with feeble reason, that he may do something to turn defeat into victory. Can he not see his stubborn insistence on staying is rooted in the sin of pride? Were he humble enough to accept the drubbing he received at Saracen hands, we might be in France governing it as we should. Instead, we wander about in the desert like the Israelites. . . .

                            M

MARGUERITE
JUNE 1252
JAFFA, KINGDOM OF JERUSALEM

Waking in the dark, I cannot remember where I am. *Caesarea? No,* I think, sitting up in bed, *we left there weeks ago. Jaffa—we are in Jaffa.*

I feel sticky and my bedcovers cling to me in the hot, humid air.

Rising, I pad naked to the nearest window and throw it full open. In the dim predawn light, I can see the garden wall but not the sea beyond. Turning back, I seek my basin. Pouring out cool water, I begin to sponge myself clean of the night's sweat. Then I seat myself at my dressing table and apply lavender water to my shoulders, neck, and beneath my breasts. One of the best things about being in Jaffa is the fact that the Count and Countess have provided me with the trappings of a civilized life and accommodations that would seem luxurious even had I not slept for weeks in a tent. Yet it is not France. There are times I cannot even remember France.

It has been three years since I first saw the coast of Egypt from my ship, two years since the majority of our party departed from Acre, more than a year since my son Pierre was born, and nearly as long since the troops Louis expected his brothers to send to his aid should have arrived. Lighting a taper, I regard myself in the mirror. Sometimes I do not remember the old Marguerite either. I am very brown now, and my hair is as light as it was when I was a girl roaming the fields of Provence. Jean loves it this way, golden and glinting. Louis has not noticed. All he thinks about is fortifying Christian cities. It was for this reason that we went to Caesarea and to so many smaller places. The Holy Father grants indulgences to those who refortify settlements in the Holy Land. By building walls and towers, often with his own hands, my husband hopes to buy back the grace he feels he lost in his disastrous military failure.

Marie, bustling into the room, starts at seeing me already awake. "Your Majesty should have called," she chides.

"Why? What have we to do today that would demand your early attendance? Watch His Majesty's knights build walls?"

"Perhaps the Mamlūk troops will come today and our knights will leave off their ditch digging and march together with these infidels against the Sultan of Aleppo."

"That is one sight I *never* expect to see," I say, rising and allowing Marie to slide a clean chemise over my head. "The Mamlūks may have been willing to forgo the balance of the ransom, free their remaining prisoners, and send back the mangled heads of our dead in order to prevent His Majesty from joining with the sultan of Aleppo against them, but they will never fight side by side with the French. They hate Christians too much."

"Is that what my Lord of Joinville says?"

Marie is right; I do parrot Jean. He has no faith in or stomach for alliances with infidels. But I do not blame my husband for his treaty promising to fight beside the infidel Mamlūks against the Sultan of Aleppo. After the sinking of the first ship that Blanche sent—the ship that had been carrying the balance of the monies owed to his former captors—Louis needed a way to recover the Frenchmen still in Mamlūk hands without paying for them.

"Speaking of my Lord of Joinville, we will take the children into the garden after Mass to meet him." This is one of the worst aspects of our arrival in Jaffa. When we were camped in tents, Jean and I were constantly in company, whether with the king or outside his presence. It was easy to pass an hour or even an afternoon together, for my only companions were Marie and my *béguines*. Now that I am installed in the residence of the Count and Countess of Jaffa, with the countess and the others in her circle for company, Jean and I must be careful once again. To make matters worse, Jean, like Louis, who refuses to enjoy better conditions than his knights, lives in the armed camp erected in fields surrounding the city.

"I TELL YOU I SAW the plans this morning," Jean says, his voice low and urgent. "Twenty-four towers. Such work will take a year or more."

I begin to cry. We are in the Countess of Jaffa's lovely garden, but I am no longer enjoying our outing. Little Jean, standing at my knee as I sit beside his father on a bench, tilts his head and regards me pensively. Then, climbing silently into my lap, he reaches up his little hand to wipe my tears away. His gesture releases my words. "I cannot stay here another year! Nor can Louis, whatever he may think. Has he forgotten his brothers are ambitious men and his mother is aging? If she dies while we are here, who will protect Prince Louis?" At the thought of my son, now eight years old, my eyes fill again. He will be a stranger to me when I return. Will he be the dragon's creature by such long association with her? Has she turned my golden prince into his father?

"He *has* forgotten everything of this world. You know that. He thinks only of making a place for himself at God's knee in the next world through charitable acts." Jean lifts our son from my lap into his own and plays with his curls absentmindedly.

Marie clears her throat. The nurse walking with Pierre on her hip draws close, completing her first circle of the garden. Jean sets our son down and changes his tone. "If Your Majesty would like to see the oranges in their groves, I am sure I would be happy to arrange it."

"I think the baby has had enough air," I say, nodding to the nurse. "Pray take him in to the wet nurse. Marie and I will bring Jean Tristan in when we come." As soon as she is out of earshot, I ask Jean, "Should I write to Blanche of Castile?"

"Why? When, if ever, has the Queen Mother taken your part against her son?"

"A fair point. But this time our interests must surely be identical. She wanted Louis home two years ago. And pleaded with him again, and even more desperately, in letters accompanying the second ship that she sent, carrying the money that finally reached us."

"Then write to her by all means."

Jean Tristan wanders away and, crouching by the base of a bush, earnestly examines a bug of some sort.

"I will not speak of my fears that Louis will be usurped. She knows her sons, especially Charles, better than anyone. Rather I will say that I fear for her grandsons born here. This is no place to raise princes of France." It is the truth; both Jean and I know it. Without the company of other children, privy to conversations that ought to be held outside his presence, and alone for hours at a time, Jean Tristan is the most solemn two-year-old I have ever encountered. Louis continues to take an interest in him, though he ignores Pierre and me as much as he can. With Louis, an interest means religious education, so little Jean has been subjected to stern lectures on the glory of God and man's unworthiness—lectures better left for an older child.

"Perhaps if she reminds him of what he should already know," I continue, "reminds him that he has discharged his honorable duty by securing the release of the last prisoners; that without more men-at-arms, he cannot seek battle with the Saracens; and that no further French troops are coming, perhaps then Louis will hear and understand as he does not when his advisers say the same things. After all, Louis is accustomed to letting his mother lead him. She can certainly bend him to her will as I never could." I give a deep sigh.

"Come," Jean says bracingly. "Let me see you smile. We cannot control the king; we cannot control the Mamlūks or the Sultan of Aleppo. All we can do is love each other and make the best of the situation." Gazing up at the clear blue sky, he turns to Jean Tristan. "Would you like to go down to the beach?"

"Yes please!" The boy runs to take Jean's outstretched hand, his habitually solemn look dissolving into an angelic smile.

"Mama." Jean Tristan holds out his other hand to me expectantly. As I take it, Jean drops the one he holds. As pleasing as the image of the three of us walking hand in hand to the port might be to Jean or me, it is hardly one we can allow others to glimpse.

"DID YOU WRITE TO OUR mother?" Louis is furious.

Summoned to his tent to find him pacing back and forth, while Jean looks on, I am caught entirely off my guard. It is impossible to believe that Blanche could have my letter yet, let alone that Louis could have received comment upon it. After all, one of the greatest woes attendant upon all our travels has been the impossibility of the regular and reliable receipt and sending of letters.

"Please, Louis!" I sink to my knees in a pool of light from the setting September sun. I can see the horror in Jean's eyes, but I do not care—or rather I am beyond caring. If I must grovel in the dust to move Louis in the direction of home, I will do so.

"Answer my question."

"I wrote to inquire about the health and welfare of our children in France."

"And to complain about the circumstances of our children here."

Startled as I am, I remain too chary to confess what I am not certain my husband knows. "Is that what Her Majesty says?"

"Our mother seems unduly worried that the princes are being raised like nomads," Louis replies. "What would put such a thought in her head if you did not?"

"What would put such a thought in her head? Our circumstances, sir!" I gesture to the spare furnishings of his tent and to the sea of tents beyond its open side. "The queen is a wise woman and a mother many times over; she needs no letter from me to imagine how we live here and to see that it would be better for Tristan and Pierre if we returned to France."

Louis glares at me; then turning to Jean, he says, "My Lord of Joinville, you see how it is. I am engaged in a great undertaking for the glory of God, and my wife would distract me from it! Remember, madam, it was woman who tempted Adam in the garden with disastrous results. I will not be turned from what is right by your complaints."

Hot tears of anger spring to my eyes. "I do not complain for myself. I would be content to live out the balance of my life in the desert if Your Majesty willed it so. But what mother would not speak for her children? And what subject would not beseech her king to think of the needs of his land?"

Now I have done something unforgiveable—I have reminded Louis of his duty to France, a duty I know gnaws at him when he cannot force it out of his mind with prayer or the exhaustion of putting rocks one on top of the other from dawn to dusk. Coming forward, Louis grasps my arm and hauls me to my feet. "Leave us!" He shoves me roughly in the direction of the tent flap. "The Seneschal of Champagne and I have more important matters to discuss than how a foolish woman thinks I ought to govern my kingdom."

Jean's face is blanched. I have the horrible presentiment that he will rise to my defense. With no time to think and no better idea, I close my eyes and let myself fall to the ground as if insensible.

"Great God, was ever woman more inconvenient!"

"I will take her back to the castle, Your Majesty." I thank God that Jean's voice, while hardly calm, remains under control. Though Louis must hear the anger in it, he doubtless thinks the seneschal is disgusted with me.

"Yes," Louis responds, his voice already cooled from its rage to an icy, detached tone that I hate even more, "get her out of my sight."

Jean's arms scoop me up. I try to let my limbs hang limp to further the illusion that I am insensate. When we are clear of the tent, Jean mutters a curse.

I open my eyes. Jean's face is as openly angry as Louis was moments ago. "I am fine," I whisper urgently.

"What?" Jean is rightfully confused by my sudden recovery.

"I did not faint; I only pretended."

His gaze meets mine. "Thank you."

And then I know that Jean was closer to losing control than perhaps even he himself realized.

"You can put me down; I am quite able to walk. Only see me to my horse, and Marie and I will ride back."

"And lose my excuse for bearing you back to the castle before me on my saddle? No. And I am not only being selfish. I need time to let my temper cool before I return to His Majesty."

I close my eyes again and rest my head contentedly against Jean's chest. I can hear his heart galloping like a horse given its reins. "I swear," Jean says softly, "if he had struck you, I would have killed him."

His words chill me to the bone. I make up my mind to plead no more. Not if we stay in the desert a dozen years. More than this, I will avoid the king as much as appearances allow. It is not as if I take any pleasure in his company and certainly he takes no pleasure in mine.

But Louis is not done with me.

As dusk falls, he comes to the castle and is ushered into my rooms. I am not even undressed for bed when he dismisses my ladies. There is no love in him. Nor any real desire that I can sense, save perhaps the desire to show me that he is my master and France's. He takes me as a warrior might take a city, heedless of how he destroys my clothing, never uttering a single word.

Marie returns to find me ruined, scratched, and weeping. She too is silent. Gently removing my torn garments, she washes me.

"Promise me," I swallow hard, my voice trembling with emotion, "swear to me that you will never tell him."

Marie knows whom I mean.

"Never, Your Majesty. For the seneschal is too much a man of honor to let such as this pass unanswered."

ANOTHER SPRING HAS NEARLY GONE and I am growing large with child again. Sighing, I watch Marie move my chair before an open window, then take a seat, lifting my swollen feet to rest on the stool she places for me. It seems unjust that I should bear a third babe in the desert, but perhaps it is my penance. Jean certainly feels it is his. "I shall have a second chance to master the quality of acceptance," he said when I first told him. "To submit meekly to God's will and to Louis's dominion over you. There will be no jealousy this time, Marguerite; I swear it."

Of course, I had not told him everything. No, never that. The morning after Louis took me so violently, as I stood before my mirror examining the scratches and bruises that my husband left upon me, a clever deceit came to me. I told Jean that my courses had come early. The abstinence demanded by such an event allowed Louis's marks to heal before Jean saw me naked again. So while Jean accepts that I carry Louis's child, he does not know the manner in which it was sown upon me.

My door swings open to reveal Jean, eyes twinkling merrily, one hand hidden behind his back. "What do you think I have here?" he asks, coming to kiss my forehead. He brings his hand forward with an exaggerated flourish; it is full of pink-blossomed Egyptian campion. "The last to be found anywhere." He bows as he hands them to me.

I smile. "And have you nothing better to do this morning than pick flowers?"

"Not when they are for you." Jean takes my outstretched hand and seats himself on the stool beside my feet. "His Majesty and I will make a circuit of the city this afternoon to examine the wall that now stretches from the sea on one side to the sea on the other like a crescent. Do you feel up to riding?"

"I am not sure Louis would approve of your extending the invitation."

"I will tell him that I adjudged you in need of some air." Louis no longer visits me at all, and I eschew the tents of his camp save to dine once weekly with His Majesty and the gathering of knights that passes for a royal court these days. But, sensitive to at least this much of his duty to me, my husband asks Jean to call on me daily and ascertain my health. It is an errand that suits both Jean and myself perfectly. "Provided you make appreciative exclamations while we are inspecting the towers, you will doubtless be very welcome," Jean continues. "After all, His Majesty built these defenses to be admired."

"I thought he built them for God's glory."

Jean laughs. "That too, that too."

"When the wall is done will we go home?" I ask.

Jean's features are at once serious. "His Majesty's mind shows no sign of turning in that direction. But I think he must relent soon before the money is gone."

I want to be convinced by Jean's argument. But in my heart I believe Louis will spend every livre that his mother sent us without even knowing it. Only when the coffers are empty will he stop this madness, and then, if Blanche or his brothers do not raise and send more funds, I do not know how we will sail home. Looking down at my swollen ankles, I say, "Much as I would like to spend the afternoon in the saddle with you, my love, I fear I am in no condition. Why not take little Jean?"

"Excellent! He can sit before me on my saddle." In his excitement Jean gets to his feet, his face alight with unadulterated pleasure. Clearly our three-year-old son's company will substitute for mine. But rather than feeling affronted, I experience a profound sense of thanksgiving—just as I do every time I see father and son together. Whatever neglect Louis has shown our children, however little it appears to concern him that we have not set eyes on Louis, Philippe, or Isabelle in five years—longer than either of the boys had been alive at the time we left them—I have one son at least who is entirely beloved of his father.

When June arrives, it is ungodly hot—hot enough to make me sometimes wish that I lodged in one of the tents where I might be open to the air. Yet, as my confinement approaches, I find myself unaccountably cheerful. Perhaps it is the diversion of having something to do other than to sit for hours sweating over an embroidery frame or a book. My ladies and I are preparing a chamber for my upcoming labor. A servant sweeps the place from corner to corner while Marie, following behind, scatters sweet hay. The Countess of Jaffa stands on a stool, humming and tying bunches of herbs to the posts of the bed.

"Where is Her Majesty?" The question echoes from the room beyond in Jean's distinctive voice. A moment later he joins us.

"Sieur," the Countess of Jaffa chides strictly from her perch, "this is no place for you!"

"Pardon, Countess, but I have been sent by the king with a

message for Her Majesty." Jean is all *politesse,* but I can see the strain in the muscles of his jaw and I know something significant has happened.

"My Lord of Joinville, pray withdraw with me and I will hear you." Gliding past him and through the door he holds for me, I admonish the others over my shoulder. "Continue with your good work. I will be back shortly."

As soon as the door is shut I ask, "What is it?"

"The king is betrayed by the Mamlūks."

At last, I think, *now we can stop waiting for them.* "Surely you are not surprised by this?"

"No." Jean shakes his head solemnly in the negative to reinforce the word. "I never believed they would join us here as promised to fight the sultan of Damascus. But there is worse. They made peace with the sultan, and even now their combined forces are marching to Sidon."

"Sidon? Where His Majesty sent the Lord of Montceliard to help the populace refortify?"

"There are too few Christians there to hold the place." Jean paces away from me. "They will be slaughtered." He pushes both his hands into his hair at either side of his temples.

"Heaven help them."

"*We* must help them. We leave at once."

"It is so far," I say in dismay. I cannot imagine riding so far in my condition. Then, steeling myself, I say, "I can be ready in an hour."

Jean's face tightens. Stepping forward, he places his hands on my shoulders. "Marguerite, you are not going."

"I know you are concerned for me, but I will be fine."

"No, you do not understand. This is the king's direction, not mine."

I stagger to the nearest stool and sink down on it. "I am to be abandoned?"

"You will be safe here at Jaffa." Jean crouches before me and takes both my hands. "When we pass Acre, I will see that His Majesty sends a ship to bring you to join us at Sidon as soon as it is safe. I swear it."

"A ship? And who will make the sea journey to Sidon with me? Or am I to manage alone in dangerous waters with two small children and a babe?"

"If I could stay with you, I would." Jean's eyes look beseechingly into my own. "I suggested as much to His Majesty."

"And what did he say?"

"He will leave a dozen knights to guard you on your passage."

"That is not what he said."

Jean ignores the jibe. "That is what he will do."

"Oh Jean, I am frightened."

"I know you are, and I am frightened for you. But remember, you are the woman who held Damietta with only five hundred men. You ransomed the king and led our people to safety in Acre. You have done great things for your kingly husband and your God. One of them at least will not desert you now. I will pray every day for your safe delivery and journey, and I will stand on the shore at Sidon to greet your ship when it finally comes, though Louis himself should seek to bar my way." Looking over his shoulder at the door by which we entered and seeing that it remains closed, Jean leans in and kisses me tenderly. Then rising he says, "I must go."

I want to cry. But Jean already feels worse than he deserves to. I know he would stay if he could. I rise, give him a quick kiss, and in a voice as cheerful as I can make it say, "Take care of your person, my lord, until we meet again. I shall be very angry at you if, when I disembark from my ship at Sidon, I find you dirty and blanket-clad as you were when your ship pulled into Acre."

FROM THE DECK OF MY *nef*, I see a castle sitting in the sea. Doubtless it is on an island, but, as it covers every inch, it appears to be floating; glimmering white in the morning sun. A ribbon of stone ties it to land, a causeway. And on that jetty the figure of a knight grows every minute clearer. He is alone, but I can see half a dozen figures on shore near a small cart at the place where we must disembark, and beyond them a city of tents flying the assorted banners of my husband's men. As we enter the harbor, we pass closer. The lone figure is Jean—another promise kept. He raises a hand in greeting, then starts briskly to join the rest of the party waiting for us.

Holding little Jean's hand, with two-year-old Pierre in Marie's charge and my new daughter in the arms of the nurse, I wait impatiently for the plank to be lowered. I can see now that the others are lackeys and foot soldiers doubtless come to carry our things. Jean is the lone gentleman here to welcome us.

I let the others descend before me. I watch how Jean greets each earnestly, even as his gaze flits repeatedly to me. When I reach the bottom of the plank, he says, "Your Majesty, welcome to Sidon."

"Where is the king?" I am not worried that Louis was killed or injured in whatever took place here, for Jean wears no sign of mourning.

Jean takes our son's hand, passes it deftly to Marie, then gives an instruction to one of the soldiers who begins to lead the women of my party toward the camp. The remaining men head onto the ship to retrieve our trunks. When only the two of us are left motionless in the sand, Jean says, "His Majesty regrets that he could not come down to meet you."

"I seriously doubt that."

"We were too late." He hangs his head as if the shame of the thing were brand-new. "The sack of the city was complete before we arrived and the infidels gone. We have been burying the dead every day since our arrival, and we are still not done."

"Dear God."

"The king carries the bodies in his own arms. No task is too loathsome for him. He blames himself." It is clear that Jean is moved by Louis's behavior. I am not.

"Another failure for which he will wish to do penance," I say with a sigh. "But surely you could not have come more quickly than you did."

"No. But when those who perished are interred, we will refortify this city in their memories."

We begin to walk toward camp in silence. All I can think about is the prospect of a prolonged stay at Sidon while Louis builds walls and towers to salve his conscience.

After a few moments, Jean says, "You look well."

"I am better for being here." And I realize as I say it, this is true. Being with Jean ameliorates every other circumstance.

He offers me a broad, open smile. "I missed you too."

"My Lord of Joinville," I tease, "you are very presumptuous. I merely missed living in tents, and having everything I wear and own always full of sand and dust."

I am rewarded with the laugh I love. "I will help you shake the dust from your clothing one of these evenings to be sure. I have placed your tents on the seaward side of the camp. Just there." Following the direction of his finger I can see my standard. "If threat comes, it is unlikely to come by water, and the sea castle is the fortress we would hold in last resort in any event."

"And I thought you wanted to give me a lovely view." I lay a hand on his arm just long enough that he can feel its weight but not so long that I might attract attention of any onlooker.

"A view and a little distance from the tents of the *preudommes* and His Majesty."

"I do like the air to stir around my tents."

The small cart with my chests on it rumbles by. We are nearly upon the camp. Our time can be measured in steps.

"I must return to the king. Shall I come tonight and take you for a walk by the sea?"

"Come tonight."

"If you need anything in the meantime, send Marie and I will secure it for you. I am lodged not far from His Majesty, across from the Count of Eu. The count's tent can be easily spotted as some fool has given him a bear." He laughs again. "The noise the thing makes is criminal, and if my people do not keep their eyes out, it will eat all my capons." Then, serious, he adds, "You must tell the children to stay away from it. They will be curious, but the thing is not tame."

"Never fear, Sieur." Allowing Jean to hold back the flap of my tent for me, I can see Marie and my *béguines* shaking out sheets in preparation for making up my bed. "I did not come all this way by sea alone to let my children be eaten by bears."

"SO YOU ARRIVED THIS MORNING with the princes and our new daughter."

"Yes, Your Majesty." I sit at dinner beside Louis on the dais under one of his pavilions. A collection of his favorite knights, Jean among them, eat at tables below us.

"Would you like to see the Lady Blanche?" Again I have named a daughter after the dragon—in irritation that her delivery delayed me in Jaffa but also in hope that her grandmother will force Louis's hand and bring us home. "I can send for her."

"Tomorrow will be soon enough." Louis's expression makes me doubtful he wishes to see our daughter at all.

"Just as Your Majesty wishes." Looking at my husband's profile, I can see that he loses weight once more. Burying the dead is dangerous work; every sort of pestilence attends them. It has long been my fear that Louis will die in the Holy Land; that, in fact, he intends to. "Will Your Majesty not take some more figs?" I lift the platter from between us and hold it in his direction. "I understand from the Seneschal of Champagne that you all work strenuously in this heat. Your Majesty must take care to keep up his strength."

Louis turns in my direction, his eyes for a moment unguarded. I see his weariness, his guilt, and his feelings of unworthiness. "We do not suffer at all compared with those we were too late to aid."

I nod my head. "Yet you offer them Christian burial, and that is a worthy task that cannot be completed without your strength."

Louis stretches out his long, thin fingers tentatively and takes a fig as if it might bite him. "I see the Seneschal of Champagne keeps you well-informed."

There is an edge to Louis's tone, as if he resents the fact. I am immediately cautious. "It was kind of Your Majesty to send him to see my ladies and me safely ashore."

"I did not, madam, but I knew where he was going when he took his leave. And as he is a gentleman of the first sort who always knows what is fitting to be done, I thought it best to let him go, even though it meant delaying my priest's sermon against his return."

The king looks at me expectantly, as if I ought to be pleased by his information; ought to thank him for his magnanimity. I am only thankful that the meal will soon be concluded and I will be away from him. It is without question easier for me to talk with and understand nearly anyone other than my husband of nineteen years.

IT DOES NOT TAKE LONG for me to feel settled at Sidon. A great part of me longs to go home, but if I must continue to live like a Bedouin, I am, for the moment, comfortable and happy. In this latest crowded camp, Jean and I live even more freely than we did in its predecessors. Louis, tired from his ceaseless manual labor in the heat, retires early to scourge himself, pray, and finally to sleep, leaving Jean and his other gentlemen to their own devices. Those men who would drink, gamble, or participate in other noisy amusements are as careful to stay away from my tents as they are to stay away from His Majesty's, so my edge of the camp is largely deserted as dusk falls. Jean comes and goes freely to pass time with me, his visits given a veneer of respectability by his position with the king and by the presence of my women, my children, or both. We play chess, talk of France, read to each other, and dine together as if we were a married couple. And when we would do the other things that married couples do, Marie admits Jean to the tent where I sleep, deserts her pallet at my feet, and crouches outside in the darkness until we are done.

Today is laundry day. My *béguines* laugh as the wind blows the wet things they are hanging into their faces. Marie has all the sides of my main tent raised. Jean Tristan and Pierre play queek, using my chessboard on a blanket on the ground. Pierre is really too little to understand the game but enjoys casting the pebbles nonetheless, and little Jean is unfailingly patient with him. The sea sparkles in the distance with a light so dazzling, it is nearly painful to look at.

Jean is not at Sidon. He left more than a week ago on a

pilgrimage to Our Lady of Tortosa. He departed in the highest of humors and left me likewise, despite his impending absence, because the king ordered him to purchase lengths of cloth to present to the Franciscans when we go back to France. Neither of us can remember Louis's mentioning his return to our country since before he left Jaffa.

I am trying to write to Eleanor. I have not received a letter from her in more than half a year, and I cannot say that she gets mine. At first I blamed the winter seas, and now I presume the fact that the king moves us so frequently from one city to the next explains this matter. I certainly know I am not the only one who no longer dependably receives correspondence. Still, writing to my sister is a habit formed over many years and so I continue, or would do if the strong wind from the sea did not try to take my page every moment.

"Your Majesty." Looking up from my efforts, I see one of my Lord of Joinville's knights. He carries a flat parcel wrapped in white cloth. Darling Jean! He must have sent me a relic, something from the shrine built by Saint Peter to the Holy Mother. I told him how jealous I was that he should see the place and I should not!

Rising, I go forward to the knight and kneel before him.

Giving me a look of utter confusion, he sinks to his knees as well.

"Pray, sir, rise. The bearer of holy relics need kneel to no one."

"Your Majesty," the knight says, blushing scarlet, which I think very odd for a man hardened in battle, "these are not relics, but rather a fine piece of camel hair cloth my Lord of Joinville sends for your pleasant use."

Now it is my turn to color. Scrambling to my feet, I try to look dignified, then abandon the attempt, collapsing in laughter into Marie's arms. Both of us shake until we weep; then, wiping my eyes, I turn back to the knight, who smiles merrily.

"Tell the Seneschal of Champagne he had best be wary of me

when he returns from the north. He is out of my graces for making me kneel to a bolt of cloth, however lovely."

"Your Majesty, you may tell him yourself, for he is not more than a day behind me."

"Be assured, good sir, I shall."

Jean does indeed arrive late in the afternoon of the following day. I only hear of the event; I do not see it or him. Jean's first duty is to call upon the king, and Louis, it seems, is not inclined to release him. As the afternoon draws to a close, Marie gets surreptitious word from Caym that Jean has been dismissed, but his respite will be brief as he is expected to return to His Majesty's tents to dine with the king.

When Louis has the tables set in his large pavilion, there is always a place for me should I choose to have it. I go when there is something interesting to be seen, as when the Greek Lord of Trebizond arrived bearing gifts and begging for a French bride. This evening, as the sun begins to slip toward the horizon and the night winds cool the air, I go because I cannot bear to spend Jean's first evening back apart from him.

Louis is in an excellent mood. In addition to the cloth he commanded, Jean brought him a strange stone that can be split into slices. When opened, it reveals a tiny stone fish, perfect in every bone and detail. Louis's enthusiasm for the marvel extends even to me. "Look, lady wife. Is it not a wonder? Stone, yet just as if it were alive and could swim away this moment."

"Wonderful!" I reach out one finger and gently touch the rock creature. "It is as if an artist painted it."

"It is better, for it is painted by Our Lord. The Sieur de Joinville is a man who knows what pleases."

He is indeed, I think to myself, and give a little shiver. After nearly two weeks without Jean's touch, I look forward to him pleasing me this evening. The stars are spread like jewels in the darkening sky, and I hope to tempt him down to the shore so that we may lie beneath them. The look he gives me when he arrives at dinner and bows to Louis suggests he will be agreeable to my suggestion.

The bowls are brought to begin the meal. As I hand over the linen with which I have dried my hands, I hear the hooves of a horse riding hard. The king's guards stiffen at their posts, peering into the oddly shaped bits of darkness that separate the light cast by the torches at the corners of the king's tent from that cast by the torches of tents nearby.

A man wearing the arms of the Count of Jaffa comes into view. Jumping down from his horse, he strides into the pavilion and stops before the king. "Your Majesty, I apologize for intruding, but my master bid me find you when I reached your camp, be it day or night."

"What is the matter?"

"This letter arrived for you from France." He holds out a most official-looking missive tattered at its edges but heavily sealed. "The man who brought it to the count had been looking for you for many months, and seemed always to arrive where you were not. He told the count the matter was urgent, and, hearing this, my master took it upon himself to see it safely to your hands."

"We thank you." Louis's voice trembles slightly. He takes the letter. Nodding to the nearest servant, he orders, "See that this man is fed." Then turning to Giles le Brun who, along with some of the other *preudommes* and councilors, has crowded to the dais, he says, "It bears the seals of both my brothers."

Jean, standing just behind le Brun's shoulder, gives me a pointed look. We have not heard from the court of France for so long that we had begun to think they had forgotten their king.

In a single deft motion Louis breaks both seals. The letter appears long, but my husband's eyes cannot have moved beyond the opening lines before he rises from his seat. "No," he keens, "no, no, no." His hands, still clutching the letter, beat his breast, then claw for the neck of his tunic. In a violent gesture he rips it open, revealing his customary hair shirt underneath. And all the time he continues to wail, "No, no," as if denial could make whatever he has read less so.

"Your Majesty, what is it?" Le Brun's eyes bulge like those of a man being hanged from a noose.

Louis stops wailing, but looks at him as if uncomprehending.

Hesitantly, I put out a hand and touch Louis's arm. His eyes turn to me, and for the first time in a long while Louis sees me rather than looking past or through me. And I see Louis the man, not the oh-so-holy king. Then his hand jerks strangely in my direction and drops the crumpled letter into my lap.

Heart beating as if I were a rabbit cornered by hounds, I pick it up. *Not the children,* I think, *please, Holy Mary, not the children.* The writing is Alphonse's, and the first words that catch my eye are "The bishop of Paris was with our mother at the end, and true to her pious nature, she put aside her crown and took the veil." Raising my face to my husband's once more, I say, "Our lady mother, Blanche of Castile, is dead."

Louis nods. Then, as if this admission by gesture reminds him of his grief, he begins to keen again and, turning, runs from the pavilion. The eerie sound he makes fades but continues, leaving those of us who remain frozen in our places.

"Go to him." My own voice breaks the horrified silence. Yet it is not my voice. For, hearing it as from a distance, I cannot imagine why it is so calm.

Jean nods. As he goes in pursuit of the king, I rise and flee as if from a scene of violence, with Marie chasing after me.

By the time I reach my tent I am shaking. Marie puts her arm about me from behind and guides me inside. Without this precaution I would surely collapse. As it is, I fall onto my bed and am immediately gripped by convulsing sobs. They roll through my body, tossing me like a galley in a storm. Gasping for air, I clutch the coverlet, balling my hands into fists and twisting the blanket.

"Your Majesty!" Marie sits down beside me, a look of wild concern on her face. "You will do yourself harm." She tries to smooth my hair, but I push her hand away and, covering my face with my hands, curl up like an animal in a hole, sobbing through my fingers. "I am going to get the physician," she says, standing up.

I lose all sense of time and cannot say, when the voice comes, if it has been moments or hours since Marie left me.

"I have heard that some women are foolish, fickle, and untrustworthy. But never would I have believed you among their number." Jean's tone is both incredulous and tender.

Taking my hands from my face, I look up to see him standing just inside the tent.

He shakes his head and continues. "What can I think but that you have lost your mind and forgotten your own interests? The woman who hated you most and whose loathing you returned measure for measure is dead; yet you weep for her as if you loved her like a true mother. It is unaccountable!"

Sitting up, I swing my feet to the floor. Jean closes the distance between us in a few strides and takes a seat beside me.

"I cry for joy because I am free of her," I explain, turning to face him. "But also in sorrow for His Majesty."

I know I can say this without hurting Jean. He understands me.

He knows that some small part of me still cares for Louis, and will always care. Jean loves Louis as well—even if he no longer blindly reveres Louis as he once did. What we feel for the man who is our king is separate and apart from what we feel for each other. Our love is that of one deeply flawed person for another. When we lie together wrapped in each other's limbs and secure in each other's affections, we are two ordinary people seeking the companionship and love that ordinary people require to face the world. We love Louis as we love God, knowing that he is above us in many ways, and that he does not need our love. Without our affection he would be as whole as he is with it. In part, it is this knowledge that holds Jean and me together with such force. We find the value in each other that appears completely lost upon Louis. "Did you see him?"

"He lies cruciform in his chapel, tearing at his hair. I tried to calm him, but he sent me away. I left him crying out his mother's name," Jean says, wiping my tears away gently with his thumbs. "It is terrible how he grieves. But it is foolish for us to dwell on it. Only God can help him in his sadness; we cannot."

"Yes." I lay my head against Jean's chest as he slips his arm behind me. The fine wool of his tunic is soft against my damp cheek. "But God will help him; he always does. And perhaps this time he helps us as well. We can go home. *Surely* with Blanche dead, Louis's thoughts and footsteps will turn to home?"

"I cannot imagine but that we will set off for Acre and our ships at once. Then you will see little Louis, Philippe, and Isabella, and you will be happy."

I look up into his face and notice for the first time that it is tracked with tears as well. I want to kiss them away but worry where that would lead. Surely some of the camp must know that he has come to comfort me. "They will meet their new brothers and sister," I say gently, reaching for his hand. "They will meet

Jean, and they will love his solemn little ways. Never has such an old soul lived in such a young body, except perhaps in his father."

"We will be parted." Another tear escapes the corner of Jean's eye, and I touch it with my fingertip. Can it be that Jean, who is never selfish, cries not for Louis but for us?

"Never."

"Yes. I must go home to see my sons, my wife." He stumbles over the last word. Not because it will bother me, but because it bothers him. I have always been able to accept the existence of Alix with equanimity, perhaps because Jean never loved her. He told me once he even tried to extricate himself from his betrothal to her. "You will reign at last in your court," he continues, holding my hand so tightly that it is painful.

"And you will return to that court to advise your king and to watch your other son grow to manhood."

"We will never have the freedom we have enjoyed here."

"That will not matter," I reply fiercely. I know as I say it, it is not true. When we return to France, Jean will become someone I love but cannot have, oddly like the king himself was in our first days, distant even as he sits beside me at table. I begin to cry again, silently, but no longer in relief.

Jean senses the change. "I will never give you up, Marguerite, unless death separates us or you send me away."

I put one hand into his curls, and, pulling his face down, kiss him with a passion very like when I kissed him the first time at Curias. "I will never send you."

CHAPTER 32

Dearest Marguerite,

Henry will go into battle. Not in the Holy Land where you languish, though it is three years since His Majesty and I began planning and raising revenues for a crusade, but in Gascony.

I do not hunger for such a war, I who bitterly remember Henry's campaign in Poitou ten years ago. But I have resigned myself to the necessity of his going. Edward must have this important part of his appanage. We cannot allow either the barons of the territory or the King of Castile to steal what is our son's birthright. It seems there comes a time when the future of the son is even more important than the safety of the father. Yet at six-and-forty, Henry does not seem so old as to be expendable either to his kingdom or to me. I hold him as dear as ever I did, and my prayers for his safety will begin the moment he is out of my sight and end only once he is back in my arms. At least he has promised me that Edward will remain here in England, out of harm's way. . . .

Eleanor

Eleanor
Summer 1253
Windsor, England

"Mother, why can I not go?" Edward has interrupted my afternoon in the gardens to plead and protest his exclusion from the campaign in Gascony. My ladies, who were gathering flowers and braiding them into chaplets, drifted out of the reach of our voices at the prince's appearance. They are the souls of discretion even if my son is not.

"Because your father says you may not."

"He treats me like a child."

"You are his child."

"But I am also a man."

"At fourteen?"

"You yourself were married a whole year at my age."

I do not know quite how to argue with that. When I arrived in England, I certainly thought of myself as a woman grown. It was not until years later that I realized I was wrong. It cannot help the present argument to tell Edward he is mistaken. On the other hand, I have neither the power nor the inclination to permit him to travel to Gascony and fight. "When you are one year married we will talk more on the subject."

"Mother! If I am married, then there will be no need to speak of it. If John Mansel is successful, I will have a bride and there will be no battle."

"If there will be no battle, then why must you fuss and fume so about going to Gascony with the knights?"

"Because they are my lands that are threatened. I have been invested with them for more than a year. My honor demands I defend them."

Edward looks so solemn when he speaks of honor. I am touched. I would never jest with such earnestness. I gently lay my hand on his arm and say, "Your honor and your duty demand that you obey your father and your king."

"Saints preserve me from argumentative women!" Edward says, shaking off my hand and lifting his eyes as if he were ancient. His expression is so at odds with his youth and naïveté that I nearly laugh out loud. "You would not contend so with Father," he complains.

I would, but there can be no benefit to myself in admitting as much. Let Edward learn when he has a wife of his own what wives can say to their husbands. "Which is why I will not press him to include you in his party."

"I will sneak aboard the ships."

"I believe I would notice were you not at my side to see them off."

Edward kicks the path in front of him in frustration, sending up a little shower of gravel.

"Find your friends and go riding," I urge. Edward is as good on horseback as he is with a sword. A few races with his friends, races he is sure to win, will blow away his present bad humor.

"Edmund will want to come."

"It is natural that your younger brother should seek to emulate you. You should be flattered."

"I *am* vexed."

"Tell Edmund that I will come and read to him and the smaller Edmund." Sanchia's son trails my youngest about much as my son shadows his elder brother.

Edward is clearly prepared to complain further, but the crunch of a man's stride on gravel prevents it. Uncle Peter rounds a hedge, his face flushed. He makes straight for me, not even pausing to greet Edward, which is most unusual.

"It is accomplished!" he says, taking me by both shoulders and pulling me to him.

"I will be co-regent?" I ask as he releases me.

"You will be sole regent."

"But the Earl Richard—"

"None too pleased at present, and destined to be but one of the sworn council established to advise you."

I twirl about as if I am a girl of fifteen instead of a woman of thirty.

"Mansel and I will be with the king, but be assured the men you are given will support Your Majesty. I am suggesting William of Kilkenny, Philip Lovel, and John Fitz Geoffrey."

"What of Geoffrey de Langley?" My uncle casts me a perplexed look. He does not like Langley and cannot seem to fathom that Henry and I do.

"Have him if you like him. There is more."

"What more could there be?"

For the first time my uncle seems fully aware that Edward is with us, silent but observing all.

"My Lord Edward," he says, clapping my son's shoulder affectionately.

"Uncle." Edward is always familiar with Peter, a habit he picked up from me but one that also suits their cordial relationship.

"Edward," I say, intervening, "did I not ask you to bear a message to your brother?"

The boy sighs. He is clearly interested in the conversation and knows he is being sent out of the way of hearing any more of it. "Fine. I will go, but first I would make a suggestion for the governance of England in Father's absence."

"Indeed?" I am curious how my son would manage the country that will one day be his.

"Lift the ban on tourneying. Such action would make you much beloved in some quarters."

"I thought you loved me already."

This comment, and the prospect that I might follow it with an embrace, is enough to set Edward's feet in motion.

When the sound of his footfall has died away, my uncle continues. "His Majesty has made a testament."

I cross myself and take a seat on a stone bench. I know that such things are important, particularly as Henry will be on the sea and then in battle, but I cannot bear to think of anything happening to him.

"Custody of all the children is given you."

"Why here is a thing more important than the governance of England," I exclaim. Though I do not believe anything under heaven save my imprisonment or the use of arms could keep me from seeing my children, to have that right legally and unquestionably bestowed upon me is gift indeed.

"The two are inseparable," my uncle replies sensibly. "And so too you shall have custody of all His Majesty's territories until the Lord Edward reaches his majority."

"Would that Henry were here so that I could thank him properly!" As soon as the words are spoken I blush as if my uncle could imagine the type of scene that might well result from my pleasure. For the first time in eight years I am past the early, doubtful, months of a pregnancy, and the prospect of a new babe makes Henry and me feel young again.

"When you thank him," my uncle says, oblivious to my embarrassment and the direction of my thoughts, "do not fail to mention his generosity as to your dower rights. For these he has also increased, and greatly."

My eyes begin to tear. Whatever disappointments I have

experienced over Henry's conduct as ruler, he is ever and always a generous husband to me. If he must brave death, he will not be easy about it until he knows that I will not be left in want should things end badly.

HENRY CRIED WHEN HE LEFT us on the sixth of August. Edward wept as well, though whether in response to his father's sentimental tears or because he continued to lament being left behind, I cannot say. I kept a cheerful countenance then, but I feel like crying now.

"How can prices be so high?" I look up from the pages lying before me, setting forth the cost of grain, wine, and other commodities crucial to maintaining an army in the field.

"The bad fall harvest caused famine in Gascony, driving up the cost of everything." Philip Lovel presses his palms together in that nervous way he has when contemplating something displeasing. I have become quite familiar with this gesture in the two months I have been regent. "And even as prices swell, the treasury does not."

"And His Majesty must have money to pay bribes," I say. "Full stomachs alone are not enough to guarantee his army satisfactory progress in Gascony."

Lord Richard nods in approbation. He is of more use and less trouble to me than I ever expected, though I saw him swallow hard the first time I took Henry's customary seat at this council table. "Your Majesty, we must raise more funds."

"My Lord de Langley, you are a man handy at extracting silver from His Majesty's Jews." I pause for a moment and shift in my seat, trying to make myself more comfortable. Only weeks away from delivering my husband's child, my belly is enormous, and my back, so much older than it was when I carried my Edward with ease, aches both day and night. "Pray see if you cannot find a way to wring some more money out of them. There must be something yet we do not tax or fine."

De Langely smiles. "There is *always* something, Your Majesty. We might borrow from them."

"No. The Queen of England does not borrow from Jews. My Lord Lovel, see which of the Florentines will lend to me and at what terms."

"How much does Your Majesty have in mind?"

"I heard from the Count of Poitiers this morning. The King of France's brother will be paid to stay out of this war. But, as he is a man of honor, he will not come cheap. It seems that three thousand pounds will be needed to make him easy in this matter."

William of Kilkenny gives a low whistle and mutters, "Heaven forefend" under his breath.

"Your Majesty wishes to borrow three thousand pounds?" Lovel asks.

"No. I *wish* we could persuade His Majesty's barons to offer more men and more money for the king's use," I say impatiently, "but we have not been particularly successful in that vein, so I must borrow what I cannot secure through less onerous means."

I do not mean to snap at my treasurer. He, as well as each of the other men seated around the table, works as hard as I to do what is necessary to promote Henry's success in Gascony. But my temper grows shorter as does the time betwixt myself and my confinement.

"And now gentlemen, what do I overlook? Is there some matter yet to attend to, or is our business for the moment at an end?" I pray no one raises any new issue, for I am desperate to stand and stretch my back and legs—perhaps even to lie down for a few minutes in a darkened room.

———

AND TO THINK *I* HAVE long been considered headstrong and stubborn! I am the mildest, the most persuadable of souls when compared with my husband's noblemen. The Earl Richard and I have spent the afternoon at their parliament, trying to convince them to grant Henry additional moneys, and finding questions and excuses where we hoped for compliance. The January wind that howls outside is not colder than the reception we received from them.

"His Majesty has succeeded in bringing half a dozen castles back into the Crown's possession in the five months since he left us. What more proof do those old women need that he makes progress?"

Richard takes a glass of wine from Sanchia and drains it before replying. "They are tightfisted to be sure but—with Your Majesty's permission I would be plain—"

"Be plain then. You above all have a duty to be, as you are more than brother at the moment, you are counselor."

"The barons know Henry is not, at heart, a military man. They believe he can purchase castles and even the loyalty of some men, but now he talks of laying siege to La Réole and they will want to see him win it, or at least not lose it, before they open their purses."

I rise in exasperation, inadvertently jostling the cradle at my feet. Darling Katherine, my little princess, begins to cry.

"Let me take her," Sanchia offers, scooping up the babe with practiced ease. Nothing calms this new child like walking. With all my others 'twas singing, but that has no effect whatsoever on Katherine.

"Pray counsel me, sir. What is to be done?"

"Henry ought to surround himself with men hardened in battle with reputations for fierceness."

"He has your half bothers with him." It is difficult to speak of these men in such moderate terms; when I consult with my uncle, they are always "those loathsome Lusignans."

"They are able fighters indeed," Richard replies, "when it is in their interest to fight. Perhaps Henry might offer them a better share in the spoils. A promise that they may keep whatever lands they take will spur them on."

"You mean leave them in possession of the castles as Edward's vassals?"

"Who would be more loyal to him than his family?"

I nod, keeping my skepticism to myself. This may be the one instance in which my need for the Lusignans outweighs my dislike for them. "But, my lord, the barons do not like your Lusignan relations overmuch. Why not draw someone into this campaign whom the barons respect and the noblemen in Gascony fear?"

"Simon de Montfort."

"Exactly. He is in France but surely would answer if Henry called for him."

"Providing that call is accompanied by payment of what the Earl of Leicester is still owed for his last service to the Crown in Gascony, I feel certain Your Majesty is right."

"Why then, my lord, here is something on which to spend whatever money we can wring from the baronage and whatever is left of my loans too."

Sanchia returns to my side and places a sleeping Katherine in the cradle. "You have such a gentle nature that you soothe her with great ease," I say. My sister appears grateful for my kind words and the look that goes with them, and my heart saddens to see that her husband does not so much as glance at her, let alone smile. The ardor of Richard's first desire for Sanchia long ago cooled beyond rekindling. Cooled though she gave him a goodly son and is as devoted a wife as I have ever seen. Henry says it is because, as does he himself, Richard likes a spirited woman—someone to argue with him and to give her opinion. His first wife was like this, and Sanchia cannot compare. So, after a decade of marriage, Richard treats her with respect but no interest and feeds his passions, whether for political discussion or for the comforts of the flesh, elsewhere. There is nothing I can do to remedy this, no matter how much I wish it were otherwise. Before I am carried away by that melancholy thought, I remind myself that at least marriage to my sister has kept Richard loyal to royal interests and that was its primary purpose from the beginning.

"Will Your Majesty write urging the king to recall de Montfort?" Richard, quite correctly, apprehends that any suggestion from me on the subject of de Montfort will be easier for my husband to accept than would one from himself.

"I will do so at once."

Richard offers Sanchia his arm, and she takes it so lightly that her hand appears to be a skittish bird on a limb, ready to take flight at the slightest provocation.

I do not tell Richard ere he goes that I mean to put more in my letter than what pertains to the pursuit of victory in Gascony. I have had word from Albert of Parma, the papal nuncio. The Holy Father proposes commuting Henry's crusading vow, which he has not yet fulfilled—raising money for an excursion to the Holy Land was no easier than raising money for this business in Gascony, and the money we did raise has been since diverted to the present campaign—and which, given the disastrous results of the French crusade, I would by all means see set aside. In return, Henry would accept the crown of Sicily in his own name or Edmund's and help to secure that kingdom by military means using money that I am very happy I am not taxed with finding at this present moment.

This Sicily business is a proposition I embrace eagerly. Our first son will surely be a king, so why not our second? After all, Marguerite and I are both queens. Yet, though Richard seemed unwilling to be King of Sicily himself when he was made an offer of the crown by the Holy Father, I suspect he will not be happy to see my son have it and thus be of a greater rank than he. On this matter, therefore, I seek none of his counsel and keep my own.

"I HAVE GIVEN DIRECTION FOR the necessary transfer of lands and estates."

Uncle Boniface has just arrived from Canterbury, come to assist in my preparations to sail for Gascony with Edward. With the arrival of March and a break in the weather, word has come from Henry that our son will be husband to Alfonso of Castile's half sister—if that king keeps his word, and I have my doubts.

"What will Edward be given?" My uncle waves away my offer of wine.

"Gascony he has already, of course, but His Majesty transfers Ireland, the Channel Islands, castles in the Welsh March, Bristol, the county of Chester, and some lesser English lands."

"The father makes much of the son."

"You sound like His Majesty's barons. They complain Henry weakens the kingship, never mind that nothing is presented without a guarantee of reversion to the Crown."

"Eleanor, you know me better than that! I merely mean the boy will be a serious force in English politics, and none of us can afford to overlook the importance of his favor hereinafter."

"His favor!" I laugh lightly and pour a glass of wine for myself, suddenly feeling the need of fortification. "When and wherefore should a mother worry about the favor of her child?" But in the recesses of my mind I consider for the first time that Edward the man and Edward the boy will not be one and the same. I cannot send Edward to Windsor to dispel a sullen mood when he is a married man.

As if he knows that we speak of him, my son bursts into the room without knocking. "Mother! They are destroying my ship!"

"Who?"

"The men who are building yours."

"By God's coif, I will see them hanged!" I say. "What could cause them to behave in such a manner?"

"Apparently they are jealous that the work on my vessel outshines their own."

I turn toward my uncle. "Your Grace—"

"I will deal with it." The archbishop moves swiftly from the room, but Edward remains, looking distressed.

"Trust your uncle. He will get to the bottom of this matter and set it to rights."

"But our sailing will be delayed."

Of course, he is correct, and I ought to be as vexed as he is. But, though his marriage is needed to bring the troubles in Gascony to a close, I find myself suddenly loath to surrender my son to this other, unknown, Eleanor. "Are you so eager to be married then?" I ask, hoping to needle him into a denial.

"Why would I not be? You have read what John Mansel writes: 'The lady is as delicate as a flower with appealing brown eyes, and the golden skin of the Castilian race.'" I am stunned that my son has committed our envoy's lines to memory. When I do not reply, Edward continues. "Did you not tell me that my father was impatient to wed you?"

"Aye. But he was a man full grown."

"Why must you make me feel like a boy?" Edward crosses his

arms over his chest and glowers at me, apparently oblivious to the fact that in doing so he looks yet more the child. "I am as much a man as my father, and when I am married you will no longer be able to ignore that."

"If that be so, surely you will not begrudge me these last opportunities to think of you as the carefree boy who ran through my gardens at Windsor? To think of you as *my* Edward?"

"You may think of me however you like, Mother," he concedes. "If only you will never say anything like that when we are in company."

I laugh. What other answer could I have expected? "I know you are eager to run off and examine your new armor for when the King of Castile knights you, but seeing as we are not presently in company, can you not embrace your mother before you go?" I push, and I know that I push. But I know also that even as he chafes to be freed from my mothering, Edward loves me. And sure enough, he puts his arms around me before he goes.

CHAPTER 33

My dearest Marguerite,

Oh how glad I am to have you settled at Tyre. After so many years of uncertain correspondence, I receive your letters quite regularly and have some hope that you receive mine. I suppose I should feel selfish in admitting this, for I know you are separated from your husband the king and most of your party, but I do not because your letters provide ample proof that you are content where you are. And who can blame you? After such an unsettled existence, to have a small house for yourself and your children must be very near to heaven in your view. . . .

Your devoted sister,
Eleanor

———— ·•· ————

MARGUERITE
SPRING 1254
TYRE, KINGDOM OF JERUSALEM

"The king is on his way." Jean sweeps into the cozy room where I sit and gives me a kiss on the top of my head. Marie does not look up from her book.

"When?" I lay the fine linen shirt I am hemming for Jean down in my lap.

"The messenger says His Majesty planned to leave Sidon after

Mass this morning. He will surely be here before nightfall. Tomorrow we ride for Acre."

"Tomorrow!" Marie exclaims, her eyes widening and her book forgotten.

"Yes, having been made to see he must go home at last, His Majesty wishes to set sail at the conclusion of the holy season of Lent."

"I will set everyone packing," Marie says, rising and scurrying out.

"And what finally persuaded Louis to leave for France? Certainly not you or I," I say as Jean takes the seat next to mine and puts his feet up on a nearby stool.

"Indeed not. I seem to remember it was your offhanded mention of departing that set us here."

"That was a fortunate mistake indeed." I pick the shirt back up and resume my stitches. "Though I could not have foreseen how it would turn out when I made it."

For two full days after news of the dragon's death no one could talk sense to Louis. On the third day he emerged from his chapel and resumed giving orders for work on the walls of Sidon. Jean and I were taken aback but said nothing. All day every day for a month Louis wrote letters to archbishops, bishops, priests, and monks throughout France, ordering them to pray for Blanche's soul, and still he said not one word about departing. At the end of that time, with nearly every royal messenger en route somewhere between Sidon and the port at Acre, I gently asked if we might not soon head there ourselves. Unlike the last time I dared to raise our departure, Louis did not rage. He merely left me where I sat without a word. The next day he commanded Jean to choose a party of his knights and escort me, my children, and my meager collection of female companions to Tyre. Ours was a terrifying trip through hostile land as the king has truce with neither Egypt nor

Damascus. The memory of what their combined forces did to the poor souls at Sidon never left us for a moment of our day-long ride. But when we arrived, this city, once the center of the Kingdom of Jerusalem and now left quiet by the rise in eminence of Acre, became a home such as I have never had since my childhood.

"Providential." Jean smiles broadly. "As to what turns the king's thoughts in the direction of home, it is money, or rather the lack of it. The Counts of Poitiers and Anjou have not sent more, despite His Majesty's request. It is amazing how quickly the barons of these lands ceased to beg His Majesty to bide once they discovered he has no further money to expend."

Taking a last stitch, I tie off my thread, break it with my teeth, and hold out the shirt to Jean. "Here, something to add to your trunk."

Jean grasps my wrist instead of the garment and kisses that place on my hand where the thumb and first finger meet before releasing me and folding the shirt. "Caym can add it later." He pauses for a moment, leaning back contentedly. Then, quite nonchalantly, he adds, "His Majesty's letter thanks me for my good service here and invites me to take accommodations on the royal ship for the voyage home."

"Jean!" I jump up and with a twirl of pure delight land in his lap.

"You are wrinkling my new shirt," he says sternly. And then, burying his face along one side of my neck, he adds, "I thought you would be happy."

"Shall I call for dinner? It should be nearly ready."

"Leave it." Jean kisses the side of my face and then takes my earlobe gently in his teeth.

"It is the middle of the day," I object.

"But everyone is busy packing and we have nothing to do."

"If everyone is busy packing, then my bedchamber is occupied,"

I tease. In the back of my mind I realize that, after nearly half a year, these are the last moments left for us to live as we have since Jean let this house in the king's name for my accommodation. Half a dozen of Jean's men lodge on the lower floor, in what would be the hall of the place if its merchant owner were in residence. But Jean spends every minute he can with me and with the children. We let ourselves pretend we are a wealthy merchant and his wife. I order Jean's dinner, make his shirts, supervise the drawing of his bath, and lie with him all night while Caym behaves as if he is in his small chamber, and Marie insists I am alone in mine. Jean gathers the children and reads to them, removes their splinters, wipes their tears. He takes me to market, talks with me of politics and theology, and shares with me his plans for his lands at home without ever mentioning that I will not live with him upon them. It is perfect bliss.

Jean drops a hand between my thighs, and I can feel the heat of it through my garments. "All right," I relent. "If this is to be our last day in paradise, then let us not think of duty or waste it packing. Where shall we go?"

"What about that little spot in the garden? The one that cannot be seen from any windows?"

In half a year one can learn a great deal about a place, and about a person.

LOUIS ARRIVES IN TYRE AS dusk falls and, surprisingly, comes directly to see me and the children while his tents are being pitched. The sight of him confirms that the life I have been living is not real. And, although his arrival means we will soon head home at last, I find I have never been less happy to see my husband. Yet, bound to pretend otherwise, I call for a cold supper to celebrate his arrival. And we sit, Louis and I, at either ends of a table with Jean between us, partaking of it together. It seems a thing unreal to look up and see the king dining at our table, or rather *my* table, I remind myself. The thought of myself in the singular saddens me deeply.

"My Lord of Joinville, I have sorely missed your good counsel. You must return with me this evening to camp so that I may share my plans for the voyage to France." Then, giving me a hard look, Louis adds, "The queen surely will be fine without you for one evening, having had you to herself these many months." Louis's tone reminds me of the distant past, when Eleanor and I used to compete for my mother's attention.

"Your Majesty will be quite safe, as I will leave my knights behind," Jean says to me for Louis's benefit. Perhaps, like me, Jean heard something odd in my husband's voice and saw it in his look. Is Louis merely jealous of my time with Jean or does he suspect exactly what goes on here? This thought nearly stops my heart.

"If you would like, Your Majesty," Jean continues, "I can wait below to allow you some private time with the queen." Yes, clearly Jean does sense something, but to offer intimacy with me to throw Louis off the scent! I would feel angry if I were not quite so frightened.

"That will not be necessary, Sieur. I have not so much to say to the queen as I have to you." I feel myself begin to relax. Surely here is evidence that Louis's bitter tone stems from his having missed his friend and nothing more. Louis wipes his hands on his cloth, and I rise to bring him a bowl as we dine without servants. "Thank you, lady wife," he says as I take the bowl and cloth away. "I hope you will not be lonely this evening if the Seneschal and I depart now."

"It is a hard thing for me to forgo Your Majesty's company," I reply, bowing my head slightly, "but I do not believe, Husband, that you or anyone could ever fairly call me a demanding wife."

WE ARE AT SEA IN a blanket of fog. Never have I seen anything like it. It is not as on land, but rather like the white smoke of a hundred fires gathered and held by some invisible means close around our ship. I cling to the rail, trying to make out the shape of the galley nearest us, but can perceive nothing. I cannot see the sun, but I know it must be sinking for enough hours of the day have passed already.

"I cannot believe that this morning we could see the Mountain of the Cross on the island of Cyprus," I remark.

"Yes, Your Majesty, as clear as anything," Marie answers from my elbow. "But never mind, my lady, just like God, it is still there though we see it not."

"I am not sure that is comforting, Marie, for while God presumably watches over us with interest, the mountain has no care for us. It does not look out for us. And, as we cannot see it and tell by its size and location precisely where we are, we may likely run afoul of the shore."

A shadow of a man approaches along the rail, gloomy and foreboding until, coming finally close enough, Jean's familiar features emerge from the haze. "His Majesty the King is saying here lies proof that we ought not to have set sail from the Holy Land."

"His Majesty has been looking for proof of that every minute since the plank was drawn up at Acre on the twenty-fifth of April."

"True," Jean says, coming close alongside me.

"I will check on the children," Marie says, slipping away into the surrounding whiteness.

With Jean pressed close beside me, the fog seems as white velvet or soft white wool, curtaining and cushioning us from the rest of the ship's inhabitants. Furtively, Jean gives me a kiss. "You should go below and get to bed."

"Bed has no appeal for me in our present circumstances." I take his hand where it hangs between us. We have been at sea three weeks today. I am ravenous for Jean; yet we have not arrived at a single practical idea that will allow us to couple. Memories of our little house tease us both at intervals. Did we appreciate the gift of that place, that time together as much as we should have?

"Well, this damp cannot be good for you," Jean replies, squeezing my hand. "You will take a chill."

"You are a fine one to talk, my Lord of Joinville! Where is your *surcote*?" Fussing over him gives me a sense of ownership, a sense I have been sorely missing since we came on board.

"I felt no need of it before this fog closed in, and I am not cold now, standing beside you."

"No more am I, for I have not only you to warm me but my mantle. Would you could come inside it." I reach up and run a hand along Jean's cheek. As my little finger trails over his mouth he teasingly bites its tip.

"I begin to think this fog is our friend," Jean says, leaning down to kiss me again. As his lips are nearly at mine there is a sudden jarring bump and I am saved from sprawling on the deck only by Jean, whose hands snatch the front of my mantle and hold me upright.

Without volition I give a little scream, and I am not alone. As the ship shudders again and seems to be arrested in its forward motion, myriad voices cry out in surprise and terror.

"Come!" Jean grabs my arm and drags me along in the direction of the ship's castle. Near it, we run upon a group of sailors with their commander, a Templar. Louis, arriving at the same moment from another direction, casts a glance that encompasses the entire scene, and Jean drops my arm.

"Lower the lead," someone orders, and, going to the rail, a sailor does so.

"We are aground," this fellow says in a voice that seeps with the fear I am feeling.

"Ahoy!" the Templar cries out over the unseen water. "Galley! Ahoy, we are grounded! Come and take His Majesty aboard!"

There is no reply, only unrelenting whiteness.

I realize suddenly that I no longer see Louis. Then I hear his voice speaking the Latin words of a familiar prayer. I follow the voice and Jean follows me.

I assume that Louis is headed to his cabin to summon his counselors and see what is best to be done. But midway across the deck the voice no longer retreats from me, and I run upon him, literally. He is lying cruciform, facedown on the deck before a makeshift altar that he had constructed before we embarked.

"Your Majesty," Jean says. Louis turns his head but does not rise. "What is to be done?"

"It is in the hands of God, Sieur. Surely you sense as much?"

"But Your Majesty, though the Lord disposes, we ought also to act, for we are not some cowering rabble but God's servants."

"What would you propose? How can we assess either our peril or the condition of this *nef* when we cannot see three feet from our faces?"

Even as Louis speaks I feel the wind rising, buffeting against me where I stand. The ship seems to skiddle sideways like the crabs I showed the children on the beach, and a loud scraping noise assures me I do not imagine it.

"Throw down as many anchors as we have so that, at very least, we are not driven by the winds and waves into worse trouble before this fog lifts."

"Give the command then, in my name if you like. But I know my place, and it is here before the body of Our Lord."

Jean turns and heads back for the sailors. So furious is the pace of his steps that I must run to keep up. Reaching the captain, he says, "Drop all anchors on the windward side."

The man does not question Jean's authority, presumably because he takes no issue with what he is being told to do, but gives the order promptly. Five huge anchors are hoisted and thrown into the sea.

"What else can be done to secure us?" Jean asks.

"Sir, I dare not try to steer the ship off whatever grounds her without eyes. I might make things worse. There is nothing to be done until the fog lifts and the light of dawn rises. God willing, we will still be here then to see our peril."

Close as he is, I can hear Jean's teeth grinding at this response— so like the king's own. Jean has not Louis's knack for surrendering himself to fate, or at least for surrendering me. "Come below," he says. "The children will be frightened."

But when we reach their cabin, all my babies are sleeping soundly, though their nurses are in the highest state of agitation. "Ought we to wake them," one asks, "so that we may leave the ship?"

"There is nowhere to go at present," I reply, laying my hand upon her arm in hopes of calming her. "It is best then that they should slumber on in comfortable innocence. What good could come of their waking? They would only hear the awful wind and see the stricken faces of those around them. If my darlings must drown, I would not have them suffer a moment of fear before-hand." Saying the terrible words out loud, admitting to myself that my children, my beloved children, might perish, takes its toll on me. My limbs begin to tremble violently.

"A stool for Her Majesty," Jean orders.

One is quickly brought. Placing it beside his son's bed, Jean leads me to it.

"Your Majesty," he says, "I swear to Saint Nicholas that if he will but rescue you and your children from the danger in which we find ourselves at this moment, I will make a pilgrimage to his shrine at Varangéville."

"Would that I could do the same! But His Majesty . . ." My voice trails off for a moment. How can I say in front of these women what I am thinking, that Louis is so far gone in his mind, so contrary to any project of mine, that should I promise a pilgrimage without his permission, he would only make me recant my vow?

It is fortunate that Jean knows the king as well as I do. He sees my difficulty and tries, God love him, to smooth it. "Perhaps Your Majesty can make a different type of pledge. Say to God that if he brings you and those you love through this fearful ordeal, you will build him a model of a ship worth five livres to remember this night by. And if you do, I will take it from Joinville on foot and shoeless to the shrine of Saint Nicholas and offer it for you."

"Yes, I will commission a ship, but of silver and worth a hundred times what you suggest, if we all live to see the dawn."

"And I will sit with Your Majesty until that dawn so that you might not count out the dreadful hours alone."

"Mama?" something touches my face. I open my eyes and there is light, glorious, glorious light. Jean Tristan is sitting up in his bed, curls tousled, eyes still drowsy, one hand on my cheek. When at last I surrendered to sleep last night, I must have fallen forward onto his bed.

"Good morning, my lamb," I say, catching my four-year-old

up in a hug and inhaling the smell of childish slumber that clings about him as if it were the finest perfume.

The nurse on the pallet at the foot of little Jean's bed stirs at the sound of my voice. So does my chevalier who has fallen asleep against the wall near the door, his head thrown back and his mouth slightly open.

As if aware of my eyes upon him, Jean opens his own and says, "Dawn."

"Let us go on deck at once."

Jean is clearly as eager as I am to see our situation in clear, fog-less day, but as he jumps to his feet and straightens his wrinkled tunic, an expression of doubt crosses his face. "Ought Your Majesty not change? What will the king think, seeing you this morning in the same garments you retired in last evening?"

"If he thinks of me at all, he might well think that, like him, I have passed a largely sleepless night praying for our deliverance." I raise my hands to my head, straightening my circlet and wimple as best I can; then, after giving Jean Tristan a kiss on the end of his nose and bestowing kisses on a still-sleeping Pierre and baby Blanche in her cradle, I join Jean by the door.

The first thing I notice in coming upon deck is that while the fog has flown, the wind has not abated. It whips at my skirts and carries the end of my veil momentarily into my mouth.

"By Christ's passion!" Jean's voice trembles, and I see why. Near the front of the ship on the leeward side a massive outcropping of rock is visible rising high above the rail. I can see Louis, his chamberlain, and the constable among the group of gentlemen and sailors assembled at the prow.

"You see," the king says triumphantly as soon as we reach him, "even the sandbar upon which we rest is the work of Our Lord, sent to protect us from greater ruin!"

Jean nods vigorously in assent, then, turning aside, asks the archbishop of Nicosia who stands nearby, "How bad is the damage?"

"The master mariner has four men in the water now. We should know when they are pulled aboard."

And sure enough, gazing down at the surface of the wind-whipped water, I can see heads bobbing, then disappearing, then surfacing again. A rope ladder hugs the side of the vessel, trailing in the water near the men who dive.

Returning my gaze to the deck, I see that all of the men look haggard, but no man's eyes are shadowed by circles as dark as the king's. Making my way to Louis's side, I say, "Will Your Majesty not come with me and have something warm?"

Louis's eyes flicker over my face. Is that surprise I see? Then they fall again to the men in the water. Finally, after a few moments' silence, he says, "I believe I will. My night of prayer was fruitful to be sure but has left me depleted in strength if augmented in spirit. My Lord of Joinville," he adds, "bring the master mariners and the members of my council to my cabin to give their report and offer their advice when the ship's condition is better known."

I am pleased that Louis has condescended to go with me. Bustling ahead of him, I give orders for something hot to be brought at once to his cabin and, reaching that location, demand that his valet bring a change of clothes and warm water so the king may wash himself. Settling down on a stool, I find it strange that Louis struggles to screen himself from my view as he changes. Does he not realize we are married twenty years?

Emerging from the corner behind his bed just as a bowl of broth with a hunk of bread in it is carried in, Louis seats himself at his table and waits for the bowl and ewer to be brought so he can cleanse his hands. That task complete, he looks at me and says, "And where did you pass the night, lady wife?"

I am startled, not because I have anything to hide but at the very fact of Louis's asking. "With Your Majesty's children that they might not be roused by all the noise and confusion."

"And the Seneschal of Champagne?"

"With me to assuage my fear."

"Very thoughtful of him."

Try as I might, I cannot tell if Louis compliments Jean in earnest or means his comment in an ironic vein. The king eats steadily and calmly without another word. If I am less calm, I hope he does not know it. Finally, sopping the last bit of his soup with the remnants of his bread, Louis says, "Are you glad to be going home?"

"My feelings on the subject are mixed, Your Majesty. I greatly long to see France and our children there again and feel it is in the best interest of both that you should return to an active reign. And yet—"

"Yes?" Louis eyes are scrutinizing me in a way they have not for many a moon. Are they seeking truth? Or are they seeking empathy with his own regrets at departing from the Holy Land? I cannot tell him the truth, but I can offer him understanding of his own truth. This I owe him as a wife and, moreover, I wish to give him, for when he is like this, a normal man with needs, wants, and fears, there is a little love left in me for him still.

"And yet, there are things about the Holy Land that one must regret leaving behind, unless one has a heart made of stone."

"So there are." Louis's eyes burn.

A knock sounds on the cabin door. A procession of Louis's advisers, with Jean bringing up the rear, enters in the company of the master mariners and a sailor who was doubtless among the divers—rubbed dry but still ruddy from the cool of the water.

Louis gestures for the gentlemen to sit, and they take the remaining stools around his table, shifting me by increments closer to the king's side. *This,* I cannot help thinking, *is how I always imagined sitting—among those closest to the king, ready to be of service.*

"Sirs," Louis says, addressing the mariners who were left standing, "what say you? What have waves, water, and sand done to this great ship of mine?"

"Your Majesty," says one of the master mariners, a man with fine hair of no particular color touched with gray at his temples, whose age could be forty or four hundred, so weathered is his skin, "I will tell you plainly—the keel is in a bad way. I fear, without repair, she will not stand the high seas but will break apart."

There is a general groan from the men around me. But Louis remains unperturbed. "Can the repairs be made?"

"Yes, Your Majesty, but might I be so bold as to suggest that before they are attempted, Your Majesty, the queen, and all attached to the royal household be ferried by boat to one of the other ships? Already they are gathering within hailing distance."

"And what say you gentlemen? Le Brun? Joinville? Shall I abandon this ship and seek another?"

"Your Majesty, we are not sailors, but these men are, and sailors of the highest skills." The constable inclines his head in a show of respect to the mariner who has just finished speaking. "If they advise that you are safest on another vessel, I will not gainsay them."

"Nor I," adds the chamberlain.

"The destiny of all of France lies with Your Majesty." Jean speaks to Louis, but his eyes are, at least momentarily, on me. "Pray make yourself safe as these good men suggest."

"And what of the rest of you?" Louis asks, looking round. "What of the hundreds of other souls aboard this ship? Shall they not be more frightened if I leave it? Shall they not wonder that I think so little of them and so much of myself?"

"Surely not!" urges Joinville. "For at least with respect to the last point, every soul on board knows that you are king, and all came on this voyage with you prepared to die for you."

"And I am humbled by that commitment. But I have lost enough men already, Joinville. And at least in battle and in captivity I partook of the same danger as they, though it pleased God to spare me. No, gentlemen, I cannot leave this ship."

"At least send Her Majesty the Queen and Your Majesty's children. They are not bound by the honor of fighting men which you insist in standing upon."

I think Jean very brave for saying this. Surely he can see that in his present mood Louis will think such a plea nonsense. Le Brun sees as much; when Jean turns a pleading eye upon him seeking support, the constable merely says halfheartedly, "It would not delay repairs a moment to transport Her Majesty to the nearest ship."

"My Lord of Joinville," Louis begins—is there malice in Louis's look or do I merely imagine it?—"I was saying to Her Majesty only this morning that you take prodigious care for her and I am thankful for it. But I have more faith in God than in the machinations of man. I am content to place my life in his hands, and so too the lives of my wife and children." Then turning to the mariners, he says, "It is settled. Begin what repairs you think prudent. All who are on board now will rest there."

"HOLY MOTHER OF GOD, HE *knows* something."

"No," I say, pushing aside the fact that I myself felt the same the morning after the grounding. "And you must not really believe so yourself, or you would not be here."

Jean is in my cabin. Having come to the conclusion that there is no safer place for us to be alone together, we have fallen back on the cover that may be given by good and loyal servants. So Caym will tell anyone seeking Jean this evening that he sleeps within his cabin while Marie sits placid in the smaller forward chamber of my own to insist that I likewise have retired if called upon to do so. Still, the arrangement is fraught with risk, and we both know that. The closer the shores of France draw, the more willing we are to defy common sense and ignore what used to be for us inviolate rules of conduct in order to be together.

"Listen to me, Marguerite," Jean replies, sitting down heavily on the edge of my bed. "When the repairs were finished this morning, and even as the anchors were being drawn up and sail raised, Louis called me to sit with him upon a ship's bench and told me that, according to the saints, such trials and near escapes are sent by God to remind us that he has the power to take our lives whensoever he wishes."

"That sounds like Louis." I stand before Jean, looking down on his disconsolate face. "But what has a religious lesson to do with your suspicions, or the king's?"

"I am getting there." Jean looks up, his eyes fairly pleading for me to be patient. "I told the king it was doubtless true that God could have drowned us had he wished. And he replied, 'Yes, Seneschal, but are we all properly chastened by this reminder of our mortality? For make no mistake, God intends us to examine our conduct for anything displeasing to him that we may purge ourselves of it. Elsewise his warning has not accomplished its purpose.'"

I draw breath audibly.

"You see, we are discovered."

Louis's little speech is harder to dismiss than I would like, but still, I can drive down the sudden surge of bile that rises from my stomach upon hearing it, and hope I can quiet Jean's doubts as well. "He could have meant a more general lesson. No man not a priest loves to preach as much as Louis does. Or he could refer to your obstinate pressure upon him during our grounding to do other than pray for our relief."

Jean shakes his head, clearly unwilling to believe me.

"If Louis knows about us, why not be more explicit? Why not move to separate us?"

"I do not know."

"No, you do not. Nor do I. All this is supposition and conjecture. Would you give me up over that?"

"I ought to," Jean responds. "It would be safer for you." I put a hand gently on his shoulder, and he dips his head gracefully to kiss it. "But, heaven help me, I am not that strong. I will cleave to you until I have no choice, and I pray daily that moment never comes."

CHAPTER 34

My dearest Marguerite,

. . . It seems wrong to complain to you who want and wait to sail, but I do not like ocean voyages. Yet the business that Henry and I must conclude, that of marrying our Edward, cannot be settled from England. And so, tomorrow morning, with Edward, Edmund, and Beatrice beside me, I will watch my English coast slip away and make sail for Bordeaux. If I am sick at sea, I shall attempt to bear it with your patience, for my voyage is nothing compared with that which you will, with any luck, soon set forth upon.

Your devoted sister,
Eleanor

ELEANOR
MAY 1254
DOVER, ENGLAND

I can see the ships from my window, magnificently fitted out and ready to go. And the wind, as if knowing I desire to be gone, is strong and favorable. I glance once more at the letter I hold telling me that the house in Bordeaux where I bore my daughter Beatrice a dozen years ago is ready to receive me again. Then Henry was ʂing in Poitou. Now we are *winning* in Gascony. Winning.

Edward's birthright is secured just as we intended. I am not much familiar with the sensation of things going precisely as we planned them, Henry and I, and the fact my husband has not been thwarted or made a fool of in Gascony causes me to feel giddy with delight.

The door swings open and I expect to see Edward, back with another of his many questions. We sail in the morning, and the excitement of the event overwhelms my eldest. Instead, it is Uncle Boniface.

"This came for you. The messenger looked as if he would have swum the channel if he had been called upon to." He holds out a letter bearing my husband's seal.

"Come," I say, reaching for it. "Surely it cannot be more than His Majesty's fervent wishes that I should have a safe journey." But my fingers shake as I try to undo the seal. Henry's hand is as familiar to me as my own, and generally it brings me comfort when he is away. This time, however, it brings word I would rather not have. "Alfonso is mustering troops."

"By the nails!" My uncle's exclamation, so at odds with his standing as archbishop of Canterbury, expresses all the astonishment and frustration that overwhelm me at the moment. "Is Henry certain?"

"His spies say men-at-arms are gathering in large numbers. It seems Gascony is not yet safe from Castilian aggression and Edward may remain unmarried a while longer." Though it hardly seems important under the circumstances, I feel a sudden twinge at the thought of my son's disappointment. In this one thing, and not much else, he is exactly like his father—he has allowed his fancy to fix on his prospective bride and swears himself desperately in love with her though they have never met.

Reading farther, my eyes are stopped dead by the words, "As I value your safety and that of my sons more even than my own life or the success of this venture, do not set out from England until you hear from me."

"We are enjoined from sailing!"

"What?"

"For our safety we are to remain in England until the battle is past." I feel like letting off a good oath myself, but instead, crush the letter in my hand into a tight ball. "How? How is it possible that we are perched on the edge of complete victory and yet may be thwarted?"

"Such a thing is always possible." My uncle shrugs maddeningly. "Eleanor, you know the way of politics—allies of yesterday will tear each other to pieces today, and the opposite is equally true." Boniface rubs his chin for a moment, then asks, "Does His Majesty command you not to come?"

I find it a strange question. Then I realize what Boniface is really asking—whether I will obey Henry's admonition.

"You think I ought to go?"

"The decision is not mine, Eleanor. I merely suggest it calls for reflection, not blind obedience."

I would laugh were the situation not so serious. When in all my years have I been known as blindly obedient? I drop the ball that is Henry's letter on a nearby table and go once more to my window. The sun is setting, giving the furled sails of my fine ships a rosy hue. These sheets are ready to open and catch the morning breeze. Everything we have worked so hard to achieve in Gascony hinges on Edward's arrival there and on his marriage. Beneath the ships, the water of the harbor offers a more glaring red, the red of blood. If I take my sons to Gascony against their father's wishes, will the blood spilt there include theirs?

I reclaim the letter and tease it into a flattened state once more, sorry for my impulsive action. Here is a missive that definitely bears rereading. When I have reviewed it, I look up at my uncle. "Henry says nothing of word from Alfonso himself. Whatever manner of man the King of Castile is, would he not feel constrained to issue a letter breaking off negotiations before attacking a man he promised to call family?"

"He may yet, once his troops are ready."

"And what of Mansel? Henry makes no mention of him. Yet who should know the King of Castile's mind better, at least among the English, than Mansel when he has all but lived with Alfonso for months while negotiating the terms of this marriage?"

My uncle nods. "But as we have just discussed, minds and plans may change in an instant." I begin to think he is pushing me to stay, despite his protestation that the decision is mine, and I am on the brink of saying as much when he continues. "This, however, may counsel as much in favor of going as resting in port. After all, no matter what the situation at this moment, it may change for the better, for the worse, and even back again in the more than a week it will take you to make landfall in Gascony."

"Well then, we will hope it changes for the better." I crumple the letter once more, and this time I toss it onto the fire for good measure. It no longer has a hold on me. I love my husband, but he is not here, nor is his judgment always the most sound.

Taking my eyes from the blazing ball of parchment, I tell Boniface, "I am not some mouse to be kept in my hole. I am regent of England, and I will not risk a peace we have nearly reached merely because Gascony is, at present, more dangerous to us than it was a week ago. After all, even if Alfonso of Castile waited on the shore with open arms to embrace us, the sea herself might swallow us up between here and the coast off Bordeaux. Life is a dangerous business."

———

WHEN WE DISEMBARK, THERE ARE none to meet us but my steward, Bezill, and some lesser noblemen. I can hardly fault Henry for this. After all, he doubtless assumed that I stayed on English soil as he requested. Still, I get a lump in my throat when nine-year-old Edmund tugs on my hand and asks, "Where is Father?"

"What news?" I ask Bezill. "Have the King of Castile's troops crossed into Gascony?"

Bezill looks perplexed for a moment and then says, "Oh, that rumor! It proved groundless. The men His Majesty's spies counted so carefully were meant for the Navarre and are there now, giving trouble to young Thibaut the Second."

Well, I think, *at least Henry will not be vexed that I have disobeyed him when he sees me.*

Bezill turns aside for a moment to give some instructions for the loading of luggage. Then returning his attention to me, he says, "His Majesty and the Earl of Richmond are at La Réole."

"And John Mansel is still at the court of Castile?"

"Yes, and Peter d'Aigueblanche with him. But have no fear, Your Majesty. Everything is ready, just as I wrote."

I try to smile gamely at my steward despite my disappointment. It seems I am the only one of any consequence in Bordeaux—at least of any consequence when it comes to matters of negotiating a peace and managing a marriage. A groom leads several horses forward and Bezill hands me up to mine. Riding through the streets of the city, where more attention is being paid to the ordinary business of the day than to our passing, I feel a sudden drop in spirits. *Look up,* I want to call at the people we go by. *A queen is passing, a woman who ruled England* toute seule *for more than three-quarters of a year.* Of course, I cannot do any such thing but must confine myself to willing them to notice me. No one heeds my silent plea, not then nor in the days that follow.

As a result, even after I have been in Bordeaux for weeks my spirits have not improved. My house is quiet and comfortable, and I feel utterly deserted in it. I know this is not fair to the ladies, faithful souls, who made the voyage with me and who sit about me talking while I stare moodily out of an open window at the afternoon sky. Perhaps my feelings are particularly unfair to my dear Maude de Lacy, who left her snug home at Trim Castle in Ireland to travel with me despite being with child for the first time by the new husband I found her. Unfair also to my Beatrice, presently out in the garden gathering blossoms for me, and to Edmund who sits at my feet playing with a small cat that seems to wander about the place at will.

Edward is not with me. He is housed elsewhere, in state, as a nobleman and future king. At fourteen he is accorded all the consequence and attention that I presently lack. And though I tell myself I am not jealous, I am not pleased either, particularly as he is surrounded by Lusignans. I have it on good authority that his uncle Geoffrey, whom Henry chose to bear royal greetings to his son and me when we arrived despite my known dislike for the man, is with him again today. Geoffrey seems to easily find the time to make the ride from La Réole. Henry, on the other hand, is too busy to make the journey. I have seen my husband but once since my arrival, and I do not expect to see him again for two more, long, boring days. And, as Geoffrey brought a handful of his Poitevin knights with him to call upon my eldest son, they are doubtless having a raucous time. Edward shows every sign of becoming as besotted with the Lusignans as his father. Apparently he forgets that only a few months ago I had to fight to keep some of his lands from being granted to that same Geoffrey who now dines at his table. Nor will Henry's half brother let the land matter rest. He continues to badger the justiciar of Ireland about that grant. If Edward is not chary, he will have his half uncle for good company, but his half uncle will have a goodly slice of his appanage in return.

Well, I think, idly tracing my fingertip along the windowsill, *Edward does not ask my opinion.* In fact, since we have been here, no one does. Henry was very glad to see me when at last he arrived here to greet me, and he was sorry I did not bring his new daughter to meet him, but that is how I am viewed here—merely as the mother of his children and the woman who hems his shirts! It is disgusting; I who raised thousands of pounds for his support and consulted with the first men of the kingdom in his absence am now firmly relegated to the role of bedmate and ornament of the court. I did not anticipate how much I would miss ruling. I hunger for the responsibilities that were mine as regent, even those that felt onerous when I was actually contending with them.

"Lord Edmund, what do you do there?" Willelma's voice startles me. Looking down, I can see that my son has been slowly and steadily pulling a thread from the hem of my gown until he has a goodly length with which to tease the cat. Under ordinary circumstances I would be angered by this, but I find myself extraordinarily disinclined to be vexed with my second son who looks up at me with a certain amount of anticipatory dread.

"Never mind," I say, taking the thread from him and breaking it off where it joins the fabric of my gown. "Here, have it." I hand it back, and, confronted with the disbelief in Willelma's face, I add, "The boy is only bored. The hem can be fixed."

Maude, sitting nearby with one hand on her swollen belly, laughs and says, "Your Majesty will, I presume, want a change of gowns before we sup."

"Whatever for?" This elicits raised eyebrows not only from Maude but from all my ladies. I am renowned for my attention to dress, and all my ladies seek my opinions on fashion. The idea that I should dine in a gown with a portion of its hem dragging must seem incredible to them.

Doubtless I will go back to coveting a fine pair of slippers or a fur-trimmed *surcote* in the weeks to come, but right now these things seem trivial. I would gladly dispense even with the new ring Henry gave me on my arrival to be with the men, buried in the serious work of pacifying Gascony.

CHAPTER 35

Dear Eleanor,

. . . How long this letter has become since I began it shortly after we left Acre in April. And how varied its content. Traveling, as it must, with me to more familiar shores before it can be set on its way to you, it has become a repository for my experiences of the voyage and my feelings upon it. Of late those feelings have taken a serious turn.

Indeed, the closer we draw to France, the more I realize that some things that were in the Holy Land will never be so again. In general this is a very good thing. Never again will I be parted from my older children as I have been by this crusade, and never will the youngest of my brood be homeless again. Nor do I expect, please God, to wake to the sound of battle again in my lifetime. Nevertheless, there are things I gained by my journey that I would be loath to lose. I hope when we arrive in Paris, all that I did to preserve the king for France will not be forgotten, either by his subjects or by Louis himself. I wish to play a greater role in the destiny of our kingdom than I did before we left it if Louis will permit it. But who can say what Louis will permit?

Presently His Majesty is lighter of heart than at any time since we came aboard. Perhaps it is the refreshing effects of an absence of bad weather, or perhaps the ghosts of those who died in Egypt have left him at last. Whatever the reason, when he is like this, I, and presumably all on board, find his company easier to bear. I wonder if others hesitate, as do I, to let down their guard entirely. I suspect so, for surely the king's councilors at least know as well as I how quickly Louis's mood and manner may alter. He is like the winds at sea, entirely undependable, one moment soft and warm, the next fierce and punishing. After twenty years of marriage, I will not put myself in a position to have my hopes and expectations shipwrecked once more.

So, I will not let Louis control my future as I was wont to let him control things in my past. Instead, I have promised myself, dear Eleanor, to take a lesson from your stubborn tenacity. I will hold tight to my newfound confidence and independence. They are my recompense for six years in the desert. I earned them by tears, by courage, and by sweat. Nor shall I be afraid to be bold where boldness is required, for bold action these last years has brought me great gifts.

Your devoted sister,
Marguerite

MARGUERITE
EARLY SUMMER 1254
IN SIGHT OF THE ISLAND OF PANTELLERIA

"My lady wife, you are very pensive." Louis's words surprise me.

"I was only wondering, Your Majesty, what island that is in the foredi025tance."

"What is that place?" Louis asks Brother Raymond.

The seafaring Templar in charge of our ship tends to trail after the king in a manner much like a spaniel whenever His Majesty is on deck. But, as he is also as good-natured as a dog, his presence does not appear to annoy Louis.

"Pantelleria, Your Majesty."

"And whose island is it?"

"It is under Sicilian rule, I believe, Your Majesty, but it is full of Saracens who make imperfect subjects."

"There, madam, now you may unfurl your brow." Louis gives me a weak smile.

He has been attempting such little pleasantries this last week. I may imagine it, but it seems to me that the closer we draw to France, the more effort Louis makes.

I hesitate for a moment and then decide there is no harm in asking. "As Your Majesty knows from his own table, our stores are much depleted since we stocked them at Cyprus. Tristan begins to suffer from little sores in his mouth. I wonder if some men might not be sent ashore to acquire fresh fruit for the children?"

"Find the master of the boats," Louis orders the Templar. "Tell him to send several with good rowers to Pantelleria for fruit." Brother Raymond begins to stride off but is halted a few yards away by Louis's voice. "Mind you tell them to be quick about their task. When my ship passes the island, we shall expect them to return to us."

"Thank you, Your Majesty." I curtsy very prettily despite the roll of the ship, for having been so many weeks at sea, I am entirely used to the *nef*'s motion.

Jean, who was at the king's elbow throughout our exchange, lingers behind when Louis moves off along the deck. "He is trying to win you."

"If it means fruit for the children, let him think he is succeeding," I reply lightly.

"He *is* succeeding."

I open my mouth to protest, but, stepping to the rail beside me, Jean cuts me off. "This is not a criticism—either of you or the king. It is merely an observation. His Majesty treats you better of late than at any time during my acquaintance with you. And you, with your better nature, cannot help but be warmed by his newfound amiableness, however late or little it be."

"You make me sound very easily won indeed."

" 'I withhold not my heart from any joy; for my heart rejoiced in all my labor.' You have striven always to be a good wife and worthy queen against much unjust resistance. If you are appreciated at last, why should you not revel in it?"

"By God's coif, Jean, you sound as if you think I should favor Louis's suit."

"I cannot lose you to Louis. You are his already—"

"His?"

"But"—Jean holds up a hand to stop me from rushing forward in my indignation—"you are also mine. As I love you, I would give much to see His Majesty treat you as you deserve."

When we are at last even with Pantelleria, there are no galleys. I can clearly see the island's port from my window where I sit curled up with Eleanor's letters—the few that reached me during my prolonged exile in the Holy Land, each of which I have read dozens of times. *His Majesty will not be pleased,* I think. And I wonder upon whom his displeasure will fall—on the sailors themselves or on me since I sent them forth. Perhaps our delay will not be long. I return my eyes back to my letters but am distracted by my perception that the ship is slowing. Laying aside the letters, I rise.

"You are not going on deck again?" Marie is perplexed by the hours I pass at the great ship's rail. She dislikes the wind, the spray, in truth every part of a sea voyage, which I in contrast find exhilarating.

"You need not come with me. Stay here and enjoy your mending."

"I will," Marie replies with a touch of challenge. "*I* do not wish to arrive in France as brown as a Genoese sailor."

I laugh. "We are all scarcely browner than we were in the desert." It has been a very long time, I reflect, since any of us has looked French. We lived in Egypt and in the Kingdom of Jerusalem, and we look like the natives of those places. Or at least those parts of us not covered by our garments do. Jean speculates on how exotic I might look if all my limbs were equally bronzed. For myself, I love the warm hue that Jean's skin has acquired, and I find the sun has had a positive effect on Louis as well. Though at forty he is no longer a young man, thanks to the sun, his hair is as golden as it was on the day we met. And the color the sun imparts to his features is far healthier looking than the gray pallor of his face when he returned from captivity.

Quite a gathering of men surrounds the king when I come out into the bright sunlight. "It is best we sail onward. Neither Tunis nor Sicily is a friend to Your Majesty," one of the gentlemen is saying.

"And the men I leave behind? What if they have been taken by Saracens?"

"Regrettable. But better a few than all of our party," says the constable.

"We will give them an hour," Louis says decisively, looking at the angle of the sun and the shadow of the mast on the deck.

The sailors disperse to their various tasks. But the king stands unmoving, a grim stare focused on the distant island. I find myself transfixed by his face. It is so fierce. And, though his eyes never turn to me, I am driven back to my cabin by this fierceness. Once there, I am of no use to myself. It is with some relief, and after trying half a dozen entertainments, that I conclude the hour must surely have run.

I return to deck to find Louis precisely where I left him. But, instead of staring fixedly ahead, he is watching one of the master mariners measure the angle of the sun with a brass astrolabe.

"I make it more than an hour, Your Majesty. Shall we raise the anchor?"

"Yes."

I can see both the mariner himself and Giles le Brun, who stands closer to the king, relax slightly.

Until Louis adds, "And turn the sails."

"But Your Majesty—"

"We will mount an attack if necessary before we leave those men behind."

My stomach sinks. All I wanted was some fresh food for my little ones. How could such an innocent request lead to battle?

At that moment Louis spots me. "Lady wife, you should go to your cabin, or, better still, below to the children, for your own safety. There looks to be trouble."

And I know in an instant that Jean is right, even without the pointed look he casts me. Such a mark of caring! And from the same man who sent me on a trip through hostile lands simply to have me out of his sight not so many months ago.

I am about to obey when a sailor high in the riggings calls out. The boats have been sighted. The king, his men, and I all rush to the rail. Our three boats can clearly be seen now, making from the island in the direction of our ship.

Even with strong rowers aboard, it takes considerable time for them to reach us. And every minute makes the king more impatient. Indeed, I cannot understand his mood. Surely the wait we are enduring is nothing compared to the time, and possibly lives, that might have been lost going on shore in pursuit of our men?

By the time the ladder is lowered and the first of the sailors clambers aboard, Louis's lips are compressed into a grim white line. I wonder that the head of the landing party does not notice, but he is busy passing aboard what they picked or purchased. Besides, he has not my familiarity with the nature of the king.

"You," the king barks at him, "why were you not true to your instructions and prompt in your return?"

"Your Majesty," the man stammers, "several among out party were so overcome by the sight of the lush gardens we found that they disappeared into them. I did not wish to leave them behind, and finding them took some time."

"And were they in some peril when you found them?"

The man hesitates, clearly embarrassed. "No, Your Majesty, they had merely eaten their fill of fruit and fallen asleep among the trees."

"Line up your men."

The sailor gives a sharp whistle through his teeth, and those still on the galleys scramble on board and form a ragged line.

"Let the men who were caught sleeping step forward."

Several men come forward at once, willing to own their deeds.

"Are these the men?"

"Not all, Your Majesty." The sailor points to two more fellows who cast him black looks but then step out of line as well.

Six men stand before the king. They do not tremble, perhaps because Louis looks so calm, so detached. But I tremble for them.

"The two who did not come forward must be lashed," Louis pronounces, "for their own improvement. Then all who were indolent in their duties will be placed in the boat that trails this ship and stay there for the rest of the journey."

There is a general gasp all around, and the men who were caught sleeping look sick. "But, surely, Your Majesty, this is too great a punishment," Brother Raymond says delicately. "You have condemned them to the same treatment given murderers. While they are lazy, good-for-nothing oafs, they are not, I think, criminals."

"They are sinners, or have you forgotten that sloth is a cardinal sin?"

"Yes, but not a mortal sin, and, like all sins, it can be forgiven."

"You make an excellent point, Brother. I suggest," Louis continues, this time addressing the men, some of whom are now quaking quite visibly, "that you use your time apart from the company of your fellows in prayer, beseeching Our Lord for forgiveness of your sin."

Then Louis turns on his heel and heads for his cabin. I trail behind, even though it is a place I do not generally intrude upon. Before he disappears inside, with Jean and his other councilors, I call out. "Your Majesty!"

"Yes, Wife?" Louis's expression is puzzled rather than threatening.

I come forward until I am directly before him and sink into a deep reverence. Keeping my eyes on the deck, I say, "I would beg for clemency for the men just dispatched to the small boat."

"Why?" The confusion in Louis's voice draws my eyes to his face.

"It was on my whim that they were sent forth and on my errand that they failed in their duties. I therefore feel some responsibility for them and ask most humbly that, at very least, the time they are relegated to the boat be shortened. The sun is fearful in an uncovered craft. The waves are high. Surely a week in such circumstances will be enough to teach them a lesson."

"Wife, your efforts do you credit, but the objects of your concern do not deserve your sympathy or intervention. I do not think less of you for pleading for mercy for others as I might think of them if they pleaded for it themselves, but nor shall I yield to your entreaties. And as for your fear that you are in part responsible for the situation in which these rogues find themselves, I command you to put that thought out of your head. You are no more to blame for their dereliction of duty than am I who ordered the boats ashore."

Perhaps Louis is right. Perhaps I am not culpable. Yet I cannot convince myself I am entirely without responsibility. That night, my prayers are full of the sailors my husband punishes, though I do not even know their names. The next morning when I go onto deck, I am quickly forced inside again by the presence of the men in the boat. Whether I am to blame for their plight or not, the sea air has been spoiled for me.

A week later in the late afternoon, Jean steps into my cabin.

"Come on deck. There is going to be a beautiful sunset."

"I am fine where I am." I give him a smile and hope that will satisfy him. This is not the first invitation I have refused in the past days.

"What is the matter, Marguerite? You have hardly been on deck for days. You tell me you are not ill, but I no longer know if I should believe you." Jean furrows his brow in the way that always makes me want to soothe him.

"Whenever I go on deck, my feet are drawn to the stern and my eyes to those hapless men we tow behind."

Jean sighs.

"Have you seen them?"

"Yes."

"Are they not pitiful and pitiable?"

"Yes.

"But your staying inside will not ameliorate their condition. You spoke to the king. I spoke to the king. Verily, I do not think there is a *preudomme* on this ship who has not spoken to the king. Louis will not hear reason." He gives another sigh and then, looking deep into my eyes, says, "All your continued absence does is attract the king's attention."

I had not thought of this. But it makes perfect sense. Louis, always a man of routine whether in his religious observations or his personal life, became increasingly obsessed with order through the course of our sojourn in the Holy Land. Perhaps because there was so much he could not control, he instituted a strict schedule for that which he could. This habit continues as we voyage home. He dines at the same hour daily and likes his gentlemen to take always the same seats. Similarly, he visits my bed every Tuesday, unless that be a holy day. This bit of regularity, at least, is a comfort to me as well as to him for it allows Jean and me to meet on other nights without fear that the king shall surprise us in my bedchamber.

"All right," I say, making up my mind that I cannot remain in my cabin for all the weeks that remain in our voyage. "I will come and see the sunset."

"DO NOT DAWDLE," I SNAP as Marie and my little *béguines* clear away what is left of our cold supper. We have eaten late this evening because the king requested I play chess with him. We passed the time quite pleasantly and Louis had not one cross word for me, even when I made a silly error. But now I am eager to forget my husband and have my time with Jean. I wonder if the sudden urgency of my lust for him is sparked by the babe that grows inside me of whom Jean as yet knows nothing, or by the moment as I left the king's cabin when it seemed he would kiss me but withdrew his lips at the last moment.

In either case, I am in a fine state. Just the thought of Jean's arrival is enough to cause a few unexpected contractions in the region that now aches for him. And as my women turn from clearing my table to undressing me, I notice with embarrassment that the profile of my nipples, pointed and pert, shows clearly through my chemise.

"That will do; that will do," I chide as one of my *béguines* tries to neatly lay the garments that have been removed from me and cover them. Seated at my small dressing table, I eagerly remove my wimple and cast it carelessly aside. At last there is nothing more to remove and my women are tucking me into bed. Marie dismisses the *béguines* to their own cabin below mine to take their rest. They presume, of course, that she will lie on the pallet at the foot of my bed and take hers, but she goes to sit in my forward cabin, waiting to admit Jean before making a bed for herself on the bench there.

I draw back the curtains on my window as soon as she is gone. The sea is splashed liberally with the light of the waning moon. The candles around my cabin, sunk deep in their iron pots for safety, cast glimmering circles of light. A feeling of enchantment fills the cozy space, mingling with my anticipation.

Impatient for Jean to arrive, I pull off my chemise and run my own hands over my body. My state of arousal is so great that I cannot resist pleasuring myself. This seems indulgent as Jean will surely come soon to take me, but I excuse myself with the knowledge that if I have already experienced the release of my lust, I will be more patient with him.

Finger between my legs, knees drawn up, eyes fixed on the moon outside, I lie, thinking of Jean and me in our little house at Tyre, when I hear the door creak.

"By heaven," Jean's voice says gruffly, "what have we here?"

"Come to me," I reply eagerly. "I am desperate to have you."

"So I see," he says, "just as this moment am I to have you." He begins to strip off his garments, his muscles rippling gracefully in the candlelight and his eyes on me as I continue to touch myself.

Coming to the side of the bed, he lies on his side next to me and begins to kiss me, his hand caressing my belly. Then, putting his mouth by my ear, he whispers, "Let me watch you."

I should feel shamed by this idea, but I feel exhilarated. He crawls to the end of the bed and settles himself near my feet. I continue with my self-ministrations, exaggerating every gesture and every vocalized moan of pleasure for his benefit. As my excitement builds, I forget he is there and abandon myself to it—eyes closed, back arching, body spasming around the fingers I have inserted inside it.

By the time my eyes flicker open again, Jean is looming over me, chest heaving. I wrap my legs around him as he pushes fiercely into me. Jean's passion is as pounding as the waves and tosses me about as if I were a ship upon him.

As he rides me, running his hands over every inch of my flesh, I smell something odd—the acrid odor of smoke. I sniff again, but I detect nothing and have no more attention for such things. Then, as Jean cries out in the pleasure of release, the odor comes again.

"Jean!" I gasp, but cannot capture his attention. "Something is burning!"

I scramble to push myself up to a sitting position even as he remains inside me. There are flames at the foot of my bed!

"Fire!" My voice is hoarse and not loud enough that anyone outside the cabin could hear it, but the dreaded word captures Jean's full attention.

Both of us are on our feet in an instant, looking around frantically.

The bedclothes, kicked off the end of my bed in our exertions, are engulfed in flame, and nearby I see one of my iron candle pots spewing flames like a torch.

I fly to the window and yank it open, then racing back, throw my *surcote*, laid aside when my ladies undressed me, over the flaming pot and cast the whole out onto the waves. Meanwhile Jean is doing what he can to beat out the flames in the sheets. Together we catch them up and shove them out the window as well. For a moment we both stand, breathing heavily.

"Dear God, the whole ship might have burned." I run to him and rest my head against his chest.

"Fire!"

The voice startles me nearly as much as did the first sight of the flames. "What?" I cry.

"It must be someone on deck or the fellows in the boat behind. They have spotted the charred and smoldering fabric we cast adrift," Jean replies.

"Go!" I cry, snatching up his shirt from the stool near my dressing table and tossing it to him. "If you are found here 'twill be worse than if the ship *had* burned!"

Jean is in his shirt and tunic in an instant. Opening the door to my forward cabin, he runs directly into Marie. She looks wildly about at the bed torn apart, the open window, and the thick haze of smoke that still hangs near the ceiling.

"I am unhurt," I shout. "Pray get my Lord of Joinville safely away."

As soon as they are gone, I pull on a chemise and find a pelisse. After assuring myself that nothing else burns—not the coverlet, though it is singed, not what remains of the chainsil that covered my clothing, nor any of the clothing itself now strewn about the floor—I remove the remaining sheets from my bed and stuff them out the window. They may not burn, but they tell a tale that those who come to witness the site of the fire must not see. Then I venture out onto the deck. Louis is there with his back to me. As I approach, I can see that he addresses Caym.

"Where is my Lord of Joinville?" Louis asks, his voice fierce.

"He has gone to the latrines, Your Majesty."

"Liar!"

"If you have need of him, I will gladly run and fetch him."

"Louis." At the sound of my voice my husband turns.

"Madam, what goes on here?" My husband's face is livid.

I rush forward as if in fear and, taking the front of his mantle in my hands, rest my head against his chest just as I moments ago rested it on Jean's. I give a little sob and then looking up say, "Husband, I know not how it came to pass, but I awoke from my slumber to find my bed engulfed in flames!"

"You slept?"

"Of course—did not Your Majesty at this hour?"

Taking my hand, Louis pulls me through my forward cabin, thankfully oblivious to the cover lying on the bench where Marie slept, and into my bedchamber. Although I left the window flung wide, there are still traces of smoke lingering.

"Light more candles," Louis orders Marie who followed us in. This she does and then begins to pick up things and make them right as Louis stares about wildly.

"Something goes on here. Sheets do not just catch fire while one sleeps."

I nod my head in honest confusion. "I have no idea how the fire started." And because it is the truth, it rings true.

Marie, who has been gathering my clothing from the day over

her arm, picks up my *couvre-chef* and then, giving me a puzzled look, asks, "Your Majesty, where is your wimple?"

She and I look in earnest while Louis stands by, searching under my dressing table and bed as well as all about on the floor.

"That must be it," I say with some satisfaction. "When I awoke, the iron pot that sat here, just next to my covered garments, blazed entirely full of flame. The wimple must have fallen into it and began all."

"And where is the pot now?" Louis asks. He must be calming, for the question is more curious than angry.

"I leapt up and cast it from the window. Then did the same with everything that burned."

"God be praised for your presence of mind!" Marie says fervently

"And you?" Louis rounds on her. "Did you do nothing but stand gape-mouthed while your mistress did battle with the fire?"

"Marie was most helpful, Your Majesty," I chime in, giving her a look. "I could never have cast all those burning sheets out onto the waves alone."

Louis peers at my lady with the eyes of God on Judgment Day seeking answers, seeking falsehoods, seeking sin. For a moment I quake inside. Is Marie equal to withstanding such scrutiny? Will she lie to the king's face, even to save me?

"It was nothing, Your Majesty," she says, coloring slightly— pray Louis attributes that to modesty. "Her Majesty gave commands; I merely followed them."

"It seems, madam," Louis says, turning back to me, "that you have saved the ship." If this is meant to be praise, it does not sound like it. "But *someone*'s carelessness put it in jeopardy. I will have to see that precautions are taken in future."

I do not like the way he says this. I do not like it at all.

I PASS THE REST OF the night with my children. My cabin needs airing, and, besides, when I am in the company of my innocent babes, who will dare to say I am with anyone else?

As soon as I am awake and dressed, I go on deck, hoping to hear what is being said about the fire. Marie is with me, and this is the first moment I have been alone with my good lady since she lied for me. Squeezing her hand, as we approach a group of men standing near the ship's castle, I murmur my thanks.

My Lord Gervase, the ship's chief cook, is speaking as we draw near. "I always thought my fire was the most dangerous on board. Who would have foreseen the queen's cabin catching alight?" He laughs slightly, though for the life of me I cannot see the jest. I clear my throat and he bows with a stricken look. "We are all relieved, Your Majesty, that the fire you suffered last night was not more serious."

"Thank you, my lord. Have you seen the king?"

The Lord Chamberlain answers, "He is in his cabin with the Seneschal of Champagne, Your Majesty."

"Thank you." I try to walk away calmly. After all, there is nothing unusual about Louis and Jean closeted together. They are close friends. But, after what I observed last night—the bile in Louis's voice as he accused Jean's man of falsehood—I am nervous indeed. I make up my mind to go back to my cabin. Surely Jean will wait upon me when he is finished with the king.

But instead of Jean, a note comes to me telling me I will find him on deck, so back I go. I spot him high on the ship's castle. Climbing the stairs to join him, I am somewhat surprised when he makes a formal bow.

"Are we here for the view?" I quip nervously.

"No. To be viewed. If I could have conceived of a place where we could more easily be seen, I would have chosen it." Jean's face is fixed in a smile, but his eyes belie it. "The king sought me this morning."

"I know it."

"Would you like to hear what he said when he found me?"

I am dumb with fear.

"He came upon me as I was talking with le Brun. We naturally turned and bowed upon his approach, and then le Brun said, 'Your Majesty, I am eager to hear what happened last night.' To which your husband, looking squarely at me, replied, 'Has the Seneschal not told you of the fire? I am all astonishment, for he knows as much of it as any man.'"

My hand flutters toward my mouth; then, recollecting that we are clearly visible to all on deck, I arrest the motion. Forcing a smile, I say between my teeth, "Holy Mary, protect us."

"There is more." Jean offers his arm and begins to stroll me down one side of the tower's top as if we are enjoying the sight of the sea laid out before us. "*En privé* His Majesty commanded that I personally make certain that every fire aboard, except the main, be extinguished every evening and that I report as much to him before I sleep."

"It sounds to me as if he is merely affrighted of what might have happened had the fire been more serious."

"Does it? Then you are not listening closely. Do you know where I will be sleeping this evening? On a pallet at His Majesty's feet. He told me his nerves are much agitated by recent events and that he might sleep more soundly for knowing that I am near at hand."

"Dear God, he knows."

"So it would seem—"

I feel as though I might retch, and I can see Marie's face where she stands, far enough away to be polite but still close enough to overhear, go pale as death.

"Or at least he suspects. But it seems to me that he gives us a warning. He wants to be given reason to conclude he is mistaken."

I wonder for a moment, might Louis love both of us, Jean and me, such that his suspicions pain him?

"As I was leaving," Jean continues, "he said to me, 'Seneschal, you are a gentleman I have valued from the first. There are none, other than my own brothers, whom I love more. So do not think I give you this commission to punish you, but rather because I know that you above all can be counted upon to do that which is right and to do it thoroughly.'"

My husband orders Jean to give me up. However else his words could be interpreted, I know it plainly. And my charitable thoughts of a moment before fade, leaving me angry. "What does Louis know of what is right?" I demand. "Had he loved me as he ought to have . . . Had he loved me with even a tenth of the fervor he shows for God—"

"Yes. But consider, Marguerite, he is not on trial here, nor need he fear being censured for his actions. We, on the other hand, are in grave danger of being called to account."

"He has not the nerve."

"Can we take that chance?"

For one wild moment I want to say yes—to defy Louis, to pin my fate and my very life on this love I feel for Jean, a love unlike any I have ever known. Then a noise calls my attention down to the deck; it is the voice of a child. My children are out, taking the air. Jean Tristan, walking just beside his nurse, is earnestly conversing with her. I can see her struggling to keep from laughing as she gives him an answer. In a blinding flash I am nearly overcome by pain—pain of the soul so intense that it manifests itself physically and in its grip I am ready to double over. Whatever I am willing to risk for the sake of my own happiness, I am not willing to risk my precious son.

Leaning one hand on the parapet to steady myself, I begin to cry. Jean looks at me helplessly. He dare not pull me to him or even wipe away my tears. I myself let them fall unhindered rather than show those below that I am crying by dabbing my eyes. "I would gladly die by any means rather than live without you."

"As I would die for you."

"But it is not only *our* lives that hang in the balance." I look down again at our son, popping out from behind his nurse's skirts for the amusement of his brother, and think of the child in my womb who may also be Jean's. When I lift my eyes to Jean's face, I find him watching Jean Tristan as well.

"Surely," I say, recalling his attention, "Louis does not suspect *all*."

"Praise God I have no reason to think so! Have you?" Jean's voice is choked with terror. Never, in all the years we suffered in the desert, have I seen him as afraid as he appears to be now.

"No. If anything, Louis shows Jean Tristan favor above all his other children. Have you not remarked it?"

"Yes. Yes, I have."

My heart is pounding in my throat. "Oh my darling . . ." My voice trails off, momentarily stilled by a sob that rises up within me and cannot be contained. "I love you beyond any man, beyond God against whom I sin in loving you, more than my own soul, which I have cast into the fiery pits of hell merely for the sound of your voice and the touch of your hand. There is only one thing that I love more than you—my children. I would lay down my life for them. Even as you *are* my life, I must lay you down to protect our son. I know you will understand this, and forgive me, for you too love the boy body and soul."

"Marguerite"—Jean's voice breaks with the anguish of the moment—"I will always love you."

"That will be enough then," I reply. It *must* be enough.

"Oh God, I warned you once that when this crusade was over we would be separated."

He is right. I can see him in my mind's eye, comforting me on the day we learned the dragon was dead. But then we thought the separation would be thrust upon us by the difficulty of meeting privately. Fools!

"When we go ashore," he continues, "I will ride at once to my own lands. Put distance between us so that Louis will forget his awful suspicions."

"But you will come back to court." My voice sounds nakedly pleading for someone who has just sworn off his company.

"Can you bear it if I do?"

"Can I bear it if you do not? Besides, if you do not, Louis will seek a reason. Come back and serve your king. You are his friend, and you can surely remain mine." Friend—how bitter the word tastes in my mouth.

"I will be everything to you that I can be save lover. Everything. I swear it."

I nod. My head hurts. The sun is too bright. I cannot endure it. Whatever oaths are made on this awful day, I know that from this moment on Jean will be an empty, aching place that no other person can ever fill though years pass—separated from me by words of love too dangerous to be repeated.

HOME.

On this occasion, I, not Louis, am the one moved to prostrate myself in prayer. I lie in front of the little altar so often used by my husband on the deck of his ship, thanking God most earnestly. It is the last day of June, and I have spotted the islands not far from the castle of Hyères in my father's own county—or rather my sister Beatrice's. There is a port near Hyères. *Provence, my first home, on your familiar soil my foot will rejoice after six long years in lands not my own.*

"Your Majesty?"

I lift my head to see Jean looking at me curiously. And, as ever since that fateful morning after the fire, the sight of him brings a cruel mix of pain and pleasure. We have continued to pass much time together, but always publicly. We play at chess, stroll the deck, and eat dinner at the king's table. But Jean passes every night at the foot of the king's bed—an homage that seems to please Louis greatly. There is rarely an unguarded moment between Jean and me, and the words of love we whisper furtively when one does arrive begin to take on tones of desperation.

"May I help you up?" Rising to my knees, I take the hand Jean offers. "I fear your prayers of thanksgiving are premature," he says in a low voice. "His Majesty declares we will not land."

"Why ever not?"

"The precise point his council has just been pressing. These are, after all, his brother's lands—"

"Says Charles of Anjou. But I say they are my sister's."

"I am sure that you do, only do not say so too loudly within hearing of the king. It will only strengthen his resolve to go on to Aigues-Mortes."

"But that would mean another month at sea!"

"Or more. The council will push him as hard as they can. But Louis is not a man for yielding. He has been kind to you of late; I have remarked it." Is that pain I see in Jean's eyes? Does it hurt him to see Louis drawing closer to me?

"His kindness means nothing to me."

"For the present it may mean you have the power to set us all upon the land. Is that not worth something? It is Tuesday."

Jean's reminder of Louis's weekly conjugal visit would nettle me more did I not know that the short time my love spends alone on his pallet at the foot of the king's empty bed while Louis is in my cabin is as torture to him.

I sigh. I had planned to tell Louis I am with child and thus relieve myself of his attentions for the next months. But now, it seems, is not the time to tell him.

When Louis comes to my cabin in the evening, I am not tucked into bed, lights out. Instead, I sit by my open window, looking at the Provençal coast by moonlight.

"Louis," I say, rising to my feet as he enters, "will you take a glass of wine with me?"

The offer seems to catch Louis off his guard, and when he says nothing, I proceed as if he has assented, filling two glasses and handing him one.

"Lady wife, you are very lively this evening."

"The sight of my childhood home, though it be but from a distance, cheers and excites me." I force myself to remain standing very close to him as I speak. This is a seduction, of the body, yes, but even more so of the mind. Hence my use of his Christian name, which no longer falls freely from my tongue as it once did, and my application of every drop of the rose water that remained in my possession. I find the scent nearly overwhelming and hope I have not gone too far.

"Your eyes are very bright," Louis remarks, looking into my face in a way that once would have thrilled me.

I swallow hard. Then, taking his hand, I draw it up to my breast, firm and round thanks to my condition, and press it there, saying, "And my heart beats like the wings of a bird."

Louis stands for a moment, breathing audibly, then downs what is left in his glass in a single gulp. I follow suit, then place both glasses on a table just behind him. The action necessitates my moving in closer still, and Louis buries his face in the hair at the side of my neck. Raising his lips to my ear, he whispers, "Do you think I am a failure?"

Whatever I was expecting him to say, it was not this. "It is impossible for anyone to think it—I least of all who have been your wife these many years."

Louis draws his head back so that he can look me in the eyes again. "I am going to return to the Holy Land," he says fiercely.

I do not believe that he will, or at least I pray it is not so. I know for certain I will never set foot there again. But I say, "Of course you will." And if it is a lie, I have told bigger ones.

"Yes," he says. Then he lowers his head to the place where my neck meets my shoulder and kisses it.

"And you will be victorious next time," I murmur. "You will cast the Saracens out from the great cities, and their leaders, driven before your armies, will convert or die."

My words unleash Louis's passion. There is no image he covets more for himself than that of the victorious religious warrior. Even as he throws me on the bed and crawls on top of me, his mind clearly puzzles over his losses and schemes to avoid them in future. "There will be no blasphemers in my next army, no men who ignore holy days, or consort with prostitutes. All shall be Christian men first and warriors second. Surely then God will be pleased. Surely then he will not deny me victory."

I make no response to these exclamations, but silently and determinedly, in a manner almost as if it were my trade, do all that I can to be certain Louis enjoys himself. Running my hands down his back, watching the muscles in his jaw tighten and his eyes clench shut, I wonder how it is I feel like a strumpet in the bed of my husband, whereas I never felt so for an instant with Jean though we were fornicators plain and simple.

When Louis is finished, I curl up beside him and put my head upon his chest; I must keep him with me if I would discuss the topic of our landing. I am drawing breath to begin when Louis says, "They want me to put into port in Provence."

"And you would rather not?"

"Will I not look like a dog, slinking home with its tail between its legs if I come to France by a back way? I ought to land as I departed, with great state, at Aigues-Mortes."

"Of course, Louis, you must do as you think best. But the Kingdom of France has waited long and anxiously for your return. It seems almost an unkindness to forestall by another month or more the event they so long for."

"Do you really think so?"

"I do. Since our dear mother's death, your people have looked to Your Majesty's brothers for justice and for law. However well-meaning those gentlemen, their judgment is not equal to your own." I seriously doubt Louis's brothers are well meaning. Charles at least would take France if he could get it. But it is safer to suggest them less able. Louis himself worries about their governance in his absence. They did not leave us on the best terms, and their "wan-ton" behavior at Acre rankles him still.

"Hm." The fact that Louis does not refute my arguments instantly is very encouraging.

"And landing at Hyères would be a kindness to me. . . ." I let my voice trail off.

"Yes?" Louis pursues my lead eagerly.

"It would give me an opportunity to see my mother, whom I have not laid eyes upon in six years."

"It is natural you should long to see your mother."

This is exactly the reaction I was hoping for. The dragon's death, having robbed Louis of his ability to see his mother, appears to have made him sensitive to my need to see mine. *Funny,* I think almost idly while waiting to see if he will say more, *that he can identify with this desire but not my fierce yearning, as a mother myself, to see our own children.*

Louis disentangles himself from me with care and sits for a moment on the edge of my bed. "I must go."

I could ask why, but I have no real interest in his staying. As he stands and retrieves the mantle he uses to cover his fine linen shirt on the walk between his cabin and my own, he says, "I will think upon what you have said and am obliged to you for making me consider my decision anew. If I find that nothing but my vanity drives me to sail on, then we shall not. After all, it would be foolish to let a failing rather than sound consideration drive my judgment."

CHAPTER 36

My dear Eleanor,

We landed in our father's county, exhausted but well. At least in body. In soul . . . Well, there I struggle to explain our present state. His Majesty is sober at the prospect of returning to French soil defeated. And I, who waited and prayed so long to be back home again, suddenly find I lack proper feelings for the occasion. No rush of joy is mine. Instead, I am hollow, haggard in spirit, as if I were a woman of eight decades, not three.

Presently we are at Aix where I found our mother well. There was some satisfaction in that, and in being once again subject to maternal care. The king invited Mother back to court, and she has accepted. In the prospect of her companionship I hope there may be remedy from my present malaise. Peace and good company are all that I long for after so much tumult. No, I lie, I long also to repair my family. Louis still dwells much on what was lost in the Holy Land, but he thinks of men and cities. I, a woman, know many things less corporal are gone as well. Time was squandered that can never be regained, and relations were altered. Will Louis, Isabelle, and Philippe know me when we meet again? I pray it is neither too late to reacquaint myself with the children I left behind nor to acquaint the three I bring into France with their father's country.

Your sister,
Marguerite

———— · ————

ELEANOR
LATE SUMMER 1254
BORDEAUX, GASCONY

"My sister is returned safe from the Holy Land at last."
I have gone to find Henry in his rooms. Every day more and more Gascon rebels revert their allegiance to my husband, the way smoothed by the clemency he now offers, so Henry is more frequently in residence at Bordeaux than he was when I arrived in Gascony earlier this summer.

"I am very glad to hear it," he says, looking up from a letter. I can guess by the telltale sketches that lie beneath the letter that it is a report on the work at Westminster. Whatever else engages him, wherever he may be, a portion of my husband's mind and heart are at the abbey where his workmen are making magnificent progress on the choir and eastern sections. "I will order a special Mass of thanksgiving in honor of the news," he continues.

"Oh Henry, what a splendid gesture." In truth I am more excited by the prospect than I might ordinarily be. The event will give my ladies and me an excuse to dress in our finest, and I need a diversion. Marguerite writes from Aix, where she has stopped to visit our mother en route to Paris. The thought of the two of them together, on ground as familiar to me as their good faces, makes my heart ache. How I wish I could be there as well! But never mind; in another month or so we will leave for Edward's wedding in Castile, and there will be excitement enough.

"I am glad you've come with your news at just this moment," Henry says, reaching out a hand to me. He smiles. "More glad even than usual." Then his smile fades, and I wonder if I imagined it. "We have something to discuss."

Something serious. This much is obvious.

"Your uncle and I spent the morning closeted together. He feels that the presence of our court here reminds my subjects in Gascony that I am more than the shadow of a king ruling from afar and that this has been beneficial to the calming of the region."

"I am glad to hear it. But I hope that when we all return with Edward's bride and the King of Castile's signature on a treaty, we sail home. I am not easy being away from little Katherine for so long." If my uncle is counseling Henry for a prolonged stay in Bordeaux, he and I will have words later.

"I fear we must both make a sacrifice—"

It is as I feared. I swear if I have to spend a year complete here, I will go mad.

"It is best we do not go to Castile with Edward."

"Not go to Castile?" I am confused. The conversation heads in a direction I had not anticipated. I was prepared to plead my case for a timely return to England. The idea of not going to Castile— well, it is absurd. I brought Edward here for his wedding. I had countless gowns made for its celebration and for his knighting. Henry and I are to travel to Castile in great state. What was the point of the time and money spent to prepare a magnificent show for the Castilians if we remain in Bordeaux? And how can my son be wedded if I am not there to witness it? "Surely you do not mean it! You would miss your son's wedding merely to placate the ever-contentious noblemen of Gascony?"

Henry looks stricken. "Eleanor, you cannot doubt I love Edward, nor that he is first in my mind. But Gascony is *his*, his birthright. You have reminded me of this often. Everything we have done here—the money spent, the battles fought, the bribes paid—has been done for Edward. How is he better served then, by having us bear him company to Castile, or by having us remain behind to see that nothing gained is lost?"

As a mother I want to argue with his logic. How can I be certain that my son arrives safely at Alfonso's court, that he is treated as he should be, that he is knighted rather than imprisoned, if all is not done under my eye? He is fifteen, yes, but still less fully a man than he thinks himself. Yet even as my heart fights my uncle Peter's conclusions, my head sees they are well drawn. Just because Henry and I do not go does not mean Edward will travel alone or unprotected. I have worked for so many years to see Gascony secured from encroachment, whether by Earl Richard or Alfonso of Castile, and handed over to my son intact. I cannot falter now.

I wipe defensively at a tear that moistens my eye. "Well, sir, my mother did not see me wed; yet the marriage stuck." I try to manage a teasing smile. "So I suppose Edward may be properly wed without us. I can wear my new gowns when the couple returns to join us and we celebrate them here."

Henry knows, despite my cavalier tone, that it is not the prospect of a delay in putting on my finery that brings my spirits down at present. After all these years he knows me better than anyone. He must know too that I will cry when Edward leaves us to head south. I suspect I will not weep alone.

MY EYES ARE MOIST WITH tears, tears of joy and pride. Edward's party rides into the courtyard, back from Castile. The hooves of their horses stir up a golden swirl of autumn leaves. I can see faithful John Mansel on one side of my son. When his eyes meet mine, he smiles broadly and gives a nod. It is done! Peace with the King of Castile must lie in his saddlebag.

At Edward's other side a slip of a girl rides. Her magnificent clothing only makes her appear younger to my eyes. Did I look so childlike when I married Henry? I must have, for this Eleanor is thirteen. I see how she looks at Edward for reassurance as the horses slow to a stop, and he dismounts and offers a hand to help her do likewise. Her eyes are adoring. She is a lamb and I love her already.

I do not wait but bustle forward. This, after all, is a meeting of family. "Edward, you look well." I refrain from embracing him as I do not know if his dignity could bear such an action in front of his new bride. Henry, however, is heedless of such things and pulls our son into a bear hug, causing Eleanor to step slightly aside.

"My dear daughter," I say, taking one of her hands, "you must be weary from the road. Come inside and take some refreshment. Edward"—I turn to my son who stands talking with his father, uncles, and the other sundry male members of the court who have gathered in a knot around him—"it is just as easy to talk sitting comfortably inside as standing in this dusty courtyard. Your wife is tired."

I expect at least a sharp look in response to this. After all, what fifteen-year-old boy wishes to be reminded of his duty by his mother? But I mean for Edward to know, I am not intimidated by his new status as landowner and knight. He is still my boy. Great is my surprise then when, instead of bristling, he pulls me into an embrace, and then, offering one arm to me and one to his bride says, "You see, Eleanor, I told you my mother thinks of everything."

Through all this the other Eleanor remains silent, but I do not like her the less for it. There will be time enough for her to find her voice and her place in this court of ours.

The sun sets on the day of Edward and Eleanor's return from Castile, but our feasting and festivities continue. When at last the evening is at an end and I make my way to my apartment, escorted by an orange autumnal moon that draws my eye out each successive window that I pass, I find I am not at all tired. No more is Henry when he arrives in my rooms for our precious private time together.

"We have a treaty of peace with Castile—how shall we celebrate?" Henry spins me around in his arms as if we are still in the great hall, dancing at this evening's banquet honoring our son and his bride.

Laughing, I fall exhausted onto the stool nearest my fire. "Let me catch my breath and we can talk of it."

Henry pours a glass of wine and hands it to me. "To the King of England and his magnificent victory in Gascony," I say, raising my glass before drinking.

"Simon de Montfort could not pacify it, but I did." Henry is beaming. Can it be that this man I love, who has tried so many political schemes and failed, has, at last succeeded at something that does not involve art or architecture? He looks ten years younger. No, in this light I swear he looks as he did when I married him.

"You did indeed."

"I know you are eager to go home, but what would you say to a journey through France? I long to see all the wonders of that kingdom that we hear so much of, and to visit the grave of my mother."

The idea delights me—not the prospect of paying a visit to my husband's dead family members but the possibility of seeing my own sister, come home from crusade alive but whose letters hint at a lassitude that disturbs me. "Oh yes, Henry, write to the French king. I will write to Marguerite. I feel certain we will be given permission for our passage. After all, so much is merely common courtesy."

"To Fontevrault first, then on to Chartres. Imagine seeing its great cathedral." Henry is clearly picturing the structure of which he has heard so much, because his eyes twinkle and the lid that droops habitually is, for the moment, wide-open. "But enough talk of travel plans," he says, looking down on me. "To bed, woman. Some part of our celebration at least need not wait for permission from the King of France."

"BY HEAVEN, LOUIS OF FRANCE is a man of exquisite taste." Henry whispers the words, for we are inside the great Cathedral of Chartres. Like Westminster, the rebuilding work here is not finished. But, as at his abbey, my husband's artistic vision is sufficient to supply those pieces yet missing. "The glass, the color—they overwhelm me." Truly my husband does seem overcome, for he turns away from his view down the church's long nave back toward the doors by which we entered.

I could point out that most of the windows were not commissioned by my sister's husband, only salvaged by him, but I do not. I am highly pleased with the King of France at the moment. Far from merely permitting our sojourn in his country as a matter of *politesse*, he makes much of us, inviting us to pass Christmas with his court in Paris.

"I see Marguerite's hand in this," I told my uncle when the letter came, "for Louis and Henry have ever been rivals who spoke to each other only in the coolest manner even before the war in Poitou."

Looking at my husband, his attention focused on the myriad of glass panels depicting the life of Christ above the central doors, I remember my uncle's reply. "It matters not whose hand caused the invitation to be extended, but rather what we make of it."

So, I will see my sister soon, but our talk will not be solely of our children and our shared history. We have peace with the noblemen of Gascony, so why not a new treaty and better understanding with France? Surely the latter will help insure that the former holds, and it will allow my husband and me to focus our attention on securing Sicily for Edmund.

One of the doors swings open. A man I do not recognize enters. His frame is gaunt but his posture is straight, suggesting that illness or fasting and not age has made him wasted. His manner of dress is very plain and no fur lines his cloak despite the December cold; yet the fabrics he wears are costly rather than coarse, and the sword at his side is extraordinarily fine. His fair hair, nearly colorless but untouched by gray, is blunt cut at his shoulders. His eyes, which seem to be fixed singularly on me, are piercingly blue.

Stepping forward, he bows. "You are Her Majesty Eleanor of England, are you not?"

"I am, sir."

"There is something of your sister's look in you. I am Louis of France."

"Your Majesty!" I drop to a curtsy. "We had no expectation of seeing you before we reached Paris." Henry has moved to my side. Louis gives him the same intense look he moments ago fixed on me.

"Henry of England, you are welcome in my kingdom."

"I am grateful for your hospitality. I have long desired the satisfaction of seeing my beloved mother's grave at Fontevrault, and you have provided it."

"This pleases me. The loss of a mother weighs heavily on her sons." Louis's eyes are filled with pain. I cannot remember the last time I saw a man look so very sad. My husband glances away slightly for a moment as if unnerved by the raw display of emotion.

"It does," Henry says. "The bond of family is mighty. And on this score I am beholden to Your Majesty in more ways than one, for my wife had the greatest desire to see her sisters and mother after a separation of nearly a score of years, and your gracious invitation makes that possible."

"And she shall see them sooner even than she thinks." Louis turns his attention once more to me. The eyes that moments ago said so much are now like windows shuttered, reflecting only my own image back at me. "Her Majesty the Queen of France, the Countess of Provence, and the Dowager Countess of Provence should arrive before nightfall. They are but a little behind me."

I wonder why, if this is so, the party did not travel together? I wonder too why Louis does not simply say *"your sisters and your mother."* His manner is very unlike my Henry's, but his tone is obliging, so I do not dwell on these questions. Rather I focus on the fact that in but half a day I will see my family.

"You must join us at the archbishop's palace this evening," Louis continues. "His Grace extends me his hospitality, and our first meal together can be easy, free from the eyes and formalities of a more formal court banquet."

"Nothing could suit us more," Henry replies enthusiastically. This is typical of my husband; his opinion of men is ever changeable. The French king has been his enemy since childhood, but now, standing in this cathedral, Louis is pleasant and a novelty, so all the past is forgotten for the moment. I see that Henry will open his heart to the King of France.

Louis offers a smile by way of return, but it is wan and bloodless. I wonder, after five months at home in France, whether Marguerite still bears the marks of crusade as clearly as her husband does. Then, as if he were an errand boy rather than a king, Louis says, "I will leave you. I did not intend to disrupt you in your occupations."

"Nonsense. I wish to walk the labyrinth, but I may do it as easily another time."

"You are a king who takes pleasure in meditation and prayer then?"

"Nothing gives me greater satisfaction, save perhaps my dear family. And you are a king whose pious works are spoken of everywhere, and certainly in my England. I would be honored were you to walk the labyrinth with me and will wait upon your convenience to do so."

The smile that Louis offers this time is full. His eyes sparkle and his cheeks take on a tinge of color. "I will walk with you now since you like it. And after, if you are interested, I will show you how my mother had a portrait of me hidden in the windows here, acting the role of King Solomon."

"CAN WE NOT RIDE FASTER?"

"Would you race to the archbishop's palace?" Henry asks with a touch of a smile. "That would hardly be dignified."

"What care I for dignity when my sister and mother are so close?"

Henry laughs. "Eleanor, if you do not care for appearances, then why have you donned one of your best gowns? I know you are eager to see your family, my dear, but we will be at the palace quickly enough without riding as if we are hunting stags."

But oh the journey seems to take forever. Then at last the images of the faces of Marguerite and my mother that I conjure in my mind's eye give way to the façade of the archbishop's palace, its windows glimmering with reflected candlelight from within. We ride into the courtyard and my eyes, searching for a groom to take my horse, find Marguerite standing with the king, flanked by torchbearers. Her figure is as it was when I saw her last—slender and lithe. How has she managed this when she is thirty-three and has birthed eight children, the last only weeks ago? I am suddenly conscious of the roundness of my arms and the increase in my waist since I saw my sister last. As I pull my horse to a stop, she runs forward, and all thoughts of such trivial things are forgotten.

"My darling Eleanor, you are here." Her arms are about my neck and she is crying. I taste tears as well, but I sense a difference. Mine roll down my cheeks in tangible proof of my joy, but hers shake her in violent sobs. Something is the matter, but this is not the moment to ask what, and when she at last stands back from me, her face is composed. "This is a day of such happiness! However shall I bear it?"

"Perhaps your years in the desert have made you less accustomed to happiness than you deserve to be, but it is generally borne with a smile," I reply, squeezing her hand. "Oh, I have missed you more than anyone." Then, feeling guilty that my outburst might have been overheard, I ask, "Where is Mother?"

"Just inside, with Beatrice."

The mention of my younger sister's name stills my steps. I am not angry with her anymore; the passage of time has seen to that. But I realize that until this moment I never gave her a single thought. I had forgotten, in fact, that she traveled with the French party. I suppose this makes me a dreadful person, but I do not feel myself to be so.

Marguerite shepherds me inside. I am in my mother's arms while a lovely blond woman, sporting far more jewels than the rest of us wear, watches with sharp eyes. "Sister," she says as my mother releases me, "it has been too long."

This then must be Beatrice. I accept her stiff embrace. Nothing—
I simply have no feelings for Beatrice. "It has indeed," I reply, hoping my voice is more cordial to her ear than it sounds to mine.

Marguerite takes my hand as if we were children. "I will not
let go of you tonight," she whispers.

I wish we could scamper off, hide under a table, and talk as we
did as girls until the candles have burned down and our nurses
come to look for us. As it is, we *are* separated. Marguerite takes her
seat at Louis's side and I take mine at Henry's—the two kings
between us as they have been since they married us away from our
Provençal home.

The meal is splendid. Henry and Louis, reticent with each
other at first, are soon engrossed in talk of architecture. I gaze
across them longingly, wishing I could speak to my sister. Charles
d'Anjou is to my right. I am thankful that years of correspondence
with Marguerite have prepared me for his temperament and I can
endure his prating on with relative equanimity, even as it galls me
that such a man should govern what was once my father's.

At last the bowls are brought forward, and I hope for an opportunity to surround myself with the company of my own choosing.
The King of France rises from his seat and I do likewise. Turning
to Henry, he says, "Is there more of Chartres that you would see,
or are you well content for Paris?"

"Were I alone to be consulted, I would set out for Paris as soon
as possible. I have the most burning desire to see your Sainte-
Chapelle."

"Splendid. Let us leave at dawn."

"At dawn." Henry seems abundantly pleased with the idea, but
I have the strongest desire to kick him in the shins. If we are to rise
early, then the evening is likely over and I have not had five minutes of quiet with my mother or sister.

THE SISTER QUEENS 461

"Shall I call for your horses?" Louis asks, confirming what I suspected.

For an instant I think of begging to be left behind to pass the night with Marguerite. She is so recently recovered from her confinement that surely her husband cannot yet be sharing her bed. We could curl up in the dark and share confidences as we did as girls. But the thought is as ridiculous as it is appealing. If I am to ride through France tomorrow beside its king, I must be Queen of England and represent my own kingdom properly. I can hardly appear still clothed in this evening's gown.

As we move back toward the courtyard and our mounts, Marguerite finds my side and slips her hand into mine again. "Ride beside me tomorrow."

"What other place would be mine?" I ask, kissing her cheek lightly before releasing her hand and slipping out into the torchlit darkness.

The next day we begin our ride toward Paris most satisfactorily. Marguerite and I are side by side just behind our husbands. Henry's figure always looks best on horseback for he is long in the torso and therefore is not so much shorter than Louis when sitting down. I have made certain that he and I are dressed sumptuously in clothing that should have been worn in Castile had we gone. Our mantles are patterned with golden leopards to represent England, trimmed in ermine, and entirely lined in vair. Louis, however, again wears not a scrap of fur despite the winter chill.

"Will His Majesty not take cold?" I ask my sister. She herself is dressed in a manner more similar to my own than to her husband's.

"He prefers woolens to fur," she replies without glancing in his direction.

"And you do not worry for him?"

"What point would there be in doing so? His Majesty knows

his own mind, and it will not be changed by me. One of the many things I've learned in the course of my marriage is precisely how intractable my husband can be."

"Oh, Henry can be stubborn as well," I remind my sister. I assume this sort of commiseration is what she seeks. After all, we have been complaining about certain tendencies in our husbands for years, she and I. But rather than nodding appreciatively at my solicitous comment, Marguerite regards me as if I do not understand what she says.

"Not stubborn. Immovable." Then she continues in our native Occitan. "You may have heard that His Majesty abhors blasphemy. Since our return, he has passed a law banning it outright."

I am puzzled as to why she tells me this in the language of our girlhood, which none within hearing distance can understand. After all, a new law can hardly be a secret. "That is rather stern governance," I reply, "but surely none of us likes to hear Our Lord's name taken in vain."

My sister gives me a piercing look. For a moment she is silent, and I can see she is biting the inside of one of her cheeks. Then she continues. "Last week, he had the lips of a tradesman caught transgressing his law burned off with hot iron." Her words are spoken very low, but there is no chance of my missing them. I only wish I had. I give a sharp gasp. My sister's eyes remain pitilessly on my face. "And do you know what he said when I reacted as you do now? When I begged him to forgo such cruel punishment in future in favor of a fine or something of that ilk? He told me he would gladly be branded himself, on the steps of the Palais du Roi for all to see, if by this act he could end all wicked oaths in his lands. This is not stubbornness. It is something else entirely."

Marguerite's look as she finishes is almost triumphant. But why should she glory in relating such behavior on her husband's part?

Glory as if she detests him? I remember the happiness that radiated from many of my sister's letters while she was abroad. Clearly there were periods when she was cheerful, joyful even. There were periods when Louis made her happy, even during those years when he refused to quit the Holy Land and bring her home. If she could be happy in the dust and sand of the desert, surely there must be some hope of achieving such happiness again now that they are home in France?

"He will recover himself with the passage of more time," I say bracingly.

My sister gives a deep sigh as if I am being very difficult.

"The crusade changed him, yes. But it made him *more* of what he already was, not different. He is not like other men, not your husband, not any man you have ever known."

This seems an extreme statement, but I cannot honestly say there is a man among my acquaintance who would do as Marguerite just described. Besides, I have no wish to argue with my sister, not after being apart for so long. Nor is it my place to defend her husband, I remind myself sternly. My place is ever and always to take her part—unless, of course, there is an argument between us.

I desire to turn the conversation to safer and less troubling subjects. Casting a glance to my left, I see Maude de Lacy riding with her lord. *Here,* I think, *is a perfect topic.*

"Do you remember when you recommended certain gentlemen to my attention? The half brothers of Uncle Peter's wife? Well, there sits one, Geoffrey de Joinville, beside his wife, my close friend Lady de Lacy."

"Really?" Marguerite is transformed. All eager interest, she leans forward over her horse's neck to look past me. "I remember your writing to me that he had arrived in England and that you married him well." Then, absently, as if meaning the words only for herself, she adds, "He is a fine man, but not so handsome as his half brother."

I nearly ask her to repeat herself, but the strangeness of her remark leaves me momentarily tongue-tied. I struggle to recall the letter in which she first asked me to assist Geoffrey and his brothers. What did she say? I stretch my memory. It seems to me my sister gave me very little by way of reason for her particular interest in the gentlemen, merely some offhanded remark about their being related to one of the French king's best and most trusted knights.

"Did the knight related to Lord Geoffrey survive the crusade?"

"What?" Marguerite's attention is drawn back to me with force. My question was simple, but it has left my sister looking confused.

"Did the knight related to Lord Geoffrey survive the crusade?" I repeat.

"Yes," Marguerite says. The word is clipped, and if it conveys either pleasure or disappointment in the fact of the gentleman's survival I cannot decipher as much. I am puzzled by my sister's manner. But before I can grasp the thread of my confusion and begin to unwind it, Marguerite moves the conversation forward.

"Does not Mother look well for a woman of eight-and-forty? I hope she will remain with us in France for some time. His Majesty has agreed to set aside Castle Nesle for her use."

"I am jealous."

"You must not be." The sister I knew years ago would have said this sternly, as an admonition, but the Marguerite riding beside me today sounds a little like my Edmund when he reports some transgression to me but does not want me to be angry.

"Well, I have Uncle Peter." I offer her a conciliatory smile. "He has been a most useful companion to me these last dozen and more years. Now tell me the news of your children. When you wrote last, baby Marguerite was not taking well to her wet nurse and you thought to change her."

"Another nurse has been brought in and does better. I would suckle Marguerite myself did I not have so much to occupy my time." She sighs slightly, then looks for a moment at the pale winter sun. "That was the sole luxury we had in Egypt—time stretching on, sometimes without end. I nursed Jean Tristan entirely myself."

HOW DIFFERENT MY FIRST GLIMPSE of Paris is this time from last. The spires of the city's churches appear on the horizon, and I am neither wet nor frightened. When we reach the city gates, the sides of the road are crowded with people singing and playing upon a great variety of instruments. They call out their approbation to their own king, but he seems oblivious. When they cry out to Henry, he waves good-naturedly and scatters coins into the crowd. The streets are decorated with garlands of fabric and evergreen boughs. Glancing behind me, I watch the crowds spill into the road and follow along after the last of our train.

For every person who calls out to the King of France, another voice seems to shout a message of praise or greeting for my sister. "Preserver of kings," "mother of princes," and "jewel of the house of Capet" are phrases I hear again and again.

"Your people love you," I exclaim.

"They remember who it was that brought their king back to them," she replies, raising a hand to acknowledge the crowd, "even if others sometimes do not."

Perhaps this is it, I think, moving my mind swiftly over the cold and even angry references my sister has made to her husband since we began our journey. *Perhaps Marguerite feels slighted by her Louis and feels he has too soon and easily forgotten all she suffered for him and all she did, under great duress, to save him.* This would certainly explain much. I myself remember with pain the crushing sense of sadness that sat upon me during that single, dreadful period in my marriage when I felt forgotten by Henry. Well, at least on this point I know how to console and counsel her.

Our progress is stilled momentarily as people who have clogged the way are moved aside. A young man at the side of the road, taking advantage of the pause, steps forward and boldly kisses the hem of my sister's gown. "That one should be so beautiful, so brave, and so just is astounding." Then nodding in my direction, he continues. "That two should be so is miraculous."

By the time we reach the Old Temple where Henry and I are to lodge, I am euphoric. Henry too seems ebullient, clasping Louis to him in leave-taking, oblivious to the awkward stiffness of the French king's form.

As we are rushed inside, I raise a parting hand to my sister.

Our rooms are furnished in the greatest style. We, of course, travel with our furnishings and feather beds, but they will not be necessary. The beds are already piled high and made up with costly silks and velvets. Fires roar in every grate.

"Such a welcome!" Henry says, pulling me into an embrace and then releasing me again to examine my room. "I would do something to acknowledge it."

"Perhaps an act of charity," my uncle says from his seat by my fire.

Henry loves such gestures, but I know by my uncle's look that he is thinking of something else—he is thinking how pious Louis will react to such an action on Henry's part.

"Yes. The great hall here is of goodly size, perfect for feeding the poor. Five hundred. We will feed five hundred. Even in such a fine city as this there must be five hundred poor souls in need of succor."

Peter rises. "Consider it done, Your Majesty."

Henry takes my uncle's seat and pulls me onto his lap as the door closes behind Peter.

"We are not expected at the Palais du Roi until tomorrow. Shall we have a small supper here, just the two of us?" His hand slides up the front of my dress until it is cupped around one of my breasts.

"Henry! Surely you are exhausted by a long day in the saddle."

"Are you?" His eyes challenge me. And to be honest, I am not exhausted. So much has been made of us by the French—from tradesmen and students to noblemen—that I feel more the queen than I do ofttimes in England.

"No, I am exhilarated. I doubt I will sleep a wink tonight."

"I will endeavor to tire you, lady"—Henry squeezes the breast in his hand meaningfully—"or failing that, to entertain you well in your sleepless hours."

Henry is as good as his word. I sleep like a babe after his ministrations. In the morning we set out in great state for the Palais du Roi. Henry is invited to hear Mass with the King of France in his Sainte-Chapelle and then to examine every inch of the chapel. My husband has long anticipated this pleasure, but I have something even better to look forward to. At last I will have time alone with my sister.

Marguerite and I withdraw to her rooms where I have an opportunity to meet my nieces and nephews. I quickly see even from her manner of their presentation that my sister has two favorites among her children—Louis, a somewhat delicate but lively ten-year-old who looks a great deal like the young King Louis I met on my bridal journey to England, and four-year-old Jean Tristan. The first is completely understandable. What queen does not have a special place in her heart for her first male child, the child who secured her seat on her throne and her husband's line into the next generation? And as for the second, I suppose the partiality is explained by the fact that all of us have certain people, even among our families, whose souls are closer to our own and whom we understand better than we understand ourselves.

The children and their nurses withdraw. Then the talk begins. Words flow like wine at a banquet, ever faster and with greater abandon. Thanks to our numberless letters, we are dearest friends reunited despite nearly twenty years without sight of each other. And yet there is something so very different and wonderful about being physically together—about the sight, smell, and touch of my sister; about the sound of her voice as she relates the most recent happenings in her life. I am quickly engrossed by the details of Marguerite's travels and travails in Egypt—things she could never have committed to paper—and gratified that Marguerite is eager to hear of Edward's bride and of the recent actions in Gascony. When a servant brings word that Louis and Henry will go into the city to see Notre Dame and other sights of architectural import, we decline the invitation to join them.

"The men will not miss us," I say. "They have a shared passion for the art of building. They have long been rivals without knowing each other. Perhaps familiarity will bring more harmonious relations. I cannot say what it would mean to us if Henry and His Majesty could come to a better understanding, particularly over Gascony. I do believe, having secured it at last from Castilian aggression and the avarice of its own barons, we could hold Gascony against all if we but had a new treaty with France."

"And what of your husband's intentions in Poitou and Normandy? Will his success in Gascony make him ambitious there?" My sister does not speak the words as a challenge so much as a true question, and she waits thoughtfully for my answer.

Is it disloyal, I wonder, to speak the truth? How can it be when bravado will only keep England and France enemies longer?

"Henry has no hope of regaining Normandy," I say. "He knows this in his clearer moments. It is only pride and a deep longing to be thought a great king that keep him from admitting as much."

"He is not thought a great king in England?"

"He is presently, of course, thanks to the victory in Gascony," I say. "But as you well know, too often his barons do not show the respect for him that they ought. I am sure you are tired of hearing me complain on this point after so many years. But it never ceases to both vex and confound me. Why can they not show him proper deference? He is their anointed monarch and a good man."

"Yes," my sister says kindly, putting her hand over mine where it flutters on the arm of my chair to quiet it, "I can see that he is a good man, and also a good husband." She looks into my eyes so intensely that for a moment I wonder if I can bear her stare. "The two things are not the same—being a man and being a king." I prepare to rise to my husband's defense, surprised that my sister would intimate that my husband is an ineffectual king, even as I know it to be true myself. Defending Henry is my habit. It is my duty. And I am prepared to do it. Then Marguerite says, "Louis is considered a great king, but as a man . . . I so often find I do not like him very much."

So it is as I suspected—the affinity between my sister and her husband that clearly existed while they were on foreign soil, as witnessed by her letters, did not survive their return to France. If she is willing to so frankly own her present disappointment, I will own mine.

"Henry is a kind and loving man," I say with warmth, "but there are times when I think he would be better suited and happier too had he been born to follow, not to lead."

We sit in silence for a few minutes, Marguerite's hand resting on mine as we each stare into her cheery fire. *We have each of us half the man we wanted,* I think. It is an epiphany. "Perhaps," I say, "no man can be everything. Not even a king."

"Perhaps."

My mind wanders back to the political subjects that led us here. "If Henry were to abandon his claims in Normandy, what might Louis do in return?" In the back of my mind I can hear Uncle Peter suggesting that marks of silver would be far more useful to my husband than lands he cannot conquer or hold, especially with a crown for Edmund to pursue.

"It is always hard to know what Louis will do until he does it," Marguerite replies. "But he talks favorably of Henry on such a short acquaintance. And I believe Louis may be amenable to drawing closer to my family connections, as he never was before. After all, with his mother gone, a brother dead in Egypt, and another enfeebled by a sudden seizure while we were yet in the Holy Land, the king's own family is neither as strong nor as numerous as it once was. He feels this fact keenly. We may have the opportunity, you and I, to make one family of our two. As we have ever been the closest of sisters, let us each push our respective husbands to see each other as brothers. For our children's good as well as our own."

I nod. A knock sounds at the door. Servants bearing refreshment troop in, followed by our mother who passed the morning at the Old Temple with Sanchia, freshly arrived from England for our reunion.

"Do I interrupt?" she asks, seeing us drawn so close together.

"What, Mother? Never." Marguerite rises to offer her seat as it is closest to the fire. "Where is Sanchia? How I long to see her."

"She is exhausted from her travels and begs leave to postpone waiting upon you until before this evening's banquet."

"Of course I can wait, and I dare not even complain of the delay while I have the two of you for excellent company. But speaking of the banquet, I must make myself easy on a score of details before the tapers are lit and the first course served. If you will excuse me."

Mother and I wave her out. My mother hunts about among the embroidery frames huddled like serving girls, silent but ready, in a corner, and pulls one out.

"Very elegant," I remark as she draws it before her and prepares to work. "I fear I am no better with silk and wool than I was as a girl."

"Never mind, Eleanor," Mother says. "You excel at many other things. My brother tells me that you have a natural head for politics and that you are a most excellent mother."

This praise catches me off my guard and moistens my eyes.

"The mothering I learned from you, madam, and the facility for politics comes with the Savoyard blood."

"So it does." Her smile is as it ever was, even though she looks undeniably older than when she came to England to see Sanchia married. Can ten years really have passed since then? They must have, for I am thirty-one now, a year older than my mother was when I married.

I rise to help myself to the cold meats and things the servants laid. "Would you like something?"

"Not at the moment."

My sister's table, like her wardrobe and her castles, is of the finest sort. I am glad that where my mother is seated she cannot see the quantity of sugarcoated aniseeds I am taking. I pour myself a measure of wine and water and am about to return to the fireside, when the sound of children laughing attracts me naturally to the window.

Below in the bleak winter garden I can see the younger princes, Philippe, Jean Tristan, and Pierre, with a nurse. After a few minutes of discussion that I cannot hear from this height, Jean Tristan puts his hands over his eyes and begins to count. They are clearly playing hide-and-seek. Philippe, a strapping boy of nine years, takes off at a run to secrete himself somewhere. Pierre, too young to hide alone, is dragged off by the nurse.

I am just about to turn away from the window, when a tall man, beautifully dressed, enters the garden, walking with purpose. At the sight of the boy he stops, his face alight with a combination of frank admiration and tenderness. I have seen this same look a thousand times before on my own husband's face—this man adores my sister's son. Creeping up behind the child who is still dutifully counting, he grabs him from behind. The prince laughs in delight and opens his eyes. After an exchange of words, the gentleman swings Jean Tristan up to his shoulders. The boy wraps his one arm about the man's forehead and points with his other in the direction he wishes to go. As they begin to move off, the child leans down to say something. The dark curls on his head blend with those of the nobleman whom he rides like a pony.

"Mother," I demand, "who is this gentleman in the garden with Jean Tristan?" My mother puts aside her embroidery, and with frustratingly unhurried steps makes her way to my side. I cannot say precisely why, but it seems a matter of utmost urgency to know who the man is. I am fearful that my mother will not arrive beside me before the man and the boy disappear behind a tall row of shrubbery, but she does.

"That," my mother replies, "is the Lord of Joinville, Seneschal of Champagne, a great favorite of His Majesty's. My goodness, Louis will be glad to have him back."

CHAPTER 37

MARGUERITE
DECEMBER 1254
PALAIS DU ROI, PARIS

To have Eleanor here is a balm, I think as I hurry to the hall to check the *mouvants* for this evening's banquet. It is as if some piece of my heart long missing has been put back in its proper place. I am not whole to be sure, but I bustle and feel an energy I have lacked since returning to France.

On my way back to my rooms, I mean to stop at Louis's apartment and speak with his chamberlain. I know that Louis will wear no fur, but surely between the two of us we can contrive for the king to look better than he has of late when he presides this evening. He may be used to dining with holy men and collections of the city's elderly and infirm, a practice he has engaged in almost daily since our return, but this evening's entertainments are in honor of a king who is also my brother. I would have nothing done that is not in the best style out of respect for Henry of England and for my sister. Thank goodness the fast of Saint Martin has ended or our feasting and entertainments would be so severely curtailed as to make honoring my English kin a hollow gesture.

Nearing Louis's apartment, I hear voices. Perhaps he and Henry of England have returned. I quicken my steps and turn a corner. Not a dozen feet in front of me Simon of Nesle and Philip of Nanteuil stand with Jean between them. Fortunately, they do not see me. I am able to turn back and round the corner before my knees give way and I sink to ground. I cannot say if I want to sob or laugh, to run back to them, or to run away and hide myself. *Jean is here.* When he left us at Beaucaire to see to his own affairs and put the distance between us that we both felt prudent, he swore to me that he would not return to court before spring showed herself and the roses in my garden greened and budded. But he is here nonetheless.

I sit where I am, quite unable to move.

"So," my Lord of Nesle says, his voice infused with jovial enthusiasm, "life in Champagne was not entertaining enough to detain you."

"That is not what I hear," the Lord of Nanteuil chimes in. "My friends at the court of Thibaut the Second say you have been busy. You may not have stayed at home long enough to plow your fields but you had plenty of time to plant your wife."

"Listen to him," Nesle says. "Were you not such an old fellow, de Nanteuil, you too would be eager for the company of your lady after a six-year absence."

I hear the sound of a hand slapping someone on the back or shoulder and a great burst of laughter.

A tear runs down my cheek, and I catch it with the tip of my finger. Of course, I knew Jean must lie with Alix when he arrived home. It is his duty, and not to do so would generate talk, but I wonder if it was also his pleasure. For the first time I have a glimpse of how Jean must have felt all those years as he thought of Louis touching me. I was spoiled by his faithful devotion, by knowing he was mine alone in the desert. In France he is not.

"What will you do now?" Nesle asks. "Come! Have a drink with us while you wait for the king to return. Once he has seen you, he will not soon be parted from you. Why, only yesterday in council His Majesty mentioned the hardship of your absence."

I would not wonder if this was true. As the want of Jean has gnawed at me over the past months, it has likely also pained my husband. I am almost willing to cede that Louis loves the gentleman as much as I do.

"You exaggerate." The sound of Jean's voice—oh dear God, it is as if I were thirsty these five months and did not know it. Having taken the first sip, I would gulp greedily. My breath catches in my throat, and the skin on my arms prickles. *Only speak again,* I will him. And he does. "His Majesty has too much to occupy his mind to think of one poor servant who is far away."

"No," Nesle replies, his voice serious, "His Majesty forgets none who serve him well, least of all you. Your place in his favor was not filled in your absence."

There is a moment of silence. Slowly, and as quietly as I can, I get to my feet. If they should proceed this way, it would not do for them to find me thus.

"So, will you drink?" the Lord of Nanteuil asks.

"With your gentlemen's pardon, I will pay my respects to Her Majesty the Queen."

"Well done, Sieur. Doubtless we will see you at this evening's banquet."

I pull myself to my full height and pray that I look composed. I hear steps. Someone comes, but whether it be Jean, his companions, or both I cannot say. Steeling myself, I begin to move so that it will not appear as if I have been secreted here listening, though I have. I round the corner and nearly run into Jean.

"Your Majesty," he says; then, glancing back over his shoulder and perceiving that his companions have disappeared in the other direction, "Marguerite."

"Sieur de Joinville." Why do I say this? Is his Christian name too painful to speak, or do I fear that once past my lips they will not be stilled and I will speak a thousand words of love and longing? "You are returned to court."

"Yes." Jean pulls back his shoulders trying to recover himself. His face wears an expression of confusion and pain. I understand both all too well. My pain at this moment is so sharp that I cannot understand why I do not fall dead on this spot.

"I am happy to see you." My voice continues to sound oddly hollow, as if I have not breath enough to infuse it with life or longing.

"*Are* you?" He lowers his voice. "I was coming to wait upon you. Can we not remove to your rooms? I feel as if I am naked here."

Naked. Yes, that is the right word. I also feel stripped bare, and should anyone come upon us, I would cower from view though my activities of the moment are entirely blameless. "My sister the Queen of England and my mother are in my rooms. Oh Jean—"

"I know." He reaches out a hand tentatively as if he will touch me, then draws it back. "The pain is overwhelming. I ought to have stayed away longer as I promised. And I would have for your sake, though my thoughts every day turned in your direction, did not the circumstances of my family compel me hence."

"My lord, what is the matter?"

"I arrived home to find my finances in ruins."

In all our time together I never gave a thought to how Jean lived. Like every other gentleman on crusade he scrambled for money to keep himself and his men, but I supposed this to be but a function of extended warfare.

"With my mother yet alive—and God knows I love her too well to wish her in her grave—and in possession of her dower rights, I must support me and mine on scarcely one thousand livres a year in rents. Alix received but half her dowry, and even to secure that before I left for the Holy Land we were forced to sign away claims to the balance. I pledged substantial portions of my land when I took up the cross to equip myself and my men. . . ." Jean's voice trails off.

"Love,"—it feels good to address him so and good to take charge of the situation, for I can be queen and friend just as I promised and make things right—"if these are your worries, put them aside. You are beloved of a generous king and his queen. Make a list of those who are indebted to you and give it over to me. His Majesty and I will see it collected forthwith. Beyond that, can you have any doubt that Louis will wish to recompense you for your service now you are returned to court?"

Jean regards me with an intensity that carries me back over years to the first time we were alone in the gardens at Saumur. "You were ever my angel."

"And you were ever a man who could be counted upon." Does he remember the words as I do? Perhaps, for he smiles.

"France agrees with you. You bloom with vigor in native air."

"It is not France but the effect of Eleanor you see upon me. Verily I believe she can cure me of anything, save you."

"I can hardly wait to meet her then."

"You shall tonight. Only pray, sir, remember that once, many years ago, you assured me that if ever you knew the Queen of England, you should still prefer the Queen of France."

"To any woman on earth. My heart needs no reminding of that. It is for you that it breaks anew every morning."

CHAPTER 38

ELEANOR
DECEMBER 1254
PALAIS DU ROI, PARIS

"What a marvelous banquet!" I smile at Marguerite and take her arm. We are retreating to her apartment to pass an hour reliving the glory of the evening, while Henry and some of the French king's favorites have been invited to Louis's apartment for discourse.

"Yes, it was, though I say it myself." She squeezes my elbow, her eyes on fire. The vestiges of care and exhaustion that hung about her as a pall when I first saw her in Chartres seem to have fallen away at last. "How gallant your husband was."

Now it is my turn to glow. Henry behaved magnificently. He showed not a moment of pique or peevishness, but complimented everything and was munificent to all. The high point of my evening came as we were being seated. A place of honor had been prepared for my husband, marked by the most gorgeous saltcellar of carved rock crystal, gold, and jewels, and he stood aside, insisting that Louis take it instead. It was nobly done and all remarked favorably upon it. "Your entertainments were superb. Such voices! And the leopard, clad all in silver and black, lying down to slumber pleasantly among a field of gilded lilies while the azure cloth that was the ground billowed around them—breathtaking and, I hope, prophetic."

We have reached my sister's hall. Bowing before me, she offers her hand and together, without need of musical accompaniment, we mince through the opening steps of an *estampie*, much to the delight of her ladies and my own.

"You dance better than you did when we were younger," Marguerite says.

"I *always* danced better than you." I lower my eyebrows and mimic the sort of fierce glare I might have given her in verity when we were girls and I was subject to a challenge or unfavorable comparison.

She laughs, throwing her head back in delightful abandon. "Marie," she says, "my sisters and I will take wine together in my withdrawing room. Ladies, you may make a party here with the Queen of England's companions or away to your lovers or your sweet dreams as you like. I will see you in the morning."

We leave our collected retinues clustered in a swirl of giddy conversation and color and proceed into the next room. Our mother has retired for the evening, so we are four sisters, together as in our nursery days. Marguerite pours out the wine, dancing her way to each of us in turn as if she wished the evening with its festivities were only beginning.

"You did not dance with His Majesty this evening," I remark.

"The king does not dance since we are returned from crusade. He generally eschews such entertainments as we have enjoyed, but supported them in honor of your visit." My sister's voice is neither judgmental nor weary as it was this morning when speaking of her husband; rather it is matter-of-fact. I wonder at this and then recollect that Beatrice sits nearby listening.

"You were well partnered though by another gentleman, Marguerite. Who was he?" I ask just to see her reply, for I recognized the gentleman.

"The Sieur de Joinville."

"Ah," I say, "this then is Geoffrey de Joinville's half brother. He was in Egypt with you."

A smile softens the edges of my sister's mouth. "Yes. He remained with us when others departed." She casts a dour look in the direction of our youngest sister.

Apparently this is enough for Beatrice. She is already sullen and vexed for she did not at all like where she was seated for the evening. Such little things, Marguerite assures me, are ever giving her offense. Rising, Beatrice says, "I am greatly fatigued, Your Majesty, and with your permission would retire."

"Of course, *Sister*."—the word that when applied to me or Sanchia seems to encompass boundless warmth, sounds more like a taunt when addressed to Beatrice—"I would not detain you." When the door closes behind the Countess of Provence, Marguerite stands silent for a moment as if she has forgotten what we talked about.

"You were speaking of the Sieur de Joinville," I prompt.

"Yes." Her tone is breezy once more. "He never abandoned Louis and is the king's most loyal servant and closest friend."

"Your friend as well?"

Do I imagine it, or do my sister's eyes dart away momentarily from my face?

"Yes. The Seneschal of Champagne has been a faithful friend to both Louis and me." Marguerite lays particular emphasis on her husband's name, and I wonder what she is trying to intimate about the knight's connection to the king. "The Sieur de Joinville was oft trusted with accompanying the children and me as we moved from place to place when the king could not do it himself. But generally he and Louis are inseparable."

"How is it then I have not seen him before this evening?"

"He left us at Beaucaire on our journey home. He had his own lands and his own family to attend to."

"Does he have children?"

"Indeed, two sons. I cannot recall their names. Why do you ask?" There is a sudden hesitance in my sister's voice that I cannot account for.

"He seems fond of children," I say, shrugging. "I saw him in the garden this afternoon with yours."

For one unguarded moment my sister's face shows a tenderness akin to that I saw on the Seneschal's face this morning. Her expression could be the very like, and then it is gone. "The Sieur de Joinville is kind to every living thing."

IN THE MIDDLE OF THE night I wake disturbed. At first I think my stomach roused me, filled as it was when I retired with an over-abundance of rich food and good wine. But shifting around in bed I realize that it does not ache.

"Eleanor?" Henry murmurs inquisitively. "You are indisposed?" Sated as my husband was at the banquet, he dozed off immediately after we coupled and I let him sleep, heedless of what gossip might be occasioned in this French court when the servants find his room vacant in the morning.

"No, I am fine. Go back to sleep." I need not tell him twice. Almost at once his breathing is slow and steady again.

We are staying the night at the palace. The king and my sister had rooms made up for us and for our closest companions, so how could we refuse? Not wishing to wake Henry again, I slide out of bed. The fire is low, but I can see well enough to avoid running upon any furniture. Pulling on my fur-lined pelisse, I move to the window. The glass is frosted over, and I draw my finger across it, tracing a pattern of I know not what. The moon is very large and shines brightly through those spaces I clear, enhancing the effect.

Looking down through one of the transparent patches, I realize the view is nearly the same as from my sister's rooms. This is hardly surprising, as I am honored with a room very close to her own. The vision of a boy and a man come to me—the Seneschal of Champagne and the little prince, Jean Tristan. They are in my mind's eye as they were this morning. The man has the boy on his back; their curls touch. Their curls are just exactly the same. Then I see my sister at dinner, eyes bright, high color in her cheeks. I see Jean de Joinville coming forward so that Louis can present him to my husband. His eyes are not on the king; they are on my sister. Everything he says is the very essence of *politesse*. Introduced to me, he remarks on my gown, my beauty. It is all smooth, courtly language; nothing more. But when he pays the nearly identical compliments to my sister, spurred on by Louis who insists his wife will be jealous if she does not have her due, they have a different sound—his voice is low and halting, as if he feels awkward saying such things, or as if he feels them too deeply to speak them aloud in company.

I shake my head to free myself of these images and thoughts. I turn my back to the window and its suggestive moonlight, and try to focus my attention on the embers of the fire, but another image comes to me. Jean de Joinville and my sister are dancing. His hand is on her waist, and they are the best dancers on the floor. Why? True they are both abundantly skilled in the art and handsome of face and form. But it is *not* that. I realize with a suddenness that causes me to gasp aloud, it is because they fit together. They are a pair as if they were made for each other.

My feet begin to move unbidden. Lighting a candle at the fire,

I am out of my bedchamber and into my sister's before I know what I am doing. Like my own room, Marguerite's is very nearly in darkness. I consider for a moment the seriousness of my intrusion. What if the King of France is here? How will I explain myself? Shading my light with my hand, I approach the bed. Marguerite is there, Marguerite alone. The force of my relief causes me to realize it was not the king I feared to find.

"Marguerite," I say, my voice soft but urgent.

"Eleanor?" Like my husband's a short while earlier, my sister's voice is thick with sleep and confusion. She sits up, rubs her eyes, and swings her feet out of her bed. "What is the matter?"

Without thinking I say, "The Seneschal of Champagne is Jean Tristan's father." And though the truth of the words hits me forcibly as they come out, part of me hopes that Marguerite will voice a denial. Instead, she sits perfectly still and silent on the edge of her bed, her head tilted as she regards me. She does not so much as lower her eyes. I am crushed. My sister, whose equal I have striven to be since childhood, a woman I always thought above reproach, is an adulteress. "How could you?" I gasp. "You have a husband— God help you!"

"No! *You* have a *husband*," Marguerite snaps, jumping to her feet and nearly knocking my candle from my hands. "I have a lord who cares so little for me and for our children that he would have let us drown at sea rather than distinguish us above his other subjects; a man who does not notice me for weeks at a time despite the fact that by *my* efforts alone he was saved from finishing his life as a miserable prisoner of the sultan."

My heart pounds. Never have I seen my sister like this. Although I am taller, she towers over me in her fury. In response to her anger I feel an anger of my own. I am not the guilty party here. "Even if all you say is true," I respond, raising my chin,

" 'what God has joined let no man put asunder.' On Judgment Day what will you answer to God?"

Marguerite grabs me by both shoulders and gives a great shove, pinning me against the wall. The flame in my hand wavers as if it would go out but flares again. "*You* are not God, Eleanor. And I am not interested in your judgments! Only in your promise. You have guessed what Louis has not. Swear to me, by the bond of blood we share and on the lives of your children, that you will never tell a soul."

Her face, illuminated by the angry, flickering light of my candle, is fierce. She takes several quick breaths, then continues, her lowered voice urgent. "If the secret had only the power to destroy me, I would not care. Dishonor, death—they mean nothing to me. I have given up the man I love to secure the safety of the son I love more. I walk through life as one half-dead already." I can feel her arms shaking with the emotion of the moment, but her grip does not loosen. "Surely you understand that if you repeat what you have said, your words would cost the happiness and possibly the life of my child."

I begin to cry. I want to break free from Marguerite, to run from this room, from this palace, from France. My sister is likely damned; she is certainly miserable and I cannot help her—I cannot repair the shambles she has made of her life. But I will not, I cannot, destroy her more than she has destroyed herself.

"I will take your secret to my grave; I swear it," I whisper.

Marguerite is weeping too. She releases me, but instead of departing as I so urgently desired only moments ago, I set my candle on a nearby table and take her into my arms. "I will never tell," I croon in the same tone I might use to comfort one of my boys after a bad fall.

When Marguerite's sobs subside and she is quiet, I let her go.

She wipes her eyes on the sleeve of her chemise. "You are no doubt tired," she says in a voice so formal and out of place to the occasion that I experience the insane desire to laugh, "and will wish to return to bed."

She is trying to restore the normal order, and I, God forgive me, am eager to let her. Eager because we have nothing to say to each other that cannot bring more pain or horror. "Yes," I reply, "Henry might awaken and look for me." I reach to collect my candle and take my leave.

"No one." Her eyes search mine.

"No one," I agree, nodding.

When I am almost to the door, I turn once more. My sister stands where I left her, a figure suddenly without substance in the low glimmer of her dying fire. "One thing I must ask in return," I say. "Never speak to me of this again, nor of him. My forbearance cannot extend so far."

"Never," she agrees.

Then I go. But the heavy door falling shut behind me is not enough to banish the image of my sister's empty eyes. I can feel them on my back as I flee in search of my room.

Back beside my slumbering husband, lying as still as I can so as not to disturb him, I hear my sister's words again: "Dishonor, death—they mean nothing to me. I have given up the man I love." Here then is the explanation for all the emptiness and listlessness I perceived in Marguerite's letters since her return from Egypt, and in my sister herself when we were reunited. A part of her dwells in grief just as that emotion dogs the steps of her husband. Only her sadness comes not from the loss of armies. Does she grieve over the commission of her sin or over its cessation? In the dark, staring up into the curtains of my bed, I am oppressed almost to the point of screaming by a single thought: my beloved sister is damned. How could this man, this Seneschal, be worth that, an eternity of suffering? Hot bitter tears roll down my face in the dark, as if I, not she, were guilty of her offenses. And I suppose twenty years ago had anyone predicted which of us would be capricious even to the point of her own destruction, none would have said Marguerite; not even I.

The bells marking the hours continue to find me awake, struggling to think how I can help my sister, or at least how I can forget what I know and wish I did not. Then, there is a man at the foot of my bed. He has his back to me. For a moment I think it is Louis, for no one else of this court dresses so plainly. Then he turns. He is a stranger. He tries to speak, but his words come out mumbled and slurred. I am not afraid, though perhaps I ought to be, but rather I am frustrated. I feel that he has some explanation to make for my sister's conduct—that if I could understand his words, I could help her. "Speak up, man!" I admonish. "And hold up your light so I can see you properly." Slowly he lifts his candle until his face is bathed in its glow. His incomprehensible babble is explained. The man has no lips, only horrible, red, puckered scars where his lips ought to be.

I awake screaming.

CHAPTER 39

Marguerite
December 1254
Palais du Roi, Paris

I send Marie away with the note even before my ladies come to help me dress:

> *As you say that you love me, burn this the moment it is read. My sister has guessed. We need fear nothing from her, she being the sole person in this world whose love I can count upon as I count on your own. But what her eyes have seen perhaps others will remark as well. For the present then, let your looks be guarded and your words cold. Cordiality and decorum will be our shield, though I fear also our sword. For if your eyes obey my command and your will, and regard me as if I were any other, the wound in my heart will be deep. And the banal words of daily discourse I must utter to you without distinction of smile or jest will doubtless cut you likewise.*

All in my household are tired from the festivities of the night before. This is just as well, for it makes my low spirits less subject to observation. My mind wanders nowhere this morning. It is merely blank, wrapped in a shroud of pain. My sister despises me. My sin, which I thought to abandon on the deck of my husband's ship that it might do no one any harm, seems determined to lay waste to all before it.

Matilda is lacing up the back of my gown when her hands stop. "Your Majesty!"

Every woman but I sinks in reverence. The sudden and most unexpected appearance of my husband leaves me frozen like stone. I struggle to conjure a smile.

"Do not let me keep you from your business," Louis says to the ladies surrounding me just as Marie slides into the room. My husband comes to stand before me while my women, with some hesitation despite his admonition, resume their ministrations. "I'll warrant you were not surprised to see the Seneschal of Champagne at yesterday's banquet," he says.

No opening of conversation could be better suited to unnerve me. Tired from passing half the night crying, I must expend considerable effort to keep my knees from giving way beneath me. Even so, my arm jerks involuntarily at Louis's comment, causing the woman who is sewing me into my sleeve to prick me with her needle. She murmurs an apology, while Marie, who has come to my other side, gives me a look as if to say, *Go carefully, lady.*

"Why should Your Majesty think so?" I ask, trying to keep my tone light as if I am curious, not terrified. I am about to protest that I keep no correspondence with the gentleman, but Louis plows onward.

"Joinville told me that he called upon you yesterday when he arrived and found that I was out. Just the sort of attention to form and nicety I would expect from the knight. Goodness, I have missed him."

"Mmm," I murmur, noncommittally, as I raise my arms and my ladies slide my *surcote* over my head, conveniently covering my face so that I may collect it. How glad I am now that my defensive words were left unspoken. Still, I wonder if Louis taunts me. But no, when my head emerges, I see he is smiling.

"Your father must be happy in heaven this morning."

"My father?" My husband is in such a state of bright agitation, and his conversation jumps about so unexpectedly, that did I not know him better, I would suspect he had begun the morning drinking.

"From his seat in that celestial home, he surely observed last evening that all the most golden threads in the tapestry of Europe are related to him by either blood or marriage."

"Sir, it is kind of you to say so." What can Louis mean by such hyperbole?

"I do not flatter." The stern Louis returns for an instant. "Though he had no sons, his four beautiful daughters have married into a greatness that his sons could not have been born to. His wife is in every part a lady to be admired; his brothers by marriage, at least the Earl of Lincoln and His Grace the archbishop of Canterbury whom we meet here, have as fine an understanding of doctrine and of politics as I have seen. And his son the King of England—what can I say but that I am thankful we have had this meeting. Having fought the man in Poitou and heard reports of him, I could never have imagined King Henry as he is—a man of such devoutness, faith, and piety that I am not at all embarrassed to call him brother."

I slide first one foot and then another into the slippers that my ladies hold out. I see now how it is—Louis is dazzled by the same domestic tableau that charmed his emissaries twenty years ago, that found places for my kin in the court of England, and secured husbands for us all. He comes full late to valuing my family connections. Yet, in my husband's eager face I see an opportunity. I will throw myself into the making of peace between kingdoms. It is the season for such things being in a period of *Treuga Dei* when warfare is suspended by order of the church, and with the celebration of the birth of Our Lord, the Prince of Peace, approaching. And more than this, it is a task by which I may, perchance, make meaningful my life, which is turned again to ashes in my mouth since Eleanor left me sobbing in the dark.

"I believe my sister's husband is as Your Majesty finds, a very good man. I cannot think that such a man will march his troops into Normandy as we have been told for so many years, can you?" Here I must step delicately. It was an unquestioned pillar of my late mother-in-law's canon that Henry of England maneuvered always and in everything to retake Normandy.

"This much is certain," Louis concedes in a cautious tone. "If Henry gives me his word that he will not do so, I will trust that word as my own."

"And has Your Majesty spoken with the English king about what it would take to secure such word? Or perhaps it would be more delicate to sound out my uncle Peter on the subject. My sister tells me he is much familiar with the mind of the king." It costs me some considerable effort to mention my sister. The very thought of Eleanor conjures in my brain memories of our heated exchange in the dead of the night.

"And what else does your sister say? I had no notion that you ladies spoke of politics."

It no longer baffles or insults me that Louis thinks as he does. I have had ample time to accept that, save for his mother, Louis cannot think of members of the fair sex as political creatures. "Husband, we speak not of politics but of family. Is it not the earnest wish of every wife and mother to see her family harmonious? Is it not well within her purview to work to make it so?"

"My lady wife, what you say is entirely sound." Louis holds out his arm to me now that I am properly assembled to greet the day. "Will you walk with me to Mass?"

"With pleasure, Your Majesty."

And laying my hand upon Louis's arm, I realize I will need its support to face this day. Will arriving in chapel in company with my husband mollify my sister? Will Louis's leading me to my place make it easier for me to keep my eyes from the spot near to his own that Jean occupies? I can be certain of only one thing: both Eleanor and Jean are bound to notice the circles beneath my eyes that my husband overlooks entirely.

CHAPTER 40

The Sister Queens
December 1254
Palais du Roi, Paris

I glance over at Eleanor. She and I have come to the great hall to
help Louis and Henry. Two hundred of the city's needy gather
to be fed on this Christmas Eve day, and our kings wish to serve
the bread and fish themselves. She gives me a smile from beside a
stack of trenchers, and I try to return it.

She has been cordial these last days. As if the events of that
dreadful night, one week ago this very day, did not take place. Yet
they did, and if I cannot forget them, neither can she. I see a sign
of this in the fact that our conversations confine themselves to the
most trivial things, such as the arrival of my son Pierre's last tooth;
the fabric of a gown; the elephant Louis brought back from crusade
that the English king finds so marvelous. After so many years of
maintaining closeness across many leagues and through so much
living, we are estranged. I fear I have lost Eleanor's respect, and her
judgment of me matters greatly, whatever I may have said that
night in the dark.

I move to my sister, pick up an armful of trenchers, and say,
"Shall we lay the tables?"

She gathers an armful as well, and we set off, each along our
own trestle, placing trenchers as we go. Jean is in the hall. Louis
selected him to be one of those honored by participating in the
washing of the hands. I watched him enter, all clad in a dark green

that becomes him well, but I have not looked at him a single time since; such discipline costs me greatly. I notice Eleanor glancing about as we work. Is she searching for Jean?

When everything is in its proper place, the doors are opened and the king, who has been waiting outside with Henry of England, making conversation with the filthy, rag-covered souls whom he will now nourish, leads the way. The odor of so many filthy bodies crowding into the place is quite overwhelming. I curtsy to my husband across the room, then, going to Eleanor's elbow, say, "Let us withdraw. We have done our part, and Louis and Henry could not be happier."

"True." Eleanor shakes her head in dismay and crinkles her nose. We slide from the room unnoticed. "Heavens," she says once we have gained fresher air, "I have founded my share of hospitals and abbeys and embroidered my share of vestments for pious clergymen. But I cannot see why good works must lead to unpleasant odors."

"Oh Eleanor!"

"I am glad to think I can shock you still after all these years."

"No indeed," I protest. "In truth I admire you. You have the courage to say what everyone else only thinks."

My sister stops walking and releases my arm. She squares her shoulders and says, "I shall endeavor to prove your point. It is silly not to look at him on my account."

"I—"

"Never mind your protests; they will not convince me. For a week you have studiously ignored the Seneschal of Champagne. Nothing could be plainer. I do not doubt but if he fell down dead before you, you would step over him and proceed unhindered. It convinces me of nothing and is, I think, likely to draw more eyes to you, not fewer."

My heart pounds in my throat. "But if you detected us in only a day—"

"Have your husband and your courtiers not had a thousand times as many days and failed? I know you as no one else does, and I came with fresh eyes, having never seen you in the gentlemen's company before. Those of your own court are doubtless used to your prior conduct. They think only that you play the lady and the knight. Would you alert them by this change, this studied avoidance, to the very thing you want them least to notice?"

A serving girl, leaving the hall, passes us, bobbing her head in respect since her laden tray prevents her from curtsying. Her appearance stops our conversation. By God, no woman has less privacy than I do! Yet here is a conversation I would not abandon.

Taking Eleanor's elbow, I steer her out into the gardens. Frost covers everything, and it is doubtless foolish for us to stand out of doors dressed as we are, but here at least we are alone. Not far from where we stand is Louis's favorite pear tree. Gazing upon it, I feel very sorry for myself. How little could I have imagined, when I sat beneath that tree as a girl watching my husband's lips form Latin conjugations as if his every word were enchanting, that I would stand as I do, a woman grown and supposedly wiser, shivering in the cold, my life as empty of love as the tree is now of bud or bloom.

"Eleanor," I say, "I know you bid me never to speak on this subject, but you have begun it. Before it is quit, I swear by my very life, there is no longer anything going on between the Seneschal of Champagne and me that anyone at court might not know of. Jean and I have *never* sinned on French soil nor ever will."

"Do not tell me lies, Marguerite. I see your eyes when they chance upon him. More than that, I have looked deep into your eyes these past days as they seek to avoid him. The pain there cannot be missed. You love him still."

"You call love alone a sin, then?" I demand. "I say *not* to love what is yours is the worse sin, but I will not argue the point with you, you who have been adored since you set foot on English soil. For the simple matter is this: it is not in my power to cease loving Jean. If I bid you tomorrow to stop loving Henry as you do, could you do it? Is your heart so obedient to your command?"

Marguerite's words hang in the air, though the steam from the breath that accompanied them has fallen away. "My heart is not at issue here," I reply. "You have some practice in the task of ceasing to love. You stopped loving Louis, did you not?"

"Would you believe me, Eleanor, if I told you it took years?" she asks, reaching out a hand for mine, which I keep from her. "That I clung to some fondness for Louis even in the face of his constant neglect, like a dog will crawl back to its master again and again despite being struck or sent away?" Turning her back upon me, she takes a few steps away. Then rounding, she says, "How long can we love those who do not love us in return?"

I do not know the answer to her inquiry. I've struggled with a question of my own since the maimed man spoke to me in my dreams. I know my sister has sinned; yet my heart tells me she is still the best woman I know. How can these facts be reconciled? Marguerite has always been deliberative in nature, and just—more just than I—in her treatment of others. Can her judgment suddenly have abandoned her so entirely? Perhaps I do not see things clearly. Would that it were so! For in this instance I would rather be wrong than have Marguerite wrong. Such an admission might make me smile under other circumstances.

I look down at the ground. Near the tip of my slipper lies a broken twig with a cocoon lashed upon it. If my Edmund were here, he would pick it up and gently place it where it could not be stepped on. *"It may seem broken,"* he would tell me, *"but something beautiful might still come out."*

I pick up the twig. Marguerite looks at me oddly. She is still waiting for my answer. Her life at present is like this cocoon. Damaged, yes, but something beautiful may still come of it. I wish I could make her life better. I cannot. I pray that time can. But I will not step on her. I will have my son's heart. I walk to the nearest bush and carefully set the twig among its branches.

"I know only one thing for certain about hearts—that ours must never be separated. That is the essence of what we pledged when you left me to come to France. So many years have passed, but we have allowed neither the events that filled them nor the others of importance in our lives to sever the bond between us—not Louis nor Henry, even when they were at war. The only things to part us for a time were my stubbornness and anger. I will not make that mistake again. That the Seneschal of Champagne loves you makes him a wiser man than his king." For some ridiculous reason my eyes grow damp. "There is surely no sin in that, nor, I think, in the contents of your heart. As for your acts," I say, feeling my cheeks grow warm despite the December cold, "did Our Lord not say, 'Receive the Holy Spirit. Whose sins you forgive are forgiven them'? If God forgives you your sins, then they can be nothing to me. You are my most beloved sister as ever you were and ever you shall be."

Marguerite runs to me and, as her arms close about me and we cry and laugh in turn, I feel such a lightness of heart, such grace. It is as if the forgiveness of Christ were mine as well.

EPILOGUE

M y days with my sister have drawn to a close. The ships outside my window tell me so.

We celebrated Christmas with such pomp and gaiety that Paris
will talk of it for years. There was still sorrow in my sister's looks
in these last days. But there was also happiness without the need for
concealment. It was the same happiness, and springing from the
same cause, I now realize, as that which filled her letters from
Cyprus and the Holy Land. When Marguerite danced with the
Sieur de Joinville at our Christmas revels, I watched with joy. To
see someone you love laugh is a marvelous thing.

"Are you ready to go on board?" Henry sticks his head through
the doorway. "Ready to say good-bye?"

"It is not good-bye. My sister is always with me."

Doubtless Henry thinks I refer to Marguerite's letters, several
of which are in my *aumônière* even now. Over the years he has
occasionally poked fun at their number and frequency. But I do not
refer to these tangible objects. Walking with my husband to the
courtyard where Marguerite and Louis wait to see us on our horses,
I keep one hand ever so gently against my breast, as if guarding my
heart.

My sister greets us with open arms, clinging first to Sanchia,
who is to sail back with us, then to Henry, and finally to me. Louis

steps forward with more reserve. There is something awkward about the way he embraces Henry but something hopeful as well.

"We are brothers as all men are brothers in Christ," the King of France declares, releasing my husband, "even more so as we have taken sisters to wife. Our children, along with their cousins, will rule the greatest kingdoms in Europe and influence its history for a hundred years. You are my brother; be also my friend."

Henry clasps Louis's arm and pulls the French king back into an embrace. Over my husband's shoulder I raise my eyebrows and give Marguerite a look. How typical of men to think that by their brotherly embrace they are the authors of history and fortune. Marguerite and I know better. 'Tis sisters who shape the world plain and simple.

AUTHOR'S NOTE

Half a dozen years ago, while researching another project, I came upon a footnote in a history of Notre Dame de Paris—a footnote about Marguerite of Provence, whose kneeling image is carved over that great church's Portal Rouge, and about her sisters. I had never heard of these remarkable sisters from Provence and wondered how such extraordinary women could have largely slipped through the fingers of history. I started a folder with their names on it and tucked it away in my file drawer, vowing to come back and tell their story. *The Sister Queens* is the result of that vow.

Perhaps inevitably my finished novel focuses on the two closest sisters, Marguerite and Eleanor, and tells their tale through the lens of their relationship with each other. I am, after all, a "big sister," and my relationship with my own sister defines me and has done so since childhood. If you have a sister, you know precisely what I mean. We do not escape our sisters. I believe the same was true for Marguerite and Eleanor—they were queens, yes, and wives, and political actors on the stage of thirteenth-century Europe, but first, last, and always they were sisters.

The Christmas of 1254 when my novel ends was the first that Marguerite and Eleanor of Provence spent together after nineteen years of separation, but it was not the last. Five years later, a shared French and English holiday resulted in more than the exchange of rings and pretty presents. In early December 1259, Louis IX and Henry III signed the Treaty of Paris, and, for the rest of Marguerite's and Eleanor's lifetimes, France and England would see each other as allies, not enemies. The roots of that treaty stretched back to the Christmas of 1254 when, with the help of the sister queens, important territorial issues were settled in principle. As part of the Treaty of Paris, Henry was paid handsomely, both in money and by the grant of a number of fiefs and domains of the French Crown, to renounce English claims in Normandy and Poitou. In turn, Louis accepted English control of Gascony and Henry did homage for the duchy. The sister queens from Provence had reshaped the political relations between their kingdoms.

But more was changed than politics. On a personal level, the royal families of France and England drew together. After 1254, they increasingly provided support for each other in adversity—just as Marguerite and Eleanor had done since girlhood. In 1260, Henry of England shouldered the coffin of Marguerite's beloved son Prince Louis, acting as pallbearer on the first stage of the boy's journey to Royaumont for burial after the fifteen-year-old died suddenly. During the English Civil War, with Henry and her son Edward in rebel hands, Eleanor took refuge in France, raising money and troops for her beleaguered husband. And King Louis, who before the Anglo-French understanding might well have favored his countryman and personal friend Simon de Montfort, declared the English Provisions of Oxford null and his brother-in-law king, plain and simple. He ordered all the lands the English rebels had taken returned to the Crown and its supporters.

The importance of family, championed by two sisters from the houses of Provence and Savoy, made rival kings brothers in spirit, not just in name—quite an achievement and certainly not the end of the sisters' story. As *The Sister Queens* closes, neither Marguerite nor Eleanor has yet lived even half the years of her long, eventful, life.

A word about my two kings. *The Sister Queens* is very much the tale of Marguerite and Eleanor, but to tell that story is also to tell at least in part the stories of their husbands. These powerful men were multifaceted. I was particularly interested in exploring sides of their characters that have, perhaps, been overlooked somewhat in other portrayals. In the case of Louis IX of France, I sought to illuminate the imperfect man behind the gleaming image of the Roman Catholic saint. And I tried to show the caring husband and good father often overlooked in history's judgment of Henry III as one of the least of England's kings.

And what about Marguerite's "other man"? Did Marguerite of Provence and Jean de Joinville, Seneschal of Champagne and a close associate of Louis IX, have an affair? Storytelling involves making decisions and drawing inferences based on what we know and what we can never know with certainty. While no historian can definitively say that such an affair took place, there has been speculation and there is certainly evidence to support my inference. For example, there is the open affinity and fondness exhibited by Jean de Joinville for Marguerite in his writings in *The Life of Saint Louis*. This book, which includes Joinville's own first-person account of the crusade in Egypt, is largely laudatory of Louis IX. But of His Majesty's treatment of his queen, Joinville, notably, often does not approve, at one point writing, "It seems to me that this conduct was not becoming, to be so distant from his wife and his children" [Jean de Joinville, *The Life of Saint Louis,* translated with an introduction by Caroline Smith (Penguin Books, 2008), 294]. This is forceful language indeed when one considers that Joinville's open criticism is contained in a book dedicated to Louis's grandson, the future King Louis X. In contrast, Joinville's portrayals of Marguerite are glowing and often warmed by touches of familiarity and humor. Joinville sets forth plainly not only Marguerite's repeated neglect at her husband's hands, but the antipathy of Blanche of Castile toward her son's wife.

Then, there is the very telling fact that Louis IX himself appeared to believe that something was going on between his wife and his favorite. Joinville's writing recounts episodes of Louis's jealous behavior, most notably in the chronicler's description of the fire at sea on the voyage home from the Holy Land. Just as depicted in my story, the historical Louis was fixated on the idea that Joinville knew more of that fire and its circumstances than he was telling, going so far as to accuse Joinville's servant of lying about his master's whereabouts at the time of the conflagration. When it comes to Marguerite and Jean, I for one am willing to conclude that the smoke revealed a real fire.

Finally, a few words about the needs of plot. I am a writer of fiction. All fiction is a mixture of truth and invention. Historical fiction is no exception. In order to create a compelling story, I ruminated upon my historical research and then used my imagination to breathe life into long-dead historical figures, giving them thoughts, feelings, and voices. The words they speak are mine, and I would not want anyone to think otherwise (for example, the letters that begin each chapter are original to the novel and not excerpts of historical documents). In telling the story of my sister queens, however, I have generally attempted to remain faithful to the facts and chronology of the sisters' lives. The precise dates of a number of events from this period—including the birth dates of some members of the Provençal and royal families—are, however, far from certain or agreed upon. In cases where legitimate sources differed, I have chosen to assign dates based on the needs of the narrative arc of my novel. For example, various sources place the birth of the girls' youngest sister Beatrice between 1231 and 1234. Because I wished Marguerite (and the reader) to know the toddler Beatrice before her eldest sister departed for France, I have selected the earliest date. In a few cases, I deliberately moved an actual event. For example, for storytelling reasons I moved the attempted assassination of Henry III by one year, from September 1238 to September 1237. Likewise, the skirmish between Eleanor and Henry over the living at Flamstead was moved to an earlier date while retaining the facts of the power struggle. Additionally, though Henry did reach a truce with the Scots in 1244, which included the promise of little Princess Margaret's hand, he returned from the border in the autumn of that year, whereas I have placed his homecoming in December. In the case of Marguerite's story, I have, for example, adjusted both the dates for the battle of Damietta and the birth of Jean Tristan, but only very slightly (by weeks, not months) for narrative purposes.

The SISTER QUEENS

SOPHIE PERINOT

QUESTIONS
FOR DISCUSSION

1. Although Marguerite and Eleanor grew up together at the court of their father, Raymond Berenger, Count of Provence, they turned out to be very different women. Why do siblings raised together turn out differently? Why do you think Marguerite and Eleanor might have been so different?

2. As young women and new brides, what are the most significant differences between Marguerite and Eleanor? Which sister's personality appeals to you more and why?

3. In her own time, Eleanor was described as a "virago"—which meant overbearing or domineering. This term was not a compliment. Would she be viewed differently today? If so, why and how? How would Eleanor's behavior have been judged had she been a thirteenth-century nobleman?

4. It is said that "imitation is the sincerest form of flattery." Several times during *The Sister Queens*, Marguerite consciously behaved as her sister Eleanor would instead of going with her own instinct. Did adopting an "Eleanor approach" help Marguerite or cause her to betray her own nature? Why do you feel as

you do? What about Eleanor? Were her attempts to act "as Marguerite would" helpful or harmful to her?

5. *The Sister Queens* is very much the story of the relationship between Marguerite and Eleanor of Provence, but it is also a tale of their individual relationships with their powerful husbands. Marguerite's husband, Louis IX of France, was by all historical measures a great king. If you were transported by time machine back to the thirteenth century, would you want to be married to Louis? Why or why not? How important is professional competence/success in a spouse?

6. Eleanor's husband, Henry III of England, was not considered an able king during his lifetime and continues to rank as one of England's least effectual rulers. If you woke up one morning married to Henry, would you be happy or unhappy? Why? Would you be embarrassed, as Eleanor sometimes was, by his political/professional shortcomings? How does Eleanor deal with that embarrassment? How would you?

7. How were Marguerite's and Eleanor's relationships with their husbands a product of the period in which they lived? How were the sisters' marital relationships affected by their being not only wives to their kingly husbands but also queens to their subjects?

8. The marriages of Marguerite, Eleanor, and their two younger sisters were all arranged to bring their family political advantage and prestige. There is abundant historical evidence that such arranged marriages could turn out happily. How were historical couples able to find contentment with spouses not of their own

choosing? Do you believe expectations for marriage were different in the High Middle Ages than they are today? How?

9. Both Marguerite and Eleanor's marriages evolve over the
course of *The Sister Queens*. Marguerite began her marriage
enthralled with Louis (who was, after all, pretty darn hot). Was
she actually in love with him or merely infatuated? If Marguerite
was just "crushing" at the beginning of her marriage, did she
grow to love Louis? Do you think Louis was ever in love with
Marguerite? Or was his attraction to her only lust?

10. Feeling neglected by Louis, Marguerite entered into an
extramarital affair with Jean de Joinville, Seneschal of Champagne. How did this decision affect your opinion of her? Why do
you suppose Marguerite was willing to commit mortal sin (sin
that, if not confessed and absolved, condemned the sinner to hell)
in order to be with Jean? Would you have made the same decision
in her circumstances?

11. Eleanor did not expect to love her husband when she left
Provence for England. How did Henry, more than fifteen years
her senior and not particularly attractive, win her over? What
factors in Eleanor and Henry's marriage allowed them to live
contentedly for so many years? Are those factors still important
in modern marriages?

12. More than a dozen years into her marriage to Henry, Eleanor
found their relationship strained and stale without quite knowing
why. Was Eleanor's situation realistic and believable? Do you
think midmarriage boredom is common? What methods did

Eleanor use to try to rekindle her husband's interest? Why do you approve or disapprove of these methods?

13. In 1253, Henry chose to appoint Eleanor as regent in preparation for his travels to Gascony. He also made a will giving her custody of all their children, including Lord Edward, and control of all royal territories until Edward attained majority. The appointment of the queen as regent was not dictated by either law or custom (such an event had not occurred since the early years of Queen Eleanor of Aquitaine's reign). Why do you suppose Henry granted Eleanor such massive powers? What does the appointment tell us about his opinion of Eleanor's abilities? About his faith in her loyalty? Was Henry's faith justified or misplaced?

14. Blanche of Castile was a major obstacle to Marguerite's influence over her husband and to her involvement in the governance of France. Why do you suppose Marguerite was so slow to recognize her mother-in-law as her enemy? Once she did, how did Marguerite work to defeat Blanche? Was she successful?

15. At one point in the novel, Jean de Joinville told Marguerite, "Before coming to court, I heard that His Majesty cleaved too closely to his mother. These last days I have seen it to be true. The Dowager Queen treats the king as a boy, and thus unmans him." Is de Joinville's assessment fair? Why or why not?

16. Another obstacle Marguerite faced as both wife and queen was Louis's growing religiosity. Did Louis's religious fervor cross from a positive to a negative characteristic? When and how? Where, in your opinion, is the line between piety and religious fanaticism? Was the line different in the thirteenth century?

17. During the siege of Damietta, Marguerite was given her first real opportunity to shoulder the role of leader and decision maker. Did her handling of the crisis surrounding Louis's military defeat and captivity change her? How? What, if anything, did it teach her about herself?

18. When Louis first returned from captivity, Marguerite found herself experiencing feelings of tenderness for her newly vulnerable husband. Were you surprised by this development, and why or why not? Should Marguerite have cared for Louis? Why (e.g., out of duty; because he had earned her affection)?

19. Eleanor was aware that the King of France had neglected and even mistreated Marguerite over the years. Eleanor clearly loved her sister; yet Eleanor was horrified when she uncovered Marguerite's betrayal of Louis. Why did Eleanor find Marguerite's adultery so shocking? Is it fundamentally more difficult for a happily married person to comprehend infidelity? When the sisters reconciled, did you have the feeling that Eleanor was able to forgive the sinner but not the sin? If so, how do you feel about that?

Notes

Notes

Notes

Notes

Notes